47 hours

The coup that shook the Americas

INSPIRED BY TRUE EVENTS

Clinchandhill

For information contact address: info@clinchandhill.com

Cover design by Magdalena Adic.

http://xdmaggy.wixsite.com/magdalenaadic.

ISBN: 978-0-9964695-4-8

First Edition: May 2017

10 9 8 7 6 5 4 3 2 1

"....this course of events will inspire who knows how many books about our history and set an example to the entire world..."

Hugo Chávez, April 13, 2002

CONTENTS

ACKNOWLEDGMENTS

Special thanks and love to my wife Nathalie for her support and standing in for Mitchels wife.

--

Thanks to my editor, mentor and critic, Andrea Busfield. I do so love to work with you.

--

Thank you Rose for re- re- reading the book and keeping me consistent.

--

And thank everyone involved who was willing to speak to me on the subject.

"11 de abril, recordamos el inicio del auge y caída de la dictadura más breve de la historia, recordamos también el calvario del Cristo-Pueblo que resucitó al tercer día, nuestro 13 eterno. El 11 de abril siempre estará ahí para recordarnos cómo pretendió triunfar y fracasó la muerte, recordamos también qué clase de país se proponía la oposición mediática y contrarrevolucionaria, para no olvidar nunca la sangre que se derramó ese día. Sangre venezolana, tanto bolivariana como opositora. El golpe de abril es un punto de inflexión en nuestra historia como pueblo, que cobró conciencia de que él mismo es quien lucha y construye su propia historia, y nos demostró, para siempre, que todo 11 siempre tendrá su 13 en la Patria de Bolívar.

Todo golpe tendrá siempre su contragolpe revolucionario.

Honor eterno a nuestro bravo pueblo y a nuestros bizarros soldados."

"11th of April, we remember the beginning of the rise and fall of the shortest dictatorship in history; we remember as well the cavalry of the Christ-People who resurrected on the third day, our eternal 13. The 11th of April will always be there to remind us how he aimed to triumph and beat death, we also remember what kind of country the counter-revolutionary media opposition wanted, so we may never forget the blood that was spilled on that day. Venezuelan blood, both Bolivarian and from the opposition. The April coup is a turning point in our people's history, who then realized that it is itself, that fights and builds its own history, and proved us, forever, that every 11 will always have its 13 in Bolivar's Motherland.

Every coup will always have its revolutionary counter-coup

Eternal honor to our brave people and our gallant soldiers"

Hugo Rafael Chávez Frías, April, 2002

1 Long Live Transparency

March 2002

HINKING ABOUT IT, he had no idea how he had ended up there. Not really. He couldn't remember the details that had brought him to such a gray, dull, windowless waiting room, to find himself now sitting in this chair – even residing in this country. But that wasn't what bothered him most, rather it was the almost blind acceptance of his fate. The truth was, he had never planned on leaving and yet he did; he picked up his wife and daughter, got on an airplane and left. And now, while still trying to familiarize himself with the country's customs and habits, he was already in familiar territory; waiting in a dull, gray, windowless room for what would be his first appointment with a new shrink.

His wife liked to claim he was never the same after his involvement in the doomed rescue of the Kursk's submariners a little over a year ago. "Must have been all the dead people you saw," she would say, despite having no real knowledge of the incident, not to mention his own assurances that he never saw a single dead body throughout the disaster. And yet, he had changed. His wife was right about that. He was different to the man he was. Something inside of him had made him look differently at a lot of things, but mainly things that involved state authority, politics and borders, indifferent. For 14 months he had seen a shrink every other week and though he had come to accept that something internally had gone wrong, it was nothing he could concretely point to. As a result, his wife had lost patience and slapped him with an ultimatum – make a choice or lose the family. So, he made a choice and that choice had landed him 4,600 miles from the place he called home.

Now he was sitting, somewhat uncomfortably, in a chair waiting for another psych session, glad to be able to still call himself a family man even as he doubted the wisdom of moving to take up a desk job.

Unable to stop himself, he released a sigh, glancing at the water stains above his head on the ceiling. Almost immediately a door opened to his right and male voice broke the silence. The accent was Spanish.

"You must be James Mitchel."

On the first real sunny day of spring, life returned to the streets of Washington DC. Not far from the White House a tall man in his mid-fifties, holding a newspaper and briefcase, walked up the small staircase and into a fairly non-descript building. Above the entrance a sign read 'COUNCIL ON FOREIGN RELATIONS'. As the man passed the receptionist he slapped his newspaper under one arm and waved 'good morning'. On entering the elevator, he barely had time to press the button to the sixth floor before his cellphone rang. Juggling his suitcase and newspaper, he balanced the phone between his chin and shoulder as he answered.

"Charles Turner.... yeah... uh... uh... hmm... yes, I'm just walking into the office for a briefing on the subject."

As the elevator came to a stop on the sixth floor, the brief conversation ended. He left the elevator and walked purposefully down the long corridor until he reached a glass-walled room inside of which were eight men dressed in military uniforms and business suits sat around a conference table. *'So much for secrets and long live transparency,'* he thought to himself. He knew he was being cynical but the scene reminded him of his days as 'Chief of National Security' under Clinton. It seemed a lifetime ago now and he was glad he got out, relatively unscathed, during the Democrat-Republican handover at the White House. If those last months in office had taught him anything it was that keeping secrets was one thing while decision-making was something altogether heavier and harder to bear.

Without saying a word, Turner entered the room, opened his briefcase and took out a stack of files that he gave to the man next to him to pass around.

"Good morning gentleman, and welcome to my first official briefing as Chairman of the Council on Foreign Relations." As he spoke, Turner knew he sounded calm. Addressing groups of senior officials was nothing new to him after all. Hell, he even recognized some of the military faces at the table from his time in office. *'Nothing really changes,'* he thought *'except for elected officials, thank God'.* "May I suggest we pass on the formal introductions and get to know each other as we move on?" As Turner looked around he was pleased to see nodding heads before him. "As requested, you now have in front of you the latest foreign intelligence briefing on the Venezuelan situation. I understand through government channels that Chávez is becoming an increasing and major thorn in the side of your economic interests in the region, which is why in the past six months my office has been 'rewarding' two high-placed military officials who are challenging Chávez's rule."

"You've been paying them off?"

Turner looked towards the end of the table, recognizing Oskar Rout, the Assistant Secretary of State for Latin American Affairs. Although Turner had never discovered what role the man had played in the Nicaraguan Revolution as part of the Reagan administration he had always had his suspicions. One thing he knew for sure though, was that with people like Rout at the table, nothing and no-one could be taken at face value.

"In my business we don't pay people off," he replied coolly, making a point of the difference between his old position and his new job. "Vice Admiral Molina and Colonel Pedro Soto have been publicly rewarded $100,000 each for their services. Note the word 'publicly'." Although Turner was aiming to convince the table it wasn't simply 'business as usual' he couldn't deny his own skepticism. However, he really did want to do things differently – to be different to the man he once was. For this reason, he had promised his wife and children it would be regular office hours from now on, and no more secrets. They would finally lead a normal life, living on the outskirts of the city, away from all of those late-night meetings and house calls that eventually morphed the days into one big working week. Once he got used to the metro commute he was also pretty certain he could start each day feeling fresh and rested from the day before, unlike the old days where every new working day simply felt like a hangover from the previous one. "In your folders you'll find the details of all the payments. In accordance with the Freedom of Information Act everything is publicly notarized."

At the news, Turner couldn't help but notice the shadow of disapproval across a number of the faces before him. It was something he quietly reveled in. It was the proof he needed that things were being done differently. Or at least some things.

"Of course, not every piece of information is suitable for direct 'freedom'," he admitted, "but as insignificant as these payments are right now you don't want them 'getting out' later creating an international scandal that bites you in the ass. With that said, let's now turn our attention to some of the bigger secrets involved." As Turner paused for effect, he noticed the small ripple of relief that ran through his audience at news that some secrets still existed. "So," he continued, his tone becoming more business-like, "what did we get for our generous donations to these gentlemen?" Turner flapped his arms theatrically. It was an affectation that had earned him the nickname 'The Hurricane' in DC. "Every detail of the information we have gathered is in your folders, but I'd like to draw your attention to the fact that in February Colonel Soto, who you may recall was once an assistant to President Pérez, demanded at a public event on human rights that the Venezuelan president should resign because he had turned democracy into a dictatorship. Somewhat predictably, this has triggered a wave of discontent regarding Chávez's governance. In turn, Soto has effectively declared himself to be in rebellion after citing Article 350 of their constitution that states that the people of Venezuela shall disown any regime, legislation or authority that violates their democratic values."

"Well, that sounds like a load of bull."

"Maybe," Turner replied calmly, not even bothering to see where such a verdict had come from. Opinions no longer bothered him. He was an advisor now; a distributor of information. How people chose to interpret that information was solely up to them. "However, what we know for certain is that his actions have attracted the attention of a privately-owned media network that was desperately looking for a new face that might protect their interests, unlike their current poor-people-loving dictator. That would be in their opinion, of course," Turner added quickly so as not to sound in any way biased.

"So, what's the plan?" Rout asked.

"Plan?" Turner returned. "No plan; that's what you get paid for. We supply the information. It's up to you how you decide to use it. In that way you'll never mistake us for the CIA, DIA or any kind of other A for that matter. However, given the way we got this information and the cooperation we have received from Colonel Soto, I think it's safe to say he has started a movement that, with a little incentive, could grow to become a major game changer in Venezuela."

"And Vice Admiral Molina?"

Turner paused for a moment. Molina was an uncertain asset. Yes, he had taken the money and given them tons of information, but there were conflicting reports about the reliability of that information which raised doubts about his overall intentions. "We haven't been able to validate any credible news from him yet," Turner finally said, falling on an old political favorite in order to play safe.

2. Chávez

S ANTIAGO DE LEÓN DE CARACAS, better known as Caracas, was the birthplace of the revolutionary freemason Simón Bolívar who was considered to be the 19th century founding father of South American countries such as Panama, Colombia, Ecuador, Peru, Bolivia and Venezuela. Of course, today's Caracas looks nothing like the city Bolívar freed from the Spaniards. A melting pot of races, it is now better known for its violence and for the fact that 60% of the population live in *barrios* - slums built on the hillsides surrounding the richer part of the city that they gaze down upon. Along the hillsides, the multicolored houses look as though they have been stacked, one on top of another, in no particular order. On one side of the *barrios* government money had encouraged a number of house owners to paint their houses white so they spelled CARACAS when looked at from the distance of the city center. The aim was to resemble the famous Hollywood sign in the US, but Caracas was a long way from Los Angeles, and in more ways than distance.

Where the hillside ended, wide highways, heavy with traffic, separated the *barrios* from the high-rise homes and skyscraper offices that grace the heart of the city. On one of these roads, south of the city, a ten-car motorcade snaked slowly from the highway and into the slums. Half of the cars were open pickups, in the back of which were people brandishing automatic rifles nervously scouting their surroundings. Driving up the hillside, the window of one of the cars positioned somewhere in the middle of the motorcade rolled down. A tanned man calmly poked his head out and took a deep breath, inhaling the foul stench that filled the *barrios* as though it was the sweetest perfume.

"Please come back inside Mr. President. It is not safe."

A hand landed on the President's shoulder encouraging rather than forcing him back to the safety of the car.

"You tell me it's not safe," the President replied, not even turning to look at the man by his side, "but isn't it your job to make it safe?" He smiled to himself and kept his face in the breeze, devouring the smell of street food rising above the stench of garbage, enjoying the cacophony of yells, laughter and cries that were the soundtrack of real life. After a few moments more, he retracted his head back into the car. "Look, it's your job to keep me safe and I have absolute faith in you," he told his bodyguard, "but as you're new to my security detail I feel I should tell you that you really don't have to worry. These people love me, unconditionally. These are the people that voted for me not once, but twice. And do you know why? Because I am one of them. I was one of them, I still am one of them and I will always be – one of them. So you see, they would never hurt me. I could walk this route on foot and not get injured. I brought these people the new socialism of the 21st century; fraternity, solidarity, justice, liberty, equality and love. Hurting me would hurt them. To them I am a safe bet. With any other president they wouldn't know what they would get. But besides all that, I didn't get where I am today by being scared. So you better get used to it."

The President smiled warmly before returning to look out of the window as the motorcade turned into a small square where it was greeted by a waiting crowd of people. Men, women and children, most of them wearing red as it was the official color of his self-styled 'Bolivarian' revolution, waved small Venezuelan flags as they chanted his name.

"Chá-vez, Chá-vez, Chá-vez, Chá-vez, Chá-vez."

At 48, the charismatic Hugo Rafael Chávez Frías was running for a second term as the democratically-elected President of Venezuela. Born into a working class family, Chávez joined the army when he was seventeen. During his military career he read about the life and politics of Simón Bolívar and the Marxist revolutionary Che Guevara. After founding his own clandestine political party – the Revolutionary Bolivarian Movement-200 – Major Chávez led the MBR-200 in a coup d'état against the government of President Carlos Andrés Pérez in 1992. The coup was a failure, but during the two years he spent in jail he founded another political party, the Fifth Republic Movement, and in 1998 he won the democratic election to become the new President of Venezuela.

As the motorcade came to a halt, Chávez immediately jumped out of the car, quickly chased by his security detail. Dressed in military green overalls with the now customary red scarf around his neck that had come to symbolize his politics, he marched up to the waiting crowds and began shaking hands. Behind him, equipment was unloaded from the motorcade and frantically assembled to create an outdoor television studio, which would be the setting for the President's Sunday television show '*Aló Presidente*'. The TV show sometimes ran for six hours and was generally used by Chávez to promote his 'Bolivarian revolution'. The schedule usually consisted of various social welfare announcements, popular folk songs and attacks on Americans because they were largely held to blame for Venezuela's economic woes. Throughout the broadcast, the President would sit behind a simple mahogany desk. It was the same set, the same desk, wherever the weekly address was filmed, and this time was no different.

By the time the set was finished, Chávez had completed his tour of the square – shaking hands wherever they were offered and talking to anyone who had something to say – before finally sitting at his desk, more than an hour after he had arrived. Next to him stood his 25-year-old daughter María Gabriela Chávez. Ever since his divorce she had effectively acted as the First Lady, showing up at every national and international event. Some critics painted María Gabriela as part socialist, part power-hungry Amazon. It was not uncommon for Chávez's opponents to gleefully write about her all-day shopping trips to the luxury Centro San Ignacio.

As Chávez tapped the microphone, loud thuds echoed from the large speakers that were set up around the square. At the first sounds of the show's theme tune, the crowd started clapping and the cameras zoomed in on Chávez.

"Aló Presidente, bravo!" he cried before adding to the party atmosphere with his own handclaps, clearly enjoying himself. However, as soon as he took up position behind his desk, his face took on the gravity of a professional statesman. "My fellow Bolivarians!" Chávez stretched out his arms, attempting to quieten the crowd, many of whom were still chanting his name. "My fellow Bolivarians, friends of the Republic. Today I speak to you in a different voice than normal. Usually I'm obligated to inform you of the great foreign threat we face each day in the form of the United States and their symbol of western oppression, Mr. Bush himself. But today is different, today I must tell you of a threat that comes from the inside. I want to talk to you about the betrayal off my good friend Pedro Soto. Yes, I'm talking about my fellow army colonel who was, until recently, someone I believed to be a loyal Bolivarian who would freely give his life for the republic. But perhaps you have heard him already accuse me off tyranny and oppression, of bullying the people of Venezuela, *my* people of Venezuela. Soto called me a dictator and my government a dictatorship." Chávez waved his arms again. His face the pained mask of a man wounded. He then fell silent. Although he wasn't known for subtlety or reflection, he had planned this moment carefully. In the silence he thought about Soto's betrayal and he felt a real and very physical pain in his chest at the treachery. It wasn't so much the fact that someone would deceive him, or could deceive him, but rather the realization that he was vulnerable, maybe even mortal. He had never thought about his political life in such a way. He never imagined it might end. Sure there was always opposition – from internal political rivals to meddling international counterparts – but as long as there were more poor than rich in Venezuela he had felt assured of being loved. He was convinced the poor would forever adore him for giving them the promise of tomorrow, for letting them share in the wealth of oil. But the problem was this was the same oil that also gave the rich of Venezuela a reason to hate him, and his western political counterparts a reason to despise him for cranking up prices. After two minutes of silence, Chávez slowly began to clap. "Who loves you?" he asked the crowd. "Who will be there for you, looking out for you, sharing our country's wealth with you? This is not my answer to give, but think about it when you eat your dinner this evening or when you send your kids to school in morning."

The President continued in much the same vein for almost an hour, doing his utmost to try to convince everyone that Soto was nothing less than the devil himself; a devil under the influence of the West who may have been 'bought' by Bush himself. "I can now tell you I have had Pedro Soto arrested for insubordination, given he is a senior military officer, and also for being a traitor to our republic. But he isn't alone. There are more traitors in high places and I promise you that within the month I will expose them all. They will be dealt with and put on trial before the public."

Some three hours into the broadcast, an emotionally-charged Chávez suddenly changed tack, breaking off from the political tirade to play to the nation's sentimentality. In an unscripted move, he rose from the desk, picked up a microphone and walked towards a little boy, who couldn't have been more than three years old, who had been waving to him throughout his address. Having caught his attention, the boy intrigued the man behind the President and Chávez kneeled down to get closer to the child. He then embraced the boy with one arm, turning him towards the camera. The boy held up his hand.

"You want to give me something?"

"A cookie," the boy stammered in reply.

"A cookie. OK, so give me a cookie."

The boy immediately put his fingers in his mouth and removed what was left of the cookie he had tried, and failed, to save for the President. The crowd laughed, the child looked confused, and Chávez took the boy's small hand in his own and, without hesitation, took the remains of the cookie from his fingers and ate it. As everyone erupted in applause, Chávez kissed the boy and turned to look into the camera, tears glistening in his eyes.

"Look, children. See the generosity. Later... later comes the capitalist society that rots us with selfishness. But this boy shares what he has in his mouth. God bless him. God bless the children."

3. A Good Friend

VERLOOKING THE PARK, the wood and red brick mansion would not have looked out of place in one of America's national forests, though it actually stood in the center of Caracas. Navy Commander James Mitchel drank in the scene, feeling lucky to have a friend like José Rafael Abrantes. José had been instrumental in finding Mitchel and his family a home to rent, far away from the post-9/11 paranoia that had infected so many Americans. In recent months, Mitchel's wife Nathalie had grown heartily sick of it all. Even Mitchel had occasionally thought of cutting himself off from his politically-conscious friends, but of course this wasn't so easy given he was considered to be a talented career intelligence officer. It wouldn't have been a particularly sensible move either because, ultimately, he enjoyed his work, he was really good at it, and though the politics was a bore it was the search for truth that consistently intrigued him, that kept him going. In many respects, that search felt like a puzzle that constantly needed solving.

Of course, Mitchel was still in the intelligence business, but thankfully he was now in the intelligence business in Caracas, Venezuela. It was a country able to provide him with a relatively steady source of business and enough excitement to fuel his need to puzzle-solve. Shame then that his daughter Catherine hadn't been so keen on the move. While Mitchel had worked all over the world, the family had largely stayed put, and that meant a lot of friends for a 14-year-old girl to kiss goodbye to. On top of that, Catherine would now be required to learn Spanish if she was to get on and make new friends. In many ways, it felt to Catherine as though she were having to start her life over again – and she was frequently vocal about that inconvenience, berating her parents for the disruption every chance she got.

Nathalie walked onto the terrace to stand by her husband, noticing as she did so the damp mist rising from the trees. Before today, it had rained for three days solid so the sudden warmth and the mist made it feel as though the trees were returning some of that moisture back to the sky.

"Thanks," Mitchel said as Nathalie handed him a local beer. "Catherine home yet?"

"Not yet." Noticing the frown crease her husband's face, Nathalie controlled the sigh fighting to be released. Their daughter had an interview at the Caracas city college to discuss her options regarding courses for the start of the next academic year. These things sometimes took time. "You worry too much. The college is literally a three-minute walk from here. She'll be home soon."

"I'm not worried, just careful. This is South America, you know."

"I know, but if we want to get back into her good books we need to show we trust her. I'm afraid that's the only way we..." Before Nathalie could finish, the doorbell rang and she glanced at her husband, throwing him a 'I told you so' look. "I'll get it," she said.

As Nathalie walked to the front door, she glided through a living room that still felt alien to her. The house had been rented fully furnished and most of their personal possessions still needed to be shipped from the US. When Mitchel was offered the embassy job he had been given only one day to decide, and one week to pack before they got on the plane. As they were in no great hurry to have their memories travel with them, they left most of their belongings behind. In fact, the only clue that the Mitchel family had moved into the Caracas residence was a frame on a small side table displaying a very recent photo of the Mitchel family. Nathalie and James had bought the frame specifically to put some sort stamp on the place and that very same evening they took a family picture to fill it. It was actually supposed to represent a new start in their lives, but for Nathalie the picture simply reminded her of everything they had left behind, and she had mixed feelings about that.

As Nathalie entered the hallway her steps slowed a fraction. The shadow cast through the front door's small porthole was too tall to belong to her daughter. A little cautiously, she opened the porthole and then tried to sound enthusiastic as she opened the door, trying to make up for the disappointment she felt at not having her daughter safely home.

"José."

"*Buena tarde,* Miss Mitchel." José stepped forward and immediately thrust a bottle of Rum into Nathalie's hands. She then did her best to read the wording on the brown and orange label.

"*Diplomatico Reserva Extra Anejo, ocho 8 años.*"

"I thought it had a fitting name," José smiled playfully, "and you just keep practicing, Miss Mitchel. You'll get there."

"I'll keep practicing, but only if you start calling me Nathalie."

"Deal, Miss Nathalie," José teased. "Is Mitchel…"

Before he could finish, Catherine walked through the door, apparently in some urgency and with no intention of speaking to her mother or their guest.

"Where are you going, young lady?" Nathalie asked pointedly.

25

"To change."

"To change for what?"

"Yeah, thanks for asking; the interview went well. I even met a few friends and we are going to meet later at one of their parents' houses."

Nathalie took a deep breath. The sarcasm had not gone unnoticed, but she was desperate for her daughter to start leading as normal a life as possible, and as quickly as possible.

"Great, just run it by your father. He'll want to know where you're hanging out."

Catherine paused to check whether her mother was being sincere or not. There had been so much negativity surrounding their move and she felt most of it had been aimed at her. "Thanks, mom."

As Catherine walked to her room, José turned to Nathalie and offered a small shrug. "It's probably hard for her."

"Yes," Nathalie acknowledged. "Thanks for the rum but... did I miss something?"

"Ah, not again!" José smiled. "I am having dinner with your husband, so we might talk about his new job, but I guess..."

"He forgot to tell me." Nathalie felt irritated and yet strangely pleased by the news. This appalling absent-mindedness was something she had always loved in her husband, probably because it was so alien to her. "No problem, come in. He's on the terrace. Beer?"

"Please." José smiled and went to find Mitchel. When he found Mitchel on the terrace, his friend pointed to a chair and asked whether Nathalie had given him a hard time.

"Absolutely not."

At 38 years old, José was still single, having never succeeded in sustaining a relationship for more than a few months, six at best. He blamed his work for this because it had made him inherently distrustful of people, but it was a career he had grown up with; his own father had entered politics after attaining the rank of general in the military. And yet he sometimes longed for some of the comforts of married life. "You have no idea how lucky you are," he told Mitchel, and despite the playful tone, he meant it. He might even have explained why he thought this, but he felt a tap on his shoulder and turned round to find Nathalie waiting with his beer.

"I'll go now," she informed them both. "I'll be back around eleven. You boys be OK?"

"We'll be fine. Thanks, babe."

"Yes, thank you, Miss Mitchel." Nathalie lifted a finger in admonishment. "She likes me," he stated, after she had gone.

"It's hard to believe that you two never met in the, what is it now, 12 years we have known each other?"

"Actually it's 14 if you include the two years you spent working with my father."

"Ours was mostly a long distance relation. It also feels different because we were never that good at separating business from pleasure, in as much as we talked about things other than work."

Mitchel had never had many friends. Perhaps that was the reason he connected with José; they both shared the same initial distrust of people and their own friendship had grown as a result of the years they had worked together and the countless conversations they had enjoyed, generally over the phone.

"So, how's work?" Mitchel asked, eager to get on with the job at hand, as always.

José worked at the *Dirección de los Servicios de Inteligencia y Prevención* (DISIP) – the CIA's counterpart in Venezuela – which made him not only a friend, but also an asset given Mitchel's own role as Intelligence Liaison at the US Embassy. Before the Kursk disaster took place in the Barents Sea, Mitchel had worked for the Under Secretary of State for Arms Control and International Security Affairs. The job mainly involved intercepting foreign documents originating from South America that might possibly contain sensitive information.

This was how Mitchel first met Marco Abrantes, José's father. It was possibly the one positive he came away with because Mitchel largely considered his years on that job a failure after uncovering not one single threat to US interests. Of course Marco Abrantes was also instrumental in his friendship with José after he introduced them both at an 'arms control' dinner more than a decade ago. Despite the odds, they had managed to maintain their long distance friendship and Mitchel was now looking forward to living and working alongside his best friend though he was also acutely aware of the difficulties that friendship faced given they were, to all intents and purposes, political adversaries.

"Work is fine," Mitchel told José, "or at least it's as fine as it can be one week in. So what do you think of the whole Soto affair? You think we've seen the end of it?"

"Whoa, slow down, cowboy. No foreplay?"

José was all for sharing information, even leaking interesting snippets from time to time, but in the past it had always been a byproduct of their work and friendship, and he was not planning on changing that arrangement simply because Mitchel had moved to Caracas.

"Mitchel, you are my friend and I will help you, but you know that I work for Venezuelan intelligence while you're DIA, which means you should be, and indeed you are, my sworn enemy. Surely, even you can see the challenge and irony in that. And while we're on the subject, who exactly does sign your paycheck these days?"

Mitchel smiled. He appreciated the fact that they might be best friends, and that they were also two sides of the same coin. "Sure I see the challenge, but I could really do with some fresh facts to present during my first intelligence briefing on Monday. Even the odd insider rumor would do." Almost childishly, he then mouthed '*Please*'.

"*Bueno Cabrón*, Let's say I believe your need to impress, for now. But it's going to cost a double-topping pizza at the very least tonight."

28

"Deal." Mitchel grinned and raised his hand. José grumbled at the gesture, but then rose from his chair to high-five his friend.

"So what do you want to know?"

"First off, I want *you* to know that I will never allow our conversations to endanger our friendship. That means more to me than whatever job I might have."

Mitchel paused long enough for José to see the sincerity in his eyes. José smiled. He knew the value of true friendship and also the risks their careers posed to it. His father had always urged him never to give up on trust because to do so would be to give up on life. When he was younger, he had no idea what his father meant by this, all he knew was that he missed his dad whenever he went away on missions, sometimes for months in a row. Many times he had craved for the normality of his friends' lives and yet every time his father returned home, the happiness he felt was so intense it seemed to work to strengthen their bond rather than weaken it. Sadly, his father died a few years ago and, as a result, he had lost the best friend he ever had. José raised his beer bottle and pointed it in Mitchel's direction. "To friendship".

"Friendship," Mitchel saluted, hitting his bottle against José's. "Now, tell me something I don't know."

The two men laughed and José shook his head in mock despair. "OK, so before we even start, you need to realize that before Chávez, President Caldera allowed Washington's influence to infect Venezuela. Since then, we have seen Chávez spearhead the creation of Latin American integration and cooperation, resulting in organizations such as the Union of South American Nations, the Bolivarian Alliance for the Peoples of Our Americas, the Community of Latin American and Caribbean States, as well as the oil alliance PetroCaribe and Telesur, the region's first television network among many more social initiatives. Naturally, all this led to a decrease in Washington's influence and that is something we know they still hate him for – as well as for bringing back the wicked concept of socialism over US-inspired neoliberalism. And this is why you Americans insist on calling our President a dictator."

"And this has what to do with Soto?" Mitchel asked impatiently.

"Soto is an idealist and in many ways he's not so very different form Chávez; sharing the same ideas along with different ones, more recently. So the main problem lies in the fact that, up till now, no Venezuelan has ever called Chávez a dictator. Sure, in politics there's always a certain amount of criticism, but decrying the President as a dictator is something different and intolerable because being labeled a dictator from the inside brings two risks with it: first, there's the risk that other politicians will take up the insult, destabilizing the internal political situation; and second, the accusation that Chávez is running a dictatorship could give your own President Bush grounds to act against him, resulting in who knows what."

"So you're saying he had no choice, but to act harshly against Soto?"

José shrugged and tilted his head in a way that suggested Mitchel might like to draw his own conclusions on that matter.

"Well, Bush isn't the only one that doesn't like your boss," Mitchel replied. "Most other big – and by 'big' I mean 'Arabic' – oil-producing countries dislike him for killing oil prices, thereby undermining their own power to determine higher prices for US sales. Of course, Bush won't be too keen on Chávez's links with Castro in Cuba either, not to mention his relations with Saddam Hussain in Iraq. It's a mad world, my friend, but one that always seems a little better after a big pepperoni pizza. Shall we order?"

José nodded. "Yes, let's."

4. The Secret Discussion

THE '*PALACIO DE JUSTICIA DE CARACAS*' at the end of Bolivar Avenue consists of a couple of rectangular, grey, concrete buildings connected at the front and back by two large arches. After 10 years of service, and little maintenance, the concrete had long ago turned black giving it the scorched look of a World War II bunker rather than a modern-day courthouse. There was usually some sort of commotion taking place in the hallways, whether it was a common thief having his day in court or groups of protestors, local and international, demanding various human rights. However, this Tuesday morning when General Eduardo Valbuena sprinted along the court's hallways it was surprisingly calm. Usually when he set foot in the building he needed to employ his hat to shoo away the attentions of the waiting crowds. In a way it supported his feelings of self-importance. But this Tuesday morning, there were no crowds to negotiate and fight back. He was late. His meeting had started 15 minutes ago. Not that it could be helped, and for once the capital's traffic was not to blame; every Tuesday morning he visited his sick mother in a nursing home.

After Valbuena's father committed suicide five years ago, his mother had struggled to cope and last winter she finally suffered a stroke, one which left her totally dependent on him, her only child. In order to have her close to his place of work he had registered her in a nearby nursing home. However, the visits were never easy and some days it was harder than others to walk away from the woman who had given him life. Today was one of those days, and now he was late.

At the end of the hallway Valbuena charged through a door to descend a steel spiral staircase. At the end of the staircase was a large, bare, concrete room. At the door Valbuena slipped a pass through the magnetic lock. It released the catch with a loud thump that echoed around the room. Walking through the door, he quickly glanced at the large conference table in the middle of the room at which were three military figures and a civilian, all of whom were so engrossed with the heated debate taking place they hardly noticed the General slip into the room to take his seat at the table. After listening to the discussion for a few moments more, Valbuena decided it was time to make his presence felt.

"Firstly, I must say that I'm glad this room is soundproof and secondly, I'm glad to see you don't need me to bring fire to the discussion."

Those in the room gently laughed in response – Valbuena was well-known for his humor and sharp wit – the room then fell silent as they waited for him to take charge of the discussion.

"From the lively debate taking place I deduce that not everyone thinks it's time?"

Valbuena carefully looked at each of the faces staring back at him. Just from their eyes he could tell who was in favor of including Moises Rojas, and who was opposed. The fact was General Rojas had always been a good friend to Chávez, not to mention a political confidante. As the head of the military high command – equal to the chairman of the Joint Chiefs of Staff in the U.S. – Rojas had been a powerful ally of the President. They had also been friends since 1971 when they attended the military academy together. Chávez respected Rojas' military insights and Rojas had remained loyal all the way from the academy to the failed coup in 1992. But then last year, Rojas began to doubt Chávez for the first time when the President's approval rate dropped from 80% to 30%. As far as Valbuena was concerned, Rojas was crucial to their plans. If he could turn him he would not only have added another important general to their ranks, but also someone on the inside who was so close to Chávez he would be at the President's side while the plan unfolded.

"Moises?" Valbuena looked over to the general, keeping his eyes soft. "We've been down this road before. What can we do to take away your doubts?"

Moises Rojas closed his eyes for a second, took a deep breath before opening them again, and released a weary sigh. "There is nothing you can say," he admitted. "I know he alienates more people than ever and his government is becoming increasingly undemocratic, favoring certain parts of the population as it does, but..." Rojas paused and Brigadier General Naldo Gomez took the chance to interject.

"He's your friend, we all know that," the general said gruffly, his irritation apparent as he prepared himself for the same tired talk of past heroes again. "You have to make up your mind," he instructed. "Chávez was a hero to us all and will no doubt remain a past hero to us for the remainder of our lives, but the future needs a new and different leader."

"Six months," Mauricio Gallardo added glumly.

General Gallardo was the military attaché at the Venezuelan Embassy in Washington, and as such he was well connected to a number of influential U.S. politicians. Over the past year, he had defied Chávez several times, publicly criticizing the President's foreign policy and its increasing hostility directed towards America. Now, he was in Caracas for a month-long 'family vacation'.

"Six months?" Valbuena asked.

"In the past six months our country has fallen into a fast developing recession due to the rapid decline of world oil prices following September 11. And what did Chávez do? He passed 49 law decrees in one night alienating the rich in our country, he pushed for elections at the *Unión Nacional de Trabajadores* defying the labor party and he openly opposed the Bush administration's 'war on terror', something that might possibly throw our country into the next international crisis. You need more?"

The room fell silent for a second as everyone contemplated the truth of the general's words. Maybe they didn't have all the answers, but they believed beyond doubt that the welfare of their country was in jeopardy. What had been right before was no longer right today, not if they were to survive. And yet, the silence and furtive glances across the table revealed a reluctance to be the first to say the obvious.

"Maybe I should say something."

Every eye in the room moved to the one civilian among them.

"I know I haven't brought much to the discussion yet, but as a man of God I feel I might add a unique perspective."

Ignacio Velasco might have been the Cardinal and Archbishop of Caracas, but he was considered by some to be more politician than priest. It was a reputation he had earned through his outspoken support of Chávez in the past.

"As you know, the church has always supported the President, especially given his focus on helping the poor of our country. But now it's clear to see that he's wandered from God's chosen path. His attacks on the rich will only hurt the poor. Sadly, he's no longer able to differentiate between good politics and personal vendettas, which is why he derides anyone influenced by capitalist forces. We feel for him as a person, but the church can no longer support the President's policies and therefore we will back any responsible transition. Our only condition is that Chávez and his family are not hurt in the process."

"I think I speak for everyone when I say that we all want that," Valbuena confirmed. "But we need to understand that our plan will not be free of violence. There will be casualties. Naturally, we hope the numbers will be minimal, but these types of operations are never risk-free. So all that remains is to decide whether we're all in or we're all out – and this has to be decided now because everything is set to go." Valbuena glanced at Gallardo, looking for confirmation, and the general nodded. "So, you see gentlemen, it's now or never. Therefore, and with your consent, I'd like to ask you individually if you're on board because it is only if we are all in that we can proceed."

Valbuena paused to allow for a few mumbles of consultation to take place. Once everyone agreed to vote, he turned first to the one man whose vote he knew he could rely on, mainly because he was heavily involved in securing the participation of the United States in the plan.

"Gallardo?"

"In," he responded without hesitation. "I'm in."

"Naldo?"

"Me too."

"Monseigneur Velasco?"

"I pray for what we start here and for the forgiveness we'll need when it's done."

Valbuena nodded and turned to Rojas. "Would you like me to go first?"

Rojas shook his head and grimaced, his face etched with a pain that was very real. "Though I cannot free myself from the thought that I will regret this decision for the rest of my life I don't see any other way. I'm in."

At the needed response, Valbuena paused to let the gravity of the moment sink in. He then inhaled deeply before confirming that he was also on board. "Before we continue, I suggest we all take a moment to reflect over tea."

No sooner had Valbuena finished speaking Gallardo stood up from the table, his chair screeching upon the floor like nails on a blackboard. "Sorry," he apologized before glancing at Valbuena, who nodded in reply. Gallardo then hastily left the room. "I'll be right back," he shouted behind him, to no-one in particular.

Gallardo took the stairs two at a time before pausing to catch his breath and collect himself. He then entered the main hall of the Justice Palace and crossed over to the room adjacent, furnished with a handful of desks, at which were sat two government officials apparently stacking papers from one desk to the other.

"I need the room," Gallardo told them.

"Yes, Sir."

"Sure, General."

As both men left the room, Gallardo closed the door behind them. Next he walked to the desk furthest away from the door and picked up the phone.

"5, 5, 5, 4, 7, 8…" he mumbled. After only a couple of rings, his call was answered. "It's me," he said. "Can you put me through on a secure line?"

A few seconds later a booming voice exploded in his ear.

"Rout here!"

Gallardo and Oskar Rout had developed a mutually beneficial relationship over the years, exchanging so called 'grey information' in Washington. Rout was the Assistant Secretary of State for Latin American Affairs and the grey information they shared covered everything worth sharing that wasn't clearly marked '*Top Secret*'. In short, the sharing of grey information meant no laws were broken, meaning those who shared it were relatively safe from prosecution.

"It's a go," Gallardo succinctly informed Rout.

"All right, we'll start preparations on our side and get back you on the details of the delivery."

With everything said that needed to be said, Gallardo hung up the phone and returned to his colleagues in the basement.

"Are we good to continue?" Valbuena asked after Gallardo returned to the room and whispered in his ear, "It's done." The general nodded and Valbuena turned his attention back to the table. "So now we have one more difficult decision to make. We need to decide who will be the successor."

"Successor?" Gomez asked, the surprise evident on his face. "I don't recall anyone saying we'll need a successor."

"Well, what would you have?" Rojas asked. "A Junta, an authoritarian state with us at the wheel? Are you mad? If we were to install a military government we would distance ourselves from all of our people, the rich as well as the poor. We wouldn't survive a week."

"I agree," the Cardinal joined in. "We want to get Venezuela back on track, sooner rather than later, and we need an interim president and fully functional government to do that. We need to get back to business as soon as possible."

Gomez listened while searching for allies around the table. He found none. The flamboyant 55-year-old Brigadier-General rubbed his bald head in consternation. "I still think a military provisional government would be best for the country, though I agree, the acceptance of such a government would be very low at this time."

"All right," Valbuena said decisively, moving the discussion on because they were running out of time. "We have two main candidates, Ortega and Carmona. To keep it short, Carlos Ortega is president of the CTV, the biggest Venezuelan Workers Confederation, and he will deliver the support of the country's labor party leaders whereas Pedro Carmona is the President of the '*Fedecámaras*', The Venezuelan Federation of Chambers of Commerce, and he'll will give us the economic and military support we need." Valbuena turned to Gallardo as the others started debating the options. "Mauricio, can you please fill us in on the necessary details?"

Gallardo dutifully stood up to address the room.

"We actually need both men for the plan to work as it revolves around two demonstrations scheduled to be held in the first half of April. The idea is these demonstrations will set in motion the events that will kick start the revolution."

"Revolution? Now you sound like 'El Presidente' himself," Gomez scoffed.

"Call it what you will," Gallardo replied coolly. "But we need one of the men to start events and the other to finish."

"Meaning?" snapped Rojas, his dislike of Gallardo eating away at his patience. To some in the room, Rojas was the '*redneck*' among them. Born in the state of Zulia he was a true Zuliano and different from the rest. In general, Zulianos were poor, they spoke a different kind of Spanish, they listened to their own music, ate their own food and were well known for a no-nonsense attitude to just about everything, and Rojas was no exception. As head of the military high command he had little patience and an allergy for being left in the dark. In contrast, Gallardo was a native of the "*Distrito Capital*', otherwise known as Caracas. He was also the son of a wealthy oil baron. Therefore, it was almost expected that Gallardo and Rojas wouldn't get along.

"Meaning," Gallardo repeated icily, "there are two potential candidates that need to be convinced that they can, or rather will, be president. When the time comes only one of them will set things in motion. Whoever does this will also be later condemned for his actions – and for any casualties incurred in the transition. In short, things can go wrong and inevitably will go wrong, and when they do the new president needs to be clear of any blame. Hence the need for two candidates."

"So one of them is a patsy," Rojas concluded.

"If you will, a patsy. We did it before, so…"

"But never on this scale and with such dire consequences. Are you OK with this Cardinal?" Rojas looked at Velasco not expecting any support, but wanting to hear him voice his opinion in order to stop both him and his church from turning tail at some point the future.

"We are willing to accept the consequences regarding the two candidates as long as they and their families come out of this unharmed."

"Physically, we can be certain they will be unharmed," Valbuena stated, knowing that whoever ended up as the patsy would probably be convicted of something or at least be out of work for a while.

"Sure," Gallardo said in support before looking around for any further need for clarification, but everyone nodded in agreement.

With the doubts silenced for a time, Valbuena continued. "Of course, we now have to decide who we really want for the presidency."

"That should be simple," Gomez piped up. "If we go with Ortega we'll antagonize the military and the rich, with Carmona we'll suffer a slight disadvantage with the people. Personally, I know who I'd rather have at my side of the table when the other shoe drops."

As crude as Gomez's observations were, they made sense to everyone in the room. This was no time for crusades or even sentiment. Leadership needed power and it needed money.

"So that's it then," Valbuena concluded. "We will ask for Ortega's commitment in order to get the ball rolling, and quietly tell Carmona about the bigger picture, but otherwise – and I'm sure I don't need to say this – it's imperative we keep the number who know what's happening to a bare minimum. *Viva proyecto Evolución!*"

As the men gathered their things Valbuena walked up to Rojas and put his hand on his shoulder. "Are you OK, my friend?"

"Well, let's see," Rojas replied, his voice dripping with sarcasm. "I'm acting as a double agent between the government and some coup leaders while betraying my oldest and most trusted friend. So yes, I must be fine."

Valbuena took the comment on the chin. "I understand your reticence. This must be very hard for you, but I'm glad you understand the necessity of our task, and you've got my personal guarantee that neither your friend nor his family will be hurt. In fact, this will all be over in a few weeks."

Rojas responded with a reluctant nod, but as the five conspirators broke up Rojas's' mind found no peace. As Valbuena watched him go he knew that if there would a weak link in their plan it would be Rojas.

At the end of the day the white brick, red-roofed presidential palace, known as *Miraflores*, appeared golden under the rays of the setting sun. Built in the late 1800s, along with the adjacent '*Fernando Rodríguez del Toro barracks*' which houses the presidential guard, the palace has hundreds of rooms and dozens of passageways surrounding the large square park that sits like a garden in the center of the scene. One room, named the '*Ayacucho*' in honor of the great Peruvian city, could hold up to 250 people at a time, meaning it was largely used for official events. Chávez loved this room, so much that if he wasn't on tour he would broadcast his weekly address from the *Ayacucho*, sitting behind his usual desk, positioned under an impressive painting of Simon Bolivar. However, it wasn't the size of the room that captured the President's heart, but rather the balcony attached to it that overlooked the '*Parque Miraflores*'. In a city where every view seemed to offer nothing but high-rise blocks, the garden area was a taste of paradise and whenever Chávez needed to clear his mind he would come to the balcony and sit there for hours, simply looking at the trees. However, that night the President was waiting for someone and the picture of paradise before him failed to keep his attention. Therefore, when a loud knock disturbed the quiet, it took every ounce of strength for Chávez not to jump up from the custom-made mahogany deck chair he was sat in.

As the footsteps neared, Chávez welcomed his visitor, not even glancing behind him to be sure.

"My dear friend! Come, join me."

Moises Rojas walked onto the balcony and immediately positioned himself at the railings, pretending to gaze at the darkening green of the landscape below.

"I'll never know how you recognize people solely from their footsteps," he finally said, trying to keep his voice calm.

"It's important to know who's behind you and who's not," Chávez responded, seemingly unaware of the impact his words would have on his friend. "Sit." Chávez gestured towards a chair and Rojas sat down. The President then poured him a glass of '*Chicha*', a fermented drink made from rice, milk and sugar. He then turned his attention back to the '*Parque Miraflores*'. "Sitting here, it's hard to imagine where we came from."

"And easy to forget," Rojas added truthfully. "In fact, it's getting more and more difficult to remember the day when we first tried to rise to power in '92."

"The wrong thing for the right reasons," Chávez responded. Despite finding popularity on the back of the two years he spent in jail for the failed coup, he still bitterly regretted the loss of 14 lives in the battle to oust President Carlos Andrés Pérez. The goal had been to kill Pérez, but others fell in the process and though he recognized it had been the only way to seize control, the deaths haunted him still.

"Pérez deserved it," Rojas insisted as he saw a familiar sorrow darken his friend's mood. Bizarrely, the people knew Chávez as the eternal optimist, a man without remorse who was always in control, but Rojas knew him better than most. He was there when Chávez was released from prison by the new President, Rafael Caldera, and he saw him come out a depressed and broken man. Two years in jail had cost him his marriage and a number of military friends who had disagreed with the violence-free ideology behind his *'Movement of the Fifth Republic'*. "Doubts?" Rojas asked.

"Never about the past, but always about the future." Chávez closed his eyes before tilting his face towards the sky. "You know what I see?"

"No."

"Nothing." With a grim smile on his face he repeated, "Nothing."

Rojas opened his mouth to try and cheer his friend, but the words turned to dust before they passed his lips, and Chávez continued talking.

"In the past when I closed my eyes I could always see the future, as bright as could be; I knew where I was going and where I would be when I got there. Now there's only a blank." Chávez paused to stare at his old friend. When he next spoke, his voice was heavy with disappointment. "I know you opposed me on my 49-law reformation, but I did it to reform the land; to guarantee indigenous and women's rights, and to provide free healthcare and education…"

"Whilst practically disowning every landowner in the process and alienating anyone with money who was forced to pay for your plans."

Chávez's eyes widened, unused to such a direct response, even from his old friend. But as the words sank in, he softened and smiled.

"It's OK my friend," he said. "I deserve it. But sometimes it's hard to do the right thing."

"Yes, it is." Rojas mumbled, feeling the depth of his betrayal echo in his stomach.

5. The First Sign

Tuesday, April 2nd, 2002

A

T THE FIRST FLUSH OF MORNING, rays of light found their way along the edges of Mitchel's bedroom curtains. Nathalie was already awake, woken by Mitchel's tossing and turning beneath the sheets. She had experienced this so many nights and mornings before. Soon he would begin to shake his head, as though dodging bullets. When this happened, her first instinct was always to wake him, but experience had taught her that doing so would only disorient him whereas if he was able to wake of his own accord he would do so knowing he had been caught in a dream.

After a minute that felt more like ten, Mitchel sat up, ramrod straight, and exhaled loudly as though expelling all the bad air from the night. Nathalie immediately threw aside the blanket that covered them, threw him back onto the sheets, and placed herself on top of his naked body still hot with the sweat of his nightmare. Mitchel stared into her eyes as Nathalie took hold of his head with both hands before kissing him, first on the forehead and then slowly moving down from his mouth. As she disappeared under the sheets, Mitchel wished her "good morning," with softly spoken gratitude.

As Mitchel hit the shower, Nathalie went downstairs to fix breakfast dressed only in a long T-shirt. She knew she had exactly fifteen minutes before he would appear. He would then gulp down a glass of juice and grab a sandwich that he would eat while on the move. It was a hangover from his Navy days – quick to bed, quick to rise – and it was something he couldn't easily shake as it added some resemblance of structure to his day.

When Nathalie heard her husband's footsteps coming she picked up the glass of orange juice she had made and held it out, in the direction of the kitchen door. When Mitchel appeared he smiled with appreciation.

"Good morning again, dear." He took hold of the glass and drank the contents in one go. "I probably don't deserve you."

"You probably don't," Nathalie laughed before taking the glass and handing him a sandwich.

"I love you," he told her.

"I know. Now go."

As the sun lifted clear of the tree line, the white garage door grew brilliant against the red brick of the mansion to cast a spotlight on the red '68 Mustang standing in the driveway. The Mustang belonged to José who, in turn, had inherited it from his father Marco. He had only driven it a few times before lending it to Mitchel, indefinitely. José was more of a motorcycle man, declaring it to be the "surest and fastest way to get from A to B".

Following a loud clunk, the garage door sluggishly rose from the floor. Once the opening reached four feet, creating an angle of almost 45 degrees, Mitchel raced into view on a bicycle, carefully dodging the

Mustang as he gained speed. He was sick of spending his mornings in traffic jams and had decided peddle-power would be the best way to deal with the Caracas rush hour. The city was well-known for its snarl ups and though the bike ride would only cut five minutes off his journey, Mitchel understood it would improve not only his fitness levels, but also his mood.

Turning in his seat he waved at Nathalie who stood watching at the kitchen window before curving away, into the street. With no bike lanes to speak off, it was often said that cyclists took their life into their own hands in Caracas, but during rush hour it was probably the safest time of day to take that risk because the cars were mostly stationary. As Mitchel stood on his peddles he weaved between the still or barely moving traffic with his messenger bag swinging from his neck like a cape. Almost drowning out the constant honking of irritated drivers, the music from his iPod powered him on. 'The best 400 dollars I ever spent,' he thought. Of course, Nathalie had called him nuts to spend that kind of money on a glorified Walkman, but he was fanatical about the bands he liked and he enjoyed having them with him wherever he might go. At the opening riff of Bon Jovi's *'You Give Love a Bad Name'* Mitchel shifted up a gear to race through the traffic. Taking the quickest route he knew, he reached the halfway point at *Avenida Caurimare*. At any other time of day, crossing six lanes of city traffic would be suicidal, but during rush hour the freeway looked more like a car junkyard, parading motionless cars as far as the eye could see.

Speeding along the fourth lane, standing again on his pedals, Mitchel skimmed past an old rusty car just as the driver opened the door. By some miracle of balance, Mitchel missed the door by an inch and yet it was the Venezuelan guy who immediately got out of his car to remonstrate.

'Dumbass!' The man shouted after him, waving his fist at the sky as he did so. Mitchel gave a glance backwards, but he was too far away to properly hear the man let alone understand him so he simply gave him a thumbs up. Some twenty minutes later, Mitchel took the last bend at speed, ready for the 400-yard incline up to the five-story embassy building in which his office was located. Sunk into the bedrock of the Andean foothills, the stars and stripes welcomed every visitor, as did the security guard at the service entrance.

"Good morning," Mitchel said as he stepped off his bike. "Twenty-two minutes and thirty seconds. A new personal best," he joked while looking at his watch. The security officer didn't respond at first because he was too surprised to speak. This entrance was mostly used for deliveries. "One moment," Mitchel instructed as he searched for his ID in the bag around his neck. "Here you are."

Mitchel showed him his card. The man took it without a word, the surprise still evident on his face.

"You're not a man of many words," Mitchel observed.

"I'm sorry," the guard finally replied, "it's just that we don't get too many cyclists here. Most people find it too dangerous, I guess – what with all the traffic."

"It probably would be very dangerous if the cars actually drove anywhere," Mitchel responded with a laugh.

"First day?"

"Definitely first day on the bike."

"All right. Good luck. You can park your bike in that large wooden building 25 yards that way," the guard said, pointing the way as he spoke. "You can't miss it; it's the only almost empty structure on the premises."

Mitchel smiled, thanked the man and wheeled his bike passed as the steel-barred gate opened. Once inside the wooden building Mitchel parked his bike next to the only other bike there, one positioned next to the door leading into the building. As he walked through the door he was greeted by another guard as well as an X-ray machine that barred the way into the rest of the building. Mitchel placed his backpack and wallet onto the waiting conveyor belt and passed though the metal detector without incident.

"Thank you, Sir."

Mitchel nodded.

A small corridor led him up to the central hallway. He glanced at the United States seal carved into the marble floor and noted the number of people already queueing for tourist visas, work permits and passports.

"Mr Mitchel! Mr Mitchel!" A young man in a white linen suit shouted across the hallway before running over. "Nigel Small-Fawcett," he introduced himself, speaking fast with a clear British accent. He looked kind of nervous. "Sorry, I recognized you from your picture. You're new here, so am I, on internship, from Britain, second week, here, I mean. Welcome, welcome."

The man extended his arm and forcefully shook Mitchel's hand.

"Wow, that's quite a reception. Thank you. I guess you know where I'm going?"

"Yes I do, please follow me."

Mitchel dutifully followed Nigel as he scurried across the hallway, up the open stairs, and into an open-plan center space filled with secretaries working behind computers. Surrounding the center was a number of glass-walled offices and conference rooms, each marked by the name of a fruit.

"Here we are," Nigel said, pointing at a glass door with a sign that read '*Apple, James Mitchel, Lc Intelligence*'.

"That must be me."

"I think so, Sir." Nigel looked at his watch. "It's 8.30 now. You have thirty minutes to clean up before you're expected at the ambassador's office at nine. It's straight across the square."

"Thank you."

Once Nigel left the room, Mitchel looked around his new office, which mostly comprised of a small, but functional desk with a computer on it. Mitchel put his backpack on the desk and walked to the window to find he was directly above the place where he had parked his bike. 'I'll be OK,' he thought.

At 52, Calder Shale looked young for his age with only a few grey hairs. He also looked somewhat inexperienced even though he wasn't new to South America and the Caribbean. As a political counselor he had served in El Salvador and Chile as well as Trinidad and Tobago. Before coming to Venezuela he worked for the Bureau of Western Hemisphere Affairs, an organization officially charged with implementing U.S. foreign policy and promoting U.S. interests in the Western Hemisphere. The organization also staffed and managed America's embassies. Shale had forged quite a career 'converting' countries to the neoliberal economics of the US. However, as he was only six weeks into the role of ambassador he was still learning the lay of the land. In his first week, he had enjoyed lunch with Chávez, an invitation he hadn't expected to receive so early in his tenure, and one he felt might have been offered due to the circumstances surrounding the departure of his predecessor, Dana Hagopian. However, over lunch Chávez told him that he didn't want to talk about the past, that he wanted to start anew; to forge even better diplomatic relations between his government and the US embassy.

"Even better?" Shale had responded with typically dry humor and for a moment Chávez looked stunned. But just as Shale began to wonder whether he had committed his first diplomatic faux pas Chávez burst out laughing. He then reached over the table to slap Shale on the shoulder.

"Good one!" the President said loudly, drawing quizzical looks from everyone else in attendance.

Shale's office wasn't particularly grand for a high-flying government official. There was no mahogany desk, no American flag taking up space, and the only color came from a portrait of George Bush hung on one of the white walls. At the back of the room stood a small, white desk, which was largely redundant because Shale preferred to work on one of the two leather couches in the center of the room. And that's where he was when Mitchel knocked on the frosted glass door – sat on a couch, with his legs up, reading from a large stack of papers.

"Good morning, Sir. I believe we have an appointment," Mitchel said as he took in the surprisingly relaxed scene in front of him.

"You believe correct. Please, sit down, Take the weight off your feet." Shale pointed at the couch opposite. As Mitchel took his seat, the ambassador watched, noting him take in the décor. "Different from what you expected?" he asked.

"To be honest, it is," Mitchel replied with a smile. "Brown usually seems to be a government official's favorite color."

"I'm sure you're right, but then I'm not exactly your conventional Washington politician. So what do you say? I read your file and I'm pretty sure you've read mine. So, let's get to know each other better by you telling me what it is you've prepared for this meeting."

Mitchel couldn't help but smile again. Unconventional really was the word. "All right," he agreed, happy to get straight down to business. "It's no secret that the US doesn't like Hugo Chávez Frías. His foreign and domestic oil policy is a clear risk to US gas needs as well as international oil prices. But despite Chávez returning oil revenues to the people by selling gasoline at 10 cents a gallon, meaning everyone can afford a car, the country actually has no money left to build the infrastructure needed to drive on. Then, after 9/11 and the bombing campaign in Afghanistan, Chávez publicly declared it an act of terror responsible for the killing of innocent women and children. I think his exact words were, 'this is fighting terror with more terror'. Therefore, I'm not surprised to learn that last December this office sent a message to Washington declaring it was time for change. Pirro Carrera was put in the frame as, and I quote, 'the right man for the right time'." Mitchel paused, interested to see how Shale would react to the last piece of information he had gleaned from is friend José.

"A short synopsis finished with a piece of gossip," Shale responded coolly with a smile. "You know what happened when my predecessor, Dana Hagopian, addressed Chávez about the other issues?" Mitchel shook his head. "Well, the State Department sent her to deliver a message in person. Chávez agreed to the meeting and when she asked him to not publicly condemn the US, Chávez interrupted her with the words, 'You are talking to the President of the Republic. Regarding your position, I find you are not behaving in a fitting way to address a president. Please, leave, now'." As he spoke, Shale put on a Spanish accent and gesticulated wildly. His face then grew more serious. "Of course, you know Chávez sells low-priced oil to Cuba and refuses airspace to American military aircraft? And you know he supports the murderous regime in neighboring Colombia?"

Mitchel nodded, left in no doubt about where Shale stood on the Chávez issue, politically. But there was more to the President.

"I know all that, and I also know that when Chávez came to power he overturned the privatization of the state-owned oil company PDVSA. Before the reversal the private PDVSA sold oil abroad with only 1% profit, thereby impoverishing his own country. When he raised that profit to about 20% he gave that same profit back to the people for things like healthcare, education, employment, technology, housing, safe drinking water and pensions."

Shale grimaced and waved at Mitchel to stop.

"That's all very well," he said. "But Chávez is the first explicitly anti-establishment president in over forty years in this country. Two years ago, not long after he took office, he completely removed the country's old elite from the Supreme Court, the National Assembly as well as a number of governors – plunging this country into an early state of chaos. In 2001, he attended the Summit of the Americas in Quebec where he first met President Bush, who was there to present the Free

Trade of the Americas Act. Your friend Chávez was the only one to oppose the plan. And you know why? I'll tell you why, because he simply wanted to defy the US. Trust me on this, his attitude will put Venezuela in a state of diplomatic isolation."

"I take it you don't like the man?" Mitchel half-asked, half-joked, not willing to alienate himself from the boss at this early stage.

"Met him only once. Seemed like a nice guy. Possibly even a good friend to a lot of people, but a political leader? No. In my opinion the man is merely out to avenge the killing of his uncle who died fighting with the National Liberation Armed Forces in 1969 during their attempt to overthrow a US-friendly government. But Chávez's real crime is not his ideology but his failure to deliver on electoral promises."

"And in this case, he is unique?" Mitchel responded incredulously. "Can you name me one president who hasn't failed in this regard, including in the US?"

"Look, you're right, but coupled with his idea of wealth distribution and private property in the hands of the common people he strikes me as a desperate man with a vivid imagination rather than a revolutionary president with any political insightfulness…"

"Others might say that the Bolivarian Revolution, started by Chávez, is actually starting to take form, with the latest hydrocarbon laws allowing for a common prosperity that was denied under the old oligarchy. Furthermore, the industry is beginning to recuperate."

As Mitchel paused for breath, he could see the ambassador gearing up to fire his own arguments back at him and he was suddenly reminded that this was their first meeting, and a heated debate might not be the best start to their working relationship. So before Shale could respond, he apologized.

"I didn't mean to disrespect," Mitchel explained. "But I think we need to tread carefully. I take it you have heard the rumors about the National Endowment for Democracy (NED), a supposedly privately-funded institute suspected of having ties to US official agencies and accused of channeling hundreds of thousands of dollars, four times more than ever, to opposition movements such as Fedecámaras and the CTV Labor Federation, for the good of who knows who? Chávez is still the democratically elected president of a democratic republic."

"Democratically elected?" Shale raised an eyebrow. "I know from your file this is your first official assignment in South America, and that last sentence speaks volumes about your inexperience. Dictators are chosen out here."

As Shale paused for effect, Mitchel stayed quiet. The last remark was personal and when a conversation like this becomes personal he was experienced enough to know when to stop. But there was one last thing he needed to get off his chest.

"In 1992, Jimmy Carter, then chief of the international committee for monitoring elections, declared the '92 election in Venezuela as 'the best in the world'. And there's also that other rumor currently circulating, that Chávez might just win the next Nobel Peace Prize."

Shale smiled calmly and when he spoke, he delivered his words slowly. "With his so-called '49 enabling laws' the intent might have been for a democratizing effect covering issues of land distribution, banking reformations by micro credits, fishing rights et cetera, et cetera. But the people who provide the money will simply take it out of Venezuela thereby reducing this country to an impoverished state likely to dip into civil war. For this reason, I strongly believe that even though Chávez was elected he has gone on to act like a potential dictator. But," Shale sat back and allowed the easy smile to return to his face, "for now it might be best if we simply agree to disagree. It's obvious we both have strong opinions on the matter and since we'll be working closely together they should help us stay sharp and ahead of the game."

Mitchel nodded, despite disagreeing that he held any particular opinion on the matter. For him, his comments on Chávez came from keeping an open mind, like his father had always taught hm. He watched Shale pick up a file from the coffee table separating them and handing it to him.

"This is a copy of the new '*Venezuelan National Human Development Report*'," Shale explained. "Read it and tell me what you think."

Mitchel nodded and as it was clear the meeting was over, he left the room. All in all, he had been with the ambassador for less than 30 minutes, but it was an experience he would be unlikely to soon forget. He was also irritated at having been so easily lured into such a discussion. It was clear he had developed some strong thoughts on the Chávez issue and yet he was baffled as to how and why. He then wondered whether he had been more influenced by his friend José than he had realized.

Shale sat down at the small, white desk in his office. He was a big man and the image looked almost cartoonish. "Please get me Charles Turner on the phone," he instructed over the intercom. A few moments later, Turner was on the line.

"Charles, thank you for picking up so fast. I just met your boy."

"And how did it go?"

"I tested him a bit and I can see why you like him. He's stubborn, emotional, concerned, does his homework and wears his heart on his sleeve…. like you."

"It sure sounds like you met James Mitchel," Charles replied, the good humor evident in his voice. "But can you work with him, that's the question here?"

"I can work with him, sure, but can I trust him? That's what I'm not so certain about yet."

"He's a good man and you can trust him if he feels he can trust you. Be honest is my best advice. He'll reward you by being the same."

Shale paused in thought for a moment. "Well, if honesty does the trick I'm sure we've had a good start," he finally joked. "I'll see where we go from here. We have no easy task at hand so I guess we'll see how things develop. Thanks for your help in getting him here. Hell, thanks for getting me here!"

"You're welcome. Let's have a drink sometime when you're back in Washington."

"Will do. Talk to you later."

'*Los Pilones de Este*' was a small diner straight opposite Mitchel's office window at the '*Av. Principal de Las Mercedes.*' A little further down the road was the Hard Rock Café but Mitchel chose to meet José for lunch at a traditional Venezuelan café. When Mitchel arrived his friend already sat on the small terrace.

"What's good here?" Mitchel asked.

"Hello to you too, and how was your morning?"

Mitchel thought for a second before answering. "Different...yes, I'd go with different, and yet the same."

José smiled at his friend. "Sorry, I didn't mean to make fun of you."

"No problem, have your fun. It's just that you expect things to be different from home, in another county, with new people but it's not. This morning I got acquainted with the Ambassador, Calder Shale. You know him?"

"I know of him, but haven't met him personally, he just got here."

"Well, within five minutes of shaking hands we got into a weird argument about Chávez's leadership and his intentions for the future. It somehow felt like a test."

"Perhaps it was."

"A test for what though?"

"Couldn't it simply be that he's checking you out? I mean, you're new to the country, he's new, perhaps he's just looking for someone to trust, maybe even a friend. You're the one who's always saying we should start with trust – so – start with trust."

"Sounds like good advice." Mitchel smiled, recognizing his own advice. "Still, could you please have a look; see what you have on Shale?"

Although Mitchel's father had always told him to start with trust, he had also taught him to listen to his gut, and right now his gut was telling him something was off, but he couldn't quite work out what.

"I can look into the DISIP files for you, but I don't expect there to be much," José offered. "Up until recently Shale was an insignificant North American politician to us who only became interesting when he arrived in Venezuela."

"Still I would appreciate it if you'd have a look."

"Consider it done. *Sancocho de Gallina*," José added and Mitchel gave him a wary look.

"You better watch your mouth," he joked and his friend laughed.

"*Sancocho de Gallina*. You asked me what was good here, and this is it. It's a cross between a stew and a thick soup with cassava, yams, bananas all kinds of peas and it's finished off with lots of chicken. Trust me, it will get you through the afternoon."

"Then I guess I better take your word for it," Mitchel smirked. "It's a trust thing."

6. Accidental Discovery

Wednesday, April 3rd, 2002

A S A CAR DROVE UP THE DRIVEWAY of the presidential home – a luxurious six-bedroom villa complete with swimming pool and private movie theater in the middle of *'Parque Miraflores'* – loud music sounded across the yard. As Chávez got out of the car he shook his head and looked at his watch. 'Three in the morning,' he thought as he shook his head remembering how different his own youth had been. Growing up in the slums of Sabaneta with his brother Adan they didn't have electricity or even running water, and from an early age he planned to escape the poverty that trapped them, determined to give his family a decent life. In contrast, the only worry his two daughters seemed to have was when they'd plan their next party. 'So, I must have succeeded in something', he decided, smiling ruefully as he walked up the garden path.

"Hugo!"

A voice cried out and in the dim light Chávez took a moment to notice Moises Rojas sitting on the small staircase in front of him.

"*Qué chingados*. What the…" Chávez rushed towards his friend in alarm. "What are you doing here outside? Are you OK? It's freezing!"

"I'm not that cold. María and Rosa invited me in, but as you can hear … well … it's not entirely my scene."

Chávez shrugged his shoulders in resigned agreement and sat down next to Rojas.

"My friend, what are you doing here in the middle of the night?"

Rojas flinched slightly at the harshness of the question, unsure whether it was the shock of finding him there alone in the dark or the surprise of his actual visit that had rattled the president. In truth, Rojas wasn't even sure himself whether he had done the right thing in coming to the palace. What would it achieve? What did he expect? And as the questions wrestled in his head he felt doubt coming to smother his resolve. Never in his life had he ever felt more caught between what he wanted to do and what he thought he should do, and in desperation he gazed at his watch, hoping it might buy him more time to prepare his words. But in the end all he managed to come up with was, "That late, huh?"

Of course he was hoping Chávez would start the conversation and after a few seconds of silence, the president obliged.

"You know, I forgive you," Chávez informed him, bringing his arm around Rojas' shoulder, which immediately caused the man to panic.

"Well uh…" Rojas stammered, unsure of what to say or why he was being forgiven. Then the words started to tumble from his lips. "You remember our conversation the other day when you told me you had doubts about the future, not seeing it as brightly as you used to? Well that remark has kept going through my head ever since. I feel it too. What if we're off the right track? How can we still be sure we're doing the right thing? How do you feel?"

Chávez frowned at the insecurity tightening Rojas's voice. Something big must be bothering him, why else would he turn up on his doorstep at 3 a.m.?

"*Amigo*, let me tell you what I know and maybe that will tell you something about how I feel. I know we're both still in it for the right reasons. I also know you're having trouble supporting my latest actions, you said so, even in public, and that's OK. I also know that something is going on; something that's been going on for some time within my military ranks. There's a lot of doubt, and I know I need to make my actions a success. So what do I feel? I feel afraid, but I also feel righteous. I feel that everybody should stick to their chosen path even when sometimes we feel all alone in the game. What would have happened if Bolivar, '*El Libertador*', had given into the Spanish opposition? Venezuela would never have been freed and I would never have been democratically chosen."

Chávez's voice rose and his fist punched the air. Rojas leant back a little, to better see the man he had adored and worshipped most of his adult life. Now it felt different. Tonight, his old friend looked obsessive, as though he had lost touch with reality.

"And I'll tell you something else," Chávez continued, but before he could finish the door behind the two men opened and the music from inside drowned out any hope of further conversation. A handful of young women, talking loudly, made their way down the small staircase, almost tripping over the two men. A flurry of apologies followed and Chávez smiled broadly, brushing away their concerns as easily as his switch from political preacher to loving father. 'How can this be one man?' Rojas thought. He then turned to look at the President's two daughters, waving goodbye to their friends from the step above him. After a few seconds, Rosa bent down towards her father.

"We're going to bed, Papa. So you two old men can safely come into the house now."

"That's OK, my dearest. Just leave the old men alone on the stairs. I'll see you two tomorrow."

Rojas managed to give a small smile as he waved the girls goodnight.

"Now where were we?" Chávez asked once his girls had gone.

"We were going to bed," Rojas responded as he got up from the stair he was sat on. "It's senseless to worry at night when we can worry all day tomorrow."

Chávez didn't disagree and when he watched Rojas walk away he quietly echoed the sentiment. "Wise words, my friend. Let us worry tomorrow."

Mitchel looked at his watch as he walked into the embassy corridor and placed his backpack on the conveyer belt of the X-ray machine. 'That's 21 minutes and 40 seconds,' he murmured.

"Where have you come from?" a security guard asked while thoroughly re-checking his backpack by hand after it passed through the X-ray.

"Ciudad Universitaria," Mitchel replied in his best Spanish. "Something wrong?" he asked, pointing to the bag.

"No, nothing," the guard replied, handing the backpack to him. "It's just a random check because not everything shows up on the scanner. You're good to go, Sir. Have a good day."

Mitchel nodded. "Thanks, you too."

As Mitchel walked along through the hallway he was suddenly stopped in his tracks.

"Twenty, thirty," the security guard shouted.

Mitchel turned. "Excuse me?"

"Twenty, thirty," the guard repeated. "It should be your *tiempo objetivo,* your 'target time', for tomorrow."

"Great, thanks," Mitchel replied with a smile. "My first full day on the job and already I have a personal trainer."

As he continued his way into the central hall he noticed Nigel Small-Fawcett standing on the seal in the center of the room. Nigel saw him and walked over.

"Good morning, Sir. I hope you had a good night's rest after your first day."

Mitchel walked on while Nigel followed him.

"I did, thanks," he replied and continued walking towards his office with Nigel in hot pursuit. "So tell me, are you going to be here every day and what is it you do here anyway?"

"I'm an intern, Sir, so I guess I do just about anything they ask me. I'm not sure if and when you'll see me again, Sir."

As the two of them entered Mitchel's office, Nigel took a folder out of the briefcase he carried. "I have something for you to sign, Sir." Nigel put a small stack of papers in front of Mitchel before sitting at a desk to deliver a speech at a speed unhindered by punctuation. "Please it's the embassy's standard privacy and security statement I understand that they forgot to have you sign one please read it and when you're ready please sign it and get it back to me please have great day Sir."

"If it pleases you," Mitchel joked in reply, and Nigel looked at him for a second before laughing warily.

"Good one, thank you, Sir. We'll meet again."

Mitchel glanced through the documents, which seemed pretty standard. 'Not worth the reading,' he thought before signing them and heading back out of his office to seek help from one of the secretaries.

"Excuse me?" he asked the secretary closest to him. "I'm looking for a copy machine." He waved his papers in the air.

"You can give it to me. I can make the copies for you."

"Oh, that's no problem. If you can just show me the way, I'll do it myself. That way I'll learn my way around here. I'm Mitchel by the way, James Mitchel. All new here, on my second day."

"And I'm Doris, Doris Day."

Mitchel couldn't help but smile and the woman in the white and pink flowered dress answered it with one of her own.

"I know," she said. "Not the most creative parents, I guess."

"I'm not saying anything," Mitchel joked.

"Walk back to the stairwell. On the right side you'll see PEAR, that's our communications room. You can't miss it, but you'll need your security tag to open the door. And please, ask me anything you want."

"Thank you, I will surely know where to find you." Mitchel smiled warmly, responding to the woman's gentle flirtation, but also natural instinct; if there was one thing he'd learned in his career it was to stay friendly with secretaries in the workplace. They know how a company works, they can grant you access to anywhere and everyone, and quite often they know everything that's going on. As almost every high-placed official trusts his secretary implicitly they also get to see confidential documents. In short, if a little flirtation leads to greater knowledge, Mitchel saw no harm in it.

Approaching the only door in the room that wasn't made of glass – something that caused him to wonder 'why?' – Mitchel slid his keycard through the slot to the right of the sign which read 'PEAR'. Once the red light turned green there came the soft clank of the door opening to allow him entry. Once inside the room, the door automatically shut behind him with a clearly louder thud.

The communications room was roughly 10ft by 10ft. Alongside one wall was a number of old looking radios and computers stacked from floor to ceiling. On the opposite side there were two basic copy machines. Mitchel recognized the radios – Soviet-made communication systems from the Cold War period – and he couldn't help but wonder why they had a place in a modern US embassy. He wandered over to the copy machines. As he started to read the instructions attached to one of them, the door opened behind him to reveal the lovely Doris.

"Hi again," she said. "Don't worry, I'm not stalking you or anything; there are other people who use this room from time to time." Doris glanced at the copy machine. "You found out how it works yet?"

"I was just getting to it. I was distracted by all the old radios you have here."

Doris gave a small laugh. "I've worked at the embassy for more than ten years and when I first started work here two men constantly sat in this room, monitoring, I guess. The rumor was that the Venezuelans were using old Cold War radios and we were listening in. I guess the Venezuelans must have upgraded since then."

"I guess they must have," Mitchel replied with another warm smile.

"Anyway, it's easy," Doris said, turning to the copy machines. "You put a stack of papers in the document feeder here and a single sheet of paper here on the glass plate. When the red button turns green, you just press it." Doris duly pressed the button and the machine purred into action. Retrieving the photocopy, Doris waved it playfully in front of Mitchel's face. "And that's how you do it."

"Well, what do you know?" Mitchel replied, the teasing clear in his tone. Doris arched an eyebrow and was about to retort, but the door to the room swooshed open again and the moment was lost.

"Shale asks for you," a uniformed officer informed them with no preamble. Doris and Mitchel looked at each other, mirroring the other's confusion. "You, Miss Day. He's looking for you," the officer clarified.

"Well, Mr. Mitchel, I guess you know your way around now so don't be a stranger."

"Thanks again," he replied and smiled as Doris left the room because it was only his second day in and already he had a very useful contact to call on. "A stack of paper goes in here," he said, mimicking the secretary's instructions before noticing the light was still red. He next noticed a small red arrow pointing at the document feeder. Lifting the lid, he saw Doris had left her sheet of paper. He removed it and the red light turned green. "You see, honey, all thumbs, huh?" he said, softly referring to his wife who was always complaining about his clumsiness.

As Mitchel placed Doris's document on top of the machine he noticed the logo printed at the top. The round seal depicted a bald eagle over a compass star, and it was something he had seen many times. It was the logo of the CIA.

Mitchel wasn't especially surprised to find CIA papers in an embassy. The CIA and the DIA officially enjoyed a mutually beneficial relationship, but as a DIA man he had frequently experienced the rivalry between the agencies. Mitchel glanced over the sheet without picking it up, and his eyes were immediately drawn to the words 'Exercise' and 'Project April Showers' as well as two names: Eduardo Valbuena and Moises Rojas. There followed a piece of coded information signed at the bottom by O.J. Rout. Though Mitchel had never met Oskar Rout in person he had read a lot about the Iran–Contra affair in the eighties, when Rout had served under Reagan and Bush Sr. Rout had been in charge of the U.S. Office of Public Diplomacy for Latin America and his named had been frequently linked to the lobbying and division of money for the contras. Rout had always denied any involvement or even knowledge of the claims saying he didn't know what was happening under him during the Nicaraguan Revolution. Rout was also no stranger to Venezuela, having been a former ambassador to the country. From '86 to '89 he was highly decorated for his work and received the Meritorious Service Award, the Republic of Venezuela's Order of the Liberator, and the State Department's Superior Honor Award, and yet, despite all of the denials and all of the accolades, Mitchel had a strange feeling about the man.

Mitchel decided to make a copy of the letter and quickly placed the original back in the machine. As he pressed the green button, his heart hammered in his chest and he was reminded once again why he had never liked fieldwork – too much tension. Mitchel was no 007 or

Jason Bourne. His nerves couldn't even cope with the possibility that his wife might one day catch him drinking juice straight from the bottle.

As the photocopy emerged from the machine, Mitchel swiftly grabbed it and folded it away in his coat pocket. He then made a copy of his own document before leaving. As he opened the door, Doris stood on the other side, her keycard poised for action. Momentarily startled, Mitchel quickly recovered himself before casually mentioning she had left something in the machine. As Doris slipped past him with a smile he told her she was welcome.

From his office window, Mitchel watched the sun setting over Caracas. Evaluating the day in his head he decided there wasn't much to think through. Much of it had been spent reading about education, health, human development and income inequality in Venezuela. He probably knew more about the state of the country than most of its inhabitants, or at least he would do once he'd checked out the tourist attractions. He looked at the view before him, admiring the Andean peaks now lit orange against the thousands of hillside *barrios*. Turning away, Mitchel reached for the copy of Doris's paperwork that was nestling in his jacket pocket. He transferred it to his backpack with barely a glance, planning to read it later when he was home. Once he knew what he was dealing with he might even fact check it with José – but first he had to get it out of the embassy. If there was another random bag check, the classified document wouldn't be easy to explain.

"Have a good evening, Mr. Mitchel." He turned to see Doris at his door. "Don't be late. It's only your second day and there will be plenty of opportunity for that later."

"Thank you, Doris, and please, call me James. Have a great evening."

As Doris walked away Mitchel looked at his watch. The display revealed it was *6.15*.

"Shit," he mumbled. He had promised José he would meet him at the botanical gardens at 7.30.

As fast he could, he juggled some papers, put a few in his backpack and left his office. He then ran across the square, down the stairs and into the exit corridor. In front of him a young woman was handing over her bag to the security guard. As she walked through the metal detector Mitchel spoke.

"The other bike?" he asked, and the young woman looked at him in some confusion. "I've been here two days now and there has only ever been one other bike parked down here," he explained.

"That's me," she responded.

Mitchel handed his backpack to the officer who opened it, took out the stack of papers inside and spread them on a small table. Mitchel tried to remain casual.

"Barbara Small, Visas," the woman introduced herself.

"James Mitchel, Intelligence," he replied.

"Pleased to meet you, James."

"Likewise. You live in the neighborhood?" Mitchel tried to ignore the security guard who was looking carefully at the collection of papers in front of him.

"Why, do you live nearby?" Barbara asked.

"Uh...sorry?"

"You live nearby?

"Oh, yes. University." Mitchel could barely turn his eyes away from the guard.

"So you're exactly opposite from me. I'm in Valle Arriba, to the south."

Mitchel was about to try and respond, but he was momentarily silenced by relief as the security guard finally returned the papers to his backpack before placing it on the belt of the X-ray machine.

"You're good to go, Sir." The guard pointed to the metal detector and Mitchel walked through, still feeling paranoid. But nothing happened and with the danger passed he picked up his backpack and resumed chatting to Barbara as they made their way to the parking bay.

"So, maybe I'll see you tomorrow," Barbara said as she swung a leg over her bike.

"I'll look out for your bike," Mitchel replied before riding away. As he cleared the grounds, he felt inside his jacket and touched the photocopied letter, thanking God he had had the foresight to put it back in his jacket. Then, once he was safely in the roar of the city's traffic he cried out, "Stupid! Stupid! Stupid!"

7 April Showers

E DUARDO VALBUENA WALKED into the office of the Venezuelan Federation of Chambers, '*The Fedecámaras*'. Although he wasn't very keen on being seen in what many of his colleagues called 'The Lion's Den', he respected the natural rivalry between the military and the *Fedecámaras*. Twice a year he and his fellow generals would fight over the division of government funding, and judging by the commotion in the lobby as he arrived, the coming battle was destined to be a bloody affair. In front of a large gathering of people, a bald man in his sixties spoke from a stage, his every word documented by a bank of journalists jostling for space as they pushed to get their microphones as close as possible to the speaker.

"…and that is why I state that the Government of Venezuela, in the past three years, has systematically carried out hostile and repressive acts against our employers and their officials in order to restrict, obstruct and intervene the exercise of civic, trade union and employers' organizations and the freedoms that are necessary to defend their interests, as well as the exercise of their right to demonstrate peacefully, which is recognized in Venezuelan legislation."

Even if Valbuena hadn't been able to see the man for himself, he would have immediately recognized the words as belonging to Pedro Carmona Estanga. Carmona was a small man, standing only five feet tall, and he was highly educated, having attended schools at home and abroad. Valbuena knew Carmona from his time as the president of and major shareholder in Venoco, one of the largest producers of automotive oils. Valbuena had even voted for him when he had stood for the presidency of the Fedecámaras in 1999. He trusted him, which was partly why he wanted to personally bring him the news he carried. As Carmona continued to speak, his arms waving wildly as he hammered home his points, Valbuena allowed a tiny smile to pass over his lips.

"This repressive action includes physical, economic and moral harassment of Venezuelan employers and their officials, as well as the exclusion and marginalization of employers and organizations in the decision-making process, which affects the functioning of tripartism and social dialogue in the country. We need a change… and soon we will see a change, that I promise you. Thank you for being here and we will meet again next week."

Carmona clapped his hands and one hundred or more people followed suit before gradually turning to leave. As the crowd filtered out of the hallway, Valbuena fought against the tide to reach the podium.

"How are you doing?" he shouted up to Carmona.

"You see them?" the older man asked, waving a hand across the departing crowd from the stage. "They want to believe. And the questions they ask, more and more seem to become what we – what I – can provide the answer to. Please, follow me."

Carmona descended from the stage and led Valbuena to his office. As he shut the door behind them, he felt the younger man's hand land on his shoulder.

"Trust me, they will believe you," Valbuena assured him. "Within a week you can prove them right."

"There's a plan?" Carmona asked with surprise.

"We're working on one."

"But there is a plan?"

"Yes, and for the plan to work I need you to do two things. First, I need you to support the national strike that will take place next week. You'll need to work closely with Carlos Ortega, but he will not be given the full details, and other than working on the strike you cannot involve him any further."

Carmona looked at him, the question evident in his eyes.

"I know it's hard, but I need you to trust me on this. If you really want to start the change you were talking about, I need you to not question our requests. I also need your personal guarantee on the second part of my question."

"Which is?"

"In the past you were able to forge an alliance with the Venezuelan Workers' Confederation, as you well know, the largest labor group in the country. You were also one of the few who were able to successfully negotiate with Chávez …"

"…in the past," Carmona hastily interrupted. If the truth be known, it had been a long time since he had felt any influence over Chávez. Only in the first six months of his 12 months as chairman of the Fedecámaras had the president sent for him. It was only an occasional summons, but it had usually led to them speaking for hours in the sumptuous surroundings of the presidential palace as they tried to figure a way to bring reforms to the banking, agriculture, commerce and energy sectors. They had seldom agreed on anything, but for a while it felt like he had the president's ear, even reaching some agreement when it came to energy prices. But a lot had changed in the past year. He was never sent for anymore and whenever he instigated a meeting it would take up to a month to come about. Even then, Chávez seemed changed, a different man, preoccupied with whatever.

"I have serious doubts he still listens to me," Carmona admitted.

"It's not about that," Valbuena replied. "It's about the presidency itself." The General paused for a moment looking for any sign of emotion on Carmona's face. But the mask never slipped. As a military man he was used to people saying one thing and thinking another. That was why he had learned to *read* faces and he believed himself to be quite good at it. But Carmona's face remained impassive. "So what do you think?" he asked.

"What do I think? I think you need to make yourself clearer. What are you talking about?"

"All right, let me be clear. We, being a small group of generals representing a large part of the army, want you to be the next president of the Republic of Venezuela."

Valbuena paused to watch the surprise and fear sweep over Carmona's face.

"What are you talking about? Are you crazy?" Carmona glanced at the door to assure himself it was closed. "Elections are not due for several years, so I can only conclude you have something in mind that isn't due process?" Carmona took Valbuena by the arm and dragged him further into the office and away from the door. "You know there are already rumors in certain circles about a change in power. Do you have any idea what would happen should those rumors reach Chávez?"

Valbuena gently removed his arm from Carmona's grip. "And that is exactly why we need to act fast. The only thing I need from you is to make sure the strike will happen and to know if you are willing to step in when the time comes. That's all."

"I'll need some assurances."

"What kind of assurances?"

"That whatever transition you have in mind will be a peaceful one."

Valbuena released a sigh, slightly annoyed by Carmona's demand. "I can assure you that everyone wants a peaceful transition, and everyone involved will do everything in their power to make it so. As for any other details, trust me, you don't need to know them and don't want to know them. Anything else?"

"Who else knows about this, who are the other generals you speak about?"

"Again, that should be none of your concern for now. Really, you need to trust me if this is going to work."

"I need to think about it."

"We anticipated that, so yes, take some time, but don't take too long. The wheels are set in motion and events will not wait for your conscience to catch up. But I'll leave you with one urgent request. Whatever you do, don't tell anyone about this conversation, not your wife, not your kids nor even your shrink. For now, this needs to stay between us."

Carmona nodded and walked to the door to open it for Valbuena.

"We'll talk again soon," Valbuena informed him before raising his hand to the edge of his hat in salute and leaving.

On the *Autopista Prados Del Este* a large white chauffeur-driven sedan carried a uniformed soldier in the back as it swerved through the traffic, looking in a hurry. The flag that waved from the hood of the Chevrolet Caprice gave it a governmental look.

"Gallardo," said the general into his cellphone before breaking off to shout at the chauffeur. "I know we can be faster than this!" He turned his attention back to the caller.

"It's Eduardo," Valbuena told him. "Having trouble with your car? I thought you just got a new one?"

"Absolutely no trouble," Gallardo responded. "I love my new Caprice. I bet you didn't know that Chevrolet has been assembling these beauties right here in our country since 1948, more than 1,500,000 already!"

"Interesting, but I'm not really calling you for trivia."

"Understood," Gallardo replied quickly, stung by a slight disappointment. "And the answer is 'no'; I haven't spoken with Ortega yet. We're on our way to pick him up, though if my driver actually drove the car as it was built for I would be there already." Gallardo once again gesticulated wildly at his driver. "And you?"

"I just left Carmona's office. I think he understands. He wants time to think about it, but I'm positive of the outcome. He's convinced that something is going to happen and he's too afraid to not be a part of it. We'll have his consent soon."

"That's great news!" Gallardo shouted above the roar of the highway traffic. "OK, I've got to go. I have Ortega in sight. Talk to you later." Before the line went dead, the general heard the beginning of a plea. "Please keep me ...."

"Yes, yes," he muttered to himself before the sedan pulled up alongside a small man sporting a rather large handlebar mustache. Gallardo opened his door. "Get in, we haven't got all day," was all he said.

Ortega nervously glanced inside the car. As a labor leader he was always suspicious of the military, and he wouldn't be the first official to mysteriously disappear or spontaneously migrate to a far flung place.

"Oh, get in," Gallardo repeated. "Trust me. It's OK."

Ortega got into the car but remained on his guard.

"How are you doing, Carlos? You want a drink?" Gallardo asked cheerfully as he opened a small cabinet between the back seats and took out a bottle of Scottish whiskey. "Sixteen years old."

"No thanks, and I'm OK. How are you?"

"I'm doing great."

"Where are we going?"

"Relax, we're going nowhere. We're just going to drive around for a bit and have a talk before I drop you off wherever you want to be."

"And what do you want to talk about?" Ortega asked, feeling slightly more at ease.

"Have you heard any good rumors lately?

"Rumors, what do you mean?"

"I mean rumors about the political situation in our country."

"Can't you just tell me what this is all about?" Ortega raised his voice a fraction. "We haven't spoken since the election so I guess this isn't a courtesy visit."

"It isn't." Gallardo admitted, his own voice lowering in pitch. "In all seriousness, we need you."

Ortega frowned, shaking his head in disbelief.

"I know we don't seem to have so much in common," Gallardo admitted, "but I believe that underneath all our differences we have at least one common goal."

"And that is?"

"We both want a healthy, secure and internationally important Venezuela."

"Sure," Ortega answered still unable to fathom where the conversation might be heading.

"And that's where we might help each other. I know it's hard for a man of the people like you to trust the military. So let me tell you in absolute confidence, we have a plan for Venezuela and we want you to be an important part of it. The most important part of it."

Ortega breathed deeply before replying. "OK," he finally said. "I have two questions to start with. Who is 'we' and what is their plan?"

"Let me be blunt…"

"Finally," Ortega half snapped, evidently more confident of his position than when he first got into the car.

"You're right," Gallardo replied. "So here it is. To answer your first question, we are a small group of people with a large group of followers in politics, in the military and the Church. Secondly, we are planning to give Venezuela a new chance with a new leader that we can trust to remove our nation from the brink of disaster. Thirdly, we would like you to be that leader. Is that blunt enough for you?"

As Gallardo paused, Ortega's mind span from disbelief to opportunity. At 52 he was too far away from retirement to deny his ambition, and as a bachelor with no direct family and few friends he had no other prospects than to remain a union leader for the rest of his life. In Venezuela union leaders seldom found new careers in other industries.

"What about Carmona?" he asked.

"Good question," Gallardo replied with a smile. "Carmona is popular with the military and the rich, but we need two people on this one. And that's where you come in."

"So you want me to believe that you and some friends plan to remove Chávez from his position and you want me to take his place?"

"Exactly that. Interested?"

"And how are you planning on doing this?"

"Well, it's better if you don't know the details, but there is one thing we need from you to make this plan work and that is to just keep doing what you're already doing. Specifically, we need you to make sure the national strike that you are planning takes place in the second week of this month."

Ortega rubbed both hands along up his forehead, messing up the feathery black eyebrows that reminded Gallardo of two battered blackbirds. "I think I'll have that drink now," he said.

As Gallardo passed him a glass, Ortega took hold of his hand. "How serious are you?"

"Deadly serious."

Ortega nodded, already picturing the moment he would become president of the greatest republic on earth. "So I just do what I was already planning on doing?"

"That's right. You need to do nothing more for now. Later, when we have any updates we'll contact you. The one thing you need to know is that during the strike you will be working with Pedro Carmona. It's imperative that you don't discuss any of this with him. He needs to be totally in the dark about any plans we have." Gallardo waved his finger in the air like a schoolteacher addressing a student.

"Shouldn't be a problem. Anything else?"

"Where to?"

"Excuse me?

"Where do you want me to drop you off?" Gallardo smiled as he raised his glass to toast the wannabe president.

"Take me home," Ortega responded, and the two men clinked glasses.

Mitchel was almost back home, but still troubled by his own stupidity at taking a letter he had no right to. It was a perfect way to get fired in his first week, and what then? Move back home, find another job in Venezuela? 'Absolute moron,' he thought.

"Hi, honey." Nathalie was tending the lawn, but immediately stood up to greet her husband as he freewheeled onto the driveway. "How was your day?"

Mitchel parked his bike by the garage door before answering, and Nathalie instinctively knew something was bothering him. "Are you all right, honey?"

"Yeah sure, sorry. I was a bit preoccupied."

"So how was your second day?"

"Well let's see... it was good. The ride up and down went a bit faster than yesterday, the colleagues are still nice." Mitchel continued to fiddle with his bike.

"And..."

"And...uh... I haven't told you but yesterday I might have gotten into a teeny, tiny discussion with my boss, the ambassador, in our maiden conversation."

"All right." Nathalie spoke slowly, aware that Mitchel's discussions weren't always good for him. Last year, a discussion with her republican father on whether or not the patriot act was a good thing resulted in them not speaking again for a month. Mitchel's stance was that the act went much too far and gave too many privileges to certain government branches without legal intervention. His father-in-law was of the belief that the entire justice system should be removed from the domestic terrorism problem.

"So what now?" Nathalie asked carefully.

"Nothing, really nothing. It was just a discussion and I'm sure it will be OK in the morning. "Mitchel didn't dare telling here about the letter. "Now if you don't mind I need to freshen up a little. I have a short meeting with José planned, if you remember. I could really use his help on something."

"Sure I remember. Just leave me here all by myself again," she teased and Mitchel gave her a quick kiss on the cheek before running inside. As he glanced back, he saw her shaking her head.

As part of the hangover from his military days it took Mitchel exactly 15 minutes to freshen up, change clothes and return to the front of the house where Nathalie was still tending the garden.

"Punctual as ever," she noted, and Mitchel winced. In the past he had rarely spent much time at home, and one of the reasons Nathalie had agreed to move to Venezuela was so that they would see more of each other.

78

"How's Catherine?" he asked as he slipped on his shoes. "I expected to see her upstairs."

"She's OK, I think. She seems to have made some friends. In fact, I met some of them this afternoon. They seem like nice girls, and they all spoke amazingly good English. She went to one of their houses."

"That's really great." Mitchel sighed in relief. "It's good for her to make new connections, which reminds me; I've got to go. Give her a kiss from me and tell her I'll see her when I get back."

"Sure, will do. Have fun."

As Mitchel walked up to his shining Mustang, standing in the driveway, his hand stroked the car's apple red bodywork. Once seated he wound his window down and started the engine. For a second he pushed his back into the red leather chair, closing his eyes and reclining his head, enjoying the growl of the 289 horsepower V8 engine. 'This is it,' he thought, 'it'll never get better than this.' Putting his foot on the pedal, the car roared out of the driveway.

As it was the time of day most people reserved for eating, the roads were relatively empty, and Mitchel's to cruise along. His meeting with José was to be at the Jardín Botánico de Caracas, which was only four miles away, and so he took the long way around in order to enjoy the ride. After 20 minutes he drove through the park gates and was immediately taken by the splendor of what he saw. The gardens were huge, like a tropical forest, and completely removed the gray of the city. At the entrance of the parking lot Mitchel noticed José waiting next to a small vending cart.

"Compadre!" José shouted as Mitchel got out of the car and he waved two paper-wrapped empanadas in front of him. "You like the car?" he asked while handing over one of the meals.

"Like it? I love it," Mitchel replied, beaming from ear to ear. "What's this?"

"Your dinner. Basically it's the leftovers of a previous night's meal wrapped in a thin pancake. It doesn't sound great, but it's recycling at its tastiest. Try it, I think you'll like it."

Mitchel inspected the wrap a little more closely, noting the presence of chicken and greens, and took a bite. "Not bad."

"Told you. OK, let's walk." José pointed to a small road framed by large palm trees.

"It's beautiful," Mitchel said as he breathed in the clean air. "Do you come here often?"

"Sometimes. When I need to think or just get away from the crowds. One day we'll walk the *Cyclo de la Vida* discovery trail. It's filled with poetic explanations and comments along the way. Anyway, how was your afternoon in that little patch of the US?"

"Ok, I guess. What did you find out about Shale?"

"And we're back in business," José teased. "But that's fine. So here's what I've got; Calder Shale held numerous senior political positions, including Principal Deputy Assistant Secretary for the Western Hemisphere. He has also held positions in Chile, El Salvador, Trinidad and Tobago and even Denmark."

"That much I know," Mitchel interrupted impatiently.

"Hold your horses," José laughed good-naturedly. "I'm coming to the good stuff. After a diversity of Washington assignments, he became Coordinator for Cuban Affairs. But the best part is undeniably his position as '*political officer*' at the US Embassy in El Salvador at the height of the dirty war, backed by your country. But that you also probably know. However, did you know that this post is often used as a diplomatic cover for the chief local operative of the CIA? When Shale was there, the CIA was pretty much organizing the activities of the so-called right-wing death squads, the ones blamed for killing tens of thousands of Salvadorans during the civil war."

Mitchel abruptly stopped walking. "Are you telling me that Shale, the friendly though somewhat fanatical man I met today, is responsible for genocide in the eighties in South America?" Mitchel raised an eyebrow. "Do you really expect me to believe that?"

"No, that's not what I'm telling you," José replied tersely. "I'm only telling you what it says on Shale's file at the DISIP. What you choose to believe is up to you."

"I'm sorry," Mitchel apologized. "It's just that I'd still like to believe in the integrity of my country and those that run it. But hey, this is a South American secret service dossier, I doubt they'll be filing anything positive about us."

"Look, just watch out and keep your eyes open while you don't know who or what you're dealing with. My country is in a heated state right now so you never know what's going to happen."

"Thanks." Mitchel continued walking, reaching into his back pocket as he did so to retrieve the CIA letter he had taken. He waved it at José. "I have another favor to ask."

"What's that?"

"I'm not sure what it is. It's a CIA communiqué. This afternoon I found the original in our communications room and my eyes were attracted to some highlights, but it's not clear to me. I thought maybe you could have a look at it."

José raised his hands, palms up, refusing to accept the letter. He then glanced around to make sure no one was watching. "What are you doing handing me a CIA letter in public in the center of Caracas?" he hissed. "This is not the US. We need to watch out. It's common knowledge we are friends so there's a good chance we're being watched. Or at the very least we are of interest… and that's in regard to both sides." José grabbed Mitchel by the sleeve and dragged him to a narrow path leading to a small lake before stopping at a wooden bench. From the lake's bank he had a good view of their surroundings. After quickly scouting the area, he turned to Mitchel and told him to sit. "Are you sure you want to hand me this?"

"Yes, I'm sure. I trust you and I believe we both have the same interests at heart."

"Spoken like a true friend," José replied, and though he was reluctant to, he accepted the letter and unfolded it slowly. While reading he softly hummed. "No," he concluded. "It means nothing to me. As I read it Valbuena and Rojas are working together with Oskar Rout on a project called April Showers, which could be anything from a humanitarian project to a declaration of war. So why would it stand out to you?" José folded the letter and handed it back to Mitchel.

"Somehow Rout doesn't seem like the humanitarian type," Mitchel replied, "and I know next to nothing about Valbuena and Rojas. And then there are the numbers at the bottom. Some kind of code?"

José smiled before answering, hearing the excitement rising in his friend's voice. "Nothing has changed I see. Well, let's look at this; both Valbuena and Rojas are high placed and well-respected generals. Valbuena is head of the army and he has some family troubles according to the tabloids, but there's nothing more than that. Rojas is the head of the military high command, the equivalent of your Chairman of the Joint Chiefs of Staff. Of him I know that he's a lifelong trusted friend of Chávez, maybe even the only one."

"So what would he have to with Rout? Knowing what I know about Rout he can only be opposed to Chávez."

"That I cannot say. I know Rout is of German descent and he became a Cuban-American exile in the early 60s when his parents fled the island after Castro found out there were ties between Rout's father and Hitler. Could be the man hates everyone speaking Spanish because of it." Mitchel laughed at his friend's joke and José joined him for a moment. "But seriously, I have no idea about their connection in a project called April Showers. For that matter I've never even heard of a such a project."

"Could it be that you wouldn't know about such a project?"

"Sure, although I know about most projects I know there are deeper, secret projects conducted within the DISIP. But about the more regular projects, all senior staff members are regularly briefed so…"

"… so April Showers can only be a not-so-regular project?

"I guess so."

"And what about the code below?"

"Show me again."

Mitchel handed José the letter and took a pen and a small piece of paper from his jacket pocket. He then copied the code from the letter before giving it back to Mitchel.

"I would burn this as soon as possible," he advised. "We know what it says and it's of no further value. I copied the numbers and I'll see what I can find out. Let me pick you up at the embassy for lunch tomorrow. We'll drive to the park and have lunch there."

"That's great, thank you. You're a good friend."

"Yes. Now let us continue our walk. How's your empanada?"

8. The First Brief

Thursday, April 4th, 2002

VERY TIME MITCHEL PASSED THE WINDOW as he walked in circles around his office his eyes took in the beauty of the Andes hillside in the distance. Once past the window, his mind became a clutter of scenarios as he considered his next move. What would he do, in fact, what could he do with the information in his possession? Was it his place to act on the information and why was he so concerned by it? Eventually, after ten minutes had passed and he came no nearer to answering the multitude of questions crowding his brain, he stopped and stared at the phone on his desk. He then dialed a long distance cell number. It was one he had called many times before in the past year.

"Turner," a voice on the end of the line said.

Mitchel had kept in touch with Charles Turner ever since the Kursk debacle and he now considered him a friend – one he liked to turn to when tough decisions had to be made.

"Charles, it's James Mitchel, can I bother you for a minute?"

"Mitchel, good to hear from you. Sure, no problem. How's the South American sun treating you?"

"Thanks for asking. The sun is fine at this time of year, but I fear the worst is yet to come. I took the liberty to call you because I can use some advice."

"Always."

"It's the kind of advice you can only give me when I take you in absolute confidence. This needs to stay between us."

"Well, as long as you're not trying to overthrow the US government you should be fine," Turner replied playfully. "So, with what can I help you?"

"Well, I'm not sure how to say this so I'll just…uh say it."

"Usually works best."

"Uh… ok… well… I accidentally came in possession of a classified CIA document that got me thinking, or rather, worried. The document speaks of a project or exercise, it's not clear what, called April Showers. The project talks about a collaboration between Oscar Rout and the Venezuelan generals Valbuena and Rojas. A part of the document is also written in some kind of code."

"Doesn't sound like anything that unusual, so what has peaked your interest?"

"To be honest, I don't exactly know, but knowing Rout's reputation and the fact that the project has no official status in either country plus the code at the end… Also my first encounter with the ambassador went far from smoothly."

"Why? What happened?"

"From what I'd read about Shale, and based on his past experience in the region, I figured him to be a man with an open mind, and what with him being new in the country. Unfortunately, I found him to be, and pardon my bluntness, narrow-minded, biased and complacent. So as you can imagine, due to my own character flaws, we were drawn into a debate about good and evil in Venezuela and whether

Chávez was good or bad for the country. I guess he caught me by surprise while I was still making up my own mind about things."

"And because of that you now think that Shale and Rout are in cahoots with a bunch of local generals in some kind of secret project? Forgive my own bluntness."

Mitchel stayed silent for a moment as he ran through his own conclusions. "I'm not sure it's just that." Mitchel shook his head. "Do you think I'm overreacting?"

"As long as you're not really acting you cannot overreact, but you need to be careful who you talk to," Turner advised. "I guess you got your information on Venezuelan intelligence from your local friend?"

"Whom I trust implicitly."

"Well I don't know what you want from me, and I cannot tell you what to do, but as you know I'm a big fan of following instinct. But maybe you have a specific question for me?"

"Well, yes. There is one. Could you take a look at things your end to see if I have grounds for suspicion?"

This time it was Turner's turn to stay silent. Over the phone line Mitchel could hear him scratching at his throat, knowing he was trying to buy time before answering.

"No problem," he eventually replied. "But you must know I'm no longer in any position to get first-hand information let alone any more classified form of intel."

"I know, but I trust your network is as strong as ever, as Chairman of the Council on Foreign Relations."

"OK, I'll see what I can do, and if I may give you one more piece of advice; I've known Shale for a long time now and if there's anything he appreciates it is honesty and openness. Maybe you should discuss your findings with him."

"If you don't mind I'll have to think about that for now."

"No problem. It's your funeral." Turner laughed. "I'll get back to you later today on any findings."

"Perfect. Talk to you later."

As Mitchel put down the phone he clenched his fists and waved them in front of him, whispering, "Yes."

"Are you leaving, Sir?" Nigel Small-Fawcett addressed Mitchel as he crossed the central hallway of the embassy.

"Just going out for lunch. I'll be back in an hour or so."

"If you turn right at the entrance and take the first right again, after about half mile there's a great cafeteria called Atrium. You can be sure to find some colleagues over there."

"Thanks for the information," Mitchel said and he meant it – the last thing he wanted was to bump into colleagues when he was going to meet José.

As Mitchel left the building he noticed a rather striking 1999 blue Ducati Monster 900 City bike across the road. A buddy helmet was raised in his direction, and Mitchel responded with a smile before hopping on the back of the bike.

"Hang on!" José shouted from within his helmet, but before Mitchel had time to even decipher what he had said, the Ducati sped away. Mitchel grabbed José around the waist and with every curve he tightened his grip. Then, after a mere seven minutes, José stopped in front of a small cafeteria in a remote street where no tourists or expats would ever show themselves. As both men removed their helmets Mitchel looked at José.

"Relax," José assured him. "You'll be fine. I just thought we needed a place where no one would accidentally walk in on us. We're perfectly safe here."

"My life is in your hands, as it was for the last 10 minutes or so," Mitchel half joked. He then followed his friend into a dingy cafeteria that was no more than 20 feet deep and 10 feet wide.

Inside, at the front of the cafeteria, were four small tables, all of them empty. José walked past the counter, choosing a table at the back of the room. "Tea?" he asked.

"Please," Mitchel replied.

"*Dos té,*" José called out to the lone barman, who didn't appear to have a care in the world.

"So, here we are in the middle of...somewhere," Mitchel said. "And what's with the secret location?"

"My friend, you worry too much and think too much about nothing. I brought you here simply because the man behind the counter is Hans and Hans is married to my nephew's sister-in-law and he makes the best Pernil in the whole of Venezuela."

"And that's it?"

"Truly, you have to taste it. At least once in your life. It's made with roast pork cooked from the bone flavored with garlic, vinegar and oregano."

Mitchel looked at his friend blankly, and though José tried hard to keep a straight face he soon cracked.

"OK, yes. I'm just messing with you, though the Pernil is really excellent here."

"In that case order me some of that Peril or whatever and let's talk."

"Pernil," José corrected before pointing two fingers in the barkeeper's direction. "So down to business. I have some good news and some bad news. What do you want to hear first?"

Mitchel shrugged. He really didn't care as long as José started talking.

"All right, mister impatience. We know what the numbers resemble, but we don't know the exact contents. The code consists of three parts of three numbers. The first number we don't know and probably resembles some kind of index number. The second resembles a location code and the third number stands for a date and probably a time."

"Which means?"

"The only thing I'm pretty sure about is that the date code is April 11.

"So we know that on April 11 at a specific time some Venezuelan generals along with American politicians will start some kind of unknown project or exercise."

"Yup." José leaned away from the table as the bartender approached to place two large roast pork shoulders in front of them. Just as Mitchel was about to ask for something, José silenced him.

"Don't worry, you fake Yankee Brit. Hans will bring you some salad to go with it."

Both José and Hans laughed at Mitchel.

"It is roasted pork with garlic that will fall off the bone when you put a fork to it," Hans assured him in a heavy Spanish accent. "You like."

"Thank you," Mitchel said politely. Once Hans had returned to the kitchen he turned to José. "So what do you think?"

"I think you should eat and wait. The meat is great and there's nothing you can do for now. Did you call Turner?"

"I did. He basically said the same thing, but also promised me he would look into it."

"So there it is. Wait. Eat your meat and wait for Turner to call back."

Mitchel picked up his fork and poked at the pork causing a large piece to fall off the bone. As he ate José watched him closely.

"And?"

Mitchel chewed slowly, like a woodchuck, before answering. "This is really great, really. I don't think ..."

"Sh!" José suddenly ordered, pointing to the television behind the counter. He then shouted to Hans to turn up the volume. On the screen

Carlos Ortega was stood on a pedestal in front of his office, shouting and waving his arms widely. In front of him were twenty or more reporters.

"What's he saying?" Mitchel asked. Though he spoke a few words of Spanish and could understand most things when spoken slowly, Ortega's speech was too fast and emotional and he could just as easily have been speaking in Russian for all Mitchel understood.

"He is announcing a 24-hour strike for all government laborers that might be extended for 48 hours or even turn into an indefinite strike, depending on how the situation evolves and how the government reacts."

"What's the strike about?"

José silenced his friend by putting a finger to his lips. Mitchel waited, but grew impatient after a few minutes more and gave José a quick poke.

"Yes, yes, yes. Hold on, you impatient man." Then, once Ortega had left the screen José revealed all. "OK, so in Venezuela it's illegal to call a strike when there's a risk of weakening the government, but Ortega says the CTV has no intention of weakening the government and it simply wants the government to comply with their collective bargaining agreements and an assurance that members of the CTV will not be mistreated."

"Did he say when the strike will take place?" Mitchel asked.

"April 9th, but that doesn't mean that the end will be anytime soon. It probably depends on Chávez's reaction. There are rumors that Chávez might decree a state of emergency, a state exception, but Ortega says 10,000 states of exception will not prevent the strike from taking place. On the other hand, earlier today the management of the PDVSA went on strike claiming too much of the oil money they create is given to state welfare projects, so who knows what Chávez might do. And finally…. you've hardly touched your Pernil."

As José leaned over to pick at Mitchel's plate, the American ignored his bad manners, mainly because his mind was somersaulting with possibilities.

"Do you think this has anything to do with our problem?" he asked.

José looked Mitchel's face trying to determine how serious he was. "What do you mean exactly by 'our problem'?"

"Well, you've got to admit it's a big coincidence," Mitchel stated and José stared at him for a few seconds. This was not the Mitchel he knew. His friend from the past used to look for evidence before jumping to conclusions. Now, he was behaving like a conspiracy theorist.

"What are you doing, man?" he asked, unable to think of anything else in the circumstances.

"What do you mean, 'what are you doing'? Are you saying I'm wrong?"

"All I'm trying to say is think. Think about the way you're drawing conclusions and what they are based on."

Mitchel's mouth opened only to shut it again. He took a deep breath and nodded his head. José smiled.

"Now let's enjoy our Pernil and wait to hear what Turner has to say. Agreed?"

"Agreed."

"Do you need anything before I go home?"

"No thank you, Miss Day," Mitchel replied playfully as he looked up to see Doris standing in the doorway. "I'll be fine for now. You have a great evening."

As Doris turned away, Mitchel's cell phone rang. The number flashing on the screen revealed Charles Turner was calling. Mitchel immediately rose from his desk and closed the door to his office.

"Mitchel here."

"James, it's Charles Turner. I promised to call you back if I found out anything."

"Yes, so you found something?"

"Well, are you familiar with the Senior Executive Intelligence Brief?"

"Isn't it some kind of periodical between the government and the CIA?"

"Correct. The brief is positioned one level below the presidential daily briefing and distributed weekly to the 200 highest level decision-makers and national security advisors in the U.S. government. Now, on March 11, 2002 the top secret brief spoke of something that might be of interest to you. I'll send it to you later, but let me quote a small piece from it."

"Ok, please do."

Down the phone line, Mitchel heard Turner unfold some papers.

"Here we are... 'President Chávez is facing a continued stream of strong opposition from the media, the private sector, the Catholic Church, and his opposition political parties that are all enraged by the 49 laws he decreed last December. The opposition has not yet organized itself into a united front. If the situation further worsens and demonstrations become even more violent the military may decide to move to overthrow him.' And that's all it says."

For a second or two both men stayed silent. Mitchel was trying not to jump to conclusions, but he had a hard time doing so.

"Charles? Are you still there?

"I am. I'm just waiting for your reaction."

"If Chávez is under fire from so many parties isn't that a spark that cannot be stopped from igniting a major fire?"

"Well, you mustn't forget that Chávez is a man who has been under fire his whole career," Turner replied, noting the tremor of excitement in Mitchel's voice. "The workings of South America are vastly different to how things work in the West, but that doesn't mean something is bound to happen. Maybe you should take a step back and ask Shale about this. He's a lot closer to the source than I am and I'm pretty sure you can trust him."

"Yes, maybe I'll do that. In the meantime, please send me the transcript and keep me informed if anything new turns up in the coming days?"

"Sure I will, but only if you inform me of every move you make before you make it. I can protect you, but only if you keep me in the loop."

"Are you saying I need protection?"

"I'll talk to you later, James. Goodbye."

As the line went dead, Mitchel stared at the phone, hardly believing his friend had effectively hung up on him. He glanced across the floor and seeing the lights in Shale's office still on he started to walk towards them, only to stop halfway. 'What am I doing?' he thought as he realized he could be jeopardizing his career for the second time in only two days. Then the lights in Shale's office went off and slow to react, Mitchel found himself looking directly at Shale.

"You leaving too?" Shale shouted across the floor.

"Uh, in a short while," Mitchel stammered as his boss walked towards him.

"So how are you going so far?" Shale stopped in front of Mitchel and set his briefcase on the floor between his legs.

"The work on the Human Development Report is coming along fine. I expect to have the first draft of my findings on your desk tomorrow, around lunch."

Shale laughed. "That's not what I meant. I meant how are you settling in, and how are your colleagues treating you. Things like that."

"Ah, in that case, everything is great, Sir. The office is great, my colleagues are fine, especially Doris who is a great help in finding my way around here."

"Good. That's good to hear." Shale bent down to pick up his briefcase.

"Actually, I've been meaning to ask you something that's related to our conversation yesterday, if you don't mind," Mitchel asked, and Shale's briefcase hit the ground again with a soft thump.

"Sure. No problem. Let's have it," he grinned.

"Well it's probably nothing, but as I talked to some people and dug a bit deeper into this country's history, specifically regarding Chávez, I came across some information regarding a project named April Showers as well as intel on how several Venezuelan parties are threatening to take action against their president. I wondered whether the two might be related."

As Mitchel finished, Shale's face was a picture of surprise. "What would make you think that?"

"Well there seems to be more chatter on the subject than usual and project April Showers talks about an exercise taking place only days after the CTV's scheduled national strike. It could be a coincidence, but even for a South American country it seems more than random."

Shale frowned before allowing the smile to return to his face. "Listen," he said. "While I cannot give you full clearance on the subject and I don't know what the Venezuelans are doing or planning to do, I do know about April Showers. What I can tell you about the project is that it has to do with the pro-US oil lobby in Venezuela and the financing of that lobby. What did you expect? Did you think we only issued visas all day? Oh God, please tell me you didn't think that."

Though he was still smiling Shale's voice had raised a pitch and Mitchel couldn't gauge whether to believe him or not. Not that it made much difference. For once, he decided to err on the side of caution.

"Of course not," Mitchel laughed. "I just found it a curious coincidence. I guess I'm not accustomed to South American ways yet. I'll grab my things and go home too. Have a good evening, and like I said, you can expect my report in the morning."

"That's absolutely fine." Shale picked up his briefcase and turned away. "I'll see you in the morning."

"Hi, honey!"

Mitchel yelled towards the kitchen as he came in from the garage. Finding Nathalie bent over the sink cleaning vegetables he tried to lean over and kiss her.

"Oh my God, you smell awful," she cried as she pushed him away.

"Twenty-one minutes and forty seconds," he told her, glancing at his watch. "No kisses?"

"You better get yourself cleaned up first and get that filthy sweaty smell out of my nose otherwise there will be no more kisses for you ever." Nathalie playfully whipped her kitchen towel towards him.

"That's not what you said this morning when you were all sweaty and we...."

"Go away!"

As Mitchel walked out of the kitchen he picked up an apple from the tray. As he took a bite his cellphone rang. "James Mitchel," he managed to say despite his mouth being full.

"It's José. I have some news and I was also curious if you had heard anything from Turner."

"Yes, he called back and talked about an intelligence brief where they spoke about the continued discontent from just about all state officials in Chávez's rule, particularly regarding his 49 laws. The brief seems to suggest it's only a matter of time before parties will combine forces and take action."

"What kind of action?"

"It's not clear, but I guess you can think of a few options yourself. So what's your news?"

"You have a minute?"

"I have about five, but then I must hit the shower and prepare for a lovely meal in the company of my beautiful if fussy wife."

"I heard that," Nathalie shouted from the kitchen.

"I know, dear," he shouted back.

"I heard that too," José joined in. "Look, I'll be brief."

"You better be or she'll have me for dinner."

"I hear you. Remember I told you the PDVSA started their strike today, just before the CTV announced their own strike?"

"I do."

"Well since I found it an odd coincidence, both strikes being planned at the same time, I did some digging."

"And you found something?"

"I'm not sure, but large offices of the PDVSA were shut down along with several gasoline distribution centers and the refinery at El Palito. Now, closing the refinery could be a tricky one as the crude oil in the pipes – that run for miles – will turn into a tar-like substance rendering the pipes useless should they want to start again anytime soon. So Maria Cristina Iglesias, the Minister of Labor, went on public television to announce that all those who failed to show up for work would be fired. She said the strike was illegal. And all this made me wonder why they would start a strike if they knew they wouldn't be able to go back to work anytime soon?

"Perhaps because they know a big change is coming that will get them back to work soon or at least provide them with some kind of income in the meantime?"

"My thoughts exactly. So I contacted some somewhat shadowy colleagues of mine at the DISIP and asked them if they knew anything about April Showers."

"And nothing," Mitchel added enthusiastically.

"Ah, the catch. No, not exactly. One of them told me that he saw a memo that mentioned the project. It also mentioned that even though the US government couldn't officially participate in the exercise they could help finance it."

"But what is it?"

"That, my friend, I'm afraid we still don't know."

Mitchel thought for a second before summarizing. "So what we do know is this: The Senior Executive Intelligence Brief talks about disgruntled officers possibly planning a big scale event when parties start to work together; there's a CIA memo that describes a project called April Showers with a location code and a date set for April 11th; there are two national strikes planned that could possibly paralyze the country; and last but not least our intel says the US cannot participate officially but they can finance."

"And don't forget the involvement of Rojas, Valbuena and Rout," José added.

"Indeed. We need to know what's planned for the 11th."

"Well, we have six days to find out."

"And if we don't like it, to do something about it?" Even as he asked the question, Mitchel suddenly realized that he and José might have very different interests in the outcome.

"You know, we may find each other on opposite sides of this," José said, as though reading his mind.

"That's just what I thought," Mitchel admitted and both men went silent for a few seconds. "Look, I think we've come too far to go our separate ways now. This might change in the near future, but for now we're in this together and I believe we are much stronger working together."

"That's for sure," José added. "But we ought to keep a low profile."

"You're right. OK, let's get a good night's sleep and see what happens in the morning. With everything that's going on it wouldn't surprise me if another clue presents itself tomorrow. Let's talk at lunch."

"Lunch it is," José confirmed, and Mitchel hung up the phone.

"Shower!" Nathalie ordered from downstairs, hearing Mitchel ending the conversation.

"Going now, dear. I'll be downstairs in 15 minutes and then I'm all yours."

9. The Firing

Friday, April 5th 2002

CHÁVEZ PACED AROUND the long conference table positioned in the center of the Hall of Mirrors. A large golden sword hung from his hip. Once upon a time he used this room was for formal meetings and to welcome new ministers and ambassadors. "New friends" he used to call them. Now the empty room felt cold and he was no longer sure who he could trust or who his friends were.

'Did you know who to trust?'

It was a silent question directed at the two large paintings of Simon Bolivar hanging behind the presidential chair.

'Did you ever feel betrayed or felt you were bound to be betrayed? Did your...'

Two loud knocks upon the 20ft doors that ran from floor to ceiling interrupted his thoughts and he turned abruptly to face the noise.

"Yes!" he shouted fiercely, and two valets pushed open the doors to allow entry to a young officer who walked a yard into the room before coming to a halt with a click of his heels.

"Yes," Chávez repeated, but this time it was almost a whisper.

"General Rojas is here to see you, Sir." The officer spoke without moving even an inch of his body.

"Send him in, boy. Send him in."

The young officer signaled at the doorway and Rojas walked in. With a loud thump the doors closed behind him and the general looked startled. Returning his eyes to Chávez he found the President gazing at Bolivar's painting, his back facing Rojas.

"Thank you for coming." Chávez spoke without turning. "I wanted to continue the conversation we started the other day at my house. So, what do you make of these strikes?" Slowly the President turned to face his old friend who was still stood near the door. "Come near, what are you doing over there?"

Rojas responded by coming to stand next to Chávez, who asked again for his opinion on the strikes.

"What do you want me to say?" Rojas replied.

"I want you to tell me your thoughts, like you always did before."

"You want the truth?" Rojas wasn't intending to goad the President, but he needed time to formulate his own response because the betrayal he felt played heavy on his mind and he couldn't afford to be weak, despite wanting to still be there for the Chávez he knew from old. Oblivious to the conflict delaying Rojas' response, Chávez asked for the truth "as always", and Rojas took a deep breath before giving him it.

"Many people are not happy, and they are the ones that ought to be most feared. They are the politicians; the people with money and power. When you were elected six years after our coup you made promises not only to the general people, but also to them. Now they feel betrayed. They are sick of the high taxation and they are convinced they are picking up the bill so that you can play Robin Hood by giving their money to the poor. Internationally our country is on the brink of isolation. When Caldera was president, it's true that the US acted like a mafia Godfather. We supplied endless streams of cheap oil and the rich kept the biggest share of the profits. But ever since you ended that deal the US interest in our country, or rather our country run by you, has diminished. And then when you so publicly opposed Bush's 'War on Terror, well…"

Chávez silenced his old friend with a frown. "And I ask you again," he said harshly, "what do you think is the reason for these strikes?"

Rojas shook his head. "I'm not sure, but I do know that if you add up everything that's happening in this country right now, in regard to foreign and domestic issues, there are a lot of unhappy people about. And when all those forces gather…" Rojas paused for a second to see how Chávez would react only to be little surprised when the President finished his train of thought.

"We're back in 1992," he admitted, "when coups were being hatched, albeit unsuccessfully at the time." Chávez shared a wry smile with his friend, but they both knew there was little to smile about. "So we need a plan." Chávez took a step backwards and took the sword from his side to wield it in the air. "This sword," he half-shouted, "this sword belonged to the great liberator, Bolivar. It is made of pure gold, it shines with more than 3,000 precious stones, and it is decorated with the insignia of the last Inca emperor Atahualpa Coronad. This sword is alive and if necessary it will guide me through another Bolívarian revolution and onwards to a great tomorrow for all the people of Venezuela."

Rojas took a step backwards, half wanting to believe, half frightened to believe. Could he still be right?

"So, what are our options?" It was a rhetorical question from Chávez and Rojas felt no need to respond. "I guess I could have the National Guard raid the PDVSA offices or I could give bonuses to employees who choose not to participate in any of the strikes."

"You talk about attacking the strikes," Rojas interrupted him. "Why not think about a solution that leans more towards what they want? Give them something? An attack may solve your problems for a short time, but it will not make the problem go away."

Rojas stared at Chávez, hoping to see the return of a national hero, but the President looked straight through him and gave no answer and what he found in his eyes was not love or hope, but an emptiness fired by hate.

Chávez began to pace the room, speaking his thoughts aloud.

"I could also launch a campaign with disinformation and propaganda on public and private television and during the strikes have them show pictures of people going about their business like any regular day, or perhaps flood the highways and streets with government loyalists so there's no room for the strikes..."

"Hugo!" Rojas shouted so loud it echoed around the room, and startled by the outburst Chávez turned quickly in his direction, his face dark as thunder before softening as reasoned thought fought its way to his senses.

"I'm sorry," Chávez said. "I know I'm rambling."

"Are you OK?" Rojas stepped forward and placed his hand on Chávez's shoulder.

"I think I'm OK now. Thank you. And you're right; I need to think about what to do."

"Is there anything I can do to help?"

"You've done enough, old friend. What's left is mine to do. Go and wait for tomorrow to come when I will address the nation in *Aló Presidente.* That's where I'll deal with this problem. Go. Tend to your family. There are rough days ahead.... for all of us."

Unable to reply, given all that he knew, Rojas turned and left the room. Once the deep thump of the doors closing had gently echoed around the room, Chávez sat on the presidential chair, took the sword from its scabbard and held the hilt in front of him. He then gently bent his head forward and kissed the blade. "This too shall pass, my old friend. This too shall pass."

In the large glass conference room marked 'Pineapple' Mitchel concluded his presentation on the 2002, Venezuela National Human Development Report in front of a handful of embassy workers including Calder Shale.

"And so I think we can conclude that, generally speaking, to reduce inequalities and help increase opportunities for the Venezuelan people IT should be further explored as a tool for human development and as a means to develop powerful institutional, political, economic, and social networks, since such technologies foster communication and information exchange. The US could clearly benefit from this in the ways I have presented. Thank you, for now."

As Mitchel switched of his projector, small applause punctuated the end of his report.

"Thank you for this insightful, first presentation, Commander Mitchel," Shale commented as he rose from his chair. "If you'll walk by my office later today I have another assignment that might suit you."

"Will do," Mitchel answered gratefully, and once everyone had filed out of the room he gave the place a last look, feeling content with the job he had done there today. And then his cellphone vibrated with a text message.

'Meet me tomorrow at lunch to meet my nephew in the barrios. More news on project. Pick you up at 1300.'

At the realization that more news was to come, Mitchel lost the calm that had so recently found him and texted a reply confirming the date for tomorrow.

Ever the showman, Chávez smiled brightly for the selected crowd that had been flown to the presidential palace for the latest edition of '*Aló Presidente*'. As he took his seat behind the desk, he started to sing and his delighted fans cheered. *Cuando Yo Quiera Has De Volver,* he told them; I Want You Back.

Mitchel was sat behind his desk when he noticed a small group of people walking into the large conference room. A second later, Doris appeared in the doorway.

"The ambassador would like you to join him in the conference room immediately."

"And who am I to say no?"

Mitchel got up from his desk and followed Doris. As he entered the room he noticed that all the senior staff were present. Two large, flat panel televisions were then wheeled into the room and plugged into the wall by technicians. As all the seats were taken Mitchel placed himself against the glass wall at the back of the room just as Shale got to his feet.

"Thank you for joining me," he called out and the room fell silent. "We are here because we have it on good authority that today Hugo Chávez, during his one-man show, will address the constant threats to his governance and, if the rumors are correct, will be announcing drastic measures to deal with them. On the other screen, at some point during *El Presidente's* speech Carlos Ortega and/or Pedro Carmona will announce their strikes. This could be a very promising and dramatic morning, people. So, find your seats and have a good time."

As Shale finished, Mitchel was struck by the television host persona of their ambassador and it didn't sit easily with him. He looked at the first TV screen which appeared to be a local news channel talking about a report into the poverty of the Caracas slums. Almost immediately the sound was muted as Chávez appeared on the other screen.

"Y si no has vuelto es porque, Yo no he querido todavía," Chávez sang before opening his arms to the public before him – part entertainer, part messiah, part president. "Thank you, thank you," he repeated as he soaked up the applause and beckoned the room to quieten. *"Compadres, familia, colegas,* today I sing that 'I want you back', but I'm afraid that's not true of all of you. You see, I have to bring you more sad news. As almost every one of you knows, I work only to bring you good news, which is why earlier this year I brought you 49 laws to ensure a better life for you all. Unfortunately, those that have to give up a little of their wealth in order for you to have your better life would like you to believe our country will suffer from this. They would like you to go onto the streets and protest against me and my government. They would like to remove me from power. Well, to those who want to see the back of me I welcome your contributions during our democratic elections. We are a free country and this would be the time to seize your chance, but I will not be bullied or blackmailed into resigning. For this reason, I have given clear instructions to the president of the PDVSA that should anyone call for an illegal strike they are to be fired immediately, without any discussion. I'm afraid the time has come to take action." Chávez paused to pick up a piece of paper sitting in front of him. He then began to read, sounding like a baseball umpire throwing the book at his players. "Eddy Ramírez, until today general director of the PDVSA Palmaven division, you're out!" Chávez almost spat out the words as his arms cut through the air. "We gave you the responsibility of leading the very important business subsidiary of Palmaven, but you seem to have forgotten this subsidiary belongs to the people. Anyway, Señor Eddy Ramírez, muchas gracias, you, sir, are terminated."

As the President's audience cheered wildly, Shale turned towards Mitchel, interested to see his reaction. But Mitchel was ready and he kept his face still as a mask. While it was true that Chávez's presentation style was a little unorthodox, he was determined to keep an open mind, even as another official was unceremoniously dismissed, followed by another. Chávez then paused for a moment.

"Horacio Moroco, Manager of Strategic Negotiations... I will repeat the title in case you didn't hear it ... that is Manager of Strategic Negotiations. Well, in military terms this is a member of the high command." Chávez shook his head sorrowfully before raising a dismissive arm. "This man would be a member of the military high command? Not anymore, Horacio Moroco. You're out. You were Manager of Strategic Negotiations. Muchas gracias for your services Mister Moroco." Again, the audience cheered, growing ever louder as more names were given the chop. "And now for the last – an analyst working for the PDVSA gas projects. Muchas gracias, Señora. Carmen Elisa Hernández. Thank you so much for everything you have done, and you're out!" Chávez again paused to lap up the applause before raising his arms to silence the crowd and continue. "The seven people I have named have been dismissed from Petroleos de Venezuela. And trust me, this will not end here. Anyone who threatens the wellbeing of our nation will go."

"What do you think?"

Mitchel almost jumped out of his skin. He had been so intent on the President's performance he had failed to notice Shale sidling up to him.

"What do I think about Chávez?"

"No, about the weather, of course about Chávez!"

"Well, he's a good showman and I'm beginning to see things are a lot different in the Americas compared to the good old US of A."

"They sure are, and I think the best or worst, I haven't decided yet, is still to come."

Shale paused and Mitchel tried to decipher what was really being asked of him. "If you're wondering whether I have adjusted my opinions on Chávez, I told you I haven't formed any yet," Mitchel told him. "And that hasn't changed." Mitchel smiled as though he had made a joke.

"I know," Shale responded. "I know that when you're ready to have an opinion you'll share it with me."

Mitchel nodded just as a loud 'Sh!' echoed around the room. On the second screen Pedro Carmona appeared.

"My fellow co-workers," Carmona greeted, but the delivery lacked the natural charm of the President and dressed in a suit and tie the slow, deliberate speech might have come across as honorable, but also dull. "Today I speak to you not only on behalf of myself, but also with the voice of our friend Carlos Ortega who couldn't be here today. And let me start by saying that the strikes will happen. You might have heard…"

Before anyone got the chance to hear what it was they might have previously heard, the screen switched venues and Chávez appeared. A loud 'boo!' filled the room as it became apparent to everyone but Mitchel as to what had happened.

"This is how it works here. We've seen it all before. Every time something is aired that doesn't follow the government line it gets taken off the airwaves."

"So how about press freedom?" Mitchel asked. Off course he knew he was asking the obvious, it wasn't his first year in the business, but still, somewhere in his heart, despite all his experience, he liked to hope there were still people in power for all the right reasons.

"Don't tell me you don't know how this works? The freedom of the press goes as far as it follows government policies." And that was exactly the answer Mitchel was afraid he would hear.

"But isn't there anything the free press can do about it?"

"Sure there is," Shale confirmed. "Usually it's the government-controlled TV stations against the commercial, and the commercial stations are by far technologically superior to the government's. But who would dare defy the government? You see, that's also how it works here. Trust me, you've still a lot to learn, but you learn best through experience. We'll talk again when you've worked here for a few months."

Mitchel looked at the two TV screens in the room, both showing Chávez ranting against the "saboteurs" within the PDVSA and the CTV.

"I will take action against anyone who is blocking the advance of the revolution," he railed. Then, rather bizarrely, he picked up a referee's whistle and shouted 'Offside!' while alluding to the upcoming World Cup in Japan. "But seriously people," he continued in a more somber tone, "I have a confession to make. During the election, I made you a promise that I neglected to keep and I would like to correct that now. I promised to raise the minimum wage in our country by 20% - and of May 1st I will do just that. Every laborer, office worker and military personnel on minimum wage will receive an extra 20% as from that date and forever."

It took Chávez four hours to complete his address to the nation and during that time, many of the embassy staff quietly disappeared for lunch.

Mitchel turned to Shale as they walked from the room, "Do you remember our conversation from the other day?"

"Sure, I do."

"Well, I did some more digging and more and more I get the feeling that there's a big event coming, a real game changer here in Venezuela."

"Why do you keep digging?" Shale asked with surprise.

"Is there a reason I shouldn't?" Mitchel retorted.

"I'm not saying you shouldn't, but it's not going to change anything. These countries have a way of finding their own way. We are just here to adapt to their ways and see where we can help them, as well as ourselves. Look, do you want to grab lunch together so we can talk a bit more?"

"Sure."

"I know a neat little place where they serve nice local dishes. Fifteen minutes at the exit?"

Just as he was about to accept, Mitchel suddenly remembered he was already booked. "I have a lunch date with a friend of mine outside that I cannot cancel," he explained. "Monday?"

"Let me check my calendar and I'll let you know. OK?"

"Of course, and sorry."

"No problem. Enjoy your lunch. I'll see you later."

In the early afternoon the sun burned hot at its highest point above the Venezuelan capital.

"Again?" Mitchel cried out when he saw José standing next to his Ducati holding a spare helmet.

"Unless you'd rather take your bicycle into the slums."

"Yeah, yeah." Mitchel grabbed the helmet and climbed onto the back of the bike. "Next time I'll drive."

"Sure," José confirmed, smiling.

"Where are we going?"

"Barrio Tacagua, it'll take us about 30 minutes on the autopista."

As José started the motorcycle Mitchel took hold of his waist and with a roar they drove off. Travelling at high speed they quickly joined the highway to find it practically deserted. In the morning the four lanes were always gridlocked. Some twenty minutes later, José left the highway and headed towards tree-lined hills. Five minutes later the trees were gone and the small roadside shacks that stacked the hillside were exposed. Mounds of trash bags spilled their rotting guts onto any patch of wasteland and the overriding smell was one of a garbage dump. After half a mile, José stopped his bike next to two shacks and a path leading up a hill. As they parked up, two boys, aged about 12, came to loiter around José's motorcycle.

"You want to earn some money?" José asked the boys who nodding eagerly. "Here's five Bolivars. You look after my motorcycle and when I get back you get another five. OK?" The boys nodded again.

"You think the bike's safe?" Mitchel asked.

"I'm sure of it. For one dollar they'll defend it with their life if necessary. Let's walk."

Mitchel followed José up the path. It reminded him of a staircase reinforced with white and blue garbage bags.

"Garbage gets a second life here," José explained when he noticed Mitchel looking. "With heavy rain the water from the top of the hills runs down at speed taking everything in its path. The garbage helps hold things together."

Mitchel nodded and wondered at the ingenuity of man, even when man had nothing. "So what exactly are we doing here?"

"My sister-in-law has several cleaning jobs, one for a high-placed government official. When I spoke to her son over the phone yesterday, it's his birthday soon, he told me that his mother, a real Chavista, had a new cleaning job somewhere and the day before yesterday she came home upset. It had to do with her boss and the president, but he wouldn't give any details over the phone so... we're here."

As José finished, he stopped in front of a small red-bricked house. He banged twice on a large wooden board that served as a door. Almost immediately, a young man opened the door loudly called out José's name and the two men hugged each other.

"You must be James Mitchel," the young man stated as he took hold of Mitchel's hands and shook them warmly. "Uncle Abrantes told me much about you. I'm Adán, come in, have a seat." Adán ushered the men into the room and pointed to an old couch decorated with large red flowers. "A drink?" he asked.

"No, thank you," Mitchel answered.

"I'm good too. I'm sorry but we're on our lunchbreak so we can't stay too long."

"No problem. You come visit next week for my birthday."

"I wouldn't miss it," José replied. "So what couldn't you tell me over the phone?"

"Yes, well, as you know, my mother has worked as a cleaner now for a long time and she's a true Chavista. When she came home from her job she was all upset and didn't want to talk about it at first, but later that evening she couldn't keep it to herself any longer."

"What did she say?" Mitchel asked. Adán looked at José waiting for permission to continue.

"It's OK," José told him.

"In her new workplace she overheard a conversation. There were two people talking about some kind of major change in the government that would happen in the next week or so."

"Do you know who these people were?" José asked.

"No, but there's more. She told me she was particularly upset when she heard them say that Pedro Carmona would take over the presidency from Hugo Chávez."

José and Mitchel looked at each other with alarm.

"Are you sure she said Pedro Carmona?" Mitchel asked.

"Absolutely sure," Adán confirmed, nodding his emphatically. "So what should I do, Uncle Abrantes?"

"Nothing," José answered firmly. "You should…"

"One more question if I may," Mitchel interrupted.

"Sure," Adán replied.

"Do you know whose new household it is that your mother works for?"

"Sure, it's General Rojas'." Mitchel and José looked at each other both raising their eyebrows before answering.

"Thank you." Mitchel answered.

"Listen to me, Adán," José faced his nephew square on, taking his hands to illustrate the gravity of his words. "You must do absolutely nothing with this information. You go about your business like it is any other day and don't tell your mother that we were here. It will only upset her."

"So, what are you going to do?" Adán asked.

"I don't know yet, but please don't worry about it. Thank you for the information. Everything will be fine."

With nothing more to say, both men thanked the young man and said their goodbyes. Only once the makeshift door had been closed again did they speak about what they had learned.

"So what do you think?" José asked first.

"I think it's obvious," Mitchel answered. "There's some kind of coup being planned and Rojas is involved."

"But Rojas is one of Chávez's original friends; his lifelong confidant."

"There I have no answer for you. Maybe friendship can be bought or maybe he thinks he's doing the right thing for his country. Could be a lot of things, I guess."

"And what about the US involvement? Did you learn anything new from Shale?"

"I still can't figure out Shale. I couldn't say for sure that he's involved or that he even knows something, but he's definitely not going to help us. For now we are on our own on this one."

"Except for Turner maybe?"

"Except for Turner," Mitchel confirmed. "Although you don't sound too convinced."

"My bet would be that part of your government is involved," José explained. "Ever since Chávez was elected president US-Venezuela relations have soured, and him condemning the US invasions of Iraq and Afghanistan and threatening to cut off oil sales to the United States didn't help, I guess. Besides that, we know for sure that more than one million dollars in US government money, this year alone, has been given to Venezuelan opposition groups for so called "democracy-training" programs run by the National Endowment for Democracy, a private agency and subsidiary of the Council on Foreign Relations, led by your old friend, Charles Turner."

Mitchel shook his head as he felt his heart plummet. "I don't know who to trust anymore," he confessed. "My head is already spinning."

"OK, let's not overthink this for now. We'll go back and talk about it later."

"Good plan."

10. The Second Brief

Sunday, April 7th, 2002

I N THE HALL OF MINISTERS IN MIRAFLORES the seats were slowly filling up around the long wooden table as cabinet members and high level military officials arrived. Apart from Cardinal Ignacio Velasco, who refused to work on a Sunday for religious reasons, all the conspirators attended the meeting. In the corner of the room the generals Eduardo Valbuena and Mauricio Gallardo were softly talking as General Gomez came to join them.

"Should we call for him?" Gallardo asked.

"Leave him be," Valbuena replied. "We may only make things worse if we push him."

"So, where are we?" Gomez asked. "Are we still on for the eleventh?"

"Carmona and Ortega are both in," Gallardo confirmed. "I don't anticipate any problems as long as they don't inform each other of their individual plans." Gallardo glanced around the room. "Does anyone have any idea what this meeting is about, and why it was necessary to call us in on a Sunday?"

Valbuena and Gomez both shook their heads.

"I was only told the President had some additional information he wanted to share beyond his televised address yesterday," Gomez said.

"Nervous?" Gallardo asked looking at the others.

"A bit uncertain about Rojas, but that's all," Gomez admitted.

"Just four days left. We only need to hang in there for four days," encouraged Valbuena before a heavy bang upon the main doors stole his attention.

"El Presidente de República Bolivariana de Venezuela, Hugo Rafael Chávez Frías!"

At the announcement, Chávez entered the room dressed in military green and wearing a red beret. As well as a scarf around his neck and an armband in the national colors, he wore the ever-constant smile that had become his trademark. "Sit, gentleman, my friends. Please take your seats."

Everyone immediately hurried to their chairs in silence, knowing this was no request, but an order. Once they were all seated, Chávez walked around the table, tapping each and every one of them on the shoulder without a word. Finally, he stopped at his own seat. Yet he did not sit down.

"Why did I ask you here, on a Sunday when you should all be in church praying to God and Jesus our savior?" Chávez asked. "Let me tell you. Yesterday I went on television to publicly fire a number of threats to our republic. But this was merely a gesture; a taste of things to come. More and more traitors are among us, and I'm not just talking about the public opposition. Though 'treasonous', they have the guts to show themselves. No, much more dangerous than the official opposition is the media. The media owners, their managers and commentators are accusing me of intimidating their journalists using specially dispatched gangs. How dare they denounce their loyalty to Venezuela! How dare they publicly reveal their allegiance to be to the United States and to the advancement of neoliberalism! How easily they poison the minds of the common people through corporate propaganda!" By now, the smile on Chávez's face had long gone, and the raised voice and fire in his eyes reminded many in the room of a young Fidel Castro. "And then there's you." Chávez paused to look around the table, meeting the gaze of everyone present. "You, who I believed to be my friends. You, who I thought I could trust. Yes, I know there are friends and traitors amongst you. But as I don't know at this stage who you are, that scares me as much as it maddens me." Slamming two fists onto the table, everyone jumped in their seats at the accusation. "So what do I do with you?" he asked. "I thought about this, all night long, and I have decided to give you one chance to redeem yourselves – a chance to denounce the neoliberalism of the United States and return yourselves to the fold of decent Bolivarian Republic values, the ones we once all swore to uphold. If you don't, and I'm telling you this only once, I will put every one of you in jail on account of treason. Don't worry, I'm very close to finding out who you are, and I will have you arrested, put behind bars and tried for subversion. I hope you believe me. But for now, I want you to go and when you're ready, come back to me; show me you have reformed so that I can forgive you. But I warn you, you must show me this before I find you because by then it will be too late. I can guarantee you that."

Chávez looked around the room registering the confusion on many of the faces before him. No one dared to speak and slowly they all filed out of the room, one by one, until Chávez was left alone in the chamber. Only then did he sit down. After removing his beret, he began to pray.

Dios te salve María,
llena eres de gracia.
El Señor es contigo.
Bendita tú eres
entre todas las mujeres.

Y bendito es Jesús,
el fruto de tu vientre.
Santa María, Madre de Dios
ruega por nosotros, pecadores,
ahora y en la hora de nuestra muerte.
Amén.

A few miles down the road from the US Embassy was the International Racquet Center. On any weekday, after working hours, the eight racquetball courts were normally filled with expats blowing off steam in glass cages, a red-faced spectacle of grunting men and squeaking sneakers. Mitchel and José were two that didn't like the crowds during the weekdays but at Sunday they were such men, running around, smacking a small ball from wall to wall as hard as they possibly could.

"Ten-seven," Mitchel grunted. "Match point."

Both men were panting profusely and sweating as they walked back to the baseline.

"You have been practicing," José stated.

"Just a little, twice a week, for the past two years," Mitchel joked. He then hit the ball with all his might against the back wall. José stepped forward, stretched his arm, but the racket couldn't reach the ball on its fast return and he landed on the hard floor with a smack. "And match," Mitchel called out before stretching to help José to his feet.

"OK, you win, this time. But next time I'll be prepared."

"Sure you will." Mitchel laughed as he packed up his racket. Glancing at his Blackberry he then noticed a message. He showed it to José who read it aloud.

"*Call me, Charles.* That's Turner I guess?"

"Yep. Let's go somewhere a bit less noisy and I'll call him back," Mitchel suggested and the two of them retired to the sports center restaurant where they found a quiet corner. Once Mitchel had dialed, José moved closer to listen in on the conversation.

"Turner here."

"Charles, it's Mitchel. You wanted me to call you."

"Yes, thank you for calling. I might have something for you."

"OK, what is it?"

"Today I got a copy of yesterday's Senior Executive Intelligence Brief. It has a large portion in it about the situation in Venezuela that I'm sure will be of interest to you."

"Can you tell me?"

"I can do better than that. I'll send the complete brief to your Blackberry if you promise me to share it with no one, not even Shale, and delete it once you've read it."

"I can promise you that."

"Then it's on its way. Let me know if you need anything else or think of anything else."

"Will do, and thanks again, very much." Mitchel ended the call and his hands immediately searched for the Blackberry in his bag. "Found it," he muttered.

"Wondrous how they manage to get so much technology into such a small machine," José remarked.

"It sure is. Let's see. Ah here it is, an email from Turner."

After pushing a few buttons, Mitchel opened the email and both men inched their heads towards the small black and white screen to read.

Venezuela: Conditions Ripening for Coup Attempt

Dissident military factions, including some disgruntled senior officers and a group of radical Junior officers are stepping up efforts to organize a coup against President Chávez, possibly as early as this month.

The level of detail in the reported plans - one report targets Chávez and 10 other senior officials for arrest - lends credence to the information, but military and civilian contacts note that neither group appears ready to lead a successful coup and may bungle the attempt by moving too quickly.

Civilian groups opposed to Chávez's policies, including the Catholic Church, business groups, and labor, are backing away from efforts to involve them in the plotting, probably to avoid being tainted by an extraconstitutional move and fear that a failed attempt could strengthen Chávez's hand.

Prospects for a successful coup at this point are limited. The plotters still lack the political cover to stage a coup, Chávez's core support base among poor. Venezuelans remains intact, and repeated warnings that the US will not support any extraconstitutional moves to oust Chávez probably have given pause to the plotters.

Chávez is monitoring opponents inside and outside the military, and might use a coup to attempt to justify clamping down on the struggling opposition and tightening his grip on the country's institutions.

To provoke military action, the plotters may try to exploit unrest stemming from opposition demonstrations slated for later this month or ongoing strikes at the state-owned oil Company PDVSA. White-collar oil workers began striking on Thursday at facilities in 11 of 23 states as part of an escalating protest against Chávez's efforts to politicize PDVSA.

Protracted strikes, particularly if they have the support of the blue collar oil workers' union, could trigger a confrontation.

"Wow!" José exclaimed.

"Wow indeed," replied Mitchel as he let the Blackberry slip from his fingers to fall into the bag.

"Do you trust Turner?" José asked after a few seconds of silence.

122

"Why do you ask? He's the one that gave us the information."

"That's what I'm talking about. How can you be sure that we aren't being played? I mean, what does he think you'll do with this information and why would he give it to you?"

"I'm not sure I can think of any scenario that would play well for him should the information become public and his name be tied to it."

José rubbed his face wearily. "So shall we say it out loud?"

"Well, I'm reluctant to do so but, I'm afraid you're right. Project April Showers is somehow connected to the overthrow of the Venezuelan government."

"And it's not only going to happen soon, but it also appears your government is somehow involved," José added. "And as it starts on the eleventh, what we do now, I think, is up to you to decide."

"How so?" Mitchel asked, feeling surprised and not a little indignant at the assumption.

"To be honest, I think you need to decide which side you're on. You can't sit on this information and do nothing. If you take it to Shale, and the information is sound, he will lead you into his game."

"But what's the alternative?" Mitchel looked at the expats around them, mostly Americans, and felt like a traitor. If he chose to share the information with Shale, it would betray every democratic principle he ever stood for as his country would be interfering in a democratically-chosen republic that posed no clear or present danger to the US. On the other hand, should he choose Chávez's side, he would betray his own people to uphold his principles. Once upon a time, he had sworn to perform his duty without hesitation or doubt, yet if he did that it would require him to switch off his feelings.

"I know this is hard, my friend," José acknowledged as he saw the struggle taking place in Mitchel's eyes.

"You have no idea."

"Probably not, but I do know that problems can look very different once you sleep on them or perhaps even share them with someone."

"You mean…?"

"Yes, think about it, sleep on it and then talk to Nathalie. Don't rush into a decision, my friend. This might be one of the most important ones you ever make in your life, and once it's made there's no turning back. Either way, you choose."

"Thanks, I'll think about it. Right, I've got to go." Mitchel picked up his bag and turned to the exit.

"I'll see you tomorrow at the reception then!"

"Ah, great. I almost forgot about that."

"I know they're your favorites." José smiled and waved Mitchel goodbye.

11. The Farewell Reception

Monday, April 8th, 2002

"HONEY, WHERE ARE MY CUFFLINKS?" Mitchel shouted from the bed where he was sat trying to work out where his wife might have put the finishing touches to the white uniform he wore.

"They're on top of my dressing table, left side," Nathalie shouted back from somewhere downstairs.

Mitchel walked to the dresser, casting an amused eye over the stacks of makeup, perfumes, and hair supplies. Nathalie could be a real good housewife, but when it came to cleaning up her dresser it was an entirely different story. Searching through the clutter of cosmetics he managed to find one cufflink sitting behind a cleaning cloth. Mitchel then found the other hooked onto another piece of cloth he didn't recognize. Putting his cufflinks in place, he went to stand before the mirror as Nathalie entered the room wearing a long red dress that was pulled tight at the waist and split at both sides, all the way to the hips.

"Wow, you look great! Absolutely astonishing. But sweetheart, please keep my cufflinks out of your toolbox in the future."

Nathalie laughed, loud and sincerely. "If you succeed in keeping our clothes on a little longer than five minutes when we get back from the gala, I'll put your cufflinks wherever you want them."

Mitchel smiled, feeling guilty at the mild irritation he had felt. "I'm sorry, hon. You know I get cranky when I have to dress up."

"Hence the fast undressing," Nathalie joked and, this time, they both laughed. Mitchel moved closer to kiss his wife on the forehead.

"So what do you think?" he asked

"About what?"

"About what we talked about last night; the whole Chávez, CIA, coup thing?"

"I thought about it and I believe you'll choose the right thing to do. Like I said, you cannot set aside your principles, you're simply not that type, and the last time you attempted to do that you ended up in therapy, for months. However, I do have one request. I want to know in advance when things are about to get dangerous. I refuse to put Catherine in any kind of physical danger." Nathalie paused to point a manicured finger in the air. "I'll stand behind you and support you because I trust your judgment, although strangely there's a part of me that wants you to be very wrong about this. I hope you understand."

Mitchel looked Nathalie in the eye. "I think I do, too," he admitted. "But thank you. I really love you."

Mitchel walked over to his bedside cabinet and took hold of the copy of the letter that had succeeded in embroiling him in something he had no appetite for. He then took it to the bathroom sink and reached into his trouser pocket to find the Zippo lighter his father had given him on his 18th birthday. His father had bought it in the gift shop after taking him on a tour of Langley and it bore the blue, white and red insignia of the CIA. Mitchel had never smoked, but he liked to carry the lighter nonetheless; it reminded him of his father and of the values he stood for.

With a flick of his thumb, Mitchel set fire to the paper and once it was properly alight he dropped it in the sink to watch it wither into ashes.

"You made your decision?" Nathalie asked.

"I did, and you're right. Thank you."

"You're welcome."

For a few seconds the couple looked at the blackened remains in the sink before Mitchel turned the faucet and washed the evidence away. "We need to go," he said. He then walked back into the bedroom and put on his service cap before striking a pose. "So, what do you think?"

"Turn around," Nathalie ordered before nodding. "Yep, you look absolutely great. By the way, do you know this diplomat they're throwing the reception for?"

"Never met him. He's some high-placed Chinese official at their Embassy who I assume has made a career move elsewhere. My embassy is invited and we are the lucky ones who get to go." Mitchel took another look at his wife and shook his head. "And I suggest we go right this minute because if we stay in this bedroom much longer we might not make it at all."

The Chinese Embassy was a little more than 'just around the corner' from the US Embassy and Mitchel passed it every day on the way to work. The building didn't stand out in any way and it could have been any other regular office building.

Driving towards the entrance, Mitchel came to a stop at the valet parking sign. A small crowd of curious people was being kept at distance and a red carpet marked the way for the hoard of dignitaries whose differing styles revealed a dizzying array of nationalities present. Just before Mitchel and Nathalie were about to enter the building, sirens sounded to announce the arrival of a small motorcade, the lights of which continued to flash all the way up to the embassy's entrance with the third car – a large limousine – stopping directly in front of the carpet. From a front seat, an officer jumped out and walked to the limo's back door.

"Who will that be?" Nathalie asked and Mitchel shrugged his shoulders.

"Let's wait and see."

Mitchel took his wife's hand and they watched as a crowd of waiting reporters and photographers descended on the limo before being pushed back. Once the way was clear, the back door of the limo swung open and Hugo Chávez emerged, immediately followed by his daughter María Gabriela. Chávez was typically dressed in a dark blue suit and red tie. He stopped for a moment to wave at the audience and pose for the cameras. He then gestured to his daughter and they walked up the red carpet towards Mitchel and Nathalie. Mitchel noticed Chávez checking out his uniform and he glanced at his wife, reading the same question in her eyes; what do they do, stay or walk in fast before Chávez passes them? Without saying anything the two agreed to stand their ground, but just as it looked like Chávez and María Gabriela would pass by, the President stopped.

"Please, go on in," Chávez told his daughter. "I will be with you in a moment."

As María Gabriela entered the embassy, Chávez turned to Mitchel and stretched out his arm. "Hugo Chávez Frías," he greeted. For a fraction of a second, Mitchel hesitated, out of surprise rather than political allegiance. He then took Chávez's hand and shook it.

"Mitchel. James Mitchel," he said by way of introduction.

"And you're dressed as an American soldier?" Chávez asked.

"Yes, Sir. US Naval Commander."

"You should always lead with that, Son. That's who you are; Commander James Mitchel."

"Yes, Sir."

"And I see that you are also here with your daughter," Chávez joked as he offered his hand to Nathalie.

"Wife," Nathalie corrected warmly before giving her name.

"You're a lucky man, Commander Mitchel." Whether it was intentional or not, Chávez took his time shaking Nathalie's hand. "You're a proud and respected member of your country's military force, you have a lovely wife, and you work in the greatest democracy in the world."

"I'm proud to be here, Sir," Mitchel responded.

"Good to hear, Son. Have a great time."

As Chávez turned away, Mitchel noticed the photographers were still taking pictures.

"I guess we're going to be famous now," Nathalie joked.

"I wonder what my boss will make of the photos in the newspapers tomorrow. I can just see the headline, '*New agreement between US Navy and Venezuelan government*'."

Nathalie smiled and, hand in hand, the two of them followed the President into the building.

The reception was held in the Chinese Embassy's ballroom, a huge place decorated like the court of Louis XVI with lots of brocade, lace and gold paint. From the high walls, strung wires held small Chinese red flags and gold stars covered the gold ceiling. To the sounds of a string quartet, Mitchel and Nathalie took up position at one of the many standing tables placed around the dance floor in the center of the room.

"A drink?" a voice asked, and the two of them looked over their shoulders to find José, dressed in white trousers and an almost too-colorful shirt. He also held two glasses of champagne in his hands.

"Courtesy of the People's Republic of China," he announced with an official tone.

"Thank you," replied Nathalie and both she and Mitchel gave a small bow.

"Have you greeted our Chinese host?"

"Not yet," Mitchel answered. "I'll catch him on the way out."

"But I bet you're already having a good time?"

"Now you're getting nasty." Mitchel threw his friend a forced smile.

"Oh, don't be a spoiled baby," Nathalie said as she pounded Mitchel on the shoulder.

"Ouch!" Mitchel rubbed at his arm, laughing. "I guess I'll survive."

"Have you seen Chávez? He is here, apparently." José looked around the room, his eyes sparkling with excitement.

"Yes, we spoke to him briefly on the way in," Mitchel responded while Nathalie nodded.

"You did? How? About what? Tell me!"

"Oh, just general chit chat about the weather, with a little politics thrown in, and a bit about coups and things."

"You're yanking my chain."

"He does that," Nathalie admitted.

"I do," Mitchel confirmed. "But we did talk to him briefly. He addressed us at the entrance, said a few words and made sure the photographers took pictures of us shaking hands."

"The Americas united," José said with a grin.

"Something like that," Mitchel replied.

"So, what do you think of...."

Before José could finish, a man in Venezuelan uniform tapped him on the shoulder.

"Excuse me," he said.

"General Sanjez Valbuena, what can I do for you?" José shook the general's hand. He knew him through his father and had always viewed him as one of Chávez's main supporters, although tonight he looked almost ill. His face was sweaty and there was a tenseness about him that José was unused to.

"Can we speak in private for a moment?" the general asked.

"Sure." José pointed towards one of the doors. "We can see if there's a room free somewhere." He then turned to Mitchel and Nathalie. "I'll talk to you later."

As José walked away, Nathalie turned to her husband. "What would that be about?"

"What is it always about?" Mitchel replied, just as the string quartet started to play the Blue Danube Waltz. Handing out his hand, Mitchel invited Nathalie to dance. When they walked onto the floor there was no one else present and Nathalie felt Mitchel's reluctance so she pulled him towards her. Soon after they began to dance they were joined by Chávez and his daughter. For a minute, the two couples danced around each other, exchanging glances every now and then until Chávez suddenly let go of his daughter and offered his arm to Nathalie as she neared. With no option, she uncoupled herself from her husband and slipped into Chávez's arms while Mitchel found himself partnered with María Gabriela. The four of them then picked up the waltz as more and more couples stepped onto the dancefloor. When the music finally stopped, all the couples bowed to each other and Mitchel was reunited with his wife.

"That was odd," Mitchel stated.

"Incredible," Nathalie confirmed.

"You can say that again. You have just danced with the man considered by my boss to be America's greatest threat and potential dictator. What are you doing, girl?" Mitchel wagged his finger at Nathalie in mock fury. "By the way, did he say anything?"

"Not a word."

"She didn't either. Good dancer, though," Mitchel said before noticing José walking towards them from across the room.

"Guys walk with me," he ordered, turning them around and pointing at an empty table. "You'll never believe what happened to me."

"Same here," Mitchel responded.

"Me first," José insisted.

"Go ahead if you're that anxious," Mitchel said before darting his eyes towards Nathalie.

"Oh, no problem," José said. "I assume you did as I suggested and shared your dilemma?"

Mitchel nodded.

"Then this is something we can also share."

"OK, go on then."

"You know who that was just now?" José asked

"General Valbuena, no?"

"Right, almost exactly right. General Valbuena indeed, General Hermano Sanjez Valbuena, not Eduardo Valbuena."

"You're losing me, mate," Mitchel said shaking his head.

"Just a second. General Eduardo Valbuena was the general mentioned in the brief you intercepted at the embassy and he is not related in either blood or views to this Sanjez Valbuena. Now, this general has told me he was approached by an American named Dwight Caldwell. This Caldwell was apparently directed to the general by another guest and then asked him, somewhat nervously, why he hadn't contacted their ships along the coastline near La Guairá's main port. He wanted to know what had happened and why no one had contacted him, wondering what they were waiting for. Now, General Valbuena – Sanjez Valbuena – had absolutely no idea what the man was talking about." José paused for a moment, his eyes wide.

"He was addressing the wrong General," Mitchel said.

"Correct. Caldwell must never have met Eduardo Valbuena face to face so he simply looked at the nametag."

"So what did this Sanjez Valbuena tell Caldwell?"

132

"What could he tell him other than he would look into it and get back to him."

"And why you? I mean, why would he tell you about this?"

"Sanjez Valbuena is a Chavista and loyalist in heart and soul. We spoke about our growing concerns a few times in the past year. Not knowing who to trust and all that and then he saw me and…"

"But what does this mean?" Mitchel interrupted. "Couldn't it just be another military secret or exercise or something? This doesn't have to have anything to do with what we are doing?"

"Not necessarily, no," José admitted." But one thing I'm sure of is that the only official US vessels in our waters these past weeks should be two US coastguard ships on a joint anti-narcotics mission with The Netherlands."

"And…" Mitchel sighed, "we might now have another piece of a puzzle that we cannot yet finish."

"Are you still convinced it's a puzzle?" asked Nathalie, who had been quietly listening to the conversation.

"What do you mean?" Jose asked.

"I mean, are you still convinced that all the pieces of the puzzle lead up to some kind of danger for Chávez and his democracy?"

Mitchel and Jose looked at each other and frowned.

"Hey, it's up to you," Jose told Mitchel.

"I know, and I made up my mind earlier today. Look, I'm not sure how these ships fit into the evidence. In fact, I cannot imagine how US ships would add up in any of this, but I'm sure that all the other pieces suggest some kind of illegal activity is afoot, possibly a coup. Now I might not agree with everything that's going on in this country, but I also believe it's not up to us, the US, to interfere in countries with freely-elected governments."

"So there you have it, and here is your chance presented to you on a silver platter," Nathalie said, and both men looked at each other in confusion.

"Nothing?" Nathalie asked. "Isn't it obvious? You have information that could damage the leader of this country and here we are, in the same room, as that very same leader."

"No!" Mitchel cried.

"Why not?" Nathalie asked.

"Look, let's think about this for a second," José suggested. "What's the worst that could happen?"

"What's the worst that can happen? I can think of a few million things," Mitchel replied. "He could throw us in jail, accuse you of treason, contact our superiors, and that's to name but a few of his options."

"I have to admit, it's not without risk," agreed José, "but if we can convince him, we might get a powerful ally to investigate further."

Nathalie pointed at the dance floor where Chávez was again dancing, this time with the Chinese ambassador's wife.

"I don't know," Mitchel muttered. "It still seems a mighty big risk, even if we can get to him."

"We can think about it for a few minutes. At least until he leaves. So, what's yours?"

"What do you mean?"

"What happened to you? You said something happened to you while I was away."

"Ah that, that was nothing special," Mitchel smiled. "Nathalie was merely dancing with Chávez while I danced with his daughter."

For a second José looked at the two before Nathalie nodded in confirmation. José shook his head: "I can't leave you two alone for a few minutes, now can I?"

As he spoke the string quartet finished another waltz only to change the tempo and break into a version of 'Dancing Queen' by Abba.

"Here he comes," José said, nodding to the dance floor where Chávez appeared to be making a beeline for their table. Half expecting the President to pass by, they were all surprised when he stopped in front of Nathalie.

"May I?" he asked, offering his arm. Nathalie glanced at Mitchel before accepting the invitation. Mitchel then watched as the most powerful man in the country pulled his wife close.

"You better watch out," José joked.

"Yeah, yeah, sure," Mitchel responded with a light-hearted wave.

"Well, he's supposed to be a real ladies man. It's been said that he tried to kiss Michelle Bachelet, Chili's Secretary of Defense, as well as Queen Sofia of Spain. He even grabbed Queen Elizabeth by the arm and took her for a walk to who knows where. There are also rumors about a courtship with Barbara Walters. So truly, you better watch yourself, and her."

"Sure," Mitchel repeated, smiling patiently until the music stopped and his wife returned to their table. "You see?"

"But she's not alone," José said with a smirk. "It looks like he's coming with her."

"All right, boys." Nathalie was smiling broadly as she reached the table, and there was a sense of mischief about her. "I will get another drink and let you men talk."

"So, gentlemen," Chávez said as he came to lean against the table. "I understand you want to talk with me?"

While Chávez put on his brightest smile the two friends were flabbergasted for a second and looked at each other in despair, wondering who would talk first.

Mitchel noticed two guards standing behind Chávez, roughly 15 feet away. It was José who started the conversation.

"Well, uh, thank you for coming here. Do you know who we are?"

"Of course I do." Chávez sounded cocky. "Your name is José Rafael Abrantes and you work for the DISIP. I knew your father. And your name is James B. Mitchel recently attached to the US Embassy."

135

"Impressive. How do you…" Mitchel said.

"Easy," Chávez interrupted. "I always make it my job to go through the guest list before attending anything official. You never know who you may find on it."

"Sounds like good advice," Mitchel said. "Did my wife tell you anything about why we wanted to talk to you?"

"Nothing, but through the years I've learned that when a beautiful woman like your wife asks you something you better do it." The three men laughed loud enough to turn heads in other parts of the room.

"I'm not sure how to say this," José began before stumbling, "but uh….well, I guess…"

"We have strong evidence there's some sort of a coup being planned against you and parts of your government," Mitchel interrupted, almost breathlessly. "The evidence consists of several intercepted letters and interviews."

José looked at his friend in surprise, while Chávez grinned.

"I must admit, this is not what I expected to hear," the President said. "Now, why would you tell me such a thing? And if this is not some kind of joke why haven't I heard this through official channels instead of an American navy commander and a mid-level DISIP agent?"

"I know this must all seem very strange to you," José continued, "but the reason we come to you directly is that we don't know if we can trust the official channels."

"And it might be hard for you to believe, but not all Americans are power-crazed war mongers. Although there are a few," Mitchel said, hardly believing the words were leaving his own mouth. For a second or two there was silence, and Mitchel began to wonder when the guards would be called to arrest them. Instead, Chávez reached across the table and took Mitchel's hand between his and squeezed it.

"I like you," he said. "You got, how you call it? Spunk? You speak your heart. But why don't you tell me something new? I'm sad to say that even in this democracy there's always someone looking to take over your place when you have some kind of power. Somehow I don't believe there's anyone out there bold enough to try."

"Not one man, but with a little help from here and there," José added and Chávez shifted his attention to him.

"So, what evidence do you have and can you present it to me? Do you have names, dates?"

"We do," Mitchel said. "All pieces of a larger puzzle. But we don't have all the pieces yet. What we do know is that you don't have much time. It could be a matter of days. The evidence seems to suggest something happening on the eleventh of this month."

Chávez hid his interest well behind his smile. Of course, he had heard the same rumors, but all information was valuable. Behind him one of the guards walked up to Chávez, clearly in reaction to something he'd heard through his earpiece. Mitchel and José looked at each other while the guard whispered to the President. When the guard took a step back again Chávez pointed at his pocket. The guard immediately took a card from his pocket and handed it over.

"I'm sorry to tell you I have to go," said Chávez. "On this card you'll find the number of my, uh, personal aid, or at least that's what I believe you call it in English. Please contact him and tell him everything you know." José took the card and looked at it briefly.

"Gentleman."

Chávez turned and quickly walked away, moving easily through the crowd towards the exit.

"Well, that was weird," Mitchel said as Nathalie returned to join them.

"So, how did it go?" she asked.

Mitchel looked at José inviting him to give his opinion.

"I have no idea. I don't believe we offended him, but I'm doubtful about him taking us seriously."

Mitchel looked at Nathalie and tried to mask how he truly felt.

"But this is what you wanted all along, isn't it?" Nathalie asked.

"Like you always know what I want, dear." Although he didn't mean anything by it, Mitchel's tone sounded sarcastic. "So what do we do now? Do we proceed this way with Chávez?"

"I suggest we step back for a moment," José advised. "I think we take some time to consider all the evidence and made up our mind from there."

"Take some time to clear your minds," Nathalie added.

"Tomorrow?" Mitchel asked.

"Tomorrow," both José and Nathalie replied in sync.

12. The National Strike

Tuesday, April 9th, 2002

THROUGH THE HALLWAYS OF MIRAFLORES PALACE, a young officer ran, pushing a large TV on top of a stand on wheels, shouting: "Out of my way, move, move!"

People walking along the hallways jumped to the side as the officer ran past. Only when he reached two large doors did he stop to catch his breath. After straightening his clothes, he knocked.

"Enter."

As the doors swung open, the officer headed towards a large table, around which were sat Chávez's chiefs of staff. The President himself was seated at the top of the table.

"Bring it over here," he called out loudly while pointing at the floor a few feet from him. The officer duly steered the TV up to him and immediately began plugging in cables.

"Which channel, Sir?"

"Any of the private channels will do, son," Chávez responded, and the young men did as he was told before placing the remote control on the table in front of the President. "Thank you," Chávez said politely and the officer left the room. Once the door closed behind him, Chávez turned his attention to the others at the table. "In a few moments we'll see that traitor Carmona spilling his latest lies as he speaks about his plans to sabotage us. I want you to look at him closely. Look at his face and especially his eyes." Chávez stood up from his chair and looked around the table. As he raised his voice, his voice cracked. "Carmona's smug face and his beady eyes. Look especially at the eyes. Those are the eyes of a traitor!"

Along the table, every man reacted differently to their President's words. Some looked him in the eye. Others turned away. However, they all had one thing in common; nobody dared say a word. The intensity of their leader's sense of betrayal was frightening to behold, and everyone was afraid to raise their heads above the parapet. Thankfully, the TV gave them something to focus on as the voice-over announced Carmona's name.

"There you'll have him," Chávez muttered darkly before turning up the volume and taking his seat again.

On screen, and dressed in a typically tired and cheap looking brown suit, Carmona took up position on a small pedestal in front of the packed conference room.

"My fellow Venezuelan citizens, all of whom are in peril in these troublesome days," he began, causing a bellowing howl of outrage from Chávez. "Today, I come before you to urge you to do the right thing in the face of the latest disgrace committed by our once beloved leader. He has fired loyal employees who dared to defy him; our President, the man who vowed to take care of us, of you."

"Hypocrite!" Chávez railed, rising from his chair to take the revolver from his hip and smack it onto the table. The clatter echoed throughout the large room. No one said a word, but every eye turned to look at the gun as Chávez sat down again.

"The next week will be tough for all of us," Carmona continued. "To make things right again we first need to get everyone's attention and I'm very sorry to say that all our attempts so far have failed." Carmona took a well-placed pause as loud boos filled the room. He waved both arms in the air to silence the crowd. "As from tomorrow this will change, and it gives me no pleasure to announce that we will take new action to get our message across. We will not – no – we will never bow to an administration that uses our natural resources to gain personal wealth in a time when more than 70% of our country cannot eat a single decent meal every day. We will not bow to a president who fires everyone who dares to defy him. Let me tell you this Mr. President, you'll have to fire the entire country because we will not back down. We will see this through until decent proposals are made regarding foreign and domestic changes that will stop this country from declining."

As Carmona shook both fists in the air, the crowd went crazy, chanting that "Chávez must resign, Chávez must resign, Chávez must resign". All the while, Carmona's small fists thumped the air, urging them on. Only once the room calmed did he attempt to speak again.

"Now, as of tomorrow there will be no newspapers," he said before pausing to allow the crowd's jeers. "But the private TV channels will cancel all regular programming to continuously cover the strikes in order to show everything that's wrong with this administration. Oil production all over the country will be slowed down to a bare minimum, enough only to preserve the machinery. And if by noon tomorrow Chávez hasn't agreed to our terms then finally, finally, on April 11th – in order to protest against the increasingly dictatorial policies of our President Hugo Chávez – on the 11th we will take to the streets of Caracas. A march of hundreds of thousands that will start at the Generalissimo Francisco de Miranda Park. And I will call upon every one of you to walk with me in – "

A loud bang startled everyone at the table, their eyes now fixed on a TV screen that belched smoke and shattered glass thanks to the bullet fired into it by Chávez.

"Out!" he screamed across the table. "Out!"

It took only a second for the chiefs of staff to respond and, like rats fleeing a sinking ship, they scurried from their seats towards the door.

"Not you!" Chávez shouted and pointed at Moises Rojas. "You stay."

His heart beating in his chest, Rojas waited until the room was clear before walking towards Chávez and sitting down next to him.

"I…"

"No" Chávez interrupted. "Not today. No more debate. I only need you to do your thing, to work for me."

"Of course," Rojas replied, but his voice lacked conviction.

"I believe that the entire PDVSA staff is up to something and I need you to increase the *cadena* broadcasts tomorrow."

"But, Sir," Rojas started before pausing, unsure how far to push his coming protest. While it was obligatory to carry the President's speeches on the entire national broadcast system, the *cadena* broadcasts were originally intended for emergency warnings. Unfortunately, they had become a weapon in the President's arsenal against his enemies, a series of short political speeches that too often disrupted regular viewing. Not that Rojas was brave enough to say this. "How much of an increase do you want?"

"As much as possible. I want to shut them down effectively," Chávez ordered.

"Are you sure you want to do this? Aren't you afraid how it might look?"

"I don't care how it looks and I don't need your advice at this point, only your loyalty. Now go and take care of it."

Unwilling to argue the point any more than he had feebly attempted to, Rojas left the room. Chávez didn't watch him go, but once the echo of the man's heels had died and the doors had closed behind him, he took hold of the bead necklace in his pocket. He was worried, he had to admit it, even if only to himself. But it wasn't just the announcement of the strikes, he had been half-expecting them, but rather the date of them. It was the same date mentioned to him by the American he had met at the Chinese Embassy, and that hinted at a far more sinister threat to his hold on the country. Domestic dissatisfaction was one thing, foreign interference on this scale was entirely another. Chávez gazed at the small cross in his hands before lifting it to his lips and kissing it.

The sun was beginning its descent as Mitchel led José up the stairs of his home. "I want to show you something," he said.

Reaching the second floor, Mitchel quickly closed the door to the master bedroom trying to hide the mess of tangled bedsheets and the clothes on the floor.

"Hey, who am I to judge?" José said with a laugh and Mitchel gave him a frosty glance.

"This is it." Mitchel opened the door to an empty room. On the far wall a number of large photos and pieces of paper were stapled to the wood. A simple bulb hung from the ceiling and it gave the room a mysterious air. In one corner a computer with a printer hooked up to it was placed on the floor. In the other corner were two television sets. As José walked up to the wall he saw the photos were of most of Venezuela's army generals. There were also pictures of Oscar Rout and Charles Turner, as well as Dwight Caldwell, the man they'd met the other day at the Chinese embassy. Mitchel walked up and pointed at the wall.

"Generals, Chiefs of Staff from Venezuela and the U.S. and, over here, all the documents we found. All pieces of the puzzle; the mystery that will unfold once we connect the dots."

"You've built yourself a nice war room," José commented, before pointing at a letter tacked to the wall. "Is this?"

"Yes, it is. A copy of the letter that started it all."

"I thought you destroyed it?"

"I did. But not before I made a picture of it with my camera. So, I reprinted it."

"So, what's next?" José asked with a grin.

"Today at work I found out that General Enrique Medina, Chávez's appointed military attaché to Washington, arrived back in Caracas the day before yesterday."

"Medina turned on Chávez during his stay in the U.S." José said.

"I know," Mitchel replied. "Quite a coincidence, and that's why I dug a little deeper. It seems that Medina flew in on a joint U.S.-Venezuelan flight, carrying school aid supplies and," Mitchel paused for dramatic effect, "a special cargo in the name of General Medina. And guess what the shipment consisted of?"

"Flowers?" José joked.

"Sure, flowers. No weapons. Weapons for personal protection it said on the transportation manifest."

"Isn't that cargo diplomatically protected, meaning there should be no record of it?" José asked.

"It would be if the guns were transported on a diplomatic mission and assigned plane. But since it arrived on public transport, the cargo manifest becomes a matter of public record. But that's not everything. On the cargo letter it speaks of weapons for personal protection and names the weapon type as MK14 EBR. You recognize the number?"

"I think I do." José frowned.

"Sniper guns," Mitchel said, quickly speaking for the both of them. "American brand Enhanced Battle Rifle exclusively built in this sniper version for use with units of the United States Special Operations Command, Delta Force, Navy Seals etcetera. A real designated marksman rifle that can easily kill from a mile away. Brand new model."

"I know, but why would he make that a matter of public record? He could only ever arouse suspicion."

"That I don't know. Maybe he figured nobody would give it any thought. Why would they? It was a humanitarian flight. Or maybe he got caught in some kind of timing problem. All I know is that sniper guns are seldom used for personal protection."

"How many guns were there?"

"Twelve. A full dozen. Or so it says on the manifest."

"Wow, think of all the damage you could do with those. But why? Even if there is a coup it usually entails some close combat in the palace or governmental buildings. In those battles a sniper is hardly of any use."

"But do you agree that this is way too much coincidence?" Mitchel asked.

José looked closely at the wall and the pictures. He rubbed his chin. "Could it be that we are turning into some kind of conspiracy theorists; finding hints and clues where we want to find them?"

"I thought about it and I don't see it."

"You don't see what?"

"I've been looking at everything in every way possible," Mitchel admitted. "But the pieces all fit, we just don't know how they fit yet." Mitchel walked from one side of the wall to the other pointing at the pictures as he passed them. "From Rout, to Valbuena and Rojas, all the way up to Pedro Carmona and possibly Carlos Ortega, and now we have sniper rifles thrown into the mix, all leading up to April 11th."

"The date of the announced march."

"Precisely." Mitchel crossed his arms, and for a moment the two friends considered the wall in front of them in silence.

"What about these?" José pointed at pictures showing U.S. naval ships.

"These are just placeholders, not the real thing, but they are meant to remind us of Sanjez Valbuena's remarks about U.S. ships along the Venezuelan coast."

"We still don't know how or even if they fit in."

"Do you still have the card?" Mitchel asked

"Chávez's business card? Sure, right here in my wallet. Why, what's your plan?"

"My plan is simply that we need to somehow get all this information to him. To be honest, I think that's all we can do, at least until we know more."

"And, of course, your plan involves me doing all the work." José stabbed a finger at Mitchel's shoulder.

"Ouch," Mitchel cried.

"You baby. OK, I'll make contact first thing tomorrow morning. If you can scan all copies and send them to my email I'll be sure to send them."

"No problem, I'll send them to you later this evening."

"Great. We meet again tomorrow at lunch?"

"Sounds like a plan."

13. To Plan Or Not To Plan?

Wednesday, April 10th, 2002

AS MIDNIGHT NEARED, the streets around the PDVSA corporate office were largely empty due to the heavy rain. In the huge parking lot a handful of cars took up the executive parking spaces as their chauffeurs passed the time chatting, smoking and even dancing to the loud music coming from one of the cars. Outside, heavy cloud trapped the moonlight and all was dark save for the bright lights coming from the 17th floor where General Mauricio Gallardo was about to speak to his fellow conspirators.

"Gentleman, in five minutes it will be midnight and we have yet to hear from Chávez or the government," he said.

"And if the next five minutes don't bring a solution, what do we do then?" Rojas asked.

"Exactly what we've planned," Valbuena archly replied, and Rojas fought to bite his tongue.

"Thank you, General, for that insightful answer," he said, aware that a vein was now throbbing in his neck. "However, what I meant was, who does what from this point on?"

"Friends, let's not bicker," Cardinal Velasco pleaded as he stood up from the table to place his hands on the shoulders of the two men. "We all chose this route and now we need to see it through."

"So, let's talk about the strikes," Carmona encouraged, eager to calm everyone's nerves. "Let's evaluate how successful we have we been so far."

"A strike can only be successful when someone is suffering," Valbuena stated flatly.

"That said," Carmona quickly interjected, "my information is that we garnered a lot of attention by not printing any newspapers today. Oil production has slowed down to almost a standstill. On top of that, the TV's regular programs have made way for news about the strikes and anti-Chávez ads have been running all day. I'd say that must have been suffering enough for a lot of people."

"I guess the President's Cadena broadcasts might also have helped increase the nation's suffering," Valbuena quipped and everyone smiled apart from Rojas who looked nervously at his watch for the tenth time in the past few minutes.

"It's twelve o clock," he finally announced and the laughter immediately subsided. The men looked at each other, hoping someone would be the first to speak.

"So, what's the plan?" Rojas asked again.

"We proceed as planned," Gallardo said firmly. "First, we let Ortega start the march as chairman of the *Confederación de Trabajadores de Venezuela* from the Francisco de Miranda Park in the north to the PDVSA headquarters in Chuao. There Ortega will wait for the march before calling on the protestors to continue west, all the way to Miraflores to present the demands to Chávez."

"That has to be another seven miles," Rojas stated. "Are you sure people will respond to that?"

"The people are desperate and in need of guidance," Brigadier General Naldo Gomez replied. "If there's one thing I know about a desperate people is that they will follow almost anyone with a megaphone. Trust me, they'll walk."

"Why not announce the march in total?" Rojas persisted. "I mean, why not announce the entire eight miles from the start? That way we eliminate the risk of people leaving the march."

"Firstly, we have no permit to march to Miraflores," Valbuena told him. "Secondly, if we announce the second part of the march, Chávez may take action using local and military forces to create a confrontation long before anyone can get near the presidential palace."

Gallardo thanked Valbuena for explaining before continuing. "So, from the PDVSA headquarters we'll walk west, with Ortega still in the lead. When the march reaches the palace a confrontation with the presidential Honor Guard will work in our favor and Chávez will have no other option but to act."

"Why is that?" the Cardinal asked.

"Simple," Rojas said timidly. "Chávez will never allow his people to get in harms way..."

"...so he will either intervene militarily or resign immediately. Really, it's only a small walk into the palace and, if necessary, we remove him from office by hand, using the protesters who have marched into the palace." As Gallardo finished he spread his arms like a preacher ending a Sunday morning service.

"Won't the Honor Guard react?" Gomez asked.

"We expect the Honor Guard to be loyal to Chávez," Valbuena admitted. "It's up to them how they act, but I'll bet a month's salary that they won't fire upon innocent civilians. Chávez will have instructed them that way."

"I agree," Rojas said.

"And then it's time to play your part," Valbuena pointed at Carmona who simply nodded. "However, for now, I need you to go downstairs and face the Press currently waiting for your statement. Tell them about the success of the strikes, but also that there has been no response from the government so you are calling on all people to march tomorrow."

Carmona nodded again and stood up to go. "We'll talk again later," was all he said before leaving the room. Once he had gone, Valbuena approached Gallardo.

"How about our insurance?" he whispered.

"Been taken care of," Gallardo assured him.

"You don't think we should tell them?"

Gallardo grabbed Valbuena's arm and pulled him towards the window, further away from the other men. "You want them to know? Then maybe you should speak a little louder. What do you think would happen if they knew?"

"I don't know," Valbuena admitted with a shrug of his shoulders.

"Precisely. You don't know, and neither do I. But I do know that everyone's in on it now so why should we risk this commitment."

Valbuena softly grunted. "And what happens when they find out later, because they will find out?"

"They may find out it happened, but they will never know who was involved if we keep our mouths shut."

"There he is!" Cardinal Velasco turned up the volume of a small television to watch Carmona take his place behind a lectern and a bank of microphones. As he prepared to speak, Rojas, Valbuena, Gomez and Gallardo pulled up chairs.

"Thank you for being here," Carmona began.

About an hour after sunrise, the Miraflores palace staff got to work around a table in the courtyard, piling it high with freshly-baked bread, an assortment of fruit, Jell-O – one of Chávez's favorite foods – cuts of meat – another favorite – and various freshly-squeezed juices. The sunlight shining on the feast only added to the array of colors and general sense of opulence.

From a corner of the courtyard four men emerged, three of them dressed in uniform. As they approached, the servants went back to their chores in the palace.

"Why do you think he called us here?" one of the men asked.

"It must have something to do with the crisis."

"What crisis?"

"What crisis? Are you blind?"

"I've heard he wants to make plans to prevent the announced strikes and marches," another of the men confided just as Chávez appeared from another corner of the courtyard, dressed in casual blue coveralls and a red t-shirt. As he approached the group he waved.

"Join me for breakfast," he called out.

Naturally, the men immediately stopped their discussion and each of them took a chair at the table.

"I know, I know," Chávez said with an apologetic shrug as he got to the table and assessed the wealth of food awaiting them. "It looks a bit overdone, but I believe you deserve it."

The men at the table looked at each, the question evident in their rigid postures and wary eyes.

"I see you asking yourselves 'why?' but first, fill your plates and eat. Please eat. Eat!" Chávez pointed to the delicacies on the table. Despite their discomfort, the group felt compelled to follow the order and slowly they began to reach for the offerings laid out in front of them.

"Good," Chávez said with a smile. "And now that you all have your mouths filled with this delicious food I can talk knowing I won't be interrupted." Chávez paused to laugh at his own joke. He then turned to the man nearest him – a military man in his mid-fifties with a grey brush-cut and huge black eyebrows – and held out both hands. "General

Rafael Badillo, you were there when it all started in '92 and now you are the commander of Venezuela's elite 42nd Paratrooper Brigade – I dare to say the best fighting force in all of Venezuela – even though you've always made it clear that you stayed at my side because you don't believe in violence. I guess I must have disappointed you on more than one occasion, yet you stayed loyal to me. Why?"

Badillo's black eyebrows raised at the question. "Why?"

"Yes, why?" Chávez replied gently.

"The truth?"

"Absolutely, I wouldn't have it any other way."

"Well, to be honest..." Badillo paused as he tried to figure out if honesty was indeed the best policy at such moments, "OK, to be honest, I believe in your goals. I always believed and still believe that you can do wonders for this country. And though I don't believe violence is the answer, I do understand that sometimes there are no other means to achieve a higher goal. Of course, the overriding reason why I stay by your side is mainly to temper your more extreme tendencies and, hopefully, prevent you from doing anything stupid."

As Badillo finished, Chávez stayed silent for a second or two. It felt more like minutes and every eye in the room watched the President. Then, just as fear began to churn up their stomachs, Chávez slapped both hands on the table and burst out laughing. The table immediately relaxed and the laughter grew contagious.

"Thank you my friend, thank you for your honesty," Chávez told Badillo. "It's precisely because of that honesty that you are here. And I won't hold the fact that you're a devoted Taoist who believes in reincarnation against you." Continuing to smile broadly, Chávez looked to the rest of the men. "In fact, this is the reason why you are all here. I believe you to be honest and loyal, and these are qualities I need at my side as we come to a turning point in Venezuela's history. It's a point in which it becomes difficult for me to know who to trust, but I've come to the conclusion that is you, and only you four, that I trust."

"This cannot be it," General Lucio Reyes said in dismay.

"I'm afraid it is." Chávez's voice sank low, sounding almost timid. "And you were the first one to teach me everything about the value of trust at the military academy. You were the one that taught me to always be on my guard because in the end there will only ever be a small group of people you can really trust. *'You can probably count them on one hand'*, were your exact words, I believe."

"Your memory seems to be intact."

"Now, I know most of you were present yesterday when I shot the television, and that must have scared you. But the reason for doing it was that I wanted everyone to see that I will not go down without a fight. I also know that most of the hypocrites at the table will probably stab me in the back when it comes to a fight. More to the point. I believe there were traitors at that table already planning my demise. But then there are you. You've all proven to be my last friends; my last line of defense, so to speak. Figuratively, and literally, you represent the last loyal military line of defense."

"What about Rojas?" General Joaquin Gustavo Clemente asked.

"What about Rojas?" Chávez snapped back.

"Well, he's always been your closest friend and confidante. Why isn't he here? If there's someone I expected to see at this table it would be him."

"General Moises Rojas is still my friend and there's a good reason for him not to be here today." Chávez didn't elaborate and Clemente decided not to pursue the matter any further. The President then asked him a question. "And do you know why you are here?"

"I think so; plan Ávila."

"Indeed plan Ávila." Chávez nodded. "Plan Ávila, but also because you were always there for my family. You were the only one that showed an interest when I had family problems; when my wife got sick and when my daughters were born. You were always there when we needed you. And now there's one more thing you can do for me."

"Look, this is all well and good but...."

Chávez turned to Garcia Peroni, the one civilian at the table. "You want to know why are you here?" Peroni didn't reply, but he didn't need to. "The answer is simple. You have been the President of the PDVSA for how long?"

"A little under three months."

"And last week you proved your loyalty when I had to fire those PDVSA officials to set an example. Garcia, you are the last one, the only one, of the civil service leaders I trust. Your oil saved this country more than once from being diminished to a renegade, poor and violent state, and we can do it again."

"Actually, I discussed this matter at length with the newly appointed board members," Peroni admitted. "We all sense the mood of a national emergency and they are all willing to tender their resignations if we can avoid a crisis that way."

Chávez looked at Peroni and managed a tight-lipped smile both proud of the man's loyalty and outraged that it was needed. How did it ever come to this? How did it get this far? Only two years after his re-election and one year after 95% of the constitutional assembly, by election were appointed Chávez followers. "I am grateful for the suggestion, I really am," he told Peroni. "And if I thought it would help I would gladly accept the resignations, but I'm afraid it's too late for that; too late for gestures. It's obvious they made it personal. Your mass resignations will not change that. You'll only be out of work. And besides, I need you to save our oil installations and refineries during the strikes so that when this is all over we can proceed to create income, whoever is President." Chávez stepped back from the table to better look at the four men in front of him. "So, you are it," he told them. "The last line of defense I have. I don't know what will happen tomorrow, but if the announced march goes ahead I'll need to know I can trust you, that I can depend on you and only you. You will be my hope to resolve any issues peacefully because whatever happens tomorrow I want it to be a day of maximum tolerance without violence."

"So, what do you expect of us?" Reyes asked.

"For now, nothing," Chávez responded. "For now, I expect you to finish your breakfast because if I'm right it could be a while before we can have another one like this. All I need to know from you is that I can count on you when needed. I need you somewhere close to me during these troublesome days so I might contact you and we can meet when appropriate. That's all I need, right now."

Badillo took a sip from his orange juice before holding the glass high. "To our President and to a peaceful end to this crisis," he toasted.

"A peaceful end!"

Chávez smiled approvingly before raising his coffee cup and making his own toast: "To you, my four trusted friends, and to the people of Venezuela!"

In spite of the sun burning high in the sky, Mitchel left the embassy building fully suited and wearing overcoat. He found José already waiting for him at the curb on his Ducati.

"You know it's over 80 degrees?" José asked.

"And a good day to you too," Mitchel responded, nodding his head. "Did you watch Carmona?".

"Only the first part, which was pretty predictable."

"Where are we going?" Mitchel asked as José handed him a helmet.

"You know we agreed to hand over all information to Chávez? Well, it seems we got the attention we wanted. Hop on, and keep an eye out for anyone following."

Mitchel frowned, but said nothing as he put on his helmet and stepped onto the bike. Only once he was sat behind José did he ask about "anyone following".

"On this trip we need to be sure we're not being followed," José repeated. "Trust me on this."

"Sure, but if we die thanks to your driving before we arrive I will kill you for not telling me what's going on."

"Cry baby," José shouted, he then turned the throttle wide open and the bike sped away.

The roads José took were beset with bends and with every corner Mitchel swung from left to right, tightening his grip ever harder around José's waist. On a few occasions, he came within an inch of scraping his knees on the road. After a few minutes of this rollercoaster mayhem, José turned onto the autopista and headed west.

"Anything?" José shouted while glancing sideways at Mitchel.

"Nothing," Mitchel confirmed after checking the road behind them.

"Great."

After some fifteen minutes had passed in a blur of color and all-too frequent terror, José left the highway. Mitchel looked behind again to check if anyone was following, but as far as he could see no-one left the highway after them. On his right side, Mitchel saw the Parque Miraflores which hid the presidential palace. He had visited the place with Nathalie and Catherine the day after they arrived in Caracas. Catherine had described it as "something out of a theme park". Turning away from the palace, José took them a few blocks to the north where he stopped his bike in front of a huge, bright building.

"*Palacio Blanco,*" he revealed after taking off his helmet.

"It's white, I'll give you that," Mitchel replied, gazing up at all six stories of the building.

"The White Palace is also the official house of the government, conveniently located only a few hundred yards from Miraflores palace."

"And we have a meeting here?"

"Not quite, but almost right. Follow me." José waved his arm towards the front entrance, inviting Mitchel inside. "My department, the DISIP secret service, also has its office here."

"And yet I imagine that's not where we are going," Mitchel said as he stepped into the building.

Once inside, any grandeur that came with the regal name disappeared as visitors were greeted by a quite ordinary office hall complete with a reception area that could have been furnished by Ikea. Mitchel continued to follow José as he approached the receptionist. He had barely uttered a word before an army colonel walked up to them.

"Mr. Abrantes and Mr. James?" he asked.

"That's us," José confirmed.

"Will you please follow me?"

José nodded to Mitchel assuring him it was OK, and the three of them headed towards an elevator. Once inside, the colonel took a key from around his neck and slotted it into a control panel before pressing the lowest button on the board. Seconds later they arrived at a small room in which two soldiers sat behind a small desk, next to an x-ray machine and scan port. An empty tray was presented to José and Mitchel.

"Please put all your metals and electronics in the basket," one of the officers told them, and both Mitchel and José emptied their pockets. They then walked through the scan port without a beep.

"Good luck," the colonel said and Mitchel glanced at the trays holding their belongings.

"Your goods will be returned to you when you get back here," one of the soldiers explained. "Now, if you would like to go through this door and follow the path…"

Mitchel and José walked through the door to find a perfectly lit, white-painted tunnel leading to the left.

"What have you got me into now?" Mitchel asked as they started walking.

"You wanted the information shared and that's exactly what I did. After I made the initial contact they asked me to share everything I had on paper. Then, less than an hour later, we got this invitation."

"An invitation to what, where or who exactly?"

"A meeting."

"With?"

"I don't know for sure, but my gut says we are walking east so this tunnel probably leads to Miraflores. There have always been rumors about tunnels connecting various government buildings, but I never actually saw one until now."

The two friends zig-zagged underground for about five minutes before reaching a door which a soldier, who was stood in front of it, opened as soon as they neared. Mitchel stopped at the doorstep and stuck his arm around, swinging it from left to right.

"Looks safe," he concluded and José pushed him inside. The room looked much like the one they had left, complete with its own colonel who asked the men to follow him.

After making their way up a stairwell, they reached another corridor, but one that was decorated richly with chandeliers and paintings. The colonel opened a door and pointed the men inside.

"Please, take a seat at the table. Someone will be with you soon."

In many respects, the room resembled the corridor with its brass chandeliers and paintings of battles. Mitchel and José took their seats at the table and Mitchel helped himself to an apple from the fruit bowl in front of them.

"Great, here we are, probably in Miraflores Palace, awaiting who knows what, and you start eating an apple," José said, and Mitchel took a bite, crunching loudly.

"What was I supposed to do?" Mitchel grinned, but before José could answer, a door opened and Hugo Chávez entered the room.

"You're supposed to enjoy the fruits that are offered," the President said with a smile having clearly overheard Mitchel's question.

Both men rose from their chairs.

"No, please stay seated," Chávez said as he joined them. "So, we meet again. How is your Spanish Mr. Mitchel?"

"I'm afraid it's not too good, Sir – certainly not as good as the English I hear you speaking."

"That's too bad. As I'm sure you can appreciate, English is not my favorite language. Still, it is useful on occasions such as this. So, let's get to business. My aide showed me your documents and I must say I was surprised."

"You didn't suspect anything?" Mitchel asked.

"Well no, that was not why I was surprised. I was merely surprised that the two of you were able to collect this evidence and then even more surprised that you chose to present it to me." Chávez looked directly at Mitchel.

"It's like I said at the Chinese Embassy, Sir. I absolutely believe in democracy and the rule of sovereignty. No country has the right to meddle in the domestic affairs of another state unless serious human rights abuses are taking place. Certainly not for any kind of economic reasons.

"So, if I was torturing my people you think it would be OK to intervene?"

"Perhaps," Mitchel replied. "It would still be debatable, but more imaginable I think."

"You know what?" Chávez raised his voice a little. "You might be right and maybe I even believe you." The President laughed before turning to José. "And you, why are you taking this risk? I met your father about a decade ago. I didn't know him too well, but he seemed a decent man with his heart for his country in the right place. Loyal, but careful. You know you risk your job and possibly even court martial for high treason, punishable by life in prison, should anything happen to me and the new guys start looking for traitors and scapegoats." Chávez turned again to Mitchel. "Mr. James, did you know that Venezuela was the first country in the world to abolish the death penalty in 1863?"

"No, I didn't know that."

"So, Mr. Abrantes?"

"I know the risks," José replied.

"I'm sure you do, but why take them?" Chávez leaned over the table, looking determined to get his answer and José thought carefully about how to supply it.

"All right, I like to believe that democracy is the way to help this country get out of the situation it's in."

"And what situation would that be?"

José felt the heat rise up his neck. "I believe that the people's voices are more divided than ever creating fertile ground for a smaller group who have only their own needs and desires in mind. I also believe that this same small group of people could use the larger part of the population to destabilize our democracy, possibly throwing us back into the dictatorship of the mid last century."

"Some would disagree with you and claim our republic is already a dictatorship," Chávez pointed out.

"In that case, I say let them use their vote in the next election."

As José finished Mitchel sneaked a quick look at his watch.

"You're right," Chávez finally said. "And yes, I reviewed your so-called evidence and I must say it reads like an exciting spy novel with pieces that could be connected or circumstantial. But I'm still a bit skeptical."

"Then why meet with us?" Mitchel asked.

"Good question," the President replied. "Although I am not totally convinced by your 'proof' it could be that I simply don't want to believe it. One thing I do know, however, is that I believe in your integrity, something that's hard to come by these days. Also, I checked the Medina evidence regarding the sniper rifles and there are no official records to be found anywhere as to their official use."

"So, what are you planning on doing, if I might ask?" Mitchel jumped in before realizing he may have over-stepped the mark.

"What would you have me do? If you're right I don't know who to trust and if you're wrong, and I act on the information, it could backfire just as easily, leaving us more divided than ever before. Even worse, it may even help the enemy with their plans."

"I understand why you must be careful," José told Chávez, "but even though we don't know how everything fits together we are confident that there is a connection with the march scheduled for tomorrow."

"I'm sure you are," Chávez replied. "And I can tell you this much; later today I have a meeting with some, shall we call them 'friends', to discuss how to address the possible threats resulting from tomorrow's march. I can assure you, if there is a connection to any threat to my Presidency I will do everything in my power to avoid bloodshed. However, I strongly believe that's all I can do for the moment. Unless…" Chávez paused for a few seconds and looked both men straight in the eyes, "…unless, you are able to bring me any additional or more tangible proof that I can act upon. Proof that preferably comes with concrete evidence leading to names."

"And if there's nothing to be found in the short time we have left?" Mitchel asked.

"In that case I guess we'll have our answer by tomorrow evening." Chávez rose from his chair and both José and Mitchel followed suit.

"How do we contact you if needed?" José asked.

"I'll have one of my aides contact you about that." Chávez nodded to José and then pointed to the door they had come in by. "You'll find your way out there. Please, take some fruit with you."

As Chávez left the room, Mitchel and José made their way back to the tunnel's entrance.

"Dinner?" Mitchel asked as they began walking.

161

"Why not," José replied. "Seven at your place?"

14. Who?

Wednesday, April 10ᵗʰ, 2002
8pm

HÁVEZ WALKED INTO THE CONFERENCE room accompanied by Carola Faustina. Back in the day Faustina was the lead attorney for Chávez's defense team, securing his release from prison in 1994 after the failed coup. After she helped Chávez get elected in 1999 she became the brains behind the Bolivarian Circles, a loosely connected political and social network of workers' councils sometimes described as militias. Nowadays, she was more commonly recognized as a loyal 'Chavista' and lawmaker in the National Assembly.

At the table in the center of the conference room, Chávez's trusted friends Badillo, Reyes, Clemente and Peroni were discussing the current situation.

"Thank you for returning here so soon after our last meeting. You all know Carola Faustina?" As Chávez spoke he took his seat at the table, next to Faustina, and those already seated nodded their heads in acknowledgement and welcome. "So, why have I asked you here?

While I cannot give you any specifics at this time, you know full well my concerns about the march tomorrow. Well, I now have strong indications that the march will be used to cause unrest, with possible and extreme violence. I need you to help me think of a way that we can prevent this from happening."

"Do you have any details at all?" General Clemente asked.

"Not much. You all know the basics; Carmona has announced his 'friendly' march from the Francisco de Miranda Park to the PDVSA headquarters. That's about it. So, I'm afraid it's up to you. However, Carola Faustina has brought an idea to my attention and I would like you all to hear it." Chávez looked towards Faustina and nodded.

"Thank you," said the 55-year-old brunette before turning to the others. "As you probably know, a few years ago I helped create the institution of the Bolivarian Circles. I suggest we now use those Circles as paramilitary forces, organizing them into brigades. That way we can mobilize them into the march and break it up before anything has the chance to escalate. A brigade could also be used to surround and defend the palace, if needed, and block all major avenues to the palace."

"An act which might also create an escalation of hostilities in itself," Clemente noted. "You know that the Circles are not equipped to undertake such a mission. And you don't have time to make the preparations you need."

"So, what's your suggestion?" Faustina snapped.

"Plan Ávila."

"Ávila? Ávila?" Faustina cried despairingly. "I don't know if you recall, but Ávila was also designed as a military measure and was last used with disastrous results in '89 when the police and Guardia Nacional were overrun during the riots. The result was a bloodbath in which your men killed at least 277 civilians."

"Implementing Ávila will be a dangerous move," Chávez calmly interrupted. "It gives the military power over the people, something I solemnly promised would never happen. Therefore, should we

164

implement it, we risk dividing the people even further, which may spiral us into civil war."

"It's also unconstitutional," Faustina said. "The constitution clearly states that if an order from a superior officer – going all the way up to the president himself – violates the constitution, that order should not be obeyed. *Maldito el soldado que vuelva las armas contra el pueblo.* Damned be the soldier that raises his hands to the people. Your words by…"

"Bolivar," Chávez interrupted. "Please, don't use my own words against me." The President sighed deeply and rubbed both hands over his face. "Anyone have any other ideas?"

"We need to at least block all the roads to the palace using the Presidential Honor Guard," Reyes suggested. "At the same time, we could organize the Bolivarian Circles into a counter march from the other side of Caracas, as a distraction that might draw people away from Carmona's march."

"But the march doesn't come anywhere near the palace so I'm not sure the palace is the problem," Faustina replied. "I still think the Circles offer the least invasive plan."

"Then what is the problem?" Peroni asked.

"The problem is that we are not sure what the problem is," Chávez responded.

"Then may I offer another suggestion?" Peroni asked politely.

"Sure," said Chávez.

"What if we promise to give out bonuses?"

"Why not? Let's share the spoils of democracy one last time," Clemente said in support and it opened the floodgates to a wave of ideas from around the table, and some increasingly heated discussion.

"Silence!" Chávez banged both hands on the table and everyone shut up in an instant. He looked towards Peroni. "Let's here the man out. Please, proceed."

"Well, I could offer, say, $1,200 for every worker refusing to strike and march. That way we can break the strike peacefully."

"And that would affect how many people, 1,000 or 2,000?" Reyes asked. "It's being predicted that up to 100,000 might be joining the strike so this would be a mere drop in the ocean."

"And as you haven't paid any contribution to the federal bank's treasury, the president of the bank might not look so sympathetically upon future claims that your company is experiencing 'cash flow problems'. Might look a little bit opportunistic, don't you think?"

"All right, all right." Chávez calmed everyone down before tempers started to flare again. "Look, I like Reyes' idea of a counter march on the other side of town." He turned to Faustina. "Do you think you can mobilize the Circles to start such a march?"

"I think I can muster enough people. The march could start from Parque El Calvario in the south and move up to Plaza Bolivar in the north thereby creating a blockade should Carmona's march decide to approach the palace from the east."

"But I have one condition," Chávez said. "No weapons. I want the protesters to be completely unarmed."

"I will issue the order," Faustina assured him.

"I'll mobilize the presidential Honor Guard and issue orders not to fire at anyone until fired upon." Chávez stood up from the table. "I'll also issue a battalion of tanks to be ready at the north side of the city, but they won't roll out until they're absolutely necessary. Thank you for your contributions. I hope you'll stay available. The following 24 hours may very well define the Bolivarian Republic of Venezuela and its democracy for years to come."

In the dark of the evening, the single lightbulb hanging from the ceiling barely lit the walls in Mitchel's war room. In the middle of the center wall he had cleared a space for a street map of Caracas.

Surrounding the map were all the documents and photos collected earlier.

"Still saving on energy costs, I see," José joked.

Mitchel laughed. "You're a funny man. Any news from the palace?"

"His aid contacted me this afternoon. I'm to pick up some kind of radio later this evening. He was also allowed to tell us that the Chavistas will organize their own march in support of Chávez across the Avenida Baralt."

"Show me where that is," Mitchel said turning to the map. José walked to his side and with his finger he drew a line on the map from the north to the south, right in front of Miraflores palace. Mitchel took a pen from the table and marked the path José had pointed out. "And what do we know about Carmona's march?"

"From here," José's finger pointed at the map again. "The Parque del Este Metro station in the north to here, the PDVSA building in Chua."

Again, Mitchel traced the route with his marker. "So Miraflores Palace in the Central district to the west of the city is a long way from the march in the east. That's a lot of city between the two marches."

"About seven or eight miles."

"So, what are they up to?"

"That's the big question."

Mitchel scoured the pictures of the Venezuelan generals, picking out two photos which he pinned above the map, in the middle. "This much we know."

"Valbuena and Rojas." José stepped forward to take another picture from the wall, which he then put next to the others.

"Rout," Mitchel said.

"Indeed, Rout. The three names from the letter you intercepted." José reached for the brown briefcase he had brought with him. "I have something for you," he said, unclipping the clasp and taking out a small stack of brown paper files, which he handed to Mitchel. "Everything we have on Valbuena, Rojas, Rout and even a few others I thought you might be interested in."

"Wow, if only George W. could see us working together now!"

"He'd probably shoot us," José laughed.

"Probably," agreed Mitchel. "So, what do we have here?" Mitchel opened the top file and started to read, mumbling as he did so. "Rojas, Valbuena, ...Velasco? Who is Velasco?"

"Cardinal Ignacio Velasco, Archbishop of Caracas. He's very well known for his anti-Chávez statements."

"And he must have some more friends, I guess?"

"Sure, but that's not why he's included." José's eyes lit up knowing that what he had to say would intrigue his friend. "Over the past few weeks we have spotted Velasco, on more than one occasion, in the company of Rojas and Valbuena, and they were together with...?" José pointed at the stack of files.

"Generals Gallardo and Gomez," Mitchel responded, reading the names of the remaining files.

"And guess what? Yesterday the five of them met with our friend Pedro Carmona, in his office."

"Of all places," Mitchel noted. "But if the DISIP has all this information why doesn't it act?"

"Who says it's in their best interest to act? Relieving Chávez from power doesn't have to be a bad thing for them. A new government, a military government, will probably increase their budgets for years to come."

"So much for loyalty," Mitchel said, taking the portraits of their new suspects from their folders and putting them up against the wall. "Valbuena, Gallardo, Gomez, Velasco and Rojas all leading up to..." Mitchel hung a final picture next to the others, "...Pedro Carmona. I'm still having a hard time placing Rojas. From everything I've read, and from what you've told me, he's always been Chávez's friend, loyal to the bone."

"That's what bothers me too." José nodded thoughtfully. "But maybe he's simply more loyal to Venezuela than Chávez and feels having his friend in power is no longer in the best interests of the country."

"Could be, but for now he seems our logical way in."

"What do you mean, 'way in'?"

"I mean that if we want to try to get more inside information about what's going on, maybe we should talk to him, confront him."

"And how do you suggest we get in direct contact with him?" José looked at Mitchel and the look he returned told him he might not like what he was going to hear. "No, no, not again. How do you expect me to even go about arranging that?"

"That, I don't know. But I have every faith in you."

"Great." José shook his head. "It's not even as if I have enough time to plan something. In less than 24 hours the march will start. And what about the sniper guns? We still haven't figured how they fit into the grand picture yet."

"Correct." Mitchel tapped the picture of a MK14 EBR sniper rifle with his marker pen.

"And then there's Carlos Ortega. His name keeps popping up every now and then." José taped Ortega's picture next to Carmona's. "DISIP doesn't have much on him other than one meeting and several phone calls with Gallardo in the past week. And we still don't know where your countrymen Caldwell and Rout fit into it all either."

"Both of whom I absolutely believe to be involved somehow, probably in planning the whole thing."

As Mitchel and José wracked their brains for possible answers, they started pacing the room, unwittingly mirroring each other, like two tigers confined to a box.

"We have all these facts and yet we still don't have a clue about what their plan is or where and when it will take place," Mitchel said after a short while, sounding disappointed.

"Maybe that's where Ortega and the sniper guns fit in somehow."

"I'm sure of it," Mitchel said, walking over to the map. "The plan has to be based on a confrontation in the streets somewhere."

"But there are more than seven miles between the marches and the palace," José pointed out. "More than seven miles between any kind of confrontation."

"Do you think they'd be able to reroute the march towards the palace? You know the roads out there."

"I think anything is possible," José confirmed. "It wouldn't be the first time a large group of protesters claimed the city and its roads. And once a few hundred thousand people are marching there's very little that can stop them."

"Not even a few snipers?" Mitchel asked.

"I don't believe so. There must be another purpose for the snipers."

"So, we have five, six names and for now there's not much more we can do than get this information to Chávez."

"Including Rojas's involvement?" José asked. "Who knows what Chávez will do when he learns that one of his closest friends is among the conspirators."

"What else can we do?"

"Indeed."

It was a clear evening and a gust of warm air played gently around the balcony of the second floor of the Miraflores palace where Chávez stood overlooking the city's streets. Below him, the Honor Guard were busy placing road barriers along the dimly-lit streets surrounding the palace and erecting sentry posts at the entry points. Chávez was thinking about his own failed coup in '92 against President Carlos Andrés Pérez when he heard a voice behind him.

"Are you worried?" María Gabriela walked onto the balcony and kissed her father tenderly on the forehead.

"You think I should be?" he asked, hoping to avoid giving voice to his own fears that night.

"It doesn't take a daughter to see that you have changed during these past few days. Everybody's talking about it."

"And what are they saying?"

"I think they're becoming afraid of you. I think somehow you always seemed predictable before, but now they're not so sure anymore. That's what frightens people. I guess they like their politicians to be predictable."

Chávez nodded thoughtfully, but his eyes remained hard. "How can I be predicable if the rules keep changing?" he asked. "Maybe I'm still a rebel, like Christ, one of the greatest rebels."

"He ended up being crucified," María Gabriela reminded him.

"True, and if that is to be my fate I will accept it. Unfortunately, I believe that our people are starting to confuse democracy with capitalism. I don't blame them; it's the West and its American backers that feed such thoughts."

"Nonetheless, I think it's becoming dangerous, Papa. The church, the media, the labor unions, business leaders, and many in the military seem to support the strikes and a change of power. Are you sure you want to stay in Miraflores tomorrow?"

"What do you think would happen if they were to replace me? Would they hold new elections or would they appoint a dictator? And who would that be? And what would he be able to do more than I already did?"

"All reasonable questions, Dad, but to be honest I don't think it matters much. I'm worried."

"Don't be, my dearest. As an old paratrooper I still have a large force behind me."

"So did Allende in Chili, and of course you know how the CIA killed his military chief of staff, opening the door for Pinochet, which left him no other option but to kill himself."

"Is that what you're afraid of?" Chávez asked, leaning forward to place his hands on his daughter's cheeks. "I promise you I will not kill myself."

"I know, Daddy, but I'm afraid they'll hurt you or put you away somewhere and I will never see you again."

"I promise I won't let that happen, and in turn I would like you to promise me that you and your sister will leave Caracas for a few days. Go to see the family in Sabaneta."

"I cannot promise you that, Papa."

"Then, I cannot force you, my dear, but having you and your sister here in the city only puts us all at risk. They will touch me only if they hurt you. So please, go." As he embraced his daughter he started to sing the lullaby he had sung so many times before when she was a little girl, and a tear rolled down his cheek.

Duérmete mi niño, que tengo que hacer
Lavar los pañales, darte de comer.
Duérmase mi niño que tengo que hacer
Lavar los pañales y darte de beber.
Ese niño quiere que lo duerma yo
Que lo duerma la madre que lo parió.
Ese niño quiere que lo duerma yo,
lo duerma la madre que lo parió.

Go to sleep, my child, for I've things to do,
To wash the diapers, to give you some food.

Go to sleep, my child, for I've things to do,
To wash the diapers, to give you a drink.
This child wants me to put him to sleep,
The mother who bore him, to put him to sleep.
This child wants me to put him to sleep,
The mother who bore him, to put him to sleep.

15. The March Begins

Thursday, April 11ᵗʰ, 2002

9 a.m.

O N THE EDGE of the Generalissimo Francisco de Miranda Park the highway started to fill with people. The sun was already high and it burned the heads of those gathering with flags, banners and pictures of Hugo Chávez. Many also held placards daubed with catchwords like 'leave', 'murderer', and 'dictator'. The atmosphere was relaxed and most of them were attending with their families, giving the march a picnic feel as mothers shared the contents of the cool boxes they had brought with them. On the edge of the park, volunteers were hurriedly finishing the stage where Carlos Ortega was scheduled to kick off the march in an hour's time.

Mitchel dragged two dining table chairs into the war room and put them in front of the two TV sets he had plugged in. Without saying anything he pointed José to one of the chairs.

"Yes, boss." José smiled as he sat down.

"We might as well enjoy it now that they shut down all the official office branches for the day." Mitchel said while on one TV Mitchel chose a private news channel to watch. On the other he switched to the public national news.

"...The streets in our capital surrounding the Miranda Park are starting to fill with protesters getting ready to march from the park in the north to the PDVSA headquarters, south of the city." On the public TV channel, the footage showed thousands of people lining up, waiting for the signal to start. *"In the studio we have Mayor Freddy Bernal and National Assembly Deputy, Juan Barreto,"* the female anchor announced. *"Mr. Mayor, what do you think about the protest today?"* Bernal gave a small nod as he began to speak. *"To be honest, Sylvia, I think that the people are misinformed by the unions and the private media and Carlos Ortega and Pedro Carmona in particular. These so-called reform plans have no real chance of succeeding. The facts have been twisted to meet their agenda and we have calculated that in reality they will cost the average citizen of our country an average of 5% of their income."*

"So, Mr. Barreto," the presenter said, turning to her second guest, *"what would you tell the people of Venezuela at this time?"*

"Well Sylvia, first I would urge everyone to stay calm. In the past, we have seen how these marches can escalate. Also, I would like to ask everyone who believes in our government, in our leader, to walk with us in a counter protest that will start from the north on Avenida Baralt."

"Yes," Bernal interrupted, *"from there, all Chavistas will start their peaceful demonstration because we believe that the man who gave us 50% less poverty in the past few years will lead Venezuela to even more prosperity. But make no mistake, if necessary we will defend our democracy in any way needed."*

"What are we doing?" Mitchel asked.

"What do you mean?"

176

"I mean, look at them." Mitchel shook his head at José. "I have barely even started my job in this country and somehow I've managed to get myself entangled in a potentially violent coup. How has this become our fight, my fight? I mean, I understand how you'll want to get involved, but me? I came here because I thought I had learned a few things, that I had become wise to things."

"What brings this on?" asked José, the concern etched on his face.

"Last night, I had one of my nightmares again."

"So, what's new?"

"I'm serious." Mitchel snapped at his friend and José was immediately sorry.

"Ok, alright," he said gently. "I apologize."

"I also think that Nathalie and Catherine are starting to suffer from all of this."

"Have they said so?"

"Not as such, but they believe that the way to protect me is to give me room to move. Unfortunately, if there's one thing I've learned from the damn mandatory therapy sessions I've had it's that I can be somewhat impulsive from time to time."

"You think?" José spoke before realizing he was being flippant again, and quickly apologized when he saw the plea forming in Mitchel's eyes.

"Will you please help me and tell me when I've gone too far? Help me so that I won't make the same mistakes again?"

"I would love to help you; you know I would. But I think the underlying problem here is between you and your family. Speak to your wife and daughter if you think they are avoiding talking to you."

"Yes, perhaps you're right," Mitchel agreed, and the two men resumed watching the simultaneous coverage of the marches in silence.

On the edge of the Miranda Park, a lectern and a number of chairs had been placed on the stage, awaiting the dignitaries that would start the march. Above the stage a huge yellow banner read '*A Venezuela no la para nadie* - No one stops Venezuela'.

In front of the stage, a crowd of thousands stood waiting for the head of the labor union, Carlos Ortega, to send them on their way, but there was a carnival atmosphere to the occasion with people beating drums, playing guitars and blowing flutes and trumpets. A large section of the crowd also behaved in a way typically associated with Venezuelan *cacerolazos*; making as much noise as possible by banging pots, pans, and any other utensils they had brought with them from the kitchen. Naturally, as the first dignitaries began to come on stage the cacophony of sounds grew ever louder.

First on stage were the labor union dignitaries, followed by the generals Valbuena, Gallardo and Gomez. Then Cardinal Velasco joined them on stage and they all sat down.

"I still don't feel comfortable showing myself here in public," Gomez shouted in Valbuena's ear, trying to make himself heard over the cheers of the people.

"The point of no return has passed," Valbuena replied coolly.

"Where's Rojas?" Gallardo shouted from his other side.

Valbuena shrugged his shoulders. "And Ortega?"

"Still thinks he's going to be president soon." Gallardo smiled, just as Ortega entered the stage. Walking from one side of the platform to the other, he waved his arms at the crowd and their cheers grew even wilder. After a minute or so, Ortega took his place behind the lectern and appealed for silence.

"My family of Venezuela," he began, "thank you for being here. All of you, as far as I can see, on the left and on the right. There must be hundreds of thousands of you. I thank you." With every short pause for breath that Ortega took, the flutes, drums and *cacerolazos* resumed their noise. Ortega smiled. "Though you party here today, we know it has been a sad time for our country. The past half a year has been rough on us all. In the past six months, our government has proven to us it seeks an elected dictatorship. This must and shall end today. Firing our seven PDVSA officials was the last provocation we were willing to accept. In my hand, I hold a large list of demands that I will personally deliver to our dictator once we reach the end of our march today." Ortega waved a stack of papers above his head. "And I will not leave his palace before he accepts every single one of these demands. I will make sure we all have food in our houses!"

"We want food! We want food! We want food!" the people chanted.

"So now, we march…" Ortega's voice echoed through the large loudspeakers, but the noise was so great the instruction got lost and it took a minute or two for the chanting to subside. Ortega tried again. "We now march to Chuao. In our thousands we will show our dictatorial leader the power of the people of Venezuela. We march!" He then waved both arms up and down in the direction the march was to head in and, slowly, the huge gathering of people started to move, leaving a trail of burning flags showing Chávez's face at the side of the road.

Alone in his office, Chávez watched the newscasts from behind his desk. In front of him sat a stack of newspapers. He had chosen to spend this time alone, like he had always done before going into battle. 'And this is a battle,' he thought. Then, as he looked at the generals on stage, he began to speak aloud. "So, it's you," he said. "Your loyalty never seizes to amaze me."

He picked up a couple of newspapers. One headline read, *"End to the tyranny?"* while another announced, *"Final battle will be in Miraflores."* One by one, he read every headline of every newspaper and then he threw them all to the ground. 'It's a battle all right,' he thought. It was then that he noticed a white envelope that had been lying beneath the stack of newspapers. It was addressed *'To Mr. Chávez.'* Intrigued, the President picked up a sword-shaped letter opener and cut through the envelope. *"Dear Mr. President, I don't know when you might read this so I might be too late. These past few days have been very hard on me. On several occasions when we spoke I had planned to warn you, but I failed. I lacked the courage to tell you that forces beyond yours and my control are conspiring to force you to comply with their demands or maybe even worse. From the inside, I had hoped to be a positive influence on them, but I was unsuccessful. I wish I could have helped you, but there was nothing more I could do. As your loyal servant, and as your friend, I urge you to establish a dialogue with those who oppose you. If there's time I urge you to do so immediately after you read my plea. In time, maybe you can forgive me. I have been and always shall be your friend, Moises Rojas."*

Chávez's eyes fixed fast on the last words. Did his friend also betray him? If his best, perhaps his only comrade through life could do such a thing, what did that say about him. 'Did I change that much?' he asked himself.

"Good thing you didn't sell the bike!" Mitchel shouted as they raced through the city.

"You don't have to shout," José reminded him.

"Sorry, I keep forgetting. Your new helmet radio works excellent, by the way." Mitchel glanced around from the back of the motorbike. "I expected more people on the roads by now."

"They are still at the other end of the city. If they do in fact decide to march all the way up to the palace these roads will be filled with people in an hour or so. So, I guess it's a good thing your embassy closed because of the marches – it gives us the chance to do some sightseeing." José turned off the main street to head towards the White Palace only to find their way unexpectedly blocked by a crowd of

180

Chavistas demonstrating in favor of the government. "I might have spoken too soon," he said as he hit the brakes.

"Now what?" Mitchel asked.

"A few blocks back, we can turn north and avoid the crowd. The crowd will concentrate around Miraflores so we'll have no problem approaching from that side."

José turned his motorcycle and sped away. In the north of the city, the roads remained relatively clear and it took only minutes to reach the White Palace. After parking, they entered the building and made their way straight to the elevator that led to the secret tunnel.

"Abrantes, they're expecting me," José told the soldier guarding the way. The guard passed his finger over a clipboard he held, searching for the name.

"Indeed, you are, Sir." The soldier slotted his key into the elevator panel and a few seconds later the doors opened. As Mitchel approached, the guard stepped in front of him. "Sorry, only Mr. Abrantes is expected."

Mitchel glanced at José.

"It's OK," José nodded. "I'm sure I'll be back soon."

"You can wait over there." The guard pointed to a bench a few yards away. As the doors closed on José, Mitchel walked over to the bench and sat down. He then proceeded to impatiently inspect his watch every passing minute. Just as his mind started to wonder about all the people he saw wandering about the floor – all minding their own, secret businesses – the elevator doors opened and José stepped out carrying a briefcase.

"Everything OK?" Mitchel asked.

"I'm perfectly fine."

"What's that?" Mitchel pointed to the briefcase. José came to sit next to him on the bench and opened it slightly.

"A walkie talkie?" Mitchel asked.

"Shh! Come on, let's go outside." José then hit Mitchel on the shoulder as they made their way out of the building. "Some kind of spy you are," he hissed.

"Well, maybe you should have kept the case closed until we were outside, smartass. Where were you and what's with the antique walkie?"

"The suitcase was handed to me in front of the entrance to the tunnel. I could have stayed inside the elevator, as it happened. The soldier that handed it to me said he was personally ordered by Chávez to hand it over if I appeared. He also told me that Chávez had told him I would know what to do with it."

"And do you?"

"I didn't at first. But when I took another look at the walkie it was numbered CdP-090762. CdP stands for *'Cadena de Depredador'* or 'The Predator Network'. During the Cold War period the predator network was the analog radio system used by all official services in Venezuela. It wasn't super secure, but little was in those days. Of course, now even Venezuela has entered the digital era and replaced all the old stuff."

"So, what will we do with it?" Mitchel asked.

"Well, it's a commonly known rumor that Chávez has kept the system in use for only his most trusted loyalists and friends so that when the shit looks like it might hit the fan he can stay in touch with them. This Russian made stuff always works, no matter what hardship we expose it to. So, I assume we've been given it to make contact with the palace when we have any new information or when the shit...."

"Get Rojas on the line," Chávez demanded, and the operator succeeded in doing so in a matter of seconds.

"General Rojas, Sir."

"Where do you stand?" Chávez asked with no preamble.

"Excuse me, Sir?"

"Where do you stand, now! I need you to tell me where you stand. Can I trust you with an assignment?"

"I want to regain your trust, Sir. Please, tell me what I can do for you."

"What do you know about what's happening today?"

"The only thing I know is that they are planning to divert the march from Chuao to Miraflores."

"And then?"

"From there you will be presented with an ultimatum. That's all I know. I swear," Rojas told him.

"OK, so here's what I want you to do," Chávez instructed, needing to test the loyalty of his old friend. "I want you to deploy a battalion of tanks from our military base in Fuerte Tiuna and send them here to defend Miraflores Palace. I also want you to order a lockdown on Fuerte Tiuna. If I have any friends left they will probably be in that base. So, no-one comes in or goes out until I say so."

"Will do, Sir. I won't let you down again." And with that, Rojas hung up the phone.

In the silence, Chávez thought through the likely scenarios. In the worst case, Rojas wouldn't do as asked and nothing would change. In the best case, the palace and the military base would be defended and safe. Therefore, it was a no-lose scenario, the way he liked it best.

A loud bang on the office door announced the arrival of an adjutant.

"Yes?" Chávez asked.

"Sir, I believe there's something you need to see on television."

16. To Miraflores

Thursday, April 11ᵗʰ, 2002
11:00 am

HE SOLDIER SWITCHED on the television in front of
Chávez's desk and immediately left the office. 'What
now?' Chavez thought. On TV images of the march,
taken from a helicopter, revealed all the streets surrounding Miranda
Park were filled with protesters. People were chanting and expressing
their outrage in burnt flags and tight fists that punched the air. Chavez
glanced at the scrolling text at the bottom of the screen. *"800,000 march
against the oppression. Unconfirmed reports about dead civilians in the
streets of Caracas after pro-Chávez military confronts protesters. First
protesters to reach Chuao in 15 minutes.'*

"Guard!" Chávez shouted from his seat and the door to his office
instantly opened.

"Yes, Sir?"

"Find General Rojas, he should be somewhere in the palace, and
send him to me immediately."

"Will do, Sir."

Once the guard had gone, Chávez dropped his head into his hands and sighed deeply, but there was no peace to be had and within minutes Rojas came rushing into the room, stopping in front of the President with a click of his heels.

"You called me, Sir?" He said clicking his heels

"At ease, General." Chávez rubbed at his forehead, feeling the strain of the day taking its toll. "Do you have an idea what they are talking about when they say there are dead civilians in the streets?"

"I heard the report too," Rojas admitted, "and yet, to the best of my knowledge, there hasn't been one shot fired by our soldiers. Not one. I can only conclude, therefore, that it is the media trying to create a stir. But if the people believe it, it could be dangerous."

"You're right," Chávez agreed, and he got up from his chair to pace the room. "Any ideas?"

"As you know, the media is hard to fight and the only effective weapon we have against them is to shut down their TV stations."

"Which will simply further justify their reasons for calling me a dictator, if I shut down the Press."

"That's true, Sir. In which case, I'm afraid, there's very little you can do to influence the reports coming out, well, coming out of the private media that is."

"I could always increase the *cadena* broadcasts again, leaving no room for them to broadcast their lies." Chávez returned to his desk. "If you truly remain my old friend, I could really use your advice one more time."

"And I would give it if I thought I had any, but more *cadena* broadcasts might be viewed as sabotage so I would keep them to a minimum, if you can. Saying that, I do think the people will want to see you on public television. Many of them will be looking for your guidance; your Chavistas need reassurance that this is going to end well for them."

"I always hated that name," Chávez mumbled.

186

"Chavistas?"

"Indeed. It makes me sound like I'm some kind of religious nut – a cult leader with brainwashed followers."

"Well, that's something we can't do much about right now, but those people who believe in you are out there, right now, demonstrating on your behalf and they need your assurances. Whether you like the name or not, you don't want to risk losing the support of the Chavistas too."

"Again, you're right. I'm planning to go on air shortly. What's happening with the tanks?" As Chávez asked the question, Rojas took a step backwards. "That bad, huh?"

"How do you…?"

"I've known you longer than anyone else. When you have bad news to tell me, you always create more distance between us, like you're afraid or something. So how about those tanks?"

"Almost thirty years, Sir. We've known each other for almost thirty years now. And I have to tell you, the tanks are finding it difficult to leave Fuerte Tiuna. It seems that a number of rebelling officers have begun to block some of the city's main arteries in an effort to prevent troop movement and the mobilization of our supporters."

For a moment, there was silence in the small office. Then, with a small sigh and a nod of his head, Chávez thanked the General for the information. "You can go now," he told him. "Simply do what you can."

"Yes, Sir." And with a click of his heels, Rojas left the room.

As the march circled the perimeter of the airport, located in the center of the city, the first protesters began to reach the headquarters of the PDVSA, where the demonstration was originally planned to end. In front of the building's entrance, a stage was set to welcome the anti-Chávez dignitaries, and one by one government leaders and generals took their place to rally the gathering crowd. Amongst them was Cilia Flores, deputy of the Fifth Republic movement, and José Vicente

Rangel, the Minister of Defense. Both had formerly been extremely loyal Chavistas.

As Ortega and his own supporting generals entered the stage, the growing number of protesters started to cheer.

"So far so good," Valbuena said to Ortega.

"Indeed, but where is Carmona? I expected him here to start this second part of our journey."

"He's expected to join us later," Gallardo answered. "For now, let's enjoy the moment. Look around you."

From the surrounding high-rise buildings people were appearing at windows and balconies to cheer and sing while waving the national colors. With every passing minute, the noise grew louder until the street was so jammed with people they could barely move.

"It's your turn again," Valbuena told Ortega, and he quickly picked up a megaphone and walked to the front of the stage.

Waving an arm to gain the attention of the crowd, he shouted. "Do you think it is enough?" As the protesters grew quieter, he repeated the line. "Do you think it's enough?" He then shook his head. "I don't think it's enough. I say it's time to move on with this march to Miraflores. To Miraflores! To Miraflores! To Miraflores!"

As he chanted, Ortega pointed the way towards Miraflores Palace and everyone on stage shouted their support while waving westwards. On both sides of the street, carefully placed rally speakers took up Ortega's chants until eventually the entire protest had taken up the battle cry.

"To Miraflores! To Miraflores. To Miraflores! With the touch-paper lit, the stewards led the march passed the stage. As Ortega encouraged the crowd, his shouts couldn't scale the wall of noise that met him as the *cacerolazos* banged their drums and pans in time with the chants and the cheers of those watching from their apartments.

"And we're on our way again," he shouted, turning in the direction of the generals.

"Soon it will be over," Gallardo predicted.

"I hope so," Ortega replied.

The headquarters of Venevision – the largest privately-owned TV station and media company in the country – was a safe distance from the uprising in the north of Caracas. Venevision was well-known for its political views; during the last presidential election they devoted 84% of its coverage to Chávez and a mere 16% to the opposition. Inside the main building, company executives, reporters and producers were nervously pacing the hallways and studios as word reached them of the latest direction of the march.

"Girotti! Pedersoli!" An executive shouted across a hallway into an open office workspace. Girotti, a blond man in his late 30s with a big smile, round face and cobalt blue eyes, sat on a desk next to Pedersoli.

"I think we're being summoned," Girotti said.

Pedersoli grunted. In his early 40s, he was a big man with far too many pounds to carry. His head was almost entirely covered with black hair and it hid the hardened, wrinkled face behind it.

Girotti jumped off the desk. "Let's go see what the Chief wants."

As soon as the two men walked into the executive's office they were handed cups.

"Sit down," the Chief ordered, "enjoy your tea."

"He's way too nice," Girotti said aloud, provoking another grunt from Pedersoli.

"You're both Italian, aren't you?" At the question, both men frowned, unsure why their nationality mattered at this point in time. "Let me explain. I have orders from on high to send my most impartial reporters to a specific location to cover the uprising in the city. And since you're both Italian, well, I thought..."

"And where is this location?" Girotti asked.

"In the middle of biggest shit storm, I'd guess," answered Pedersoli.

"No, much better than that," the Chief assured them. "You'll go to the Avenida Urdaneta and Avenida Baralt crossroads and from there you will report anything related to the marches taking place."

"The Llaguno Bridge?" Girotti asked. "I can't see anything newsworthy happening there, but it's your call. Which truck do we take?"

"You don't need a truck. There'll be no live broadcast. You'll tape everything and bring it back here for editing as a backstory to the evening news."

"Great, now we've become the impartial backstory team," Pedersoli grumbled.

"At least we won't get in harm's way," Girotti laughed. He then pointed at the TV screen in front of him "What's that? Turn up the volume, will you?"

On the screen, General Lucio Reyes stood in a TV studio surrounded by other friends loyal to Chávez. "We – General Badillo, General Clemente, Garcia Peroni of the PDVSA and Carola Faustina, lead attorney – represent the military high command as well as leaders of industry and government."

"This is live on all the public TV channels," the Chief informed them.

"Friends of Venezuela," Reyes said, speaking directly into camera. "I appear before you in these troublesome times, standing here to represent all that's fair and decent in our country. Today you will hear and see many stories about what's happening in Caracas. But we are here to tell you that nothing has changed and nothing will change. Although today there are forces at work trying to dissolve our democracy, your chosen leader will not allow this to happen, and we will not allow this to happen. All rumors about what's happening, including the ones that say that our leader has been arrested are false. I can also confirm that our military is solidly in support of our Commander in Chief. Besides a few areas of disturbance, the situation in our country is normal and in a short while our leader will be here to tell you this himself."

"Sure, nothing special's going on today," Pedersoli joked darkly.

"Let it go," Girotti told him. "We'll get our gear and head out."

17. Llaguno Bridge

Thursday, April 11ᵗʰ, 2002
2:00 pm

P EDERSOLI AND GIROTTI stood on the Llaguno Bridge, looking down on an unusually deserted Baralt Avenue. Either side of the road stood blocks of high-rise buildings made up of offices and apartments, yet all was quiet.

"Well, this is exciting," Girotti joked, spreading out his arms to invite his colleague to survey the scene. "No cars and not a single soul in sight."

"Enjoy it," Pedersoli replied. "On a regular day we would need a gas mask by now to survive the smog."

Girotti frowned. "I don't like it. What are we doing here?" he asked before kicking a soda can over the railings. It was so quiet the men heard it clatter on the street 20ft below them.

"Cute," Pedersoli commented before pointing ahead. "Look, let's just do our job. The garage on the corner has a ladder and a flat roof. If we set up over there it will give us a clear view of the bridge and the road below."

Girotti saw the sense of the plan and with a small shrug he picked up his gear and started walking. "You climb up first," he said when they arrived at the garage.

"Why do I have to go first?"

"Because you're heavy and this way when you get stuck half way I can give you a push."

Pedersoli grunted in reply, and despite Girotti's teasing he was on the roof a minute later and setting up a large video camera on a tripod. Once the equipment was ready, Girotti looked through the viewfinder and panned the streets around them. "Do you see that?" he asked, pointing towards the road below the bridge. Pedersoli took out his binoculars.

"It looks like a cordon of uniformed men, police perhaps. The road behind them seems to be blocked with cars. Whoever they are I guess they're not planning to let anyone through."

"Miraflores is some 200 yards behind that line," Girotti stated.

"This could get interesting after all," Pedersoli concluded before scouring the rest of the area for signs of any ensuing confrontation. It didn't take long. "Over there, to your right," he instructed Girotti, who moved his camera in time to catch a small crowd approaching from the north. As they filmed they saw more protestors arrive, slowly gathering on the bridge, armed with picnic baskets, a few banners and musical instruments.

"I gather they are the lazier protesters that don't fancy the long walk up here now the road has been cut off to cars," Girotti said. "I'll shoot some scenes of the empty roads and then..."

"...and then we wait," Pedersoli finished.

"Indeed. We wait."

"Coffee," Nathalie announced as she entered the war room carrying a tray with mugs on it.

194

"Great," José said, throwing her a smile as he turned briefly away from the two TV sets vying for his attention.

"You're a life saver," Mitchel told his wife as she handed him a mug.

"So, how are you doing?" Nathalie asked, eliciting a sigh from both men.

"So far so good, I guess," Mitchel answered as he pointed at the two screens. On the left set, the members of the Bolivarian Circles marched along the streets near Miraflores. Dressed in their leader's favorite blue and red they waved pictures of Chávez while yelling, *"We love Hugo Rafael Chávez Frías our leader, our father, Hugo Rafael Chávez Frías!"* The screen on the right revealed a more chaotic picture, taken from a helicopter, where the ground was carpeted with hundreds of thousands of people swarming through the streets like ants in an ant farm.

"A lot of people are on the move," José said. "But so far everything seems calm enough. A few broken windows and flipped cars, but that's about it."

"So, that's good news, isn't it?" Nathalie asked.

"It's going to be a long day," Mitchel replied.

"Then, I'll leave you pessimistic boys alone in your man cave," she said as she walked towards the door. "If you need anything, I'll be here the entire day. You won't see me out there today."

"Thanks, dear. Good idea staying inside. Catherine still in her room?" Mitchel asked.

"She is; sulking. She wanted to go to a friend's house but..."

"It's for her own good," Mitchel said. "I don't expect it to be this calm outside for much longer."

"You think we're safe here?"

"I'm sure of it," José told her, thinking it might sound more convincing coming from him rather than her husband. "We are miles away from the marches and well tucked away in the park with no points of interest nearby. No-one's going to come here. Trust me."

"Trust us," Mitchel added smiling.

"I do. You behave now," Nathalie told them, and left the room.

"What do we do now?" José asked. "Or rather, what can we do now?"

"We can try one thing, I guess."

"Which is?" José looked at Mitchel who picked up his cell phone and started punching numbers. Putting the phone on speaker he crossed a finger in front of his mouth silencing José.

After a few seconds, a voice was heard. "Turner."

"Charles, it's James Mitchel, how are you?"

"All's great here. But how are you over there? I've been thinking about you. I hear you're having quite a day of it."

"We are indeed. There's a lot of ruckus going on in the streets, but so far no big incidents."

"Are you in the neighborhood of the disturbances? Are you and your family safe?"

"Yes, we are safe. No problems in that regard."

"So, what can I do for you."

"Well, I was just wondering if you had heard anything relating to today."

"Not really, no. There was one rumor going around that the religious leaders of Caracas took sides with the opposition."

"Including Velasco," Mitchel responded.

"Correct. The Cardinal has rarely missed an opportunity to criticize Chávez's policies in the past, and Velasco has been seen with quite a few of the opposition recently. Chávez called him an outlaw, a criminal and immoral."

"So why would he be of interest to the US?" Mitchel asked.

"I can think of a few reasons, but that's really for you to find out," Turner said. Mitchel looked at José who shrugged his shoulders.

196

"You're going to let me figure it out by myself? Even with the clear threat there is? Even taking our past into consideration?"

For a moment there was silence and Mitchel and José stared at the phone in anticipation. Eventually Turner began speaking again.

"The obvious reason, of course, is the people of Venezuela. If the Church endorses a change of government it would make for an easy transition."

"That one we had figured out by ourselves," Mitchel interrupted.

"Do you want to hear what I think?" Turner snapped.

"Sorry, please continue."

"The other reason I can think of, with regard to any possible US involvement, is that if there is a sudden change in government in Venezuela, the Bush administration cannot endorse it if it looks like a coup in a democratic country. And if they can't endorse the government, then there's no cheap oil. They could, however, endorse it if it isn't a coup and what better way to show the world it's not a coup than with a blessing from the church?"

"Thank you," Mitchel said.

"And you're on your own now, kid. Though I'm curious about the outcome of anything going on over there, I don't want to know what you're planning on doing. Still, I wish you and your friend, I guess, all the best."

"Thanks, again. I hope we see each other soon."

As the line went dead, Mitchel pressed heavily on the 'End Call' button of his phone just to be sure the connection was severed. "So, that solves any unclarity about Velasco."

"It sounded very plausible," José confirmed. "So, what do we do now?"

Before Mitchel could answer, the footage on both TV sets was interrupted by a national broadcast. Standing behind his desk, in front of the portrait of Bolivar, Chávez held Bolivar's sword in his hand as he spoke.

"People of our great nation. Today you march for what you believe is right, right for this country, right for you. And you have that right; the right to demonstrate and express yourself is firmly stated in our constitution. Peaceful demonstrations are our way of life. But I know that unfortunately there are forces at hand that want to use these demonstrations in another way." On the TV tuned into the privately-owned TV station, Chávez disappeared and a cartoon took his place. On the TV that was tuned into the public broadcasting channel Chávez continued to speak.

"What's that all about?" Mitchel asked.

"Looks like the private media has decided whose side to take," José replied, frowning as he did so.

"So, what should we do with the information about Velasco?"

"Nothing. Chávez already saw him on stage at the beginning of the march. Add that to the fact that he didn't trust him anyway and our information won't change anything." José looked at his watch. "Damn, I need to go. I need to check in."

"Now?"

"Yes, now. I have a job that requires me to check in from time to time. We're different from the US embassy dorks that get a day off every time a soldier breaks wind."

"I'll go with you."

"Now why would you do that? You need to stay here with your family. They need you."

"I know they need me, but what kind of a friend would I be if I were to send you outside today on your own?"

"A good friend. I'll drive around all the excitement and I'll be back here in a few hours."

"You better be."

"I will. Thanks, friend."

On Baralt Avenue, Chavez's voice could be heard in the distance, blaring from loudspeakers set up in the grounds of the palace.

"Are you taping this?" Pedersoli asked while looking through his binoculars.

"Taping what?" Girotti asked, glancing at the empty street below him. "So far there's a small group of people having a picnic on the bridge, below which a few others are doing their daily grocery shopping. There's nothing else to see. Not much of a story here. Sound?"

"Running. I guess the empty streets with Chávez's voice in the distance could make a decent background story."

"Wait! Look there!" Pedersoli waved towards the north of Baralt Avenue where the counter-march of the Bolivarian Circles could be seen advancing."

"So, they are coming through here. Finally we'll get to see some action." Pedersoli smiled before a loud bang suddenly drained the color from his cheeks. "Gunshot?"

"Don't know," Girotti replied. "But it sure sounded like it."

Bang, bang, bang, bang, bang.

Another five shots followed and the small gathering on the bridge began to panic. In the confusion, it was impossible to say where the shots were coming from and people ran for shelter behind the bridge's solid walls.

"Make sure we're taping this!" Pedersoli yelled as more shots rang out. "Is it the police or the Honor Guard or whoever it was that you saw at the end of the street earlier?"

"It could be the Honor Guard, but I don't think so. They are still too far away and the gunshots seem to be coming from the top of the surrounding buildings."

"Shouldn't we get out of here?" Pedersoli shouted, now fighting to be heard over the screams of the people below.

"If the shots have come from the rooftops we are pretty safe here as long as we keep our heads down," Girotti assured him. "Walking the streets would be far more dangerous right now."

Through his camera lens Girotti followed an old man running along the road, below the bridge, with two younger men, possibly his sons. A second later a gunshot was heard and the man collapsed. The two younger men swooped down to shake the fallen man's shoulders. As more shots were fired, they grabbed him by the arms and dragged him under the bridge to safety. Meanwhile, all about them, more and more people fell to ground, writhing in agony as they were peppered with bullets. On the bridge a number of people, apparently carrying arms, began to take turns firing into the street with no real understanding of where they were aiming for.

"Does everybody in this blasted country carry a gun?" Pedersoli screamed.

"It's perfectly normal to carry a gun over here!"

"Now you tell me?" Pedersoli pressed down on the rooftop, praying it would swallow him up. "What are they shooting at?"

"The people shooting at them! Looks like it's coming from the rooftops, but a very long way from here."

"Snipers?" Pedersoli cried out. As the men on the bridge emptied their magazines in the vague direction of their assailants, an increasing number of people were still getting shot beneath them as they scurried for safety or tried to drag the injured out of harm's way. In the commotion, the Honor Guard crossed the cordon they had set up and moved up the street, firing teargas into the fleeing crowds.

"What are they doing?" Pedersoli shouted.

"I guess they also don't know what's happening so they are trying to clear the streets."

"Did you get that?" Pedersoli asked, pointing at some graffiti painted on the wall of the bridge which read '*Pena es de la CIA*', 'Pena is with the CIA'.

200

"Who's Pena?" Girotti asked

"Alfredo Pena, the Mayor of Caracas. He was a Chavista until he joined forces with the opposition."

"Never a good move."

On the street below them, the two men could see people starting to vomit from the effect of the teargas. Among the chaos, a policeman tried to pick up a wounded girl only to be shot in the process.

"What a mess," Pedersoli said to himself, all the while the shooting continued.

"What are we doing here? Shouldn't we somewhere near the Palace?" General Gomez asked.

"The Venevision headquarters is as close as we can get," General Gallardo answered.

"Besides, from this room we have a good view of the streets surrounding the palace and we also have updates from all the news channels," added Valbuena.

Gomez shrugged. The conference room on the top floor of the Venevision tower did indeed give a good view of the streets below, while a bank of TVs on the opposite wall broadcast the coverage of every network in the country.

"Where are Carmona and Ortega? Won't they be joining us?" Gomez asked as he paced the room, occasionally glancing out of the window.

"Yes, where are they?" Cardinal Velasco also wanted to know.

"Carmona will join us later," Gallardo answered, "and Ortega is still leading the march."

"And Rojas? Still no word from Rojas?"

Gomez's nervous tone clearly irritated Gallardo and he barked his reply with undisguised irritation. "We must assume he's back with Chávez."

"But that would mean Chávez knows everything." Gomez stopped pacing the room and slumped into a nearby chair."

"Stop panicking, man." Valbuena turned in his direction. "It really doesn't matter."

"Doesn't matter? Doesn't matter? He could have told Chávez everything by now and you say it doesn't matter?"

"No, it doesn't." Valbuena turned Gomez's chair to face him. He then placed his head just a few inches from the panicking general's. "It doesn't matter because I firmly believe that Rojas will be careful with whatever he says. He knows that one wrong word could cost him his life. Furthermore, it really doesn't matter what he says because it's simply too late. It won't change a thing. Everything that's set in motion is irreversible. The march can't be stopped, a confrontation near the palace is imminent and there's no-one left for him to call for help. The only thing he can now do is wait."

"The same as us," the Cardinal added.

"Look, it's started." Gallardo turned up the volume on one of the screens. The scrolling banner below the presenter read, '*Unarmed opposition demonstrators in the streets shot and killed by Chavistas.*'

The news anchor fiddled with an earpiece before saying "*More news coming in from the White Palace grounds.*" The scene then switched to the park where people could be seen setting up first aid posts. The camera panned to a reporter. "*More dead and wounded are being brought here in search of help. As you can see behind me, more and more tents are being put up. With hospitals virtually unreachable by protesters still filling the streets, more and more people are being brought here. This first aid post was originally intended for protesters with minor injuries, heat stroke and such, but instead people are turning up with gunshot wounds.*"

"*Do we know who the shooters are?*" the anchor asked from the studio.

"Well, eyewitnesses claim not to have seen the shooters, but they believe the shots were fired from the direction of Miraflores Palace, which would suggest it is the presidential Honor Guard that has fired upon the unarmed protesters, presumably in an attempt to avoid the march reaching the palace."

"Thank you for your report. We'll come back to you later." The anchor returned to the screen and looked directly into the camera. *"We are just getting word that we have reporters on location who have footage of what happened. As soon as we have the material ready to go in the studio we'll present it to you."*

"It has started," Gallardo said, trying to hide the smile on his face as the men turned away from the TVs to look out of the window and onto the streets below. At the height they were at, the only indication of trouble they could clearly see were the plumes black smoke, presumably from car tires the protesters had set fire to.

"It must be hell down there," Gomez said, and Velasco suggested they might all want to pray.

18. The Edit

Thursday, April 11th, 2002
5.00pm

A S THE SUN BEGAN TO SINK below the gable, Pedersoli and Girotti sat on the garage rooftop packing away their gear. The streets below and around the bridge were empty. In the distance, every now and then, a gunshot could be heard – the only indication that violence still troubled the city – but in many ways it sounded like an aftershock rather than a continuation of the nightmare that had visited them.

"This is really creepy," Pedersoli said, climbing down the ladder.

"What is?" Girotti asked.

"The silence. It's as if nothing ever happened. It really creeps me out."

"You're absolutely right. Let's head back as fast as we can," Girotti urged, trying to keep his eyes from the blood-stained asphalt that was now the only proof that something dreadful had happened during the past few hours.

On their return to the office, Pedersoli and Girotti were greeted by their boss at the main entrance to Venevision's headquarters.

"There you are. We were getting worried. What happened? Are you OK?"

"Thanks for your concern, Chief," Girotti grunted.

"You can give the tapes to him," the chief said, turning to an aide at his side. "He'll take them up to the editing suite. We're on the air in thirty."

"We better hurry then. Which studio do you want us?" Girotti asked.

"That's the thing, guys. We don't need you at montage. You deserve some rest. Take the rest of the day off. We have a team upstairs perfectly capable of editing this piece."

"That's the thing, Chief," Pedersoli snapped back, "we tend to take care of our raw material. We don't just hand over our babies to anyone."

"You know we got shot at, a lot, to get you this?" Girotti added.

"OK then, let me tell you something." The Chief rubbed at the vein throbbing at the side of his forehead. "You shot this material on the instruction of Venevision, which means we now own it and can do whatever we want with it. You sold your babies, men."

Pedersoli and Girotti looked at each other.

"If you think that…"

Girotti put his hand over Pedersoli's mouth before he could finish and pulled him away

"It's useless," Girotti hissed. "We all know how the news is made."

"What's with that man?" Pedersoli grumbled. "If he thinks that he can handle us like this he's in for a surprise."

"Let's just accept his generous offer and go have a drink somewhere."

"Only one?"

Girotti slapped his friend good-naturedly on the back and, resigned to the fact that their hands were tied, they handed over their bags and left the building. Four floors higher, up in the conference room, the conspirators were still watching the news.

"The palace." Gomez pointed to the screen where the marchers could be seen arriving at the corner of Avenue Urdaneta and Tenth Avenue. On Tenth, the road was closed by the Honor Guard standing both in front of and behind the palace fences.

"Where are the counter-protesters?" Gallardo asked.

"They must have been dispersed by the march." Valbuena walked up to the screens. "There's not one of them left. Everywhere you look now you see our protesters. There must be over a million."

The door to the room suddenly burst open and Cardinal Velasco entered, stealing everyone's attention as the door banged shut behind him.

"I just heard there was a big shoot out near the Llaguno bridge," the Cardinal informed them breathlessly. "Dozens of casualties and deaths have been reported."

"Must have been those damn Chavistas," yelled Gallardo, banging his fists on the table.

"I seriously doubt that," the Cardinal responded, the anger evident in his flushed cheeks.

"What do you mean?" Gomez asked.

"What I mean is that I heard that the shots were fired from the rooftops using high caliber rifles. While I know everybody in Caracas seems to carry a weapon, high-powered rifles are not very common. And besides, the Chavistas were protesting in the street, not on the rooftops. There's something suspicious about all of this. So, what's going on?"

The Cardinal turned his steely gaze on Valbuena and Gallardo.

"Yeah, what's going on?" Gomez demanded, clearly confused.

Valbuena tilted his head towards Gallardo.

"It's your call," Gallardo told him.

"What's your call?" Gomez asked, the unease catching in his throat as he approached the two generals.

Valbuena took a deep breath, looked up to the ceiling for a second and then sat down at the table. "All right, please sit." Once everyone found a chair he continued. "Remember we told you we were convinced that our plan would succeed? Well at that time we were almost certain it would."

"Who's we?" Gomez asked and Valbuena glanced again at Gallardo.

"The two of us," Valbuena replied softly. "Just the two of us. Anyway, since this is a one-time opportunity we had to make sure there wasn't any room left for failure."

"So, you had shots fired at civilians?" the Cardinal asked.

"Are you totally out of your mind?" Gomez half-screamed, his face turning red as he clasped his hands to his cheeks. "What the fuck have you done?"

"What we have done is made sure you got what you wanted," Gallardo told him icily.

"And did you not think there would be an investigation into what happened, into how the violence started? And what do you think will happen if we fail in the end?" Gomez raised both fists towards Gallardo.

"First of all, we will not fail," Valbuena insisted. "And second, any investigation carried out will be carried out by us."

"Which means, we're pretty sure what the outcome of any investigation will be," Gallardo informed them.

"But we agreed to keep casualties to a minimum, with preferably none," the Cardinal protested, glancing at Gomez who had lowered his fists to place his shaking head between his hands again.

"That's exactly what we did," Gallardo said.

"You're absolutely nuts."

Gomez stood up from the table and left the room, slamming the door shut behind him. As Valbuena rose from his seat to fetch him back, the Cardinal stopped him.

"Let him go," he said, and Valbuena paused. "There's nothing you can do for him right now and there's nothing he can do to make matters worse."

Acknowledging the sense of his words, Valbuena returned to the table.

"So, congratulations, gentleman," the Cardinal said, his voice dripping with sarcasm. "You have managed to alienate the first two co-conspirators."

"My fellow citizens, men and women of Venezuela, a very good afternoon."

Surrounded by lights, cameras and monitors Chávez sat behind his desk flanked, as ever, by the portrait of Simón Bolívar and the Venezuelan flag. On a monitor, the live broadcast could be seen together with a banner at the foot of the screen reading, *"This is a special broadcast from the Ministry of Information and Communication."*

"As always, here I am in the government palace of Miraflores, for you. As always, here in the palace, we are taking our responsibilities seriously. I come to you via this special radio and television broadcast to send a message to all of you, my fellow Venezuelans. I direct this message to all of you, and especially I ask God that the small number of Venezuelans who are also our countrymen, but who do not want to hear, who do not want to see, who do not seem to want to accept the reality, also listen." From his desk, Chávez picked up a large leather bound Bible and waved it in front of the camera. "I use the name of God to begin this message because with His help, His guidance, and His illumination we can still make it. So, with this invocation and His spiritual guidance, I want to begin this message. For more than three years now the whole country has borne witness to the huge endeavor this government has undertaken with dignity. In 1999, when we started, we had a difficult year, but even in fiery political debate we have always been constructive. Our Constitutional Assembly was elected and later endorsed by referendum, the people came out, and from then on every sector of the country was able to participate in the national debate. We never disrespected anyone. No one was ever ignored and everyone exercised their rights to express themselves: political groups; individuals; economic and social groups; religious groups; nongovernmental organizations and anyone else in the country I may have forgotten. Everyone gave their opinions and the majority always decided in a democratic way, the Bolivarian way."

As Chávez talked he was handed several slips of paper, updating him on the situation outside of the palace. If the contents caused him concern, he somehow managed not to show it.

As Catherine walked down the stairs, on her way to the kitchen, the doorbell rang.

"Will you get that, dear?" Nathalie called from upstairs.

"Sure, if I can't go out you can always use me as a servant," Catherine grumbled and made her way to the door. As she opened it she saw José taking off his helmet. "I see they let you out," she joked and José frowned in confusion.

"Excuse me?"

"Oh, nothing. Come on in. You know they are holding me hostage here? They won't let me go out to see my friends. It's too dangerous, they say. What do you think?"

"Well, most of the city seems quiet enough..."

"You see!" Catherine shouted towards the staircase.

"I'm afraid that's not everything," José told her. "There are reports of violence and gunfire in the streets in the northwest. I just tried to get to work, but the streets were filled with people. There's no getting through."

"I hate not being able to go outside," Catherine continued to complain, tugging at her hair as she did so.

"I understand that, but it will be only for a day or two. You'll see."

"Is that you?" Mitchel called out from the top of the stairs.

"Who's you?" José shouted back while winking at Catherine who managed to give him a small smile.

"Smartass," Mitchel said. "Come up here."

Before walking up the stairs, José took Catherine in a bear hug before patting her on the head.

"You take it easy, young lady. Your time will come soon enough."

José then walked to the foot of the stairs, glancing upwards to find Mitchel waiting for him.

"That was fast. How did it go at work?"

"It didn't go," José responded with a shake of his head. "There was no getting through. The streets near the government center are completely blocked. Nothing is getting through there."

"Good thing we have television then," Mitchel said and the two of them headed back into the war room.

"So, anything good on TV?"

"Have a coffee first," Mitchel said, handing him a thermos and a mug.

"Thanks."

"So, what have you missed? Well, your president is now on all channels declaring how he, with a little help from God, has been working on your wellbeing throughout the democracy."

"I can see," José confirmed, looking at the two TV screens both showing Chávez preaching from behind his desk. "As long as Chávez is speaking the TV stations aren't allowed to show anything else."

"He's hijacking the airwaves," Mitchel concluded.

"Correct. And in theory, he could go on for hours."

"Well, if you're ever bored, I'm taping it all." Mitchel pointed at a large stack of video cassettes next to the TVs. "Both channels. You want to watch some TV with me?"

"Of course," José said and he settled into a chair to watch Chávez deliver his message, over and over again, in varying word formations.

"In '99 we started the Constitutional Assembly and the beginning of this peaceful, tolerant, open, democratic, constructive, in no way destructive, revolution. It was a revolution of love, and dreams for our future generations, to enable us to climb back from the tragedy the country had fallen into, especially for the weakest and the poorest of our society. To do that we needed, and still need, everyone – everyone from every class, from the middle classes, the lower classes and the upper classes. I've said it countless times before, Venezuela will be a great country for all classes."

As the camera zoomed out, a small gathering of dignitaries could be seen standing next to Chávez's desk.

"Who are they?" Mitchel asked.

"I guess Chávez wants to show that he still has some powerful allies. I recognize the lead attorney Faustini, Chief of the PDVSA Peroni and the Generals Badillo, Clemente and last, but not least Moises Rojas."

"Rojas?" Mitchel jumped up from his chair and walked to the wall towards Rojas' picture. "What the hell is Rojas doing there?"

"Maybe he's undercover," José smiled.

"And he'd risk being exposed? You really think so? Chávez knows about his involvement."

"Sure, we told him. So, either Rojas told Chávez everything and returned to the fold or Chávez is using him as a show of strength even though he might still be a mole for the opposition."

"Another riddle," Mitchel said.

Suddenly, on the TV tuned into the private channel the screen split in two. While on the left side Chávez continued his speech, the sound was muted. On the right side, images from the massacre at Llaguno bridge were broadcast.

"What's that?" Mitchel asked softly.

"This right in," a voice over announced. "While today was meant to be a day of peaceful demonstrations we now regret to inform you that up to a hundred people were severely injured and more than a dozen of people were killed in the streets of Caracas today by Chavista guns. We must warn you about the graphic nature of the following footage."

"What now?" José asked.

"This could be it." Mitchel moved his chair closer to the screen as the footage filmed by Pedersoli and Girotti was shown. At first there was nothing but empty streets until a small crowd of people began to gather below the bridge. The scene then cut to the civilian Chavistas on the bridge, hiding and shooting in turns. People, young and old, could clearly be seen falling as the streets turned red. As others ran to help the injured, they too were shot.

"Oh my God," Mitchel muttered.

"This is a disaster." José rubbed his hands over his face. "All those people. Why?" On the TV, people were now being shown trapped below the bridge while, from the west, a police cordon moved up the street firing smoke and teargas.

"Those people are trapped down there. This is a seriously well-coordinated action," Mitchel said. "If anyone might have still been looking for an excuse to start a local war, here they have it."

"I cannot believe Chávez would order such a thing. Not with civilians," José said, forcefully rising from his chair, sending it falling backwards with a clatter. "This is all the proof the opposition needed."

While Chávez continued to speak on the left-hand side of the screen the image on the right switched to the parks surrounding the neighborhood where all the wounded were being brought for first aid treatment. There was a constant flow of people on stretchers lying beneath bloody sheets. Chávez – still on split screen – was handed another slip of paper. At that same moment, the split screen changed into a full image of the tragedy.

"Now they have cut him off completely," José said.

"I guess this was all the proof they needed. He still continues on the public channel. Turn the volume up."

After reading the latest notification, Chávez fell silent for a few seconds. When he began to speak again, his voice was heavy with emotion.

"A disaster has hit our capital. While our democracy gave everyone the space for peaceful demonstrations, the same people that want you to believe I'm the devil, have created death and chaos on our streets. I don't know what happened, but I assure you I will find those who are responsible…"

"What else can he say?" Mitchel asked cynically.

"You don't believe him? After everything we found out?"

"To be honest, I don't know what to believe. You've seen the evidence."

"Evidence can be tampered with," José stated fiercely. "We know Venevision is one of the greatest supporters of the opposition so… Can we watch the footage again?"

Mitchel walked up to the VCR and rewound the tape. On the screen the bloodbath played backwards to when the streets were peaceful and empty. Both men sat in complete silence as they then watched the video again and again and again, scrutinizing every second of the tape.

"Nothing, I don't see it," Mitchel said as José gave a big sigh.

"One more time, please."

"Sure," Mitchel said. As the footage played over, Mitchel walked up to the wall, looking at the photographs as the sounds of screams filled his ears.

"Wait a second," Mitchel said a minute or so into the video. "Here." He handed José the remote before walking back up to the wall, facing away from the screen. "Rewind for me, all the way to the beginning, with the empty streets."

Once again, the footage played. When the first shot rang out, Mitchel asked his friend to rewind and play again.

"Yes boss, one more time coming up. What is it you're hearing?"

"Shh," Mitchel pleaded. With closed eyes, he tilted his head to the ceiling. "Did you hear it?" he said after a minute.

"Hear what?" José asked, completely baffled.

"Here, give me that." Mitchel reached for the remote in José's hand. "What do you think I've been doing these past few hours?"

"Uh, watching television?"

Mitchel walked up to the second screen and looked through the stack of video cassettes next to it before selecting a tape.

"Well, yes, I have been watching television," Mitchel confirmed. "For the past few hours I've been watching television and watching Chávez going on and on, mostly repeating himself, but…" he waved the video tape in front of José's face.

"What the hell are you talking about, man?"

"Ok, one more time. Tell me what you hear." Mitchel played the tape again from the beginning.

"Empty streets and then shots?" José tried as Mitchel stopped the video after a minute.

"You're not listening, you're still looking. Close your eyes." Again, Mitchel played the tape.

"People talking, it's indistinct, not clear," José said, trying to make sense of what he could hear with his eyes closed. "There are birds, speakers with Chávez in the background…"

"That's it, that's it." Mitchel's voice rose a pitch.

"Chávez in the background?"

"Yes, that's it! Now listen, listen again to what he's saying in this next part." Mitchel fast forwarded to the part where the Chavistas were shooting from the bridge. "Listen good. In between the shots."

"Um, something about God helping him in his quest for a better Venezuela."

"Ok, now listen to this." Mitchel fast forwarded to the part where the first man was shot in the street.

"Democratic election, 1999, reforming government," José repeated.

"Ok, and the last part of the film, where the wounded are getting aid in the park."

"Not sure, it's very hard to hear, but there's something about dark forces trying to undermine his work. Look, are you going to tell me what's going on?"

"Sure, give me a second." Mitchel walked up to the VCR and replaced the tape. "Be quiet for a minute," he said while constantly rewinding and fast forwarding. "610, 712, 813," he mumbled, then after a few more seconds had passed, "alright. Here we go."

"I can't wait."

"Now, listen to the next part of Chávez's speech number one," Mitchel said as he pressed play.

"Democratic election," José said, excitedly giving his answer as though he were a contestant on a gameshow.

"Correct." Mitchel fast forwarded to the second part.

"God's help in his quest."

"Correct again. And now for the last part."

"Oh, that's a difficult one," José said playfully. "Uh, uh, dark forces!"

"Correct again. That's three in / out of three."

"What did I win?" José asked.

"The truth, my friend. Don't you get it yet?"

"Sure, I do. You found the corresponding parts to the happenings in the street."

"And?"

"And?" José said starting to get irritated.

"They're in the wrong sequence! I just played you the three items in the correct sequence. Which means…"

"Which means that the footage shown is in the wrong sequence."

"Yup. In the correct sequence it would show that a number of minutes past between the first man falling to the ground and the people shooting from the bridge."

"Which means someone else took the first shots."

"The people firing into the streets from the bridge where reacting to someone else shooting."

Mitchel switched tapes again and played back the TV footage of the people on the bridge firing. "Look. What are they firing at?"

"It's hard to see, but it could well be that they are not firing into the street but higher up."

"They're firing at the buildings, not at the people below. That's just a suggestion added by the montage."

"God dammit," José cursed as everything suddenly became clear. "The sniper rifles!"

"The sniper rifles," Mitchel repeated.

"My god. What do we do?" José asked.

"It's your president, but if I were you I think I would like to get this information to him."

José looked at him frowning.

"Your antique radio. Call him," Mitchel urged.

"The predator network."

"Ok, yes. That sounds way better."

"If only your spoken Spanish was as good as your understanding." José joked. "I'll give him a call."

Across the street from the Venevision building, Pedersoli and Girotti propped up the bar inside a local restaurant. Behind the bar, their footage played continuously on a TV screen as various people from the studio made comment, more often than not, castigating the acts of a dictator, accusing the President of denying any form of free speech and of slaying all resistance.

"There goes our background story," Girotti said. "It just got edited into a commercial for some kind of civil war."

"Should I say it?" Pedersoli asked.

"Sure."

"I told you so."

19. The Palace Siege

Thursday, April 11th, 2002
7 pm

"**N**OTHING?"

"Absolutely nothing."

José walked around the gardens surrounding Mitchel's house waving his large, portable radio high and low while clicking the talk button on and off. Nothing, but static sounded from the device.

"I thought these vintage devices always worked?" Mitchel sneered.

"It must be the distance."

"So, how do we get the evidence to Chávez? Do we go closer?"

"We can try, but it could be dangerous on the streets. I couldn't get near the palace earlier and the riots have only gotten worse since then."

"If distance is the problem we might not need to get too close to the palace. It could be enough to get just a little closer. If we take the

Ducati you can drive and I can try getting the radio to work from the buddy seat."

"It's worth a go, I guess, but at the first sign of trouble we head back. I don't want to get into a fight with Nathalie."

"Speaking of Nathalie… You start the engine, I'll be right there." Mitchel walked up to and through the open front door, shouting to his wife, "Honey, I'll be going out for a moment."

"And just where do you think you are going?" Nathalie replied, hurrying to the door. "Are you nuts? What are you going to do?"

"We need to get the evidence to the palace, but the radio signal doesn't stretch to Miraflores so we need to try to get a bit closer to get it to work. Don't worry, dear. At the first sign of trouble we'll head back immediately."

"You promise?"

"I promise. Now give me kiss." As Mitchel grabbed his wife's head between his hands to give her a firm kiss, he heard José's motorbike roar into life outside. "Don't worry, I'll be back in a bit."

"You better be," Nathalie replied, wagging her finger to show she was serious.

Mitchel flashed a reassuring smile before turning away. Walking up to the bike, José reached out to hand him the predator radio and a helmet.

"Thanks, but I'll leave the helmet off for now since I need to use the radio while driving."

"All right then, I'll leave mine here also so we can talk while on the move. Let's go."

"What route are you going to use to get us closer?" Mitchel asked as the Ducati pulled away.

"I'll try the Autopista Fajardo and then move west to try to approach the palace from the south."

"Ok."

As the motorcycle circled the botanical gardens Mitchel noticed how empty the streets were with not a single car, bicycle or pedestrian in sight. On the fence of the gardens, sat a small group of brightly colored parrots that served to assure him there was at least some kind of life in the city. Still, the silence around them was almost eerie and it reminded him of the post-apocalyptic horror stories he liked to read. In fact, the more he looked around him, the more he felt he was in a true-life horror story.

After a few miles on the autopista, José pointed into the distance towards pillars of smoke rising up from behind a number of tall buildings.

"I see it," Mitchel confirmed and clicked the radio. "Still nothing."

"No problem. It looks like we can get a little closer without any trouble. In other news, I've just discovered the upside to all this."

"Which is?"

"It's 7 pm and I'm driving 70 miles an hour on one of the most crowded highways in Venezuela."

"Always the optimist," Mitchel joked and José opened the throttle of his bike.

As they accelerated Mitchel had a hard time holding on to José with one arm while holding the radio in the other, but after turning right José brought them to a halt in the middle of the empty road. Mitchel played with the radio again and shook his head.

"That's strange," José said. "The palace is less than a mile up there to the north. The radio should easily cross that distance."

"Can we get any closer?"

"I don't think so," José replied and he walked to the roadside. "Look, over there," he said pointing to the road below them.

"Oh my God," Mitchel gasped as he came to his friend's side. In the distance a huge swathe of people could be seen covering every inch of asphalt and pavement. "There must be hundreds of thousands."

"I'd say so. And if they're up here then you can bet your life that every street between here and Miraflores looks the same."

"Hmm," Mitchel replied, nodding his head in agreement. "So, why won't the radio work? Are you sure it isn't broken?"

"I'm sure the radio works so I don't have a clue what's going on. But there's little we can do here. Home?"

To José's surprise, Mitchel shook his head. "You said this predator network was based on old school, Cold War technology. Soviet technology?"

"Probably Soviet, yes. And I don't like it one bit when you talk like that. You're up to something, aren't you?"

Mitchel kept his counsel for a moment as he tried to work through a few points in his head.

"See," José said despairingly, "you're up to something."

"Pear."

"What?"

"Pear," Mitchel repeated. "Remember my first day at the embassy? I told you about the tour I got. They name all their public rooms after fruit. 'Pear' is the name of the old communications room. It's now a copy room, but it was once the domain of listeners snooping in on the Venezuelan airwaves, in the good ol' days."

"And where are you going with this, exactly?" José asked a little impatiently as he eyed the swarms of people not so very far away. "We need to get out of here."

"Ok, one second. In the Pear room all the original devices – radios, tape recorders and more – were kept in their original state. Well, a radio doesn't depend on anything but power, does it?"

"I think I see where you are going with this."

"So, we just need to get there and plug it in. What do you think."

"You think they'll let me in?"

"As my guest, sure. And once in, it should be easy since most embassy personnel have the day off."

Mitchel grinned from ear to ear and José could only go along with the plan.

"OK then, so what is it you're waiting for? Hop on."

"One second more," Mitchel pleaded. "I need to call Nathalie and tell her what we're up to." Taking his cellphone from his pocket he started to dial. "That's strange," he said, punching in the numbers again. "No connection. Nothing."

"Indeed, that is strange, but is it a coincidence?" José took out his own cell phone. "Dead too," he confirmed.

"I don't think today is a good day to start believing in coincidences. My money would be on someone jamming the airwaves."

"Jamming all of Caracas? Not us. There's no technology in Venezuela that would be able to do such a thing."

"Who said anything about Venezuela?" Mitchel asked. "You remember Dwight Caldwell from the Chinese embassy?"

"Sure. What about him?"

"Caldwell asked the wrong general about why no-one had contacted the ships along the coastline near La Guairá's main port. The US ships."

"And you think those ships have something to do with the communications blackout?"

"I'm not sure, of course, but in combination with well-placed satellites they would surely be capable of it."

"This just keeps getting better and better." José took another look at the radio. "Worthless piece of junk. So, what about the embassy? Will the radio there work?"

"Honest to God, I don't know. It'll probably have a much bigger transmitter so I think we should try at least."

"Ok, hop on. Let's get our asses to the embassy and get you home a.s.a.p. before Nathalie gets worried and I have to pay for it."

Once both men were back on the Ducati, José quickly turned his bike around to take them to the embassy – speeding away like ghost riders on an empty highway.

As the dying rays of the sun bounced off the red roof tiles of Miraflores palace, the guards made a full retreat into the outbuildings sat behind the fences, knowing the opposition had gained full control of the grounds around them.

"What are they waiting for?" Chávez asked, pacing the Hall of Mirrors. At the conference table Moises Rojas had joined the last of the President's loyal friends.

"I believe we'll know very soon," Rojas answered.

"What's he doing here?" General Badillo asked, no longer able to hide his irritation.

"I asked him here," Chávez replied, leaving no room for any further discussion of the matter.

"But he..," Faustina tried, until one look from Chávez silenced her.

"What were you saying?" Chávez asked Rojas.

"That I think we'll know soon enough what their intentions are."

"What do you know about their intentions?" Clemente asked.

"Not much, only that they always said they wouldn't use violence once they arrived at the palace unless it was to meet violent resistance," Rojas replied calmly. "I expect we'll receive their demands shortly."

From the window, Chávez watched the masses gather around the palace grounds, chanting and lighting small fires. On the TV the screen suddenly showed a red background within which white text revealed, *'This is an official broadcast from the Venezuelan government.'* A fanfare then sounded and General Valbuena appeared on screen, in full uniform. Stood in front of a group of men in uniform holding a piece of paper in his hand, he started to read.

"Venezuelans, the president of our republic has betrayed the trust of his people. He's massacring innocent people with rifles. Just now six people were killed and dozens of others were shot and wounded in Caracas."

"Where is he?" Peroni asked.

"Looks like a TV studio," Badillo answered.

"I know where he is," Chávez said coldly, moving closer to the image of the man who had betrayed him.

"He's trying to use parts of our glorious army to repress the public march," Valbuena continued. "Despite the fact that he himself said, on numerous occasions, that he'd never use the armed forces against his own people. This is intolerable. We cannot accept a tyrant; a dictator to run our Republic of Venezuela. Therefore, we offer ourselves to the people and ask you – no, we tell you – that you no longer have to recognize the current government and the authority of President Chávez and his military high command. Given the deaths of our people in the confrontation that took place in the city center, and in accordance to the constitution to avoid more bloodshed, we are now demanding the peaceful departure of the president to be replaced by the high command. Therefore, we have a special message for the president – Mr. Presidente, within the hour we will be at the front door of the palace, we will be armed, but we will not use violence if you don't force our hand. You will let us in and you will peacefully surrender yourself and your government."

The screen turned black as Chávez switched off the television set. In the ensuing silence, the tension was so thick it could be cut with a knife.

The parking lot at the embassy was all but deserted with the only sound and movement coming from the front of the building where a huge flag bearing the stars and stripes of America flapped in the breeze.

"It's almost creepy," José noted as they walked up to the front entrance. Behind the large rotating doors, empty hallways were guarded by two soldiers. Behind the soldiers, a woman at reception looked up to welcome the two men.

"Good evening, gentleman."

"Evening, uh…" Mitchel leaned forward to check out the nametag on her blouse while flashing his ID from the inside pocket of his wallet, "…Dolores. I need to check in a guest."

"No problem," Dolores said. "Just sign this register and I'll get you a day pass."

Mitchel quickly filled in the form and handed it back.

"Thank you, here's your badge," Dolores said, barely glancing at the completed form.

"Well, that was easy," José remarked as they walked away.

"I have a trustworthy face," Mitchel joked as they headed for the stairs. "That, and the fact that we'd already made it passed the soldiers and the metal detectors and we left the luggage on the bike."

"I would have stopped at the trustworthy face," José replied.

"Here we are." Mitchel stopped at the door marked 'Pear' and swiped his card through the reader.

"Wow!" José gasped as they entered the room to be confronted by the huge radio that stretched from wall to wall. "I don't recall us having this much radio power back in the days."

Mitchel walked up to the wall searching for a power plug. "Let's see if we can fire it up. Ah, here we are. Now, let's see what happens." As he plugged in the radio, a red light came on. With a simple click of a few switches, a soft crackling sound filled the room. "Do you have the frequency?"

"Here," José said, showing him a piece of paper. "It's on the old UVB-76, 4625 kHz frequency."

"Put it in here." Mitchel pointed at a large wheel and José dialed the numbers.

"Ready," José stated.

"The honor is all yours," Mitchel said, handing José the microphone.

"Abrantes calling Miraflores, Abrantes calling Miraflores. Over." José releasing the speak button and the crackling sound returned.

"Try again," Mitchel urged.

"Abrantes calling Miraflores, Abrantes calling Miraflores. Over."

"Miraflores here. Sergeant Bardem speaking." At the faint reply, both Mitchel and José felt their hearts skip a beat before they shared a triumphant smile.

"Sergeant Bardem, this is José Rafael Abrantes from DISIP. Can you please connect me to your superior? Over."

"No problem, Sir. We've been expecting your call. Give me a moment."

Mitchel looked at José with a big grin on his face. "They've been expecting your call."

"And all that without a trustworthy face," José joked.

"Mr. Abrantes, please come in. Over."

Mitchel and José looked at each other surprised.

"Is that?" Mitchel asked.

"I believe so," José answered.

"Talk to him!" Mitchel cried, waving his arms to hurry along his friend.

"Abrantes here, Sir. Over."

"Good to hear from you, Mr. Abrantes I hope you're doing OK during all this. Where are you and what can I help you with? Over."

"Good to speak to you, Mr. President. I'm doing OK. I am uh…" Mitchel shook his head. "I am on the road, Sir, but safe. Can we talk freely?"

"You're on public speaker and I'm here with my most trusted advisors so please feel free to speak. Over."

"Thank you, Sir. We've tried to reach the palace, but all the roads are closed. We have some new information that concerns the events happening right now. I don't know if you've heard or seen the latest allegations against your government regarding the incident at Llaguno bridge? Over."

"We've been watching the news, yes. Over."

"Well, the evidence presented in the video is doctored. We've discovered that the sequences in the video have been altered so it would look like the Chavistas and the police fired first, but in truth the first shots were fired from somewhere in the distance, probably from the rooftops. You remember we sent information about the sniper rifles that had come into the country? Well, we now believe those rifles were being used to provoke a reaction that lead to the events we saw. Over."

For a moment, there was nothing, only the crackle of the airwaves, and José nervously asked the President if he was still on line. A second or so later, he got his reply.

"Thank you, Mr. Abrantes, for bringing me this news. I'll take it into consideration. Over."

"Thank you, Sir. I felt you needed to know. Is there anything else we can do for you?"

"As a matter of fact there is. Maybe it's a lot to ask, but I would appreciate your cooperation in this matter. Should anything happen to me can you make sure all the information you have gathered gets to the Vice President? Over."

"Sure thing, Sir. Over."

"Thank you again, Mr. Abrantes. Also, thank your friend from me. I hope to meet you again under better circumstances in the near future. Over."

"I hope so too, Mr. President. Over and out."

José laid the microphone on the table.

"Well, that was invigorating," Mitchel said. "I just hope your promise doesn't backfire on us."

228

"It's my promise," José assured him. "Just as my promise to Nathalie is to get you back home a.s.a.p. and in one piece, so I guess we better get going."

"Wise idea," Mitchel agreed as he switched off the radio.

"Take it," Chávez ordered, handing the radio to the adjutant.

"Do you think it's wise to have them deliver the evidence to the Vice President?" Badillo asked.

"The Vice President is a good and decent man. Besides, it doesn't really matter. If, for some reason, he isn't good then it doesn't change anything. And while we're talking about good and decent men..." Chávez walked up to Rojas who remained seated at the conference table. Standing behind him he placed his hands on his shoulders. "Why?" he asked.

"Excuse me, Sir?" Rojas replied, afraid to turn around.

"Why the bloodshed to simply make a point? You knew I would never condone such actions."

"I swear, Sir, I knew nothing about any plans to shoot at civilians. The plan was simply to move the two marches towards Miraflores thereby forcing a confrontation. I never knew anything about any shootings or snipers."

"Can it be that you are so naïve you didn't think the opposition wouldn't secure the outcome? What other plans do they have? Will they kill me and my family? What else do you know?"

"I swear, Sir. I told you everything I know. I know nothing about harming anyone." Rojas felt the President's fingers dig deeper into his shoulders before releasing.

"I believe you," he said. "But I cannot have you here now. I'll confine you to your quarters and we'll see what happens later, depending on the outcome of the day." Turning to the soldiers in the room, Chávez told them to take Rojas away and the men duly escorted him from the room. The President then looked at the others still seated at the table. "I'll be right back," he told them before he too exited the room.

With Chávez gone, Badillo switched on the TV again and hopped from one news channel to another. Most of them were dominated by the coverage of the Llaguno bridge incident. Badillo paused a little longer at the Venevision channel that had so recently broadcast Valbuena's demands. This time a General Carlos Alfonso Martinez took the podium to distance himself from Chávez. He was quickly followed by the entire National Guard leadership. Even the leader of the DISIP declared against the President. Then, after calling for Chávez's resignation, he suggested that a provisional junta should be installed to govern the country, something that would initiate procedures for modifying the constitution to "return us to what we have always been – the Republic of Venezuela, and to remove the word 'Bolivarian'." The DISIP leader then went on to announce the defection of various regiments throughout the country, at which point Chávez returned, dressed in a camouflage uniform complete with sidearm. For a moment, he surveyed every face in the room.

"This is your last chance," he told them, "the last chance to make a choice. I call on anyone who no longer believes in our democratic revolution to leave. If you don't believe anymore now is the last chance you can go." Everyone in the room looked around the table, but no-one moved. Chávez nodded. "If you stay, you should know that I gave orders that if the traitor Valbuena wants to enter the gates they are to let him in. I want to give him one last chance to stop this madness."

"And if he refuses?" Clemente asked.

Chávez slapped his holstered sidearm. "If he refuses, me and my gun are ready to keep them from stealing this revolution."

"What if they detain you, or take you out of the country?" Faustina asked. "Bush did it to Noriega and he now rots in a US cell.

They could get their cheap hands on our petroleum again and who knows what else."

As Faustina talked, Chávez didn't seem to hear. He kept his eyes on the tanks rolling down the road outside, taking up positions around the palace.

"Here's what we do," he said after a few minutes. "We'll let the opposition think we are ready to negotiate or surrender while we work out the details for a counterstrike. Outside, tanks are surrounding us, but I believe that the only reason they haven't attacked us yet is that a large part of the military still hasn't made up its mind about which side it's on."

"What are our options?" Badillo asked.

"First, you could try and contact your base in Maracay and see if they're still loyal to us. Your men are the best trained in Venezuela and if they're still loyal we might have a chance. We could transfer command to Maracay and have them mobilize as many loyalists as possible. If that works, we only need to stall them here as long as we can."

"Have you considered surrendering?" Clemente asked but before he received an answer the doors swung open and the generals Valbuena, Gallardo and Gomez entered the room accompanied by Cardinal Velasco.

"I believe I'll have to get back to you on that," Chávez told Clemente.

"Mr. President," Valbuena said, "it's my obligation to hereby demand your personal, complete surrender and withdrawal from power."

20. Surrender Or Resign

Friday, April 12th, 2002

T HE MIRAFLORES CONFERENCE ROOM smelled of sweat and fear. On the table, as well as on the ground, stacks of papers, garbage and empty plates determined the scenery. On one side of the table sat Chávez and his loyalists, supported at their backs by armed members of the Honor Guard. Across from them, Valbuena and his company were seated with an evenly balanced number of armed soldiers behind them. No-one spoke and if not for the exhausted faces, the smell, the shouts, and rumble of tanks outside the room, it could have easily been mistaken for a normal cabinet meeting.

"We've been at it for..." Valbuena looked at his watch, "five hours now and we've been over and over the situation, again and again. I think it's time you made a decision. I'm willing to give you another 30 minutes, no more, no less. And if you don't decide to resign within those 30 minutes we will leave and order a military attack on the palace and the palace grounds. You know what that means, Hugo."

Chávez tilted his heavy head up from the table and stared at Valbuena. The general knew exactly why. Valbuena had made things personal by calling him by his first name and by dragging in his family who lived on the palace grounds. Though the stare made Valbuena visibly uncomfortable, the general didn't flinch.

"Thirty minutes," he repeated.

"I need the room," Chávez came back. "I need the room to consult with my staff."

Valbuena looked around and nodded, to the left and the right, before standing up. "We'll be right outside," he said before he and the other conspirators left the room.

Once they had the room to themselves, loud sighs broke out around the table.

"What now?" Peroni asked. "I came here to stand by you, but we cannot allow them to take Miraflores by force. The consequences of life and limb could be disastrous."

"Now, we fight," Chávez curtly informed him. "But first I need a few minutes to myself. I'll be back soon." The President left the room through a side door that led to his work room. Sitting down behind his desk he picked up a photo frame with a picture of him being kissed on the cheeks by both his daughters. Softly, he offered a prayer to Mother Mary. When he was done, he picked up the telephone and pushed a button labelled '*FACR*'. The initials belonged to Fidel Castro who he had considered to be a friend and an ally from the moment they signed their first trade agreements. After a few seconds, a voice answered his call.

"One moment, please. I'll put you through."

"Compadre! It's good to hear from you," a deep voice boomed from the other end of the line. "I've been expecting your call. How are you and how can I help?"

"Thank you for speaking to me. We are OK here, for now. I take it you've seen the news."

"Yes, so I'm glad you called. The news we've heard is that they are trying to take you out, that your palace is besieged and they're forcing your hand to surrender."

"That pretty much sums it up, yes. I'm stuck here at the palace with a handful of loyalists. Outside my door the traitors await my answer to their demand that I resign along with my government. They have given me thirty minutes to do so or they will use violence. They have even threatened my family."

"What forces do you have there with you?"

"Somewhere between two and three hundred men of the presidential Honor Guard."

"Any tanks?"

"None. The only tanks nearby surround the palace and they are currently in the hands of the traitors."

As Chávez continued to talk, his eyes kept glancing at the clock, steadily ticking away the minutes he had been gifted.

"My friend, I find it hard to give you advice," Castro finally said. "I can only be totally honest with you, but I don't think you're going to like it. Do you still want it?"

"Always. Your advice has always been invaluable in the past so if you please."

"Ok, I can tell you what I would do. I would save the life of those who are still loyal to you and your family. Create your own conditions for an agreement, don't sacrifice them or yourself."

"And how would you do that?" Chávez asked.

"Do not resign, but state your own demands for a peaceful retreat and leave the country. I can send planes to come and get you as well as your most trusted loyalists and your family. I'll bring you all here to Cuba. Once you're here we can figure out how to fight this."

For a moment, Chávez stayed silent and Castro admitted again that he didn't think his old friend would like his advice.

"It's not that," Chávez assured him. "It's just that I was not seeing myself on Cuban ground trying to fight this from some kind of exile. But I really appreciate your advice and I'll promise to think about."

"Well, whatever you do, do it fast. Time is your worst enemy in this, my friend."

"I'll do so. Thank you. I'll keep you informed and let you know when I can."

"Take care of yourself, compadre. We'll talk soon."

As the line went dead, Chávez looked around the room feeling an acute loneliness descend on him. Even the quiet felt somehow treacherous. Taking some deep breaths, he stood up and returned to his friends in the other room who he found anxiously waiting for him. No-one could speak, and they looked to Chávez to break the silence. In the end it was Badillo who spoke first.

"I'm afraid I have some bad news," he said. Chávez looked at him and nodded for him to continue. "The military in Maracay joined the opposition. I made some calls, but I'm afraid we lost most of the larger military bases."

"It's not the men," Clemente added. "We're convinced most men are still loyal, but under the influence of the local leadership generals they follow orders."

"And we can't get to them," Chávez concluded.

With 15 minutes to go before deadline, and following a single knock on the door, General Gallardo entered the room carrying a telephone that he handed to Chávez. "It's for you."

Chávez hesitated, but eventually took the call. "Yes?"

"Mr. Chávez, this is Air Force General Fuenmayor."

Chávez remained silent.

"That's ok, just listen," the general said. "I understand that you refuse to resign and retreat from the palace. Let me be brief and very clear. If you don't resign within fifteen minutes I will order a squadron of F-16s to attack and bomb Miraflores regardless of who is still in the palace or the grounds."

Chávez moved the phone from his ear and handed it back to Gallardo without a word. The general immediately left the room again.

"What was that all about?" Badillo asked.

"More threats, more defectors. We need to make our own plan. Sit down everyone please. I have an idea." As everyone took their seats, Chávez placed his sidearm in front of him on the table. "I think it's time we surrender."

"What?"

"Why?"

"What are you talking about?"

"Please, keep calm and don't raise your voices." Chávez put a finger to his lips. "Listen carefully to what I'm saying. I think it's time we surrender, not resign."

"What's the difference?" General Reyes asked.

"I think I know where you're going with this," Faustina then said, bringing a halt to the discussion around her. "Let him talk."

"Thank you," Chávez said before continuing. "They want me to resign which I have no intention of doing. What I can do, however, is surrender to their forces and lay down conditions for my resignation. That way we buy time and, at a minimum, I think I can keep you and my family safe."

"What conditions are we talking about?" Peroni asked nervously.

"Yeah, and what if they don't agree with your demands?" Badillo added.

"First thing's first. Three, no four, conditions. Can someone please write them down for me?"

Faustina immediately picked up a pen and piece of paper from the table and nodded.

"First, I demand that whatever happens the constitution is respected."

"That's clever," Faustina replied. "That way the resignation will have to be presented to the National assembly."

Chávez nodded. "Secondly, I need assurances that the physical safety of everyone in my government is guaranteed. Thirdly, I demand that all of you, as my trusted advisors, my family and myself leave the country together. I have already cleared our way to Cuba so we can continue our work from there. And my final demand is to address the country live on national television."

"You know they will arrest you immediately once you make these demands," Reyes told Chávez.

"That they will, but if all goes well it will only be for a short time. In any case, it will not be an official resignation. I will not sign anything so this action will officially be a coup in a democratic republic."

"And what foreign country will endorse a coup?" Badillo asked.

"Precisely." Chávez managed a tired smile for his old friend before turning to Faustina. "You got it?"

She handed him the piece of paper, which Chávez briefly read before handing it back.

"Now we wait," he said.

Nathalie and Catherine were sat on the couch watching television when the front door opened and Mitchel and José entered the room. "Thank God you're home!" Nathalie cried.

"I told you I would bring him back in one piece," José joked.

"Where have you been?" Nathalie asked.

"That's kind of a long story," Mitchel answered.

"Well, looking at the news we have some time before we'll be going out again."

"Indeed, it might be some time before it's safe out there again," José agreed.

"Catherine and I were worried sick," Nathalie told her husband even though their daughter's eyes didn't stray from the TV.

"I can see that," Mitchel responded dryly. "Anyway, for now we have done all we can do and it's out of our hands."

"We've been following the news. Do you believe it's true what they say?" Nathalie asked. "Earlier, Ari Fleischer from the White House and Phillip Reager of the State Department were on TV saying the situation here had come as a complete surprise to them and, to the best of their knowledge, Chávez had triggered the violence, leaving him with no option other than to resign. It's hard to imagine that's the same man we met the other day if he did what they say he did."

"We know he didn't," José answered.

"The so-called evidence they showed is fake. We found proof of it and we delivered that proof to Chávez," Mitchel explained.

"You went to the palace to see him?"

"We talked to him on the radio from the embassy. We were perfectly safe all the time. I promise you."

"Look," José said pointing to the TV.

On the screen, freed from his captivity by the opposition, Rojas stood on the stairs in front of the palace ready to give a statement to the gathered Press.

"People of Venezuela, good day," he started. "I speak to you on behalf of the members of the military high command of the National Armed Forces. We stress that we condemn yesterday's regrettable events. Because of these facts, we have asked the president of the republic and his cabinet to resign their posts. For the sake of all of you, I can now tell you that Chávez personally has accepted. The members of the cabinet and the military high command are, as of this moment, tendering their resignations. From this point on, we will talk about how to move on, how to establish new authorities and governments. To finish, I call on you, the magnificent people of Venezuela to stay calm. Go home and tend to your daily business as calm and normal as possible. Reject all provocations to disorder and violence and have confidence in your armed forces."

When Rojas turned to walk back into the palace, the Press shouted questions at him, which he ignored. The camera then panned from the stairs to the ecstatic crowd waiting in the palace grounds. Chanting and playing loud music they celebrated the news that Chávez had resigned.

"Do you believe it?" Mitchel asked José.

"Hard to say, but if he did it, he did it to keep the people surrounding him safe. I'm convinced that if it was only him he would fight to the end."

"So, what now?" Nathalie asked.

"Does that mean we can go home?" Catherine added and both Mitchel and Nathalie stared at their daughter. Mitchel then looked at José who shrugged his shoulders.

"For now, we do nothing," Mitchel finally told Catherine.

"Remember your promise," José told him, which brought a menacing look from his friend.

"What promise?" Nathalie immediately wanted to know.

"Thanks," Mitchel snapped at José. "Well, uh, I kind of promised Chávez that if things were to go wrong we would get the evidence we have to the Vice President."

"James Everson Mitchel…" Nathalie warned as she rose from the couch. "Are you completely nuts? What are you trying to accomplish here? Are you determined to ruin your career and possibly risk your life?"

"I'm not risking anything, dear. I promise you I'll be back before being in any real danger. Besides, we don't even know where to find the Vice President."

"You better not be risking anything because if you keep going like this I cannot promise that Catherine and I will still be here when you next disappear."

240

As Nathalie stormed out of the room, José whispered to Mitchel, "Well, that went well."

"Yeah, remind me to thank you for that later. So, what do you think will happen now?"

"Well, for starters we don't know if Rojas is telling the truth. He may just be trying to calm things down for now. In any case I think we can be sure that Chávez doesn't stand a chance and the race for the filling of new positions has begun."

"Doesn't the Vice President take the presidency now?"

"Vice President Desiderio Clemente should, according to the constitution, become president for thirty days until new elections can be held. But since this isn't a normal transition, and with the vice president also in hiding, who knows."

"Maybe he also resigned," Mitchel added. "You think we can find him?"

"The Vice President? I wouldn't know where to start. Who could I contact, who can I trust?"

"There might be one thing we can do." Mitchel took his cell phone from his pocket.

"Are you sure you want to do this?"

"What do you mean?"

"Knowing you I guess you're thinking about calling your friend in Washington."

"So?"

"So, did you ever think about the possibility that one day he might ask you for a favor in return."

"Isn't that what friends are for?"

"Friends, yes. In politics, well?"

"In for a penny, in for a pound, I guess. I'm already indebted to him so I guess one more call isn't going to change much."

"It's your funeral," José joked.

"Smartass. We'll call him in the morning. For now, let's get a few hours of sleep. Who knows what we might run into tomorrow."

21. The Island

Friday, April 12th, 2002

3am

WHILE ROJAS, GOMEZ AND CARDINAL VELASCO sat on a small wooden bench in front of the conference room, Valbuena and Gallardo paced the hallway.

"What if he doesn't resign?" Valbuena asked.

"I'm convinced he will," Gallardo answered confidently, if only to ease the nerves of Valbuena. "What choice does he have? The only friends he has left are here in the palace grounds and he'll do anything to protect them."

Valbuena stopped and took hold of Gallardo's shoulders, turning the man towards him. "But what if he doesn't?"

"Look, it really doesn't matter," Gallardo answered. He removed Valbuena's hands and started walking again. "If he resigns we have our hands free, but if he doesn't, well, I guess Rojas has taken care of that part. Thanks to his statement, the people already believe he has resigned … which reminds me, where is that loose cannon?"

"I don't know," Valbuena replied, looking at the bench at the end of the hallway. "But he's partly the reason I'm so concerned. I don't think we can trust him to stay silent throughout all of this."

"We'll cross that bridge when we come to it. For now, the thirty minutes are almost over and we must decide what to do with Chávez. I guess we have a few options."

"Which are?"

At that moment, on the other side of the corridor, a door opened and general Badillo appeared.

"I guess we'll have to decide soon," Gallardo told Valbuena, he then walked towards Badillo, who was clearly waiting for the two generals to join him. In his hand he held a tired-looking piece of paper.

"We've drafted our demands," Badillo stated simply before holding the note out for whoever wanted to take it. "Our demands are not negotiable and the President will only tender his resignation after all of them are met."

Cardinal Velasco took the paper from him. "I think it's best I take this."

"You know where to find us," Badillo said flatly before returning to the conference room.

Velasco looked at the paper in his hands, mumbling the words as he read.

"Aloud please," Gallardo urged.

"All right. It's a four-point list. Whatever happens we are to respect the constitution. We must also secure the safety of those in the current government. We are to allow Chávez, his family and advisors to leave the country, and finally, Chávez wants to make one appearance on national television. That's it."

"We cannot let him go on television," Gomez said with some exasperation from his seat on the bench.

"Agreed," Valbuena replied. "The same goes for the first demand; if we respect the constitution it means we have to install the vice president as the new president."

"So, what can we agree to?"

"I think we need to agree to them all," the Cardinal told them calmly, and all eyes turned to him. "I'm serious. If you don't agree, he won't sign and then what will you do?"

"You keep saying 'you'," Gallardo replied with barely concealed irritation. "You're just as much a part of this as we are. You're not some kind of impartial mediator, Cardinal."

Velasco nodded, and attempted to take the heat out of the situation. "All I'm saying is that if *we* don't agree to his demands at this stage we need to take other measures, probably violent ones. Are *we* willing to do so?"

At the challenge, all of them men looked at each other, trying to assess the general consensus before committing. In the end, Gomez spoke first, his voice rising in panic as he rubbed at his forehead.

"So, what can we do?"

"I think the Cardinal is right," Gallardo told them. "We agree to the terms, but delay on the execution."

"Which means?" Valbuena asked.

"We tell Chávez he can only speak to the people on TV after he resigns, and we agree to let everyone leave, where ever they want to go, unharmed and in one piece, except Chávez himself."

"Why?" Gomez asked. "I mean, why would we keep Chávez here?"

"So we can decide what to do with him later on because we might need him to justify all of this. You see, if we let him go to some foreign country he can contest a new government in exile. We would never be free of him. However, if we keep him here we can try him for crimes against humanity or turn him over to the U.S. authorities who may want to bring their own charges, just like they did to Noriega. There are enough US ships along the coast, courtesy of Oskar Rout, for us to extradite him at any given moment."

"We can't do that," Valbuena stated. "The US has never asked for his extradition and the ships are not here in any official capacity. We would only embarrass the US and force them into doing who knows what."

"It really doesn't matter." Gallardo sighed. "The important thing is that we proceed for now by agreeing to everything. We let everyone go, start a so-called search for the vice president, never to find him, and we ship Chávez from here to some other place so we can control things from Miraflores."

"And where do you suggest we take him?" the Cardinal asked.

"Maybe we can take him to Fort Tiuna," Gomez replied.

"Too close by," Gallardo told him. "We need a place where we can be sure there are no friends left to help him."

"You'll never find such a place."

Everyone turned to the corner of the hallway where they found Rojas watching them. Slowly, he approached the group.

"So, you decided to come back?" Gallardo called out. "Where have you been?"

Rojas ignored the question, instead addressing the group as a whole. "I'm telling you now you're going to have a hard time finding a place where he doesn't have friends."

"Then we take him to the furthest place possible where he has as few friends left as possible."

"How about Isla Orchila?" Gomez offered.

"That's actually not a bad idea," Gallardo admitted.

"What and where is this Orchila island?" Velasco asked.

"It's a small island some 100 miles off the coast," Gomez explained. "It has been said that from the air the beaches are pink and in the past it has been disputed by the Dutch and Spaniards. They lost. We now have a small military base there complete with a landing strip."

246

"All right then, Orchila it is," Gallardo decided.

"If it's ok with you I would like to go with him," the Cardinal told the group.

"I don't see a problem with that," Valbuena confirmed. "We also need a diversion for the Press. We must avoid any contact between Chávez and the Press for now."

"For now, the Press think he has already resigned," Gallardo countered. "So, I suggest we keep it that way and draft a press release stating that we have special planes standing by at Francisco de Miranda Air Base, to take members of the old government and the Chávez family to wherever they want to go. Then we drive everyone to Miranda Air Base, except Chávez, who we'll bring to Orchila Island by chopper."

"Sounds like a plan," Valbuena concluded.

The sun sat high above the trees surrounding the botanical gardens. From his back porch Mitchel enjoyed the view, conscious of the quiet that made the day seem peaceful despite the events that had, and still were, taking place not so far away.

"You want another juice?" Nathalie asked Catherine.

"Sure, what else is there to do?"

"The schools will re-open again soon," Nathalie assured her daughter. "Perhaps, if everything stays quiet you can visit some friends later this afternoon."

"You promise?" Catherine asked, her eyes suddenly lighting up.

"If, and it's still a big if, everything stays quiet. Agreed?" Catherine gestured towards Mitchel.

"Sure," he said. "But we bring you and pick you up again. I don't want you roaming the streets alone."

As Catherine took a breath, her retort was silenced by a joyful welcome coming from the side of the house.

"Good day!"

"Good day!" everyone replied, almost in harmony because they recognized the voice.

"You are in a good mood," Nathalie shouted.

"Ha, yes. After I contacted the office to find all DISIP employees have been suspended from duty until further notice, I decided to consider this day off as a well-earned holiday."

"And you wanted to spend your day off here?" Catherine teased him.

"I see I'm not the only one who's in a good mood," José replied, and Catherine smiled.

"Juice?" Mitchel asked.

"Please."

Mitchel handed him a glass. "Shall we make the call from the living room then?"

"What call?" Nathalie asked.

"You remember the promise I made? Well, I need to make a phone call to see if we can find out where the Vice President might be."

"And then what? What's next."

"I don't know, honey. We're taking this one step at the time."

"You just remember that you also made a promise to your wife and daughter."

"I won't forget. And even if I could I still have this so-called friend to remind me." Mitchel slapped José hard on the back causing him to cough into his glass. "Are you ready?"

José shook his head before following Mitchel into the house and into the kitchen. Mitchel picked up his cell phone and pressed a few numbers before putting the phone on speaker and placing it on the table.

"There you are again." Charles Turner's voice sounded from the other end. "I trust you're still OK?"

"I am, thank you."

"So, how are things out there? We're getting a lot of garbled information, but nothing definitive. CNN is having a field day though with one piece of breaking news after the other."

"The embassy is closed and we don't have satellite television. Cable stopped transmitting all the foreign channels yesterday. What are they saying?"

"For hours now, every fifteen minutes or so, there's another general or politician renouncing his loyalty to Chávez. The latest news is that Chávez resigned and that he and his family are leaving the country by plane."

"Any news on the vice president?" Mitchel asked.

"Diosdado Clemente? Why do you ask?"

"We might have some information for him. Do you know him?"

"Only by reputation. They call him 'the octopus' because he has his tentacles in just about anything important going on in the better part of South America. There's even a strong suspicion he has ties to international drug trafficking cartels."

"Any idea where he could be?"

"I'm pretty sure that if he had the time he'd flee to the Cuban embassy. One of his tentacles, you see."

"Great," Mitchel said, the gratitude apparent in his voice. "I'm in your debt."

"I know that. Anything else I can help you with?"

"Not now, thank you, but please feel free to call me if you hear of anything news worthy."

"I'll do that. You just take care over there."

"Thanks, will do." Mitchel picked up the phone to close it. He then turned to José. "Do you have the number for the Cuban embassy?"

"In my phone," he replied, reaching into his jacket pocket. "Here it is."

He showed the phone's display to Mitchel who proceeded to punch more numbers into his own phone, before putting it on speaker.

"The number you dialed cannot be reached. Please try again later."

Mitchel looked at José before redialing, only to get the same automated message.

"It wouldn't surprise me if they cut the telephone lines and locally jam cell phones, isolating the embassy from the outside world," José said.

"In which case I need a ride to the Cuban embassy," Mitchel replied.

"I was afraid you were going to say that. You better tell Nathalie first."

"Leave her to me. But let's take it easy for now and first enjoy some breakfast. You in?"

"Well, it is my day off." José smiled. "But in truth, I don't think it's wise to try and get to the Cuban embassy right now. There are still a lot of protestors out there, many of whom are very angry men, especially near the political center."

"How about later today?"

"Sounds like plan."

"Then later it is."

While local TV networks struggled to keep up with the news and the procession of players either military or civilian who were wheeled out every 15 minutes to speak in support of the new regime, members of the opposition started to gather at Miranda Air Base hoping for a glimpse of Chávez.

At Miraflores, Chávez found himself separated from his friends as Valbuena promised him that all his demands would be met.

"We first need to get you to safety, Sir," Valbuena told him as he watched his friends disappearing down another hallway.

"Where are you taking me?" Chávez tried to sound calm but the tension in his voice was evident.

"It's better you don't know, Sir. It's for you own safety. Not everyone in the opposition cares about your wellbeing the way we do."

"And what about my family?"

"You don't need to worry about them. At this moment they are being picked up to be taken to a plane waiting at Miranda Air Base."

Chávez heard the words, but for the first time in years he felt fear, but fear for what? As he was led out of the palace, he tried to rationalize the fear for what it was, telling himself everything would be OK as long as his family was safe.

Outside the palace, the entrance to Miraflores Park had been totally cleared but the chants of protestors could still be heard in the distance, as could the rumble of a waiting helicopter. Chávez had always loved travelling by helicopter despite fearing it might make him look decadent. But this time was different. Instead of feeling the luckiest person on earth, he now felt fear – the fear of not knowing, of not being in control, maybe even fear for his life.

As they got closer to the helicopter the rotor blades picked up speed until the sound became overwhelming. At the helicopter, Valbuena stopped and stretched out his arm offering Chávez his hand. For a second Chávez faltered, unsure as to whether to shake the hand of a man who had betrayed him. Then, just before Valbuena retracted his hand, Chávez grabbed it in both his own and drew the general close to him, bringing the man's ear to his lips.

"This isn't over yet," he shouted.

Valbuena didn't answer. Instead, he freed himself from Chávez's grip and nodded to the soldier next to the helicopter door. As the soldier opened the door Chávez noticed Cardinal Velasco sitting inside.

"I'll be joining you for the trip," the Cardinal shouted as Chávez climbed in without showing any sign of hesitation. A second later the door was closed and within minutes they left the ground, rising high above the palace grounds. Chávez looked out of the window to survey the surrounding streets, still flooded with people. 'Was this the last time I would see my home?' he asked himself.

Miranda Air Base at the east of Caracas was a single strip airfield completely surrounded by highways. In 1992, during his own coup attempt, Chávez seized the airbase hoping to capture President Pérez as he tried to flee the country. Now the tables had turned once again, and at the airbase entrance a gathering of opposition supporters were already waiting, waving banners saying, 'Chávez killer' and 'Never come back.'

On the runway two airplanes appeared to be getting ready to leave while at the main gate a motorcade arrived escorted by armored cars and manned by soldiers with machine guns. As the motorcade drove through the main gate, the guards had a hard time keeping the people back and out of the base.

Stopping on the runway, two cars next to the first plane and the other next to the second, the doors opened and Chávez's family and closest friends hastily made their way up the stairs and into the planes. At the second plane, María Gabriela got out of her car. Before climbing the stairs she glanced at the protesters shouting behind the gate. Almost immediately after boarding, all the protesters melted away.

Chávez looked from the helicopter window and noticed they were flying north over the ocean.

"You're taking me to Orchila?" he shouted to the Cardinal sitting opposite him, who nodded without saying anything.

Some 20 minutes later, the pinkish shores of Orchila island came into view. After flying over the barren interior of the island, the helicopter came to land close to a small cabin-like building. As the rotor blades slowly ground to a halt, the door was opened from the outside.

"Naldo Gomez!" Chávez shouted, recognizing the general who greeted him with a welcoming committee of five heavily-armed soldiers.

"Mr. Chávez, Cardinal, if you'd care to follow me," Gomez said.

Over the rocky sands, they walked to the white-painted cabin that looked more like a holiday home than a military installation. Surrounding the cabin, barren land stretched as far as the eye could see and it made the island appear bigger than it actually was. The group walked into the cabin and into a small corridor leading to three open doors, all of them furnished with a single table, some chairs and a bunk bed.

"Please take a seat." Gomez pointed to one of the chairs in the first room. As Chávez entered the room Gomez and the Cardinal stayed outside. "Please be patient. We'll be back soon."

As the door closed, Chávez walked up to the one small window at the far side of the room. Opening it, he saw the window was just large enough for him to escape. But what about the guards, and if managed to avoid the guards, where would he go?

For almost an hour Chávez waited on the bunk bed, staring at the ceiling. If only he could sleep. Suddenly the door opened and Gomez stepped in.

"Are you comfortable?" he asked, handing him a bottle of water.

"What do you want?" Chávez got up from the bed and sat down at the table to drink.

"I'm officially informing you that you are in the custody of the Armed Forces."

"I am an elected official. You accuse me of being a dictator while you detain me here unlawfully."

Gomez put a folder in front of Chávez on the table. "We need you to write your resignation letter and sign it like we negotiated."

"I will not sign anything until I have proof that all my demands have been met."

"I'm not sure I'm able to get you such proof at this time, but you have to trust me that…"

"Trust you?" Chávez interrupted. "Trust you? Why would I trust you? You and your so-called comrades have just committed a violent act of terror killing innocent civilians in the process. Trust will not be what our talks are based on."

"I see you need some more time to come to your senses. I'll leave the folder here."

As Gomez opened the door he came face-to-face with Cardinal Velasco who was about to enter. "Maybe you can talk some sense into him," he grumbled before leaving.

"Mr. President," the Cardinal greeted Chávez, bringing a smile to his lips. "Why are you smiling?"

"It seems you are the only one who still calls me Mr. President."

"And why won't you sign the papers, Mr. President?"

"And why are you involved Cardinal? I know we had our differences in the past, but a coup d'état sanctioned by everything I consider holy?"

"The Church has but one thing to take care of and that's the wellbeing of the people it stands for. It is my conviction Mr. President that your leadership, possibly despite your intentions, has failed, leaving the country on the brink of a terrible and non-reversible future."

Chávez shook his head wearily. "Where's my family? Where are my friends?"

"They are all safe. Your family has been taken to their hometown of Barquisimeto and your trustees have gone to their homes. Your daughter María Gabriela got on a plane to Cuba. That's all the information I have at this time."

"And, again, I have to take your word for it."

"Sign the papers Mr. President and within the hour you'll be on your way to whatever place you call safe in any country you want."

254

"You know my conditions, and I need proof that they've been met."

"For now, would you be willing to sign a statement saying you've abandoned the presidency?"

"Why would I do that." Chávez asked, feeling increasingly irritated.

"A show of good faith. It would buy me some time with the generals to try and get the proof that your demands have been met."

"As long as the statement doesn't contain any reason why I abandoned the presidency, I'll consider it."

"Thank you, Mr. President. I'll have a statement drawn up and get back to you."

The Cardinal knocked on the door and it was opened from the outside. As he walked out of the room, a young soldier took his place inside.

"What's your name, soldier?"

"Sergeant Alejandro, Sir, Roberto Alejandro"

"Are you a Ranger soldier?" Chávez asked, recognizing the sign on his cap.

"321st Ranger Battalion, Mr. President."

"Ah, General Sena's battalion. He's a good man."

"That he is, Sir."

"You like being in the army, son?"

"It's my life, Sir. It was my father's and grandfather's life. I love working for the freedom of my country and I regret being here, Sir. I'm sorry, Sir."

"Don't be sorry, son. For now, just follow the orders given. I promise you there'll come a better time and a clearer future."

"Thank you, Sir. May I say something, Sir?"

"Of course, son. Speak freely."

"Don't sign anything, Sir. Wait as long as possible before signing anything. The future, as you say, may be unclear right now, but I hear that almost every soldier finds it disgraceful what's happening. So, hang in there, Sir."

"Thank you, soldier. That means a lot to me."

22. Ortega vs. Carmona

Friday, April 12th, 2002
5am

C HÁVEZ LAY ON HIS BUNK BED, fully dressed and
fast asleep when the door opened with no warning and
someone turned on the light. Sergeant Alejandro shook
his shoulder to wake him up.

"Good morning, Sir."

"It's 5am," Chávez said, squinting at the single lightbulb as he
spoke.

"I know and I'm sorry, Sir, but I have orders to wake you up and
tell you to get ready to be transported. I have brought you a bowl of
water and a towel to freshen up as well as breakfast, which is waiting
for you on the table. You need your strength, Sir."

Chávez rolled onto his back before dragging himself from the bed
to the table, where he found a meagre meal of bread and butter waiting
for him and a cup of coffee.

"I know it's not much, Sir."

Chávez grunted. "Do you have any idea what their plans are, Sergeant?"

"Well, Sir, I have only overheard fragments of conversation. There have been heavy discussions about 'removing you'. I cannot be sure, but I believe that in the end they plan to take you back to the mainland. I have no idea what they are planning from there on in."

"Thank you, Son," Chávez took a bite of the bread. "Do you have a piece of paper and pen I could borrow?"

"Sure, no problem." Alejandro searched his pockets and eventually handed him a pen and a wrinkled piece of paper with what looked like a grocery list written on one side of it.

"Thank you," Chávez looked at the list. "I hope I won't get you into trouble at home?"

Both men smiled as the soldier confirmed he should be OK.

"I have a request to make," Chávez said. "It could be a dangerous one."

"All right, Sir. What can I do for you?"

"If I were to write a message on your grocery list could you try and get it to the United Socialist Party of Venezuela?"

"How do you suggest I get it there, Sir?"

"I'll give you a fax number. If anytime soon you can get to a fax you can send it."

"But isn't the office of the Socialist Party in the palace, Sir? So won't it be found by the opposition?"

"It's a Hail Mary, son, but I don't know of any place else I can find someone I can trust."

"No-one?"

"No-one I know how to get hold of. Besides, I don't think the opposition will spend a lot of time at the offices of the Socialist Party so maybe, just maybe."

"I'll do my utmost to get the message faxed, Sir. I promise you that. Now, I'll leave you to finish your breakfast. They'll probably be here soon to pick you up."

"Thanks for everything, Son," Chávez said softly as Alejandro left the room, leaving him alone again. On the back of the grocery list Chavez started writing.

"To the dear people of Venezuela..."

After a few minutes, the door opened again and the Cardinal stepped into the room. Chávez hastily hid the piece of paper without the Cardinal noticing. "Do you have the declaration you need me to sign?" he asked as the Cardinal sat down at the table.

"There's no declaration to be signed. You're going back to the mainland, to Turiamo Naval Base," the Cardinal replied.

"Why's that?"

"I'm not sure," the Cardinal admitted, causing Chávez's mind to try and second guess that of his enemies. 'They must have a plan by now,' he thought. 'When they removed me from the mainland yesterday they wanted me out of the way, and now they want me back. Why?' As Chávez racked his brains, the only thing he could think of was that they needed him for some reason, and they needed him to be there physically. Perhaps they had come to understand that having him disappear might afford him a martyr status that would make the formation of a new government problematic. And if this was the case, they needed to show him, perhaps even vilify him to vindicate their actions further with a public trial of some sort or even extradition to the US.

"It's time, Sir." Alejandro stepped back into the room and Chávez quickly splashed some water on his face before rubbing it dry. He then straightened his uniform, ran his fingers through his hair and walked to the door.

"Let's go," Chávez said and he headed out of the cabin, noting as he did so, the sound of slowly rotating helicopter blades not very far away.

"I'll be right by your side, Sir," Alejandro quietly reassured him as the small group, including the Cardinal, walked up to the helicopter platform where they were joined by a handful of soldiers.

In the dark night, the Miraflores Palace garden glowed orange under the glare of the surrounding streetlights. By now, the roads were all empty with only a handful of tanks strategically placed around the palace to suggest the recent unrest. Inside the palace, the hallways were much busier; crowded with military and civilian personnel locked in discussions about what to do next. Inside the Hall of Mirrors, Valbuena and his collaborators looked as tired as they felt.

"Soon we can sleep again, gentlemen, but right now we have to make some decisions," Gallardo told them.

"Did you see all the vultures out there? Everyone celebrating and congratulating each other while lobbying for positions in the new government," Gomez said with undisguised irritation.

"We all need to eat," Valbuena said.

"First we need to agree on how best to introduce Carmona as the new President," Gallardo said sternly.

"That's sure to create some bad blood on the first day," Gomez muttered.

"Ortega won't be pleased, but the people don't know anything about the two contenders so I think they'll quickly get behind the new leadership."

"Ortega did conduct the march yesterday," Rojas interrupted.

"Yes, and for that he will always be remembered, and all of us, including Carmona, will publicly thank him for that," Gallardo replied and the tone of his voice made it clear he wanted an end to the discussion. "So, what's the next decision to make?"

"We need a story about the Vice President."

"Still no word from him?" Rojas asked.

"Nothing." Valbuena looked at Gallardo to see if he had any other news.

"Nothing here either. I suspect he is in hiding. Earlier tonight we started broadcasting on all TV channels asking him to report to the palace, but he's not come forward."

"So what if we move on and he shows up?" Gomez asked.

"Well, there's nothing we can do about that so we'll just have to deal with it when it happens, if it happens," Gallardo told him.

"I agree," Valbuena added. "We need to address the nation as soon as possible and let the people know we have a new president, albeit a transitional one. I think that we also need to decide what to do with Chávez."

"He still hasn't written his resignation letter?" Rojas asked.

"No. The Cardinal persuaded him to write a letter saying that he was no longer in power, but I put a stop to it because it wouldn't serve our purpose."

"Why not?" Gomez asked, baffled.

"Because we need him to say quite clearly and simply that he quit his office and as a result he doesn't work here anymore. Otherwise, it could still look like he was forced to step down; making the transition a coup."

"I'll get the letter," Gallardo said, much to the surprise of the other generals. "If we need the letter, I'll get us one. Leave that to me."

"OK," Valbuena accepted, simply relieved to have an end to the topic. "But what do we do with Chávez? He'll be flying into Turiamo any minute now."

"I've arranged comfortable quarters for him there," Rojas informed them, feeling the need to take control of this part of the operation, if only to ensure his old friend's safety.

"Then that's where he'll stay," Gallardo stated firmly. "We don't have to decide anything now. There's nothing he can do from there and our attention needs to focus on the transitional government. We need to put everything in place before Carmona goes public."

"All right," Valbuena said. "We all know what to do. Let's finish this as soon as possible so we can all get the rest we deserve."

At 6am, the helicopter carrying Chávez landed at Turiamo Naval base just outside of Caracas.

"Good morning, Colonel," was the base commander's welcome, referring to Chávez's original military title, which was clearly a demotion from President. "Sergeant, Cardinal, if you'd all care to join me inside, there's hot coffee."

Shadowed by soldiers, the three men walked into the main building, heading towards the back where two armed guards stood at a door. "I believe you've been here before?" the commander asked Chávez.

"Last year I made an inspection of your base when your predecessor was still here. The base was in tip top shape then."

"I assure you that nothing much has changed."

"I'd beg to differ on that score," Chávez replied icily.

"If you please." The commander pointed the way through the open doors that closed behind them. The room appeared to be an office with regular windows and a small kitchenette in which a pot of dark black coffee was steaming.

"As you can see we have done everything possible to make you feel as comfortable as possible. In the back is your sleeping quarters and a bathroom. In the bedroom closet you will find fresh clothing and uniforms. Sergeant Alejandro will stay with you and be at your disposal as your adjutant."

Chávez nodded.

"Oh, and I don't think I have to say it, but I will anyway; there will be guards outside the doors and windows 24 hours a day. There is also video surveillance." The commander pointed at the cameras watching them from every corner of the room. "I'll have some sandwiches brought to you in few minutes. I trust you'll have a pleasant stay." The commander then left the room with Velasco, leaving Chávez alone with Alejandro.

"Please, sit down," Chávez said, bringing the young soldier a chair from the dining table.

"Thank you," Alejandro replied. As Chávez sat down he took a pen and the soldier's grocery list from his breast pocket. He gave the camera a quick glance, looked at Alejandro and started writing. After making a few scribbles he crumpled up the paper, walked to the door and threw it in the trashcan next to it. Walking back to the table, he nodded to Alejandro before sitting down.

"Sergeant, could you please take a look at what's holding up those sandwiches?"

"Of course, Sir." Alejandro walked to the door. Before opening it, he dropped the pen he had taken from the table and as he bent to pick it up, being careful to shield his hands from the camera, he reached for the paper in the trashcan and then left the room.

The main office of the workers' organization CTV was located a few miles east of the Miraflores Palace and the main government buildings. Carlos Ortega had frequently walked the short distance for meetings with politicians and even the president. Now he was alone in his office, pacing up and down the room and switching between television channels, waiting for the call he expected. On TV the news about Chávez's alleged resignation was the one and only thing all channels were reporting. "It's Over! Chávez Resigned!" El Universal reported. "The Assassin Has Fallen," Asi es la Noticia pronounced on a banner below the footage of the previous day's shootings. "Goodbye, Hugo," the Tal Cual network broadcast every 5 minutes, full screen.

Suddenly Ortega stopped as the screen showed a new announcement – 'Breaking news from Miraflores Palace.' Standing next to the presidential desk the camera zoomed in on Cardinal Velasco.

"People of Venezuela, Fellow Christians. As your religious leader, I stand before you. In my hand, I have the official resignation letter written by your former president Hugo Chávez Frias. I'll put it here on the desk so the camera can get a close-up so you can all read it." As the camera zoomed in the letter was shown full screen.

"Yo, Hugo Chávez Frías, CI 4258228, ante los hechos acaecidos en el país durante los últimos días, y consciente de que he sido depuesto de la Presidencia de la República Bolivariana de Venezuela, declaro que abandono el cargo para el que fui elegido legítimamente por el pueblo venezolano y el que he ejercido desde el 2 de febrero de 1999.

Igualmente declaro que he removido de su cargo, ante la evidencia de los acontecimientos, al vicepresidente Ejecutivo, ing. Desiderio Clemente Rendón.

En La Orchila, a los 12 días del mes de abril de 2002".

"I, Hugo Chávez Frías, CI. 4258228, knowing the events that occurred in the country during the last few days and being aware that I've been deposed of the presidency of the Bolivarian Republic of Venezuela, do declare that I quit the position which I was legitimately chosen for by the Venezuelan people, a position I've practiced since February 2nd, 1999.

In the same way, I declare that I've removed, upon the evidence of events, the executive vice president Desiderio Clemente Rendón from his position.

In La Orchila, April 12th, 2002."

For almost a full minute the letter was shown without a single sound before the camera panned back to the Cardinal.

"As you can read for yourselves, your country, for now, is without a president. Here in the palace, politicians and military personnel have been working all night on a way to best deal with this situation. Since the vice president is not available, Pedro Francisco Carmona Estanga will later today be installed as the transitional president of the Venezuelan Republic and he will form a cabinet until new elections can be held."

Ortega felt his heart skip a beat. He switched off the television and threw the remote at it, which smashed into pieces on impact.

"Fuck! He betrayed me. They betrayed me. Fuck!"

Slumping into a chair, Ortega picked up the phone and started punching in numbers.

At the palace, Carmona looked at the screen of his cell phone. Taking a deep breath, he excused himself, left the room and answered the call with as much positivity as he could muster.

"Carlos, I'm a bit pressed for time, but what can I do for you?"

"You lying sack of shit!" Ortega exploded. "You think I wouldn't notice? You think you'd get away with it? That the people will blindly follow you?"

"Take it easy, my friend." Carmona tried to sound amiable. "You have no idea what has happened so I would very much appreciate it if you would keep calm until I can explain everything to you."

"What is there to explain? I did all the work and you get to be president."

"I promise you, there's a lot more to this story than it would seem. If you come to the palace later today, I can explain everything."

Ortega stared at the ceiling in silence, clenching his fists.

"Are you still there?" Carmona asked.

"Yes, I'm still here. As soon as I hang up the phone I'm heading in your direction and you better be there to receive me."

"No problem. You just get here and I'll explain everything."

265

Unable to control his temper any longer, Ortega ended the call.

"So, is Carlos going to give us any trouble?" Valbuena asked when Carmona walked back into the Hall of Mirrors.

"How did you know it was him?"

"I saw his name on your telephone before you ran out. What did he say?"

"It would be an overstatement to say he was happy. For now, he has agreed to meet me here later today so I can give him an explanation."

"Then, you better think of one quickly," Gallardo chortled.

At sunrise José arrived at Mitchel's house on his motorcycle, turning off the engine for the last 100 yards so as not to wake the whole family. After walking around the back, he found Mitchel already sitting on his porch sipping hot coffee and enjoying a second breakfast.

"Good morning, I see you started the day OK."

"And a good morning to you, too. There is no better time of day than when the early birds are chirping and the fresh smell of morning dew still hangs in the air."

"Agreed," José said, coming to join him at the table as Mitchel poured him a coffee.

"Help yourself." Mitchel pointed at the sandwiches on the table.

"Don't mind if I do."

"I tried to reach the Cuban embassy again by phone, but no such luck. I think you're right; the phone lines are cut off. So, how is it out there, on the streets?"

"It looked pretty quiet on the way here, but I've no idea how it is downtown. Of course, now they've installed a transitional president, I suspect we'll hear a lot more this morning. How did Nathalie react to the news that you are going out again?"

"She wasn't very enthusiastic, but she understands. Although I'm sure that when this is all over there will be further talks about the future."

"So tell me again why I am still single?" José joked.

"Because nobody will have you?"

"Says you. So shall we find out?"

"Find out why you're still single?"

"Quite the comedian this morning, aren't we? Shall we find out how the streets are downtown or not?"

"Sure, let's go."

Mitchel took his coat from the chair and together they walked up to the Ducati. After putting on their helmets, José started the engine and they moved away from the house making as little noise as possible.

The Cuban embassy was some six miles east, close to the airport in Chuao district, and therefore completely reachable by highway. As the men drove, they were struck by how relatively normal the morning traffic was, although either side of the freeway the streets remained empty save for a handful of pedestrians going about their business.

After a few minutes José headed for the exit nearest the embassy, which was located three blocks away on the Calle Roraima. Directly below the exit ramp, a police roadblock could be seen one block from the embassy, behind which a huge crowd was protesting, smashing the windows of adjacent buildings and trashing cars. Some 30 feet behind a high metal fence, armed guards protected the embassy. Clearly, no one was going to get to the Cubans that way and so José turned his bike around to drive two blocks away before parking up.

"Wise decision," Mitchel agreed as he stepped off the back of the bike.

"Safety first, even if only for my bike. I guess we can try and walk up there, but I suspect we'll have a hard time getting in."

"But if we don't try…"

José nodded and without another word, the two men walked up to the first barricade and stepped over the wooden fence. The majority of the police were more concentrated on the barricade in front of the embassy.

"Do you have any idea what they are protesting about?" Mitchel asked.

"Who knows? It seems that these days there's always a reason for a good protest. Still, I guess we'll know soon enough." José pointed at a man shouting through a megaphone as he stood on top of a white sedan. He was surrounded by television cameras.

"Show us Clemente! Give us the traitor!" the man demanded.

"I know him," José shouted to Mitchel.

"Who is he?" Mitchel shouted back.

"Henrique Capriles Radonski," José replied. "Founder of the Chávez political opposition party, 'Primero Justicia'. He's also the mayor of this particular district. And it looks like we're not the only ones who know or think Clemente is in the embassy."

At that moment, a stray bottle smashed on the pavement only three feet from them.

"I guess it's now or never," Mitchel said and the men made a run for the police barricade, pushing themselves through the shouting and chanting crowd.

"Buenos días," José shouted at a young policeman. "We have important information that we need to get to the embassy." He took an envelope from his jacket pocket and pointed it at the policeman. "Could you hand this through the fence and ask if they will immediately read it. We will wait here for an answer." The young man nodded and took the letter from José and walked to the gate.

"You came prepared," Mitchel said.

"Always." The two men watched the policeman hand the letter to an officer through the gate. "I wrote about Chávez's wishes and gave a hint of the information we have, so now we wait."

268

"I don't think we can stay here much longer," Mitchel replied, nervously watching the protestors who were inching closer to the barricade. "In two minutes we either go in or we go away, back home."

As it was, they had to wait barely a minute before a civilian came running from the door of the embassy to the gate, shouting at the guards who immediately waved at a policeman. Instructions were given and, soon after, Mitchel and José walked through the barricade.

"Thank you," José said.

"You are OK?" the aide at the gate asked.

"We're fine, though I'm pleased you didn't take any longer."

"Please, follow me quickly." The man pointed towards the entrance. "I'm afraid we are in a bit of a mess here. They have cut off the water, electricity and phone lines so we are completely disconnected from the outside world."

"We thought as much," Mitchel replied.

Inside the building, the scene was far from grand and the embassy looked pretty much like any other downtown office with a reception area and a number of small offices along a hallway. The men were taken along the corridor to an empty conference room made all the more austere-looking by the bare concrete walls.

"Here you go, please sit down. I'll be with you in a minute." The man pointed to the empty chairs before leaving the room.

"Talk about minimalistic," Mitchel joked as he looked around.

"Looks a little like your 'war room'," José teased.

For the next ten minutes, José and Mitchel paced the room, occasionally stopping to watch the protestors from a window as the demonstration grew ever more violent. Then, just as Mitchel checked his watch, the aide reappeared.

"Will you please follow me?" he said.

"That was fairly quick," Mitchel said and he turned to follow the man through the hallway, up the stairs and into another hallway that was decorated with old paintings and a plush red carpet. Half way into the hallway the aide opened the only large double doors present on the floor.

"Please enter," he told them.

As Mitchel and José walked in they were overwhelmed by the splendor of the room. Huge old masters decorated the walls and the mahogany furniture, finished off with brass, gave the room a presidential look – or at least a look fit for the Cuban ambassador, German Sanchez Otero, who was sat behind a desk.

"Sit down, please," he said, pointing to a dark wooden table bordered by Louis XVI chairs where Venezuela's missing Vice President also happened to be sitting. "I believe you know Desiderio Clemente."

"I know of him," Mitchel replied, reaching forward to shake the hand of Clemente, who looked taller and heavier in person. "Pleased to meet you."

"Pleased to meet you too, Mr. Ambassador," José added.

"Please, just ignore me," the ambassador replied. "I'm just the host with a room available. Conduct your business as if I were not in the room."

"I only wish we would have met under better circumstances," Clemente told the men as they took their chairs.

"I hope you don't mind if I keep the television on while you talk," Otero said. "It's our only way of knowing what's happening outside since all our communication lines have been cut off or scrambled."

"No problem," José answered politely. "But I thought you had no power?"

"We have some power from back-up generators. It's not enough to keep everything working, but enough to provide us with the essentials and as you may know…"

"TV has become an essential in this media coup," Clemente finished. "Only now have the public television channels started broadcasting again, so maybe we will finally get some honest and truthful broadcasting."

"I see you have read our evidence," Mitchel said.

"Briefly," Clemente replied. "But I think I've seen enough to know the coup was carefully planned and the media played a crucial role in stirring it up."

"That about sums it up," Mitchel agreed. "So, what are you planning on doing next?"

"Well, there's no way I'll be able to leave this building unseen and even if I could I would be arrested as soon as someone recognizes my face. There is, however, something that might be of help. Some hours ago, just before the communications outtage, I received word that the president had managed to write a statement, which has been faxed to the office of the United Socialist Party of Venezuela."

"And do we know what the statement says?" José asked.

"Well, the rumor is – and forgive me, but it has come from a reliable source who heard it from someone who can't be identified – but they say the statement reveals the president didn't resign."

"That's something," Mitchel said. "And if it's true it would prove the resignation letter is false."

"And together with the evidence of the sniper rifles and the video montage it would present some pretty strong evidence of foul play," José added.

"This fax, it was sent to the Socialist party, you say? Where is their office?" Mitchel asked.

"You're not going to like this," José answered, and Clemente shook his head in agreement.

"The office of the United Socialist Party is in the east wing of the Miraflores palace," Clemente said with a sigh.

"Ah." Mitchel shook his head, immediately recognizing the problem. "And if it's in the palace, what are the chances of it not being intercepted by the wrong people?"

"Gentleman, maybe you should see this," the ambassador interrupted, turning up the volume on the television.

"We now switch live to Havana where María Gabriela Chávez will give a brief statement."

In what appeared to be a television studio, María Gabriela looked directly into camera. She was dressed in jeans and a green t-shirt and she looked tired and weary.

"Friends of my father. I'm here to tell you that everything that's being said about my dad is based on false rumors. My father is a great man and a great president who never betrayed his country and never wanted anything other than the best for its people. This was a clear and obvious coup supported by foreign aid. Furthermore, I want you to know that my father, your president, would never resign. I assure you that the resignation letter you have been shown is false, a fake. And I urge everyone who has doubts to demand to have handwriting specialists check his signature. I also assure that this is not the last you have heard about your president, my father. Thank you."

"That was brief," Mitchel said as María Gabriela disappeared from the screen.

"And from what we've heard at this table, no doubt truthful," José added.

"I believe you asked how big the chance was of the fax being discovered," Clemente said, returning to their previous conversation. "I think the chances are slim. All the workers at the office of the Socialist Party would have been the first to leave the palace when all hell broke loose and the opposition has no business there. The offices are tucked away, far back in the palace so…"

"So there is a chance," Mitchel said.

"Here we go again," José groaned.

"I'm just saying that if there's a chance…"

"You'll need help," Clemente warned. "If you are planning on getting anywhere near the palace you'll need all the help you can get."

"We could try and contact any generals still loyal to the president and see if they might help us," Mitchel replied enthusiastically.

"And how are we going to know who to contact?" José asked.

"That shouldn't be a problem," Clemente assured him. "Those who you don't see fighting over cabinet positions or publicly distancing themselves from Chávez will be the ones you need to get into contact with."

Mitchel looked at José.

"I know," he said. "This sounds like a plan."

"Do you have a safe way to get us out of here?" Mitchel asked.

"Yes," the ambassador replied. "Please, follow me."

23. The Carmona Decree

Friday, April 12th, 2002

7.00am

AT DAWN, THE STREETS OF CARACAS were once again calm following the exodus during the night in which thousands of Venezuelans, mostly the poor, packed their things, gathered their families and fled their homes into the country, afraid of what was about to happen next. Here and there, smoke pillars from the remnants of burning car tires served as reminders of the previous days' riots and by the time the sun was fully up the first protesters were arriving at the palace fences – only this time it wasn't the supporters of the opposition, but a small group of some hundred or so men, women and children waving banners in support of the ousted President.

As Ortega drove past placards reading 'Bring back our President', 'Viva la Democracia' and 'Carmona Traitor', he kept his eyes trained on the guards ahead. On reaching the main gate, he rolled down his window.

"Carlos Ortega here to see Pedro Carmona. He's expecting me."

The guard looked at his clipboard. "I don't have you on the list," he said. When Ortega told him to check again, only to be given the same reply, he told the young guard to call someone.

"One moment." The guard walked to his booth and picked up the phone.

"This cannot be happening," Ortega whispered to himself, while noticing the guard shaking his head before walking back to the car.

"I'm sorry, Sir. The President asks you to return later in the afternoon or early in the evening."

Ortega banged both fists on the steering wheel.

"I must ask you to turn away from the gate and make room other visitors," the guard said firmly as another soldier approached, having seen Ortega's reaction.

"And, clearly, I'm not a visitor," Ortega snapped before reversing at speed and driving away with his wheels spinning. "I'll get you for this!" he yelled.

In the richer suburbs of Caracas, most Venezuelans waited out the crisis glued to their televisions, anxiously following the latest news as it happened. Then, at the prearranged time of 7.30pm, all channels switched to a live feed from the Ayacucho room in Miraflores Palace. It was Chávez's favorite room.

For the occasion, all the furniture had been removed so as to accommodate the almost 400 invited dignitaries who now filled the place. Behind the stage the familiar painting of Simon Bolivar had been removed from the walls on Carmona's demand. However, he had kept the same wooden desk that Chávez always used for his weekly address, and he was sat at it, Bible at hand, center stage.

For a few moments, Carmona sat smiling and waving to the audience as Daniel Romero, a 43-year-old lawyer, walked into the room to take up position at a lector close to Carmona's desk. Romero had been a personal assistant to one of Chávez's predecessors, Carlos

Andrés Perez, a president who had been forced to step down in 1993 for embezzling 250 million bolívars. A personal friend of Carmona, Romero was a capitalist who had always stayed loyal to Perez and who was known to have close ties to the Bush administration.

"Ladies and gentlemen, distinguished guests." Romero looked around the room and everyone quietened. "As Acting Attorney-General I am proud to stand here before you to make the following announcements. First of all, we hereby dismiss the former President Hugo Rafael Chávez Frías for corruption and for compromising our democratic principles, as well as property and human rights violations." As the crowd cheered, Romero paused. He then continued to catalogue the so-called crimes against the people that went on for a least a minute or more. "We decree that a democratic transitional government will be established and the national assembly dissolved." Once again, Romero paused to allow for the cheers and applause that met the news. Meanwhile, Carmona remained at his desk, smiling broadly at the crowd's reaction. "We will also dismantle the office of the attorney general, the supreme court, the central bank, and we will dismiss all members of the national electorate," Romero continued, whipping the crowd into a frenzy. As fists punched the air and the cheers grew ever louder, Carmona tried to calm the hall with a wave of his arms, but it took a few minutes for the audience to settle. "We further decree the following eleven articles including the appointment of Pedro Carmona as president of the Republic of Venezuela and the removal of the word 'Bolivarian' from Bolivarian Republic of Venezuela."

As Romero went on to list the other nine articles, the audience again struggled to contain itself and even Carmona waved his fists triumphantly in the air. Romero promised elections would be held within a year and stated that the president would have the power to remove and name new officials at any national, state, or local post in order to guarantee governability. He then finished with the announcement that the 49 reforming laws that Chávez had passed with the Enabling Law five months previously, would be suspended.

The smell of coffee and sweat filled the warm war room where Mitchel paced in front of the wall lined with pictures, juggling a marker pen in his hand. Behind him José sat in a chair, holding a cup of coffee, trying to stay awake.

"Before we contact anyone we need to be absolutely sure that whoever it is, he or she, that they are still loyal to Chávez."

Mitchel was startled from his thoughts by the sound of José's cup smashing on the floor. When he turned around he found his friend hanging in his chair, eyes closed, mouth open, and softly snoring.

"Wake up!" Mitchel walked over and shook him firmly by the shoulders.

José grunted in response before opening his eyes. "Why do you do that, man?"

"You dozed off! I can't turn my back on you for a second, can I?"

"Do you have any idea when we last had more than a single hour of sleep?"

"A few days ago at most, so will you please try and stay awake and focus?"

"Yes, boss," José replied jokingly.

"So, who de we have so far?"

"To contact? Hard to say. We'll never be able to determine with any great certainty which people are still loyal to Chávez."

"We only need one," Mitchel responded, trying to remain positive despite understanding the difficulty. "And this is where I need you, José. You're the expert here. You know these people."

José sighed and rose from his chair to walk to the wall.

"Give me this," he said, grabbing the marker from Mitchel's hand. "Valbuena is working with Rout." José drew a line through Valbuena's picture on the wall. "Rojas? Nope. Our friend the Cardinal? Nope…."

One by one, José crossed off the faces pinned to the wall. He then stood back to get a clearer view of who was left.

"And?" asked Mitchel, who was leaning on the opposite wall watching José at work.

"Well, I have three possible options."

"Just three?"

"I'm sure there are more out there, but these three might possibly be in a position to help. I hope. Or at least one of them will be, again, I hope."

"Doesn't sound too convincing."

"I'm not convinced at all," José replied honestly. "But hey, you wanted to see this through so maybe you should choose."

"OK, point taken." Mitchel rubbed at his forehead, also feeling the strain of the last few days creeping up on him. "So, who do we have?"

"General Rafael Badillo."

Mitchel walked over and circled the man's face. He glanced at the file notes again: Badillo was commander of Venezuela's elite 42nd Paratrooper Brigade, once Chávez's own brigade. If there was a single Chavista left, it was likely he would be a paratrooper.

"Badillo hates violence and he was with Chávez from the beginning," José explained. "Furthermore, he plays a hell of a horse when little kids are on his back."

Mitchel stopped in his tracks, looked at his friend and mouthed, 'What?'

José grinned. "Uncle Badi, that's what we used to call him back in the day. He was a close friend of my father's and he lived around the corner. Our families were close once."

"But not anymore?"

"Not since my father died. I haven't seen the man in ten years or so."

"Do you have any idea how to get in contact with him?"

"Well, he might still live at the same house."

"And do you trust him?"

"I believe he's the surest bet of the three left. Do you want to hear more on the other two?"

"Not if your bet is the surest I feel I can get. Where is this house?"

"Just five blocks south of here. Walking distance."

"All right, let's go. And I suggest we take the car just in case we need to get somewhere fast."

As Mitchel headed for the door, José reached out to pull him back.

"If you don't mind, I would like to do this alone," he said softly. "Without you there I'll be able to find out more easily whether he can be trusted or not before we reveal our information."

"OK, I get that," Mitchel agreed. "You go, but please, let's be careful out there."

It took more than five minutes for the room to calm down enough to allow Romero to speak again. All that time Carmona had sat quietly behind his desk smiling.

"When I call your name, I ask you to come forward and sign this decree," Romero told the crowd. before reading down the list of 27 representatives from various political parties including members of Chávez's former right wing adversaries 'Democratic Action' and 'Copei'.

One by one those called walked up to a table at the front of the room to add their name to the decree. The first to sign was Cardinal Velasco who, after signing, walked onto the stage to shake Carmona's hand and pose for the cameras. Forty-five minutes and 26 handshakes later General Badillo walked up to the table. After signing he simply gave Carmona a friendly nod.

Once everyone had retaken their seats, Carmona sat tall and pulled the microphone towards him.

"Comrades, comrades," he greeted, almost immediately having to calm the room again. "Thank you for everything; for everything you did here today and for everything you did to get us here. It is my honor today to present myself to you as your new president. As you know, it's customary for a president to be sworn in by the president of the National Assembly, but as you have all witnessed there is no National Assembly anymore." Carmona placed his hand on the Bible in front of him. "So, filled with humility, I place my hand on the Bible and accept this responsibility as President of Venezuela."

A loud cheer interrupted Carmona's speech, reaching deafening levels as it bounced off the high ceiling. Carmona sat quietly, enjoying the adulation for as long as he thought seemly. "Thank you, thank you. Please, let me finish," he eventually said. "I promise you, I will reestablish the legitimacy of the 1999 constitution. I promise you a new broad-based government that will serve only you and not itself, I also promise you freedom and respect for the state of law. This responsibility is not a responsibility I have sought and I want you to know that nothing I did in the past was done in the hope it would lead up to this moment. But now that I'm here, I swear to you that I'll use all my powers to be here for you. Thank you for your trust. I will now hand you back to Daniel Romero who I hereby appoint Attorney-General and who will read the list of new ministers that will help us make Venezuela great again."

Romero duly took over and named a short list of ministers appointed by Carmona, all of them conservative party members. Meanwhile, Carmona got up from his desk to mingle with his supporters, shaking hands, slapping backs and clearly having the time of his life.

At Turiamo, Chávez walked up to the TV that hung from the ceiling at the wall and pushed the 'on' button. There was nothing but static. Looking for a remote, he started turning over the room, eventually throwing a fruit bowl against the wall in frustration. Immediately the door opened and Sergeant Alejandro rushed in.

"Are you OK, Sir?" he asked, as Chávez dropped onto the couch.

"I'm fine. I was just looking for the TV remote when the bowl got in the way."

"I see." Alejandro looked at the shards of broken glass among the oranges on the floor.

"Could you please have a look to see if there's a TV remote to be found anywhere?"

"I'm pretty sure they don't want you to look at the TV at the moment."

"I know," Chávez replied, tilting his head a little like a dog.

"I'll see what I can do." Alejandro nodded before leaving the room again.

With little else to do, Chávez walked up to the window and watched the ships in the harbor, noting that the military continued to go about their business as if nothing had happened. 'What's going on out there?' he wondered. 'What are they going to do with me and where is my family?' Before his mind had time to make up the answers Alejandro walked back into the room.

"I've got it," he said. "I stole it from the cantina. If anyone asks, please don't tell them you got it from me."

Chávez nodded before asking, "Do you think they got it?"

"Sorry? Who got what?"

"The fax. You did send the fax, didn't you?"

"Sure I did, but I don't know. I mean, the fax was delivered, of that I saw the proof, but I cannot be sure anyone read it let alone the right people."

"You're right. You're absolutely right. Besides, who's to say who the right people are in these times?" Chávez laughed out loud. "Now, let's see what's out there."

Taking the remote from Alejandro's hand, Chávez pointed it at the TV and switched channels. "Join me, please," he said, tapping his hand on the seat on the couch next to him.

"Are you sure?"

"Sit down. There's nothing to be nervous about. It's not like you are sitting next to the president. Haven't you heard? I resigned."

For a few seconds, Chávez jumped from one channel to another before settling on a newscast featuring the US press secretary Ari Fleisher, addressing the Press from the White House.

"...We know that the action encouraged by the Chávez government provoked this crisis. According to the best information available, the Chávez government suppressed peaceful demonstrations. Government supporters, on orders from the Chávez government, fired on unarmed, peaceful protestors, resulting in 10 killed and 100 wounded. The results of these events are now that President Chávez has resigned the presidency. Before resigning, he dismissed the vice president and the cabinet, and a transitional civilian government has been installed. This government has promised early elections...."

"Liars!" Chávez shouted before flicking to the next channel where he saw US ambassador Shale at Miraflores Palace. Leaving through a side entrance, he smiled at the handful of reporters waiting for him.

"...It's ridiculous to say that the US had anything to do with the events in Venezuela in the past days. Today, President Carmona and I met to exchange messages between our governments. That's why I was here. I just informed him about the situation in Washington and the Organization of American States and about some evaluations on our part."

"Can you tell us more about those evaluations?"

"It's a private evaluation, diplomatic and very private. The only thing I am willing to say about it is that I urged President Carmona to restore the national assembly as soon as possible."

"President Carmona!" Chávez sneered. "That man, if it wasn't for me he would have been discharged as president of the Federation of Chambers of Commerce long ago. The little weasel always stood on the shoulders of giants instead of creating something himself."

On TV, the report was interrupted by the image of a newscaster, pressing at her earpiece, as she looked earnestly into the camera.

"We have breaking news coming from Venevision Studio Four where Carlos Ortega, President of the Venezuelan Workers Confederation, is present to publicly announce his resignation." In the studio Ortega appeared next to the reporter and took a seat. *"Mr. Ortega, welcome to the studio and thank you for being here."*

"Thank you for having me."

"I understand that you wanted to make a public statement regarding your resignation as president of the Venezuelan Workers Confederation."

"Yes, indeed. But first I'd like to react to the events that led up to this decision, to everything that has happened in the past 24 hours in this country. What happened in Venezuela is nothing less than a coup d'état. There is no doubt about it. The Inter-American Democratic Charter and the Washington protocol have been clearly violated here."

As Ortega spoke, the newscaster's eyes widened in panic, clearly unaware of how to handle the situation as she waited for guidance through her earpiece.

"I would also like to state that President Hugo Chávez did not resign and even if he had, it would not have been legal unless he did so in front of the National Assembly. In such a case he would have been succeeded by the next in line, the vice-president, and after him the president of the National Assembly. It is my conviction that the coup leaders conspired with the United States. I can present evidence of..."

Before Ortega had chance to reveal his evidence, the program switched to a commercial.

"Finally, someone who dares to say what really happened," Chávez muttered, waving a fist at the television. "Did you see that?"

"I did," Sergeant Alejandro confirmed and he patted Chávez on the shoulder.

"I feel it!" Chávez called out. "Mark my words, this is the first sign of a true democracy at work. Son, do you have a cell phone?"

Alejandro looked at Chávez and shook his head.

"I do have one," he revealed. "But I have to check it at the door every time I get here."

"Then maybe I should ask you, if next time you come here, to bring two cell phones."

Chávez smiled.

While Mitchel drank coffee with Nathalie and Catherine on the back porch they heard the sound of José's Ducati parking in the driveway.

"Good to see you back in one piece," Mitchel noted as José walked into the garden.

"Please, sit and have something to eat or drink," Nathalie said, while Catherine automatically poured him a glass of juice.

"Thank you."

"You're welcome," the girl responded.

"So how did it go? Did you see Badillo?" Mitchel asked.

"He wasn't at home, but his wife was and she put me on the phone to him."

"So what did he say?"

"He's agreed to meet with us later today at his home. I left a copy of the evidence there." José answered, the excitement clear in his voice until he noticed Mitchel's face. "What's the matter?"

"A few minutes after you left I watched Badillo sign the Carmona decree on TV. Whatever he was, he's now one of them."

"That's what's worries you, my friend? I wouldn't worry too much about that yet. Signing the decree will keep him close to the government, allowing him to possibly work from the inside. Knowing the man, I'm unconvinced that Badillo is capable of turning to the dark side. When I spoke to him on the phone, I asked him if he was willing to meet us regarding evidence of a premeditated bloody coup. In his voice, I recognized the 'uncle' from before."

"You better be sure, if you drag my husband into this man's home later," Nathalie responded icily.

"I hardly have to drag him," José answered. "But trust me. I've known the man my entire life. He didn't turn."

"What time is the meet?" Mitchel asked looking at his watch.

"Three this afternoon."

"That gives us a few hours to get some sleep then."

"At last! God knows I can use some."

24. Operation Rescue National Dignity

Friday, April 12, 2002
3pm

A RUMOR THAT CHÁVEZ was being held at Turiamo naval base spread like wildfire through the capital and even though the base was all but hermetically sealed from the outside world, not to mention a good three-hour drive from Caracas, a large crowd of protesters soon gathered at every entry point to the base.

"Free Chávez! Free our leader! Free Chávez! Free our leader!"

Waving banners, flags and posters of Chávez, the protesters tried to move in on the base, but as soon as they passed the yellow lines drawn on the asphalt by the guards manning the gates, warning shots were fired into the air. Meanwhile, inside the base, in the cantina of the building where Chávez was being held, Gallardo and Valbuena frantically discussed their next move.

"If we don't watch out things could get out of hand fast," Valbuena stated before sucking on his cigar and reclining into a big leather chair.

"You look worried," Gallardo noted, "and at the same time you don't." He paused to pour himself a cup of coffee. "I mean, you seem pretty relaxed in your chair smoking your cigar."

"I'm just saying that outside the gates the crowd is getting increasingly violent, by the hour, and I hear that in Caracas more and more people are coming out to protest against Carmona."

"So, what do you suggest we do?"

"I think we need to decide what to do with Chávez."

"And what do you think we should do with him?" Gallardo asked, clearly starting to lose patience.

"I've no idea, but either we do something with Chávez or we do something about Carmona. I'm afraid he's moving too fast, practically nullifying every piece of legislation Chávez implemented in the past two years. At this rate, he'll burn the house down before we put in the furniture."

"Damn," Gallardo growled. "OK, you stay here and work out the options for Chávez. I'll fly back to Miraflores and see what I can do about Carmona; see if I can slow him down a little."

"Are you ready?" Mitchel asked José.

"Yup," José replied. "Car?"

"Indeed. Let's take the car. It's getting noisy out there again and it looks like the fires have been relit." Mitchel pointed at the black smoke rising above the trees in the distance. Turning to his wife, he kissed her tenderly on the forehead. "I'll see you soon," he told her, and before she could protest he headed out of the door followed by José.

"You take care out there!" Nathalie called after him.

"We'll just be around the corner, dear. Don't worry," replied Mitchel before hastily getting into the car. As all eight of the Mustang's cylinders roared into life like a lion, he turned to José, grinning. "Don't you just love that sound?"

Before his friend had time to answer he drove out of the driveway at a speed best that was perhaps best reserved for the racetrack. So, when the car came to a halt outside Badillo's house, José joked, "That was a great two minutes."

Mitchel smiled. "Right then let's see where this path takes us."

The two men got out of the car and walked up the path to Badillo's front door, only to have the man himself open it before they had chance to knock.

"Welcome, gentleman." After reaching forward to shake their hands the general invited them in.

As Mitchel and José walked through the hallway, they noticed three other men and a woman in the room. Registering the men's surprise, Badillo smiled.

"I'm sorry," he apologized. "Let me introduce you to Generals Lucio Reyes and Gustavo Clemente, Garcia Peroni, the head of the PDVSA, and Carola Faustina, the trusted lawyer of Chávez."

Mitchel and José shook everyone's hand before turning their attention back to Badillo.

"First of all, I – no, we – would like you to know that everyone present in this room is a friend of democracy and of Hugo Chávez."

"If you don't mind me asking ..." Mitchel started, but a look from José immediately silenced him.

"I know what you're going to ask," Badillo said calmly. "What was I doing signing the Carmona decree?"

"Well, yes," Mitchel confirmed.

"And it's a reasonable question," Badillo replied. "You have to know that in a situation like this you're either in or you're out. And when you're out you really are out, which means you get no information, no nothing. The new regime will not allow for any opposition yet. All of which meant, the only way for me to stay close was to sign the decree."

"You have to know," Faustina added, "that we were with Chávez right up until the moment he was transported from Miraflores and we made a promise to do everything possible to get him back into power again."

"Anyway," Badillo continued, "we'd like to thank you for the evidence you have given us. We reviewed it earlier and we are impressed with the findings."

"Thank you," José said. "Any idea what you'll do next?"

"We've discussed it at length," Faustina told him, "and we believe that we now have the means to set up an operation to restore the balance of power to the way it was."

"Operation Rescue National Dignity," Clemente added.

"You have a name for it?" Mitchel asked, not meaning to but obviously sounding incredulous given the punch he received to the shoulder from José.

"We have more than that," Peroni replied, smiling. "We drew up a manifesto describing the five main goals of 'National Dignity'."

And now it was José's turn to look surprised, but before he could say anything Faustina started to explain.

"The five main points of the manifesto are: end the terror being exercised by the metropolitan police in the barrios of Caracas; reinstate the constitutional order; avoid a military confrontation; seek the immediate resignation of the current, illegal government; and, finally, rescue Hugo Chávez from his imprisonment."

"Sounds good," José agreed. "But do you have any plans in place to execute this manifesto?"

"The key factor in whatever we do is knowing for sure that Chávez didn't resign," Faustina replied. "If, somehow, there's any merit to his resignation, for instance if the resignation letter they show isn't a fake, we could be in legal trouble."

"We need the fax," Mitchel muttered.

"So, how do you stand?" José asked the group. "I mean, are you able to count on support from the military and elsewhere?"

"Fortunately, there aren't a lot of countries that have expressed support for the new government," Clemente said before taking a piece of paper from his jacket pocket and reading from it. "Over 19 countries have officially condemned the undemocratic coup and demanded either the reinstatement of the old government or speedy elections. In fact, the only country that has shown any sympathy for the coup at this point is the United Sates. Mexico, Cuba, Libya, Iran, Iraq and Argentina have all said they refuse to recognize the Carmona government."

"And local non-military?" José asked Peroni.

"Not so easy to say, I'm afraid. We know there's a lot of opposing views. I'm sure that most of the staff of the PDVSA will support the old regime since they are all newly appointed by either me or Chávez himself. We also know that public television has always favored Chávez and since they are on air again this is helpful. As for the rest, it's hard to say, but I believe that if we are to do this we have to start with the military." Peroni looked at Badillo.

"I'm quite positive about the loyalty of the military," he told José. "At the very least I'm sure we can rely on the paratrooper regiment at Maracay, after all, Chávez himself was a paratrooper and he always kept in close contact with them. Also, we have several battalions within Fort Tiuna and I personally can vouch for my old battalions. We also have the presidential Honor Guard at Miraflores – they were all hand-picked by Chávez and they can be counted as his most loyal troops, which makes it surprising that the new regime didn't replace them."

"Without doubt, that's one of the first and biggest errors they have made," Clemente added.

"So, what do we do?" Mitchel asked.

"You don't have to do anything," Badillo replied. "You've done enough already. You have our thanks and we can take it from here."

José glanced at Mitchel, anticipating a reaction that indeed came instantly.

"I'm sorry, but we've come this far, we've gathered the evidence you are about to use and we've aligned everyone and everything, including the VP and Chávez himself. Besides, if the Honor Guard is indeed still in place we know how to reach them, so if you don't mind we'd rather stay on board."

Although Mitchel sounded decisive he looked towards and nodded at José for confirmation.

"Well, I'm glad we had this discussion," José said, frowning.

"So, what's your plan?" Mitchel asked the group.

"Our plan is to fight them with their own weapon," Badillo answered. "They started this coup by manipulating and using the media, and I suggest we do the same; that we use the same media to end it. Public television is back on air so we can use it to spread the word."

"Wont they cut it off again as soon as they notice the first transmissions?" José asked.

"They have to cut transmission from inside the studios as the radio tower is on the roof of the building," Clemente told him. "Carmona's military is being gathered at Miraflores to defend the palace if necessary. From the studio, we make a public announcement calling upon the paratroopers and other faithful regiments to join our resistance to the coup regime, and then we have to hope that others will follow. Next, we call on the people to demonstrate peacefully in the streets as we need to create a momentum. And then, finally, we feed CNN with regular updates from loyal generals speaking in favor of Chávez."

"But won't they try to take down the network again as soon as they notice the transmissions?" José persisted.

"It should be easy to defend the studio with a small army," Clemente replied. "I believe they'll think twice before starting a war in front of the studio."

"You hope," Faustina added.

"I'm pretty sure," Clemente stated.

"But what about the private TV stations, won't they just throw out more propaganda for the coup leaders?" Mitchel asked.

"Here's where I come in," General Reyes responded. "In contrast to the public network, the private networks like Venevision are on cable and not the airwaves. I have a close tie to the TV infrastructure company that manages cable and my contact assures me that with a simple flick of the switch they can take out all the private TV channels."

"Meaning we end up controlling the only available TV channels," Clemente finished.

"Of course, this is all good and well, but one of the first communications we need to get out there is that Chávez did not resign and is being held prisoner," Faustina told the men. "And for that we need the fax as proof and to get to the fax we need the help of the presidential Honor Guard to get into the palace."

"Maybe we can help out with that," Mitchel offered. "When we were at the Cuban embassy so see the VP, transmissions were being locally jammed. That means there's a chance that communications surrounding the palace are also jammed. However, we have another way to contact the Honor Guard."

As Mitchel finished he felt all eyes in the room on him.

"Is that so?" Badillo asked, not sounding especially convinced. "Well, it's clear we need a few men to get into the palace, find the fax and, with the help of the Honor Guard, find their way through the palace to confront the Carmona clan with our evidence, which we will threaten to make public through the media."

"That could be a definitive blow against them," Peroni acknowledged. "But why not get the fax, show it to a TV station and immediately throw all the evidence out there?"

"We could do that," Badillo agreed, "but it would confirm the identity of the traitors instantly and who knows what they might do in order to save their own skin. However, if we confront them we can give them a way out with some kind of dignity and in doing so, hopefully, not force them into resorting to violence."

"They will probably flee the country," Faustina said.

"Possibly, but I still think it's the safest way to do this if we are to minimize any risk of casualties."

"Ever the peaceful Taoist," Reyes joked.

"And what if we get caught or killed after entering the palace?" Peroni asked.

"Give us a few good men," Mitchel interrupted, pointing at himself and José.

"I can do better than that," Reyes replied. "When you contact the Honor Guard, try and contact either Sergeant Gonzalez or Captain Manet. I can personally vouch for them as loyal to the cause. If you manage to reach one of them they can set you up with a few men to escort you into the palace. Of course, it's a plan that is not without risk."

"If it's true we can trust them how can we be sure that we will actually be talking to them?" asked José. "I mean, on the walkie talkie anyone could say he's Gonzalez or Manet."

"That shouldn't be a problem," Reyes answered. "I can give you a few questions only they will know the answer to."

"I believe the risk is minimal," Mitchel told his friend. "Anyway, if they capture us we can always present the evidence."

"And if we get killed first?" José asked.

Mitchel didn't answer. Instead he looked to the others waiting for them to react. "So, what do you think?"

"I think we have a plan," Badillo told him.

"Good," Mitchel replied. "Now the only thing left to do is work out the timing and the details."

25. The Fight Back

Friday, April 12, 2002

9 pm

I BROUGHT YOU YOUR SOUP," Alejandro announced as he walked into the room.

"Thank you, but I don't recall…"

Alejandro pressed a finger to his lips, effectively shutting Chávez down before sitting next to him on the couch and handing him a cup of soup.

"I know, Sir. But I do believe you asked for…"

Alejandro took a cell phone from his jacket and with his back to the camera handed it over.

"Great, that's fantastic," Chávez responded with a whisper as he quickly hid the phone.

"I borrowed it from a colleague who's probably looking for it now. We don't have much time. Who are you going to call?"

"My wife."

"Your wife?" Alejandro was clearly surprised. "Forgive me, but I didn't know you had a wife."

"So, where did you think my children came from?"

"No, uh, it's just that…."

"At ease, Sergeant, I'm just messing with you. My wife Marisabel and I don't share a lot of our lives these days so it's very well possible you haven't seen us together."

"So, why do you want to get in touch with her?"

"The phones of everyone else I'm close to will either be tapped or confiscated by now, if they are reachable at all. Everyone that matters knows that my wife and I are more or less separated so I suspect they won't be watching her too closely. Now, if you don't mind?"

Chávez walked into the corner, knowing it was the camera's one and only blind spot. Alejandro immediately left the room and Chávez started punching numbers.

"Ola?" It was a man's voice and it threw Chávez for a second.

"Who is this?"

"Carlos Abarca. Who are you?"

Chávez quickly hung up without a word and, a little more carefully, dialed his wife's number again.

"Ola?" answered the same man.

For a second Chávez considered his options before replying. "I'm looking for Marisabel."

"There's no Marisabel here, you must have dialed a wrong number."

"I'm sorry."

Chávez hung up for a second time, the confusion evident in his face. He was convinced he had the correct number; remembering numbers had never been an issue for him. Pressed for time, and constantly checking the door for movement, he tried to remember any phone number from the past that he hadn't simply logged into his phone's memory. The only number he could think of was that of a neighbor from his hometown of Sabaneta. They had lost contact some time ago, more than five years, but he had nothing to lose.

"Ola?"

"Alberto? Alberto Pomoamasa?"

"Yes. Who is asking?"

"Alberto, it's Hugo, Hugo Chávez."

"Who is this?" Alberto asked again with some irritation.

"It's me! I'm telling you it's really me, you have to believe me."

"Hugo? But how?"

"Well, that's a long story, Alberto. But believe me when I tell you I don't have any numbers where I am and yours was the only number I knew by heart. I'm trying to reach Marisabel."

"Where are you? Are you OK?"

"I'm fine. I'm being held at Turiamo and I need you to do something for me."

"I don't have Marisabel's number."

"That's fine, but maybe you could find her and give her a message to pass on to General Rafael Badillo?"

"You know I'd do anything for you. I still cannot believe it's you."

"Thank you, old friend. But quickly, I don't have much time."

"What's the message?"

"Tell her I'm OK and I didn't resign or sign anything else. Badillo will know what to do."

"I knew it!" Alberto cried out. "Sure, no problem. General Rafael Badillo, you said?"

"That's correct. Thank you, Alberto. I hope we'll have more time to catch up in the near future. I have to go now."

"Thank you, Mr. President. I'll take care of it."

"Thank you."

Chávez quickly killed the line and walked back into the camera's view, hoping no one had missed him.

"Wake up! Wake up! Wake up!" Catherine yelled as she jumped on the couch where José was taking a nap.

Startled, José bolted upright in one swift movement

"What the…"

"Mind your language!" Nathalie shouted from the kitchen.

"You little devil," José growled as he pulled Catherine towards him and threw her onto the other end of the couch before jokingly warning her, "You better watch out!"

"Ready for some late supper?" Nathalie asked as she came to join them in the living room carrying a large plate with pizza slices on it.

"I certainly am," José replied. "Pizza! Did you know this was originally a poor man's dish first made by the Vikings?"

"Shut up and eat," Nathalie said before switching on the TV. "How does the couch sleep?"

"It's not so much the sleeping as the waking up. Where's Mitchel?"

"He woke some time ago and went out to get some fresh air. He'll be back soon. Eat, don't let the pizza get cold."

"Honey, I'm home!"

Nathalie looked at José. "How does he do that?" she asked in mock exasperation just as her husband walked into the room.

"Ah, pizza! I'm starving. Any news?" Mitchel nodded towards the TV.

"We just switched it on," Nathalie said. "But it seems nothing has changed. They are still broadcasting interviews with gloating opposition leaders."

"I don't like you going out again today, Dad." Catherine looked at her father, the worry evident in her eyes.

"I promise it will all be over soon," Mitchel answered.

"She's right, you know," Nathalie added. "It's not safe out there."

"But if we don't do something now there's a very big chance it won't be safe out there anytime soon."

"Can't you talk some sense into him?" Nathalie asked José.

"You know I can't," José answered. "But what I can say is that I also believe this will be over soon, whatever happens."

"You see…" Catherine said quietly. "…it's the 'whatever happens' bit that worries me."

"I'll take care of your father," José assured her.

"Thank you," Mitchel said with a grin. "Look, it's really going to be fine."

He was going to say more, but everyone's attention was suddenly taken by the television that had lost transmission, leaving the hiss of white noise to fill the void. Catherine leaped from her seat to change channels, but every private channel was off air. Mitchel and José look at each other.

"The game's afoot," Mitchel said. "Can you please switch to one of the state channels."

"But there's nothing working," Catherine replied.

"Trust me."

Catherine clicked onto one of the state channels. "You see, snow."

"Please, leave it for a moment. If all goes well that will soon change."

"No problem." Catherine shrugged and returned to her pizza. Within a few minutes the TV screen turned red and a message was displayed reading, *'This is an official broadcast by the Bolivarian Republic of Venezuela'*.

"I thought they had stripped 'Bolivarian' from the country's name?" Nathalie mentioned.

"That was the idea," José answered smiling.

After a few more seconds, General Badillo appeared on screen, sitting relaxed in a comfortable chair opposite a journalist.

"That's our cue," Mitchel stated. "Ladies, we need to go out for a bit."

"Do you have to?" Catherine asked concerned.

"It's just to do some reconnaissance," José told her. "No scary stuff. I promise you."

While Mitchel and José put their coats on, they continued to listen to Badillo as he boldly declared the coup to be illegal before revealing the details of Operation National Dignity.

"…We, the collective of loyal Chavistas will bring an end to the terror being exercised in the barrios of Caracas; reinstate the constitutional order; seek the immediate resignation of the usurping government; and rescue our democratically chosen President Hugo Chávez. I have personally spoken to the wife of our president who has told me Chávez contacted her via a smuggled telephone. He told her that he never resigned."

"But how are you planning to restore democracy?" asked the journalist.

"At all costs, we want to avoid a military confrontation," Badillo replied. "So we need the Venezuelan people to achieve this themselves. We know that only a small group of elitists support Carmona's government whereas the large part of our population is outraged by what happened. So, I ask the people to go into the streets, wear a red beret or something red as a sign of loyalty, and show you're outraged peacefully. As for my fellow generals, I would ask you to speak out in support of our President, Hugo Chávez, especially all you paratroopers out there. Show yourselves in favor of the man that is your leader; a man who is one and the same as you." Badillo stood up from his chair and clenched his fist in the air. "We will restore our national dignity!"

As Mitchel and José made their way to the tunnel entrance at the White Palace, they watched increasing numbers of people leaving their homes to take to the streets to protest. All of them were dressed in red and shouting for the return of their leader. Just around the corner from the tunnel entrance José stopped the bike.

"That's a good place." Mitchel pointed at a closed fast food stand. "We can hide behind that."

Once behind the stand, Mitchel took the Cadena de Depredador from his backpack. "Let's try this," he said, handing the walkie talkie to José just as his cell phone rang. "Hold on, let me take this," he said with a shrug. "James Mitchel speaking. Yes sir... Yes, that's true... yes, I understand... he did know... I think that's good news, Sir, ... I really appreciate that ... thank you for the call.... I will ... thank you, again."

"And what was that all about?" José asked after Mitchel hung up.

"You're not going to believe this," Mitchel said, still looking at his phone in disbelief. "That was my boss, the ambassador. He told me that somehow US intelligence has got hold of a message that came directly from Chávez addressed to his wife."

"The same message we know about?"

"Yes, that he didn't resign and to spread the word but I guess it wasn't common knowledge when he called."

"And why do you think he called you with that old news?"

"Who knows? He just said he thought I would want to know and told me to be careful."

"Then I assume he knows you're up to something."

"Probably, but for now this doesn't change a thing. So, come on. Try the walkie talkie."

"Right." José put the device to his ear. "Is anyone out there? Over."

"Is anyone out there?" Mitchel mimicked incredulously. "Is that your call for the President's Honor Guard?"

José pointedly ignored his friend. "Anyone receiving this call, please respond. Over."

"Are we sure this thing works?" Mitchel asked as José's appeal continued to go unanswered.

"Anyone there? Over."

"Hello, who is this? Over."

At the reply, José and Mitchel felt their hearts beat faster. "I can't give you my name right now, but I'm looking for Sergeant Gonzalez or Captain Manet. Over."

For almost a minute the radio stayed silent.

"Captain Manet here. Over."

"Captain, good to hear from you. Is everything OK there? Over."

"Who is this? Over."

"I have a message from General Reyes, Sir. He says 'hello' and he wants you to know that the drinks at the bar will have burned out by now. He says you will know what that means. Over."

"Thank you. It means that I know that Reyes really sent you. Over."

"He also told me to ask for the names of the two pool ladies at the hotel. Over."

There was a pause for laughter on the other end of the line. "María and Gabriela," Manet said. "Though I don't believe they were their real names."

"Thank you, Sir." José replied. My name is José Abrantes and I work, or probably worked, for the DISIP."

"Good to talk to you." Manet Replied. "You say you have a message? Over."

"Yes, Sir, but firstly, what's the situation over there? Over."

"The entire Honor Guard is still in place and we are laying low, working with the current government while we wait for a chance to restore the situation. Over."

"We have a plan that might do just that, Sir. We believe we have enough incriminating material that, once presented, might take care of everything, but we need your help. Over."

"What can we do? Over."

"The plan is to enter the palace through the tunnel at 11am tomorrow, Saturday morning. From there, we need you to guide us, unseen, to the office of the Socialist Party to pick up something and from there take us to see Carmona himself. At the same time we need you and your palace guards to position yourselves at strategic points throughout the palace and be ready to take over and secure the grounds as soon as possible. Over."

"How many of you will there be? Over."

"Just the two of us. Unarmed. You think it can be done? Over."

"If you can reach the tunnel entrance by yourself I believe we can take you from there and take up positions unnoticed. Over."

"That's great, Captain. We'll meet you there in about twelve hours. Please take care of yourself in the meantime. Over."

"Not a problem. We'll be ready for you. Over and out."

José handed the walkie talkie back to Mitchel. "That's settled then, are you sure you want to go through with this?"

"Wouldn't miss it for the world," Mitchel answered.

As the two returned home, the streets of Caracas looked increasingly restless with ever greater numbers of people arriving in support of Chávez. Despite the initial call to keep the demonstrations peaceful, in many of the poorer neighborhoods rioting and pillaging had broken out as Chávez supporters vented their anger on public infrastructures and display windows.

26. Grasping at Straws

Saturday, April 13, 2002
Midnight

VEN IN THE MIDDLE OF THE NIGHT the streets of
Caracas remained restless. With news of the manifesto
spreading fast, more and more people gathered to be
heard and members of the Bolivarian Circles began to surround
Miraflores Palace. On TV, a dizzying number of generals were giving
statements. For every general that went on private television stating his
support for Carmona, public television tried to show at least two other
profile figures denouncing Carmona and speaking out in favor of
Chávez. Those who were able to receive CNN through satellite TV were
treated to a stream of updates, carefully orchestrated by Badillo and his
friends, with images showing people dressed in red, demonstrating in
the streets, waving banners and pictures in support of Chávez. Other
footage showed Carmona's generals speaking out before driving out of
the city in their expensive cars, symbolizing the retreat of the
Venezuelan elite. Meanwhile, Venevision continued its anti-Chávez

coverage despite the growing number of Chavistas now knocking on the door.

In his office at the palace, Carmona watched the news, zapping nervously between the channels, as Gallardo tried to keep him calm. Unfortunately, he was getting tired of having to adjust to the constant flicking between news reports.

On CNN, a statement by Chávez's wife Marisabel declared her husband had not resigned and that he had been imprisoned at a naval base. Then, over on Venevision, a reporter interviewed a woman in the street who appeared to have misread the script. "We just want to be heard and the media to show what's really going on. We are here in the streets in protest and that is what is really happening. Show the people the truth," she demanded.

Carmona cursed loudly. "How can our own TV channel show this woman? I thought we owned the private networks? Isn't it bad enough we lost Badillo to this group of dissidents?"

"Take it easy," Gallardo told him. "We never had Badillo, and even without him we got this far, so we don't need him now."

"But what do we do?" Carmona asked, almost timidly.

Gallardo looked at him closely, his mind already working on a Plan B in case Carmona should fall apart at the final hurdle.

"I need you to take it easy," he said. "Nothing has changed, you just need to hang in there a little longer. In the meantime, we continue with our preparations to swear in the new ministers later this afternoon."

Carmona looked outside at the gathering protesters. Then, taking a deep breath and firming his resolve, he nodded at Gallardo. "That's exactly what we'll do, and more."

"What do you mean 'more'?" Gallardo asked surprised by the sudden burst of positivity.

"If you don't see that our little plan is in trouble then you're more naïve than I thought."

Before Gallardo could protest, Carmona picked up the phone.

"Yes, it's me," he said. "Are you all still there? Great. Please join me immediately in the conference room." Carmona hung up the phone and turned to Gallardo. "You too, please."

"No! No! No! No! No! No! No!" Valbuena slammed his fists onto the table to hammer home his point. "If you do this I promise you can kiss your presidency goodbye."

"And what's your bright idea?" Carmona asked quietly before looking around the table at each of his fellow conspirators. "Or your idea? Or yours? What about you? Anything?" There was nothing but silence, and Carmona shook his head. "We've been at it for more than three hours now, and what have you come up with?"

"It's political suicide if after only one day you start to haggle with your own decree," General Gomez told him.

"And just what would you have me do?" Carmona asked.

Gomez shrugged his shoulders.

"I'll tell you what you should do," Gallardo interrupted. "I think you should use the force of the military to disperse the crowds surrounding the palace and clean the streets in Caracas. Just give the order."

"And risk a civil war?" Carmona yelled in exasperation.

"Are you out of your mind?" Cardinal Velasco agreed, shaking his head wildly. "The Church cannot and will not condone such an action. Do what you will, do nothing for all I care, but I don't want any part of this."

"Don't worry, Cardinal," Carmona said, trying to calm things down. "I will never give such an order risking more lives. Listen, the transition of power is in danger. If you don't see that, I can't help you. In my opinion doing nothing will result in failure and, frankly, I don't know if doing anything is going to prevent that."

"So?" Gallardo demanded impatiently.

"So, we fight, but not with guns, with words. In the past few hours we have listed all the main objections to the changes we proposed. I see no other way than to give the people what they want."

"So, we give them Chávez?" Valbuena muttered sarcastically, bringing a withering look from Carmona.

"No, we don't give them Chávez. But we will reinstate the most important of Chávez's reforms. What we'll do is draft a new statement and I will announce it, live on television. We'll invite all the major networks, both national and international."

"And what will you say?" Gallardo asked.

"What we discussed before, nothing more, nothing less." Carmona banged both fists on the table.

"We won't recover from this," Valbuena warned him one more time.

"This is what will happen," Carmona said defiantly, and everyone remained silent. "I will write the statement myself. You can go now."

As the men left the room, mutely shaking their heads, Gallardo approached Valbuena.

"You have a minute?"

"Sure."

"Walk with me." As the two moved along the hallway, away from the others, Gallardo asked for Valbuena's opinion about what had just happened.

"To be honest, I don't know what to think," Valbuena whispered. "I know the coup is in trouble, but what to do? I honest to God don't know what's going to happen."

"The question is not whether you know what's going to happen but if you want to wait for it to happen?"

"What do you mean?"

"What I mean to say is that we have a choice to make. We are the ones that put him in place and if we regret that decision this is probably the last moment to do something about it."

"And do what exactly?"

"It's simple," Gallardo said breezily, "we stop Carmona from making his statement and order troops onto the streets as we suggested."

"You suggested," Valbuena corrected.

"Listen, for now, we can count on the loyalty of the military, but we don't know how long that will last. If the pro-Chávez sentiment in the street keeps growing the military may turn."

"If you can even count on them now," Valbuena muttered, unconvinced.

"Now may be our last chance."

"OK, I think you're right; this may be our last chance. But did you think about what will happen next if we do as you suggest?"

As Valbuena spoke, his anger caught the attention of others in the hallway.

"Lower your voice," Gallardo told him as they stopped walking.

"I will not lower my voice," Valbuena spat back. "Because if we do as you suggest, every man and woman who ever had any doubts about Chávez will immediately become a Chavista. We will have to crush a civilian uprising, then another and another, and then, when the streets are finally clear, we will face the first of many resistance cells who will kill innocent soldiers simply for the crime of guarding some kind of military installation. A dictatorship will drown this country in years of violence and the killing of innocents." Valbuena took a deep breath. "And all because you didn't agree with some political reforms made by our president, and our next president."

"You also disagreed with Chávez's politics so don't start now. I think…"

"It doesn't matter what you think!" Valbuena interrupted. "I want no part in yet another coup. This has gone far enough and I'm going to let it play out, but I promise you that if you try to steer this boat in any other direction than the one Carmona wants to take it, I will use every loyal soldier under my command to stop you."

"OK, you made your point." Gallardo glanced at the handful of people in the hallway listening to their conversation. "We'll let it play out. But I promise you, if this goes as I'm convinced it will go, by this time tomorrow we will either be in jail or on the run."

"Well, if you're that convinced and you don't want to wind up in jail, you better start packing," Valbuena told him before walking off into the maze of halls within the palace.

In the living room Nathalie, Catherine, José and Mitchel were either watching television or reading a book or newspaper after breakfast. If it wasn't for the presence of José, it could have been a regular day at the Mitchel household.

"Shouldn't you be preparing for something?" Nathalie asked.

"Yeah, shouldn't you?" Catherine added.

"You're making far too much of this," Mitchel replied dragging his eyes from CNN for a second. "There's really nothing to plan."

"You know I don't like to agree with Mitchel," José joked, "but this time I think he's right. In a few hours we take a tour through the palace, present the evidence and return home."

Mitchel nodded as he put his arm around Catherine.

"Don't worry," he told her. "By the end of today this will all be over."

"*We now go live to the Miraflores palace in Caracas where the newly-installed President of Venezuela will make a statement.*"

"Shhh!" Mitchel hissed, silencing the room as he inched closer to the TV where Carmona could be seen sitting behind the presidential desk, grinning.

"People of Venezuela," he started. "In the past 24 hours we have seen a lot of change, a lot of emotion and also a lot of anger. I understand that anger, and this morning I come before you to prove to you that this new government listens – and not only listens, but also acts."

"Uh-oh," Mitchel muttered.

"I wouldn't worry too much." José replied. "I doubt there's much he can do to make the country suddenly fall in love with him. Too much has already happened and if he was planning on going to war he wouldn't announce it like this."

"I hereby pledge that the transitional government will be based on the 1999 constitution. We will withdraw the April 12th decree and respect human rights. We will also restore the National Assembly and coordinate the social forces of our nation to set up a transitional government that is marked by pluralism. We will formally restore the members of the army high command and their subordinates. We will maintain our regional and local authorities who were legally elected and I personally guarantee that all benefits generated though the social programs that we were running in the old government will also be honored." Carmona paused. Even without a live audience he felt the need to allow time so all the information might sink in.

"That doesn't sound too bad," Catherine offered.

"It sounds like he's panicking," Mitchel replied.

"I agree," José said. "It feels like he's grasping at straws."

"Well, you know I don't like your plan, but I think you are right," Nathalie told them.

"He would never roll back so many reforms if he was even a little sure of himself," Mitchel concluded as Carmona continued with his speech.

"I also will respect and official recognize the supreme court. We will construct a society without exclusion, where everyone can express all criticism and protest. The only thing I demand is that every protest should be conducted in a peaceful manner without weapons; the way it should be conducted in a democratic society."

"There we are," Mitchel spoke out loud. "He's afraid."

"And finally," Carmona said, starting to wrap up his speech, "I guarantee the safety and respectful treatment of Lt. Colonel Hugo

Chávez and his family. We will honor Lt. Colonel Chávez's request to leave the country and we will show live television images of him doing so in good health. I thank you for your attention and I promise that together we will make this country great again. In a few hours, we will be back with you for the swearing in ceremony of our newly-appointed ministers. Until then..."

"I half-expected him to leave the screen singing," Mitchel joked. "I mean, he's clearly going the 'Chávez way' so why not sing a song?" They all started laughing.

"Do you need to go?" Catherine asked.

"I do, honey," Mitchel replied. "I need to see this through to the finish. I'll be back before you know it."

"You better be," Nathalie warned, but with a smile.

27. The Palace Run

Saturday, April 13, 2002
11am

PLUMES OF BLACK SMOKE stained the Caracas skyline as chaos descended on the city. People with and without political motivation were looting stores, taking advantage of the situation to enrich themselves. As the violence grew in intensity, local police struggled to maintain order and they began to suppress demonstrations using brute force, teargas and weapons, mostly fired into the air in an attempt to disperse the crowds. In the street, tactical police vehicles armed with water cannons cleared the way for heavily armored policemen to patrol the capital.

As the city burned, Carmona looked out of the window only to see the palace surrounded by hundreds of thousands of pro-Chávez demonstrators, dressed in red, lighting fires, waving banners and chanting slogans against him.

"For the sake of our children we want our president!"

"We'll stay, even if it costs us our lives!"

General Gallardo looked up from the table where he was sat eating breakfast with General Valbuena and Cardinal Velasco while trying to ignore the chants outside. "What are you planning to do?" he asked.

Carmona rubbed his face and continued staring out of the window for a few seconds more before turning to the table.

"What can I do?" he replied, sounding close to desperate. "My only question at this time is 'should we withdraw our law enforcers and let the looting play out to prevent more bloodshed?'."

No one at the table reacted, and Carmona gave a wry smile.

"Anyway, I'm glad to see you're enjoying the fruits of our labor," he sneered.

"You are expected in the Hall of Mirrors in thirty minutes," the Cardinal reminded him. "I think you should stick to your schedule."

"And act as if nothing has happened?"

"The people want stability," Valbuena told Carmona. "The only chance you have is to continue with the swearing-in of the new ministers and hope the people will see it as a sign of stability."

"So suddenly it's 'my chance' instead of 'our chance'. What happened to the 'we are in this together' line?"

"Bad choice of words," Valbuena admitted. "I'm sorry. Of course, we are in this together. If you fail, we all fail. I think it's our best chance to continue what we've started."

"I agree with Valbuena," Gomez added. "Swear in the ministers, and after that decide what to do with our law enforcement officers. With any luck things will have cooled down by then."

"What do you think?" Carmona asked the Cardinal, who up until that point had kept his counsel.

"I'm just a humble observer in this process," he replied carefully. "You should do whatever results in the least casualties."

"A humble observer?" Gomez repeated with some irritation. "Is this really the card you want to play now? You've been part of this deal from the start. You wanted Chávez out as much as everyone here at the table, maybe even more."

"What I'm trying to say is…"

"You're trying to cover your ass," Gomez interrupted. "Just in case things go south."

"Stop bickering!" Carmona shouted. "If this is the only help you can offer, then I know what I have to do."

Grabbing a stack of papers from the table, Carmona stormed out of the room slamming the door behind him.

José steered his Ducati through the streets of Caracas with Mitchel on the back. Everywhere they looked, civilians hiding behind scarves, shawls and balaclavas were looting stores, demolishing cars and setting fires.

"Shit!" José cried out as he turned the corner onto Urdaneta Avenue only to find the road blocked by a tower of burning tires. José hit the brakes and span his bike around, leaving a skid mark on the asphalt and nearly losing Mitchel in the process. When his friend secured his seat again, José drove into a smaller back street, but the scene was just as chaotic and he had to weave between burning stacks, thrown bricks and rioters. At the next corner, a swat car almost completely blocked the road as policemen shot smoke and teargas grenades into the crowd.

"Hang on!" José yelled as he skillfully swerved his bike, missing the swat car by inches.

"Fuck!" Mitchel shouted as the bike plunged through a cloud of teargas.

"That was close!" José shouted as they sped away from the confrontation.

Some one hundred yards up the road, the scene was calmer and he stopped his bike. Filled with adrenalin, both men looked behind them to watch the policemen advance into the riot, trying to disperse the crowd with the weight of their batons.

"Way too close," Mitchel said with a shudder. "Any closer and we would still be there. How far away are we?"

"Just a few blocks. If we approach from the north we should avoid the crowd at the palace. Ready?"

"Let's go before the adrenaline wears off and I change my mind." Mitchel held onto José's waist again and as the bike set off he glanced back one more time to see the police clash with people they had once sworn to protect.

Despite a couple more, lesser, altercations, it took only two minutes to get to the White Palace. Barring the entrance was a large group of heavily armed soldiers, but they barely gave the Ducati a second glance. As José parked up, Mitchel pointed towards the crowd some 100 yards away closing in on Miraflores palace.

"Look!" he shouted over the noise of the protestors, and José followed his gaze.

"Let's get inside quick!" Grabbing Mitchel by the shoulder he pushed him towards the entrance.

As the two of them hurried to the doorway, the soldiers on guard continued to pay them little or no attention and they passed through the entrance with no problem. When they reached the hallway, a soldier called out.

"José!"

"You know him?" Mitchel asked as the man walked up to them purposefully.

"Not a clue." José shook his head, but when the man reached them with his arm outstretched he took his hand.

"José, how are you? And Mitchel. It has been a long time, friends. Far too long."

Mitchel and José looked at each other blankly before the soldier moved closer to whisper.

"Please, just say anything."

"It's good to see you too!" José half-shouted as his wits managed to catch up.

"Yes, it is," Mitchel agreed. "How's the family?"

"Good, good. Please, follow me." The soldier pointed the way towards the elevator. Without a word the three of them walked in and descended to the basement floor.

"How's the family?" José mimicked Mitchel, who merely shrugged.

"I'm sorry to surprise you like that," the soldier finally said. "My name is Manuel Gonzalez, Sergeant Manuel Gonzalez. I believe you spoke to my captain before. I had to act like we knew each other so we could bring you down. We control the area below the ground, but above we cannot be sure who to trust."

"How did you know who we are?" Mitchel asked.

"We don't get many Yankee and native couples visiting us these days," Gonzalez replied with a laugh.

"Fair point," Mitchel agreed just as the elevator opened. The men stepped out and into the small room they had visited before. It was almost dark this time with only a single gas lamp on a small desk shedding light on the room. Where before soldiers had guarded the entrance, the x-ray machine and scan port, there was now no-one else in the room.

"They've cut the power to the tunnels," Gonzalez explained as he picked up a flashlight from the table. "I'm not sure why."

"Nobody uses the tunnels now?" José asked.

"Not to get in. We had more than a few people fleeing the palace via the tunnels this morning, but no-one really wants to get into the place at this time."

"I can imagine," Mitchel said.

"Can I take that for you?" Gonzalez pointed at the backpack Mitchel was carrying.

"If you don't mind, I would like to hang onto this," Mitchel replied with a smile.

"No problem. Please, follow me. Though I understand you've been here before."

Gonzalez walked through the non-functioning scan port and into the tunnel. In the dark, the single beam of the flashlight gave the place an eerie look.

"We visited your president via this route a few days ago," Mitchel told the soldier.

"A lot has changed since then," he replied, and his answer made the walk through the dark tunnel seem far longer than before.

"Almost there," Gonzalez said after a few minutes and as they took the last bend, his flashlight found the door. Walking through and into another small, dark room lit by a single gas lamp, they were greeted by another soldier who was sitting in a chair at the desk, trying to read a book in the dim light. The soldier got to his feet when the men arrived.

"Captain Manet," he said by way of introduction.

"James Mitchel."

"José Abrantes."

"Welcome to Miraflores Palace, gentlemen. I understand you've been here before?"

"Under slightly better circumstances," José said.

"I'm sure of it," Manet replied.

"What's your status, Captain?" José asked.

"Military-wise, the palace is ours. The entire Honor Guard is loyal and they are the only military power in the palace except for some generals who are playing at politics. I have a team waiting upstairs to take you wherever you want to go."

"So, we shouldn't run into any problems moving around the palace?" asked Mitchel.

"Not so much from the military, but always keep in mind that half of the politicians you'll meet upstairs will be armed with a gun. This is still Venezuela."

Manet laughed as José smiled and nodded to Mitchel.

"Great," Mitchel said, feeling less enthusiastic about the joke, if that was what it was.

"Shall we go?" Manet asked. "First stop, the office of the Socialist Party?"

"That's it," José responded and they left the small, dark room and walked upstairs.

Though the stairs were also dark, light coming from above indicated the way, and as they ascended the voices of people going about their business in the hallways of the palace grew ever clearer.

"Just act as if you belong here and we should be fine," Gonzalez instructed. At the top of the stairs they were met by four soldiers who fell in line with them as they moved deeper into the palace.

To Mitchel's surprise there were fewer people around than he expected and nobody seemed to take any notice of them.

"It seems quiet enough," he remarked.

"In this part of the palace it is," Captain Manet told him. "Everybody is gathered in the Hall of Mirrors where Carmona will be swearing-in the new ministers at any moment. Anyway, we're here."

Stopping in front of a large green door bearing a sign that read. 'PSUV', Manet took a quick look around before taking a set of keys from his belt. He quickly opened the door and the group walked into the room.

"I'll keep guard outside," Gonzalez said before closing the door behind them.

"You know what you're looking for?" Manet asked.

"A fax machine," Mitchel answered.

The office was large with ten desks neatly lined up in a row. They all looked exactly the same except for one large table at the back of the room that was covered with stacks of papers and what looked like a printer and fax machine.

"That must be it," José said, and Manet told him he would guard the door while he and Mitchel took a look.

Taking a stack of papers from the machine, Mitchel handed them to José. "Your Spanish, my Spanish," he said with a smile and José started reading. About half way through he stopped at a short, handwritten note. Putting the other papers down he read and translated aloud.

'*To the Venezuelan people...and whomever it may concern.*

I, Hugo Chávez Frías, Venezuelan, president of the Bolivarian Republic of Venezuela, declare:

I didn't quit the legitimate authority which people gave me. Forever!!'

"That's simple enough," Mitchel said.

"It's good enough for me!" Manet called out from the other end of the room.

"OK, let's do this," Mitchel replied. "You send the fax to every military base in the country and I will start making copies. Captain, do you think you can spare a few men to distribute the fax to as many people as possible outside the palace?"

"That shouldn't be a problem," Manet told him.

"All right then. Let's get this done and move on to the second part of the plan."

As Carmona entered the Hall of Mirrors, he saw the room was filled with dignitaries from all over the country. On stage, his desk was flanked by two men of the Honor Guard who kept their eyes trained ahead, ignoring the world's Press at their feet. As Carmona walked up to the desk, he put on his best smile and waved at the people in the room who were loudly applauding. Taking his seat, he tapped the microphone in front of him a few times.

"People of Venezuela," he began, "welcome. We are gathered here today to formally swear in your new cabinet ministers; the people who will guide you through this trying time of transition."

Members of the Honor Guard moved quickly through the tunnels and out into the palace gardens, armed with copies of the fax bearing Chávez's declaration. As they disseminated the papers, an unmarked car slowly pierced through the huge crowd to get as close as possible to the palace. Once within 50 yards of the palace gate, the vehicle stopped, unable to move any further. A few minutes later, General Badillo accompanied by two soldiers, appeared and began to make his way through the crowd and up to the gates. The protesters were too busy shouting *Carmona Out* to notice the general, who was dressed in full combat gear and a red beret. Arriving at the gates Badillo motioned to one of the soldiers to hand him one of the copies of the fax he was sharing.

"General, good to see you," the soldier said, handing him a sheet of paper. "But aren't you on the wrong side of the fence?"

"Thank you, son, but I'm exactly where I should be for now."

Badillo shook the man's hand. He then smiled as he read the fax. To his left, a few yards from the fence, standing on a stack of wooden pallets, a man was shouting through a bullhorn at the reporters in front of him. Badillo walked up to the man who immediately recognized him and invited him onto the makeshift stage.

Taking the bullhorn, Badillo addressed the crowd.

"Friends! Friends, hear me out! I am here to tell you that your leader is still Hugo Rafael Chávez Frías." Badillo raised a fist into the air before continuing, holding his copy of the fax aloft. "I will now read you a short statement written by the President himself. 'To the

Venezuelan people...and whomever it may concern. I, Hugo Chávez Frías, Venezuelan, president of the Bolivarian Republic of Venezuela, declare: I didn't quit the legitimate authority which people gave me. Forever!!'." Badillo waved both arms above his head, whipping the crowd into a frenzy. "That is your leader," he shouted. "And I pledge to you that I will not leave this fence until our president is back on the other side of it. Together we'll protest, watch, and wait."

As Badillo climbed from the stage he noticed copies of the fax moving from hand to hand through the fever-pitch crowd.

"*Hijo de tu puta madre*, Son of a Bitch. There you go."

Chávez jumped from his seat where he had been watching Badillo on TV. "What do you say, Alejandro?"

"What do you mean?" Alejandro asked.

"What do I mean? I'm asking you, what do you think of all this because I have a strong feeling it won't be long before we celebrate."

"You might be right, Sir, and I hope you are right. But I tend to be cautious. We don't know how Carmona and his men will react. It's still possible he'll send the military after the protesters."

"Don't be a buzzkill, he hasn't got the balls. And if he did have the balls I'm sure the army would refuse such an order. That's general Rafael Badillo at the gates of Miraflores, Son. Without a doubt, one of the most popular generals in Venezuela. Trust me, it won't be long before all this is over. I feel it in my every bone. Alejandro, I'm going to take a shower."

"You do that, Sir."

As Chávez walked away, he began to sing loudly.

At the swearing-in ceremony, Carmona had planned to call his chosen few onto the stage, one by one, taking a moment to say a few personal words before shaking hands in front of the bank of cameras and addressing them publicly by their new titles.

"Thank you General Rafael Damiani Bustillos, Interior Minister; thank you Jose Rodriguez, Foreign Minister."

However, by the time he called the third minister onto the stage, an increasing number of journalists were packing up their gear having been notified about the intensifying rioting taking place beyond the palace gates.

"That should be it," José said as they finished sending the last of the faxes.

"I guess this is the moment of truth, then," Mitchel replied, sounding nervous.

"You could stay here while we go and meet with Carmona," José suggested.

"And let you have all the fun? No thanks. I was simply wondering what will happen when we confront Carmona – last minute stage fright if you like. So, come on, let's get going while the moment is upon us."

"Do we walk?" Captain Manet asked.

"We walk," Mitchel confirmed, only to be shocked by the deserted hallways when they left the room. "Where is everyone?" he asked Gonzalez.

"I heard that a large crowd has left through the tunnels. Whatever you did in there already seems to have had some effect."

"That's good news," José said. "And it should mean we have no problem getting to Carmona. Let's go."

As the group headed for the Hall of Mirrors, Mitchel turned to Manet. "Captain, we have one more thing to ask of you once we get to Carmona."

"Which is?"

"I assume the room is guarded by your men and you shouldn't have any problems getting in?"

"No problem," Manet confirmed.

"In that case, we need you to get this message to Carmona, telling him it's urgent and that he should read it."

Mitchel took a piece of paper from José and handed it to Manet. "That's it?"

"That's it," Mitchel confirmed.

"Not a problem," Manet agreed before coming to a halt.

"Why are we stopping?" Mitchel asked.

"Because we're here," Manet replied. "After this turn it's a 15-yard dash to the doorway of the Hall of Mirrors."

"This is it then," Mitchel said, taking a deep breath.

"You know what I thought of just now?" José said, turning to Mitchel. "What the hell are we going to do if it doesn't work? What's our contingency plan?"

"And you think of that now?" Mitchel said with some exasperation.. "I thought we were sure this was going to work."

"I'm sure it will but what if?"

"I have a backup plan for you," Manet interrupted and both Michel and José turned to hear it.

"If anything should happen, you run like hell!" Manet laughed loudly, as did the other soldiers, before reassuring both men that he had their backs. "Seriously, if anything should happen, Sergeant Gonzalez here will lead you the shortest way back to the tunnels and you'll be out of here in no time. Is that reassuring enough?"

"I'll take it," Mitchel said while José simply nodded. "Let's go then."

Turning the final corner, the group walking up the hallway towards two large doors guarded by Honor Guard soldiers.

"At ease," Manet told the guards as they stood to attention.

"Gentlemen, wish me luck," Manet said.

"Good luck, Captain," both José and Mitchel said simultaneously and the two guards opened the door to let Manet through.

"Thank you, Hector Ramirez, Defense Minister."

Carmona continued smiling as he shook the Vice-Admiral's hand, failing to notice Manet who approached the stage from a side entrance. As the Captain walked towards him with no sense of hesitation, the smile fell from Carmona's face. With a nod to the two Honor Guards flanking Carmona, Manet handed over a folded piece of paper. Without saying a word, Carmona opened the note and started to read.

'We know what you did and have irrefutable proof of it. If you don't come out of this room now, we will come in and reveal our proof on live television. General Rafael Badillo.'

His face visibly paling, Carmona looked out, over the room, first at the row of ministers he had just sworn in, then at the Press and finally at the Honor Guards present. For almost five minutes, he didn't say or do anything, he simply stood on the stage, shaking his head. The moment wasn't lost on the audience. Carmona read the note one more time before refolding the piece of paper and placing it in his jacket pocket. He then got up from his chair and walked up to Manet, who told him to follow.

As the two of them walked to the exit, on the other side of the door Mitchel and José were waiting anxiously.

"What's taking so long?" Mitchel asked, just as the door swung open and Manet and Carmona appeared.

"Who are you, what is this?" Carmona asked abruptly.

"Is there somewhere we can talk?" José replied ignoring the man's questions.

Carmona looked at Manet who immediately directed the group to an empty office further up the hallway. When they entered the room, José invited Carmona to take a seat behind a desk. As he sat down, Mitchel took a large folder from his backpack and, without saying a word, he placed it on the desk. After a second or two, Carmona opened the folder and he went through the papers before him, reading the main points of each page from the first letter describing Project April Showers to the evidence of the sniper guns and finally the doctored video footage proving that it was not Chávez's men, but the coup leaders who were responsible for the violent deaths at Lugano Bridge. Some ten minutes later Carmona closed the folder and shoved it away from him.

"What do you want?" he asked, the defeat evident in his voice.

"You know what we want," Mitchel replied.

"And here's what will happen," José added. "You have thirty minutes during which no-one in the palace will prevent you or anyone else affiliated with you from leaving here in peace. If, after that thirty minutes is up, you or anyone of your comrades are still here, you will be arrested by the Honor Guard for treason and for conspiring to overthrow the democratically-elected government as well as the abduction of the President of the Bolivarian Republic of Venezuela."

"We have a safe way for you and your people to leave the palace," Mitchel offered.

And Carmona struggled not to cry.

28. The Ride Back

Saturday, April 13, 2002
1pm

NEWS THAT CARMONA WAS LEAVING spread fast through the palace and it triggered an unseemly race for the exit by his supporters. Within minutes, the hallways were deserted, leaving only the Honor Guard and lower-level staff on the ground. Beyond the palace fence, the protestors had yet to hear of the developments and the atmosphere was tense as Mitchel and José, flanked by two Honor Guard soldiers, walked towards the barrier. As the Honor Guard struggled to keep the crowd back, some of whom were beating at the gate with sticks and metal bars, José shouted to Mitchel.

"We need to get Badillo in!"

"Do you see him?" Mitchel yelled back, peering into the mass of people before them.

"There!" José pointed at the front gate, straight in front of them.

"The answer is always right in front of you!" Mitchel joked and followed his friend to the gate.

"Can you please let the general in?" José asked the guards.

Even though they complied with the request, it was a battle to get the general in and keep the protestors out.

"Easy! Easy!" Badillo ordered as the guards forcefully kept the crowd back as they pulled him inside the gate, quickly closing it behind him. As he straightened his uniform, he thanked the men for their efforts and asked how the confrontation had gone inside the palace.

"Everything worked as planned," José replied with a grin. "Most of the collaborators have left the palace. The Honor Guards are in control."

"And Carmona?"

"Last we heard he was seen entering the tunnel," Mitchel answered. "Shall we go inside? We have what's left of the Press waiting in the Hall of Mirrors."

"What do they know?" Badillo asked as they all made their way to the palace entrance.

"There has been no official statement of any kind. They're waiting for you, Sir," José told him.

As he spoke, the general reached into his pocket and took out his vibrating cell phone. "General Badillo," he answered. "Yes… ok …. yeah… uh… uh… hmm… yes… perfect. Thank you." Finishing the call, Badillo turned to José and Mitchel. "That was General Reyes. He told me that we now control the Fourth Armored Division including four artillery groups, four brigades, five tank battalions and six battalions. We also control Libertador Air Base, where our F-16 fighter planes are stationed. It's a question of time now before we retake control of Turiamo naval base where we suspect they are holding the President."

"That's great news," José replied, and they headed for the Hall of Mirrors feeling more victorious than ever. Of course, the Press was aware something major was happening and had lined the corridors ready to ambush Badillo as he approached.

"What can you tell us about the situation?" a reporter asked, thrusting a microphone in front of the general's face.

"Is it true that President Carmona has left the palace and Chávez is on the way back?" another journalist asked.

"If you follow me to the Hall of Mirrors I will provide you with a brief statement," the general said by way of answer.

"What do you think?" José asked Mitchel as they followed him to the great hall.

"I don't think anything," Mitchel answered honestly. "I'm still waiting for it all to sink in. I guess I've been acting on pure adrenaline up until now, and I'm slowly starting to realize it's really happening. It's all over."

"Surreal, isn't it?"

"It really is." Mitchel shook his head as the Honor Guard swung open the doors to the Hall of Mirrors and applause followed.

Inside, the remaining palace staff was gathered behind a large press cordon. Badillo, clearly enjoying the moment, walked into the room waving his arms above his head and clapping his hands. As Mitchel and José remained at the door, Badillo walked up to the stage and took the microphone from the table. He then jumped off the stage and headed for the Press.

"Thank you, thank you," he said, urging the room to calm down so he might speak. "Thank you. I have a brief statement prepared, but before I read it I would first like to thank all of you here for your loyalty to your President, Hugo Chávez Frias." The gathered crowd went wild at Badillo's words, then, taking a piece of paper from his pocket, he began to read the prepared statement. "Today, Saturday, April 13th, 2002 at," Badillo paused to glance at his watch, "at one-thirty pm, the loyal Chavista armies relieved the pseudo-government of Pedro Carmona from his duties, reinstating the democratically-chosen President, Chávez Frias, and his government. Mr. Carmona and his followers have left Miraflores palace and the people of Caracas and the

Honor Guard have retaken the palace and its grounds awaiting the return of the constitutional government and President Chávez."

At that point, the doors opened and an Honor Guard member walked into the room to whisper something into Badillo's ear. The general nodded before addressing the crowd. "I have good news," he revealed. "I have just heard that…" before Badillo could finish all eyes and cameras turned away from him to the door where Vice President Desiderio Clemente suddenly appeared. Almost immediately, staff members ran passed the Press to welcome Clemente with handshakes and hugs. Badillo then walked up to him and handed him the microphone before joining Mitchel and José standing at the back of the room.

"Good job, General," Mitchel said.

"I guess there's always a more popular guy," Badillo joked.

"Wait until Chávez returns," José replied, laughing.

Badillo took his phone from his pocket and checked his voice messages.

"Any news?" José asked and the general smiled.

"We've retaken Turiamo and Reyes is en route to meet President Chávez. We should hear more soon.

In his room at Turiamo, Chávez smiled as he watched Clemente addressing the Press on TV. Having already heard Badillo speaking of Carmona's retreat he was overcome by a sense of elation but also relief. It was the first time in two days he had been free of fear; fear for himself and for his family. Now knowing that fear had passed, he couldn't help but cry. Just as the tears fell, the door opened and Cardinal Velasco walked in with Sergeant Alejandro.

"President Chávez," the Cardinal greeted him. "I'm so pleased to be able to tell you it's over."

Chávez glanced at the Cardinal before pointedly ignoring him as he walked passed to shake the hand of Alejandro. Pulling the young man into a hug, Chávez whispered, "I will never forget what you've done for me."

At that moment, General Reyes entered the room and Chávez let go of the sergeant.

"Mr. President." Reyes saluted and Chávez saluted back. "I'm so very pleased to see you."

"And I'm so very pleased to see you, General."

"Are you OK, Sir?"

"Aside from some of the company in this room, I'm absolutely fine."

"That's great, Sir. I'm here to escort you by helicopter back to Miraflores. Whenever you're ready."

"How about right now?" Chávez said with a smile. "There's no time like the present, as I've learned lately." Picking up his red beret from the table he turned to Alejandro. "I would be honored if you'd join me, Sergeant."

"The honor is all mine, Sir," Alejandro replied.

As they walked through the door Chávez glanced behind him. "Cardinal, please," he said, inviting Velasco to follow them.

Outside, Chávez was met with loud applause. Visibly enjoying the attention, he walked with purpose to the airfield. In front of a waiting helicopter, Chávez turned to look one more time, waving enthusiastically at the gathered crowd. As the rotor blades began to rotate, Chávez invited Alejandro and the Cardinal to take their seats in the helicopter. For a moment, Chávez felt almost detached from the scene. The noise disappeared and calm returned to his mind. It was a great feeling. Seconds later, he shook his head, forcing himself back to the here and now, jumped into the helicopter and strapped himself in. After a minute or so the helicopter rose above the airfield, giving the men a great view of the crowd from the air. From the corners of the airfield, another four helicopters took to the skies to escort Chávez home. And as Turiamo slowly faded in the distance, Chávez sat back in his seat and closed his eyes.

"What are you thinking?" José asked Mitchel as they stood on a balcony that overlooked the helicopter pad in the palace park. Having been completely sealed off, the place was deserted.

"I was just thinking, we did well."

"We sure did."

"We should do it again someday," Mitchel joked and José punched him in the shoulder. For a second his attention was taken by the continuing roar of protestors beyond the gate. "Have you noticed that the sound of people celebrating sounds exactly the same as when they were demonstrating?"

"This is Venezuela, man!"

The two men laughed out loud.

Below them, signs of life were happening at the helipad, and a few seconds later General Badillo came to join them on the balcony.

"How are things going, General?" José asked.

"He's only a few minutes out."

"That's great," Mitchel replied, feeling a surge of satisfaction at the news. "Just out of curiosity, what will happen to the coup leaders, the other generals and Carmona himself?"

"I guess that's up to Chávez," Badillo said. "But as far as I know the man, nothing much will change." Noticing the skepticism in Mitchel and José's eyes, he added, "Seriously, a few days ago his approval rate was below 30 percent. He was no popular president anymore. If I had to guess now, I'd think his approval rate would be 50, maybe 55 percent."

"That's a lot better," José admitted.

"It sure is," Badillo confirmed. "But it also means that about half the people wouldn't choose him and just might choose someone like Pedro Carmona."

"So, what better time to embrace your enemies than in the face of their defeat," Mitchel said.

"Sun Tzu?" José asked.

"Mitchel Everson James," Mitchel replied, leaving the men smiling.

In the distance, the sound of chopper blades reminded them of the moment.

"I guess the circus starts now," Badillo said.

As the sound grew louder, the people at the front of the palace started moving towards the back of the park, hoping to get a glimpse of the returning president. As they approached they began to chant, "*Llega llega!*" He arrives, he arrives!

"It's amazing." Mitchel said. "Just 47 hours ago they were shouting 'Se va, se va!' He's going, he's going!"

"Again, this is Venezuela," José replied. "Shall we go down?"

As they walked to the park, the first helicopter neared the platform to land. As soon as it touched down, the doors opened and a small group of military exited.

"Who are they?" Mitchel asked.

"Guards and dignitaries," Badillo answered. "Five choppers left Turiamo. We're not sure which one Chávez will be in."

"Just in case someone wants to shoot him down?" Mitchel asked and Badillo and José looked at him knowingly.

"I get it," Mitchel told them. "This is still Venezuela."

Within a minute of the first chopper landing, the second one touched down with more soldiers on board.

"Three to go," José said as the third neared.

Once again, more soldiers and dignitaries exited. Then, as the fourth chopper approached and landed, and just as the crowd was growing tired of screaming its welcome, Sergeant Alejandro appeared, quickly followed by Cardinal Velasco. Both men then waited. About thirty seconds passed with nothing happening, then, just as the crowd fell silent in mute anticipation, Chávez appeared, dressed in civilian clothes. The 50,000 people crowded into the park went wild and a quickly-assembled military marching band, complete with red berets, began to play Gloria Al Bravo Pueblo – Glory to the Brave People – the Venezuelan anthem.

As the helicopter quickly lifted off, Chávez walked up to the crowd waiting to see him behind the mobile fence. He shook as many hands as possible, clearly enjoying the moment and basking in the cheers and tears of his adoring supporters. As Chávez completed the circle, General Rojas exited the palace, passing by Mitchel, José and Badillo on his way to Chávez.

"Where the hell did he come from?" Mitchel asked.

"I guess he waited for his moment," Badillo replied.

"He must have been hiding somewhere in the palace," José added as Rojas worked himself through the crowd. When he got to the President he placed a hand on his shoulder. Chávez turned to Rojas, and he took the President's hand and shook it while looking around to see whether it had been noticed by the Press photographers. Chávez didn't flinch, but he immediately let go of Rojas's' hand to return to the people at the fence.

"That went well," Mitchel said, and the others smiled.

After half an hour spent shaking hands, hugging and singing, Chávez found his way to the palace entrance where he stopped. It was the first time he noticed Mitchel and the others. Without saying a word, Chávez took Badillo's hand, pulled him in and held him firmly. After the hug he turned to Mitchel and José and shook their hands.

"I understand I owe you a lot," he said.

"The pleasure was all ours," José answered.

"And you?" Chávez said grabbing Mitchel by the shoulders with both hands. "You, of all people! I remember a few days ago that you were a proud member of your country's military working in the greatest democracy in the world. Well, thanks to you we can still call it the greatest democracy. I thank you for that."

"You also told me I have a lovely wife," Mitchel replied.

"Yes, I remember her too," Chávez said with a smile before disappearing into the palace.

"You also told me I have a lovely wife?" José and Badillo teased Mitchel as soon as the President was gone.

"Shut up," was all he said.

29. Reinstated

Saturday, April 13, 2002

3pm

C ATHERINE POINTED AT THE TV EXCITEDLY. "Look!" she yelled, hardly believing it was her father on screen. He was walking alongside José as they followed Chávez into the palace.

"The crazy men did it," Nathalie said, shaking her head as Catherine came to wrap her arms around her neck and shed a tear. "He'll be home soon," she reassured her daughter.

"I know. What will we do when all this is over? Will we stay here or what?"

"We'll talk about it later when your dad is home again, honey."

Once inside the palace, Chávez walked straight to the Hall of Mirrors shaking every hand that was offered to him in the crowded hallways.

"Where do all these people come from?" Mitchel asked as he and José tried to keep up with him.

"I have no idea," José replied. "But why are we still here? Our work is done."

"Are you mad? I wouldn't miss this for the world," Mitchel said excitedly. "We will be talking about this when we're old and living in some kind of assisted home wondering what has happened to everyone involved."

"If we'll ever know," Jose remarked.

"Indeed, if we'll ever know."

As they walked up to the door leading to the Hall of Mirrors Chávez stopped, closed his eyes and bowed his head.

"*Dios te salve María,*" he said, offering a quiet prayer.

After making the sign of the cross, he placed his hand on the doorknob and paused, looking doubtful. Then, just as Mitchel and José were about to look at each other and question what was going on, Chávez straightened his back and pushed open the door. The clicks and whirrs of cameras immediately met them and they were almost blinded by the number of flashbulbs going off.

Stepping confidently into the room, Chávez greeted the deafening applause and cheers with a wide, heartfelt grin. Walking onto the stage, he sat down in front of the picture of Simon Bolivar that had quickly been reinstated. On the desk, Bolivar's sword was carefully placed in the center. For a minute or two, Chávez got back to his feet to better absorb the enthusiasm in the room while a number of his dignitaries took their seats. Cardinal Velasco positioned himself next to the presidential desk. Mitchel, José and Badillo were the last to enter the room and, after closing the door behind them, sat themselves by it. Chávez looked at the closed door before picking up the sword and before speaking he waved it in front of him.

"El Comandante Chávez is back!"

The crowd cheered and, after a minute or so, Chávez put down the sword and waved both arms to silence the room. Within seconds everybody returned to their seats, but the hundreds of thousands of people celebrating outside the palace could still be heard in the room.

With all national and international cameras broadcasting live Chávez started his speech.

"People of Venezuela and all supporters of democracy all over the world, it's good to be able to say to you, 'it's good to be back'. Render unto God the things which are God's, unto Caesar the things which are Caesar's, and to the people, the things that belong to the people." As Chávez spoke, his voice raw with emotion, there was none of the usual cheers at every pause, but rather a silence that marked a deeper and more profound respect for a leader who had so nearly been lost. "It is with those words that I want to begin," he continued. "These past few days have been trying for everyone. I must confess, I'm still stupefied. I'm still taking in everything that has happened. So many feelings run through me as I am once more here again. These past few days, 47 hours to be precise, this process that, well, a process, if we can call it that, which will inspire who knows how many books and films, describing our history as an example for the whole world to read and see. This was a process of counter-counter revolution and I send a message from the depth of my heart to Venezuela and the world that this palace of the Venezuelan people stands for. The people have spoken and retaken this palace; never to be removed!"

As Chávez hit his stride, the crowd reacted to a familiar charisma by cheering. Once they had settled, Chávez continued in a softer tone. "Haven't I made mistakes, you might ask. Sure, I have. And I know we must make decisions and adjust many things. Soon we'll make those changes, but always with respect, dignity, and without retaliation. There will be no witch hunts and I will never tolerate disrespect for the liberties we have won. I return to you, spiritually charged with a great love. I loved you two days ago, but now perhaps even more after these historic events, after the extraordinary demonstration to the world of how a people and its soldiers can stop a violent counter-revolution and fulfill a successful counter-counter-revolution without even firing a single shot. Without bloodshed, you restored democracy. Well after this, how can I do anything else, be anything else then, more than ever, in love with you. Love will always pay for itself with love. I especially want to thank Cardinal Ignacio Velasco who visited me while I was in captivity on Orchila island and kept my faith constant, assuring me of my family's safety. I also want to thank everyone, foreign and domestic, who behind the scenes made it possible for me to return."

As he spoke, Chávez looked over at Mitchel, José and Badillo, gave a nod and started applauding. Everyone in the room followed. After a minute, once the claps had faded, he continued.

"I am, of course, president of everyone, even of the minority that doesn't want me. *I'm not a gold coin that everybody likes*," Chávez said before bursting into song.

Mitchel turned to José. "That's our cue," he whispered.

"I believe you're right," José replied.

Mitchel then turned to Badillo and held out his hand. "Thank you, General, for everything."

"It's me who should thank you," he replied.

"No, really, it has been my pleasure." Mitchel smiled.

"And mine," José added.

The two of them then quietly opened the door and left the room. Making their way to the exit they passed a number of people going about their business as if nothing had happened. Once outside the palace, however, the scene couldn't have been more different and as far as the eye could see thousands of people gathered to celebrate the return of their president. "

"Where's your bike?" Mitchel asked as they joined the crowd.

"Follow me."

******

"I'm on my way to Maiquetía airport."

Carmona spoke into his cellphone from the back seat of a parked limo.

"There's a plane waiting to take us to Bogota… I'll be there in 20 minutes… Please, make sure you're there… I will… See you there, dear."

As the limo drove away from the palace, Carmona turned in his seat unable to tear his eyes away from the people thronging the streets until the scene of his defeat finally faded in the distance.

At the sound of the Ducati pulling into the driveway, Nathalie and Catherine rushed from the couch to the front door. Before Mitchel had chance to get off the bike, Catherine grabbed him around the waist and hung onto him, almost knocking over the bike. Carefully, Mitchel got off the bike, keeping his daughter close to him.

"It's OK, it's OK," he whispered as she softly cried. "It's over now."

Catherine then came to join them in a hug and for a few moments the family simply held each other close until a polite cough called for attention.

"And what about me?" José joked.

"Go," Mitchel said smiling, and in two bounding steps Catherine jumped into José's outstretched arms.

"Thank you, thank you, thank you," she said.

"You're welcome."

"Shall we go inside and have a drink?" Nathalie suggested.

"Sounds like a plan," José replied.

"Enough with the plans!" Mitchel teased. "Though I could sure as hell use a drink."

With his daughter in one arm and his wife on the other, he led the way into the house.

"Looks like he's still talking," Mitchel observed wryly as he saw Chávez on TV, still sitting behind his desk addressing the nation.

"Knowing Chávez there's a chance he will go on for another few hours," José replied.

"So, how have things been here?" Mitchel asked Nathalie.

"The ambassador called," she informed him. "He told me to congratulate you on your endeavor and made me promise to tell you he expects you to return to your normal duties on Monday."

Mitchel smiled as he shook his head.

"We saw you on TV," Catherine then remarked.

"Your father's famous now," José teased.

"Were you ever in any real danger?" Catherine asked quietly.

"Only from his driving," Mitchel joked, pointing at José.

"But where did all the, uh… bad guys go? Were they arrested?"

Mitchel looked at José, suggesting he might be better placed to answer such a question.

"As far as I know, nobody has been arrested," he said. "Chávez will want to pick up things in as peaceful a manner as possible."

"And what about all the faces on the wall in your war room upstairs?" Nathalie asked.

"That's a good question," José admitted. "I suspect nothing will happen for a while and Chávez will use the law to try those responsible."

"I thought you also proved there was US involvement?".

"I'm afraid our proof won't make it that far. Not even Chávez has anything to gain by alienating the US any further. Maybe in the future, in some kind of election, the proof will surface to denigrate some candidate, but until then…" He took hold of the beer Nathalie handed him and raised it to Mitchel before asking, "So, what's next?"

"Next?" Mitchel asked, his frown revealing his confusion. "Not much I guess. Tomorrow is Sunday, so we'll rest, and on Monday, well, I guess we pick up things where we left them a few days ago."

"Like nothing ever happened?" Nathalie asked.

"I guess so, only now we start doing what we came here to do."

"Which is?"

"Have a normal steady job, get some well-deserved rest, start anew and be a normal family."

As Mitchel took a sip of his beer, the blackberry on the table started ringing. Picking it up, he looked at the screen and smiled.

"Who is it?" Catherine asked.

"It's an email from my therapist rescheduling my Monday appointment."

"You're still going?" Nathalie asked.

"Of course, I'm going. Like I said, it's time to get back to normal."

On the TV, Chávez finally stepped away from his desk, only to pick up Bolivar's sword and stand in front of it.

"May I?" José asked as he turned up the volume.

"So, before I leave here to take a really long nap," Chávez joked, "I will pledge my loyalty to all of you one more time, proclaiming the Bolivarian oath." As he kneeled down he took the sword from its scabbard and put it in front of his face. "I swear before you, in the eyes of the God of my parents, I swear for them, I swear for mine and your honor and for my motherland that I will not rest my arms nor my soul until we have finally broken the chains that oppress Venezuela as an inheritance of the powerful who destroyed the motherland before. I swear that I will fully dedicate my work to the Bolivarian ideology, to the common organization, to common mobilization, to common power. I promise to never abandon the struggle every day and every night that I have left with the Bolivarian circles in the Bolivarian web, in the Bolivarian current, in the Bolivarian forces and in the Revolutionary Bolivarian Movement that was born again after 19 years, by the will of the Venezuelan people. I swear that I will fight without rest for the defense of the revolution, even if I have to sacrifice my life, for the glory of Venezuela. I swear that we will consolidate forever the Bolivarian revolution and the motherland of our children. That I swear."

30. Afterword

OST OF WHAT HAPPENED before and during
Venezuela's 47-hour coup will probably stay secret
forever. What we know for sure is that the office of
the *Defensoria del Pueblo* (Defender of the People), in their final report
about the coup, reported 19 fatalities on April 11, 2002. Most of those
killed lost their lives at or around the Llaguno Bridge. Seven of the dead
were members of the anti-Chávez demonstration and another seven
from the pro-Chávez demonstration. Five fatalities were non-involved
bystanders. The number of wounded officially stands at 69. Unofficial
reports claimed casualties into the low hundreds.

Four months after the coup, an independent court passed a ruling
that declared the events of that day were not a coup, but a "vacuum of
power". Subsequently, none of the generals or admirals involved could
be prosecuted.

The civilians involved weren't as lucky. Pedro Carmona fled to
Colombia where he gained political asylum in 2002. In that same year,

he became a professor in Social Communication at the Sergio Arboleda University.

Carlos Ortega stayed in Venezuela and went into hiding. After a year, he was arrested and sentenced to 16 years in prison for treason and civil rebellion. In 2006, Ortega escaped from prison and a year later received political asylum in Peru.

So, what happened at the Llaguno Bridge and what was the involvement of the United States, if there was any?

On April 11, in a local hotel near the bridge, seven people were arrested by the DISIP. Most of them had fake Colombian identities. All of them appeared in court on the 13th, but the case was postponed until the 16th when a judge found there was insufficient evidence to hold them. They were all released, never to be heard from again.

In 2005, lawyers Jeremy Bigwood and Eva Golinger, as a result of a Freedom of Information Act request, proved that the CIA had knowledge about a coup being planned in Venezuela. In the five 'Senior Executive Intelligence Briefs', freed by the act it showed that between March 5 and April 8, 2002, the Bush administration was aware of plans for a coup. There was never any proof that the US was involved. However, Chávez later said in an interview, "I am being objective about this. I can't be launching accusations and I want to believe that a government that has stood so strongly behind democracy is not involved in this tyrannical, macabre coup."

General Pedro Soto, who Chávez had arrested for treason and insubordination earlier in 2002, was released from jail on bail and immediately fled to the US, supposedly with the help of the CIA. In June 2002, he contacted the Immigration Service in Miami to apply for political asylum, stating he feared for his life.

Ignacio Antonio Velasco García, was the cardinal and Archbishop of Caracas at the time. He was appointed Archbishop in

1995 and held that position until his death in 2003. Known for his criticisms of Hugo Chávez he was the first to sign the Carmona Decree. After his death, Chávez stated that the Cardinal was "burning in hell".

In 2006, Chávez was re-elected for a new six-year term after winning 63 percent of the vote. In 2011, he declared on television that he had a cancerous tumor removed in Cuba. From that time on, he regularly traveled to Cuba for treatment. In 2012, he revealed his cancer had returned, but later that year he was declared completely free from the disease. That same year – after winning a referendum that could have seen him re-elected indefinitely – he also won another general election, assuring his time in office for another six years. In December that same year, he announced his cancer had returned and in March 2013 the Venezuelan government announced the death of President Hugo Rafael Chávez Frías .

There are numerous versions of Venezuela's 47-hour coup including a theory that Chávez planned everything himself in order to purge the military of his opponents. There's no evidence for any of the versions, which suggests the truth may never be revealed. On one hand, that's a shame, on the other it provides writers with the opportunity to let their imaginations run free and write books about it.

"....this course of events will inspire who knows how many books about our history and set an example to the entire world..."

Hugo Chávez, April 13, 2002

List of Abbreviations

CB: Cadena Broadcasts. Short messages broadcast at irregular intervals in between regular TV programs. Originally intended for emergency warnings, they became a weapon in the President's arsenal against his enemies and grew into a series of short political speeches that all too often disrupted regular viewing.

CdP (-090762): CdP stands for *'Cadena de Depredador'* or 'The Predator Network'. During the Cold War period the predator network was the analog radio system used by all official services in Venezuela. It wasn't super secure, but little was in those days.

CTV: *'Confederación de Trabajadores de Venezuela'*, the biggest Venezuelan workers' association.

DISIP: *'Dirección de los Servicios de Inteligencia y Prevención'*. The CIA's counterpart in Venezuela.

FACR: The initials of *'Fidel Alejandro Castro Ruz'* that were found on the speed dial of Hugo Chávez's phone.

Fedecámaras: '*Federación de Cámaras y Asociaciones de Comercio y Producción de Venezuela*', The Venezuelan Federation of Chambers of Commerce.

MBR-200: '*Movimiento Bolivariano Revolucionario 200*'. Revolutionary Bolivarian Movement-200. The political and social movement founded by Hugo Chávez in 1982. The '200' was added in 1983 on the 200th anniversary Simon Bolívar's birth.

MK14 EBR: 'Sniper gun'. An Enhanced Battle Rifle exclusively built in a sniper version for use within units of the United States Special Operations Command, Delta Force, Navy Seals etcetera.

PDVSA: '*Petróleos de Venezuela*, S.A. Petroleum of Venezuela is the Venezuelan state-owned oil and natural gas company.

PSUV: '*Partido Socialista Unido de Venezuela*', The United Socialist Party of Venezuela. A socialist political party in Venezuela which resulted from the fusion of political and social forces that supported the Bolivarian Revolution led by Hugo Chávez.

UVB-76, 4625 kHz frequency: The frequency on which the '*Cadena de Depredador*' broadcasts.

www.ingramcontent.com/pod-product-compliance
Lightning Source LLC
Chambersburg PA
CBHW020640030726

47498CB00002B/296